THE BLUE BOWL

THE BLUE BOWL

a novel

GEORGE MINOT

Alfred A. Knopf New York 2004

This Is a Borzoi Book Published by Alfred A. Knopf

Copyright © 2004 by George Minot
All rights reserved under International and Pan-American Copyright
Conventions. Published in the United States by Alfred A. Knopf,
a division of Random House, Inc., New York, and simultaneously
in Canada by Random House of Canada Limited, Toronto.
Distributed by Random House, Inc., New York.
www.aaknopf.com

Knopf, Borzoi Books, and the colophon are registered trademarks
of Random House, Inc.

Library of Congress Cataloging-in-Publication Data
Minot, George, {date}
The blue bowl / George Minot. — 1st ed.
p.   cm.
ISBN 0-394-57348-X
1. Conflict of generations—Fiction.   2. Parent and adult child—Fiction.
3. Brothers and sisters—Fiction.   4. Fathers—Death—Fiction.
5. Trials (Murder)—Fiction.   6. New England—Fiction.
7. Painters—Fiction.   I. Title.
PS3613.I66B56 2004
813'.6—dc21   2003047579

Manufactured in the United States of America

FIRST EDITION

For Mum, Dad, Carrie, Susan,
Dinah, George, Sam, Ellen,
Chris, and Eliza

Blue, blue window . . .

— NEIL YOUNG,
"Helpless"

PART ONE

My brother, like a bird, in his annual spring migration up to Maine, stopped off, as usual, at the other end of my buzzer in New York, wanting a place to stay for the night.

Simon, was all he said when I asked who was there.

His crooked grin when I opened the door broke my heart. A split wound in the bruised fruit of his big, lonely head. His troubled expression, as our eyes met and slid apart, was something right out of the silver memory of my own mirror. *Am I like that?* His nose is sharp, like a beak, unlike anyone else's in the family—as if sharpened by misadventure. He was panting, smiling. I could picture him rushing up the stairs, leaning forward, taking them two at a time with eager, tight, stretching strides. His clothes were dirty, red discount jeans, his dick showing, yellow shirt with a pointed collar. His shoes were shot.

We hugged. He smelled like a homeless person, which he kind of was. He had his stuff, not much, in a black heavy-duty garbage bag.

He slid through the doorway as if pulled on a string, dipping one shoulder slightly as the other shrugged up.

I asked if he wanted to take a bath.

No thanks. Let's eat. I'm really hungry. I haven't eaten for like three days.

We went to a little Mexican place around the corner, fluorescent lit, bad decor, Mexican pop music blaring, really good fajitas.

This isn't real Mexican food, Simon commented in between bulging mouthfuls. He ate a huge, heaping plate, and part of mine.

I asked him how his painting was going.

Good.

Conversation isn't easy with Simon. He spends most of his life alone, and isn't used to talking. Though once he warms up, he's fine. He can be effusive and sweet. Or he gets going on these really negative riffs. As older brother, I'm both lifelong rival and confidant-for-life. I used to explain things to him— our childhood heads on pillows on adjacent beds, awake, at night—how things worked. He runs his plans by me, or gets me to draw things out of him, as if for paternal review and approval. Then, of course, he resents me for prying, or judging, and answers in monosyllables, as if he's being interrogated. I'd just as soon not go into those things at all. He reports to me; but at the same time he wants me to butt out, let him live his own life. Which I do.

I asked him about New Orleans, where he spent, as far as I knew, the past winter.

It's okay, was all he said. Lots of rain. And stray cats.

Like him.

We touched, barely, on baseball, Red, Timmy, and Bob Dylan's bootleg album.

Yeah, it's really good.

I asked him what his plans were, this being my role. Where he was going from here. Though I knew the answer.

North, was all he said.

I let it rest, and watched him eat. His agate eyes were bloodshot. His self-cut hair was short, a little nappy. He ate like a pig.

He wasn't supposed to go to the house in Maine—Dad didn't want him there—and he knew it. He was going there anyway—*Dad would never know*—as he had many times before. Dad always knew. The house in Maine is a summerhouse, left to Dad by his father.

Simon felt like it was his house as much as it was Dad's, and he felt like, Why should I pay rent somewhere else, where I don't even want to be, when the house is just sitting there, empty? It's my home. Too bad if Dad doesn't want me there. I'm going anyway.

This was their routine. Simon going and living in the house for a couple of months before Dad got there, maybe slipping back in when siblings arrived, then the full run of the place again for the fall, after Dad left. Washing, before the water was turned on, in rainwater gushing from a broken gutter, eating food left over on the shelves, bundling up with blankets till it got warmer. Dad hating it, but not really doing anything about it from his Massachusetts distance. Haplessly telling him not to stay there, leaving it at that. Shaking his head in dismay. Mostly avoiding each other when they were on the island together. When Dad was there, Simon slipped off to other places he could stay. Like at sort-of-friends', or good ol' rent-for-work type deals. Or out on Burnt Island, his salvation.

Simon was basically obsessed with Dad. His whole life was one big troubled emotional reaction to Dad. Sooner or later, when you were talking to Simon, he always came around to his catalogue of grievances against Dad. Plus the abiding list of wrongs, inexcusable offenses, totally alcoholic actions, the fucked-up parental moves, missteps, omissions: timeless in their immediate potency.

You know what they're gonna do? he whined.

They being Dad and his brother and sister, who jointly owned Burnt Island, having inherited equal parts from their father. Eighty-eight acres of pristine wilderness, smooth-rock beaches and dense fir forest, complete with wall-to-wall moss and needle carpeting, crisscrossed with narrow, crooked deer paths, and quietly populated with nimble white-tailed deer and the full range of little animals and birds native to an island in Maine—Mum saw a fox one camp-out night, returning from the outhouse—watched over by ospreys, circling on high, beeping down at you, and settling, wings up a moment, the mandatory weapons search, before settling, unseen, in their fat stick penthouse nest; plus all the berries and bugs, ferns and flowers, the black cake earth, the low-tide mud, the miraculous, unseen processes of growth and decay, the subtle arias of sweet smells you move through, the soft, mingled woods and beach sounds, made mostly by the wind, the water; the fog, like a ghost, forgotten when gone, and then, one night, it returns, its lugubrious voice, periodic, faraway, a lingering, alto *om;* the few choice sunny bedroom meadows, hidden amid the connected, cool corridors of the interior, and the many million-dollar views, bright, glazed blue, gray-day gray, out to the vastly air-conditioned bay, table to toy boats, and other fir-hatted islands, the views like open windows wrapped around the rocky perimeter, which, facing all directions, constantly eats the arriving ocean, as it steadily, spiritedly, stupidly, ceaselessly repeats its thwarted efforts to come ashore . . .

Simon loved Burnt Island. He felt that Burnt Island was his, too, as much as it was Dad's. *More.* It was his legally, like according to *natural law,* or like *eminent domain,* and it was his spiritually, especially. He'd stay in the little house out there, a little brown prefab cottage from the Sears catalogue, erected in the thirties by Dad's father, the grumpy, leonine Pa. Or to be precise, put up by islander workers Pa hired. There's a series of photos on the wall in Dad's side of the house on North Haven, showing the raising of the cabin. The barge that carried the stacked panels of walls, floor, and ceiling to the island, the different black-and-white stages of construction. Dad and his brother standing around squinting in their long shorts, skinny arms, and crew cuts, looking a lot like me and Simon in pictures taken on Burnt Island a generation later: Dad with his chain saw, us snapping, and getting snapped at by, dead branches, dragging away spiky limbs and logs he cut, grimacing in concentration, his forearms flexing, with a steady rocking motion, like sex, like a raucous guitar, modulating that gnawingly expressive, whining, monster mosquito roar.

Burnt Island, his one true home, Dad-allowed or not. North Haven was his home address, if he had one—Manchester, Massachusetts, where he grew up and Dad still lived, sure wasn't; and nowhere else really was, either—and Burnt Island was his real home, his God-appointed home in nature, on earth, in the cosmos: like a kid'd write for his address inside a crisp new, fresh-smelling, sharp-papered textbook. He'd live in the cabin for days and sometimes weeks on end—island boy: wake to the birdies, step outside onto the cool, wet grass, the perfect morning out there, take a steaming pee on the ground wherever, walk around barefoot, make some coffee, make paintings. He kept his food cool in a bucket lowered down into the perpetual refrigeration of the old well, overgrown but rediscovered by him, cleared out, and covered with a piece of warped gray plywood he got from the dump, to keep things, animals, and nosy people out. The well water was great to drink, cold and totally pure; it tasted really good, and was great to wash with; it was like soft water. His pot plants were hidden somewhere nearby.

Dad and his brother and sister decided, the shadow council of evasive elders, without consulting or informing anyone else, that the cabin was a dilapidated eyesore, beyond repair, and it would be torn down. Simon was livid. He heard about their plan not from them, but from our cousin Didi's kid, Bear, who was hired along with his islander uncles to do the demo. Their plan was to cut the swing tree and another one down, felling them in an X over the cabin, crushing it, then come back in the winter and *torch it!*

They were crazy. The cabin was in good shape. Raised on little stacks of flat rocks under the corner posts, and the joists and junctures underneath, it was a testament to simplicity and perseverance, stolidly surviving, alone, quietly observing the passing play of the elements, down through the seasons, the decades. A musty chapel to the rustic ideal, old New England, pure Thoreau: a brittle sage seated in the purple evergreen shade, a hidden box camera patiently recording the life and light, the lack of both, the neighbor islands across the reflective or textured water, passing boats and birds, groaning, square-cabined lobster boats, sleek summer sails, side-gliding gulls and exhausted, waterlogged cormorants, pumping low over the water, prehistoric, like black arrows indicating the single direction of the past and the future, the blue wind wrapping around the world . . .

The windows, which could still be opened and closed, all panes intact, were always shiny clean, as if someone came and washed them, every time, before you visited. Spruce needles from the tree, from whose reaching branch a swing used to hang, outside the cabin door, had accumulated and rotted through the roof juncture. Squirrels had gotten in, and chewed lower parts of the paper indoor walls into confetti, but hadn't made the place their home. That was all the damage. The kitchen needed only a little help, a propane tank, clean the rust off the stove, get it going. Otherwise the cabin was in perfect condition, waiting for new life—or quite content without. There was no way Simon was going to let them destroy his home, in a like criminally destructive act of pure alcoholic-oblivious sickness. Dad and the other two knew how much Simon loved Burnt Island, and that he used the house. They'd seen the perfectly good mattress he got at the dump and dragged up there, flopping it over the Whaler and somehow driving it to the island. That was probably why they were doing it, like get him out of there.

So he came out of hiding and confronted Dad about it.

It's none of your business, Dad said, and tried to dismiss the subject, and Simon, by walking away. But Simon persisted. Dad didn't want Ginny to see—it'd upset her—so he hurriedly put a halt to Simon's hectoring by saying it wasn't his decision: if Simon got the other two to go along with it, he'd happily agree to let the structure stand, on the condition that Simon saw to the necessary repairs and maintenance.

So it's mine, then?

If you can secure James and Melanie's consent, you have mine—yes.

So all's I have to do is fix it up and it's mine!? *To keep! Always!*

This was his dream come true. Maybe Dad wasn't so bad, after all—all the time. He walked up the hill and talked to Aunt Meanie, having cocktails on her deck with Uncle Pete, with his white sideburns, who put up his hands and said in his throat-scratchy voice,

Whoa, I'm not part of this, when Simon got right to the point.

Oh, that old heap. She waved her hand at it. It's a hazard. We'll build you a tent platform.

Simon told her what Dad said, that he'd fix it up. He loved it there—

Her watery eyes enlarged in her large, magnifying-glass glasses, Melanie shrugged, which brought down the corners of her mouth, at the same time pouting out a glossy lower lip.

They called James from there. Simon started in on him, and he asked to speak to Melanie, please. By the end they agreed, each acting like it was the other two who wanted the cabin destroyed in the first place.

Simon was over the moon. The cabin was his now! He immediately got to work fixing it up, which he'd kind of done, half-assed, before; but now he really did the repairs. As well as he knew how. He put a little skylight in the roof, using a perfectly good window someone threw away at the dump, and patched the roof with wood also salvaged from the dump—his, like, free store. He even painted the floor, and the inside walls and roof-slanted ceiling, white—as far as he got anyway. At low tide he'd carry his supplies across the mudflats and seaweedy rocks from the eastern shore of North Haven, when he couldn't use the Whaler, to the moss-padded paths in the woods where Mum and Dad were walking around on their honeymoon, forever young, Dad holding a branch back for her, Step gingerly, my dear, and he stood in the tall, black-columned shade, white sleeves furled to the elbow, with a cowlicked, freckled Simon on his shoulders, holding on to Dad's bald forehead with both hands, knocking his glasses a little off, as in the framed black-and-white photo in the downstairs bathroom in Manchester . . .

Walking back from the Mexican restaurant, Simon slid behind me when other people came toward us on the sidewalk, to let them pass. I didn't want to mess with his apparent new lease on life, but I had to say something, and said something like,

Simon, don't you get tired of sponging off the family?

His face went cold.

I don't have to stay here, he said.

That's not what I meant. But I do wish you'd at least call in advance, and ask if you can spend the night, instead of just showing up all the time.

I don't want to stay here, he said. He took a threatening step toward me, glaring. You're just like Dad, he said, then walked away.

He took a bus that night, north. Ordinarily for me, it'd be, out of sight, out of mind. It pains and disturbs me to think of Simon, off in his pathetic life. He must be so sad. But he always assures me he's fine. I don't call him, and he doesn't call me. Except when he runs out of money—usually in March, when he's blown the wad he made the summer before, selling paintings in Maine.

Years after my mother died, my aunt, her sister, a real character, boasted that she could "do" Mum really well, as a mimic or an actor—or a sibling—can "do" someone. When I asked her to show me, she hesitated, then decided not to, I'm sure because she knew it was mean. Before she hesitated, though, her hand fluttered up to her hair in a flighty way as she spontaneously began to go into her imitation. Maybe the unerring realism of that gesture—definitely made me think of Mum, distracted, her sunglasses up on her head—stopped her short, because she knew she was right on. She was her sister and, without thinking, could do her like no one else.

I'll start with what happened, then go back and forth between the aftermath and what happened before, leading up.

Simon asked Dad if he could stay at home until his new apartment deal in Boston opened up at the beginning of the month, and Dad said absolutely not and stop asking, so Simon said fuck him, I'm going anyway, and took the train out to Beverly Farms, and walked home along the tracks, his old stomping grounds, past the backs of houses with lawns under trees, behind different fences connected into one long one on either side of the tracks. After the crossing by West Beach the marsh begins under wide, open-armed sky, and the track runs straight through the blond grass, then curves gradually out of sight around the home hill, beyond the far crossing at the other end of the marsh, where Mum got killed. From out on the marsh the hill of home looks like Burnt Island up there, kind of, with its knit hat of fir trees, and the house hidden in there, like behind hair, with its big window eyes looking out over the lawn to the ocean, with its spacial eternity changing colors every day and moods all the time, and its long horizon broken only by islands named House and Misery.

The marsh is like a big meadow with dug straight streams and oaks along the edges, egrets out there sometimes like little white flags. Maybe a gaunt, grandfatherly heron sticking up like a stick. This was one of his places where he'd come as a kid, walk around, the sharp grass collapsed over the marsh like dog's fur, the sponginess underneath, find stuff. Down through the ties of the bridge you can see the little river coming out of the marsh. One of the dogs, Joe-dog, who was a golden retriever and was like Simon, with a like rasta spirit, would just come like trotting, *dum-de-dum,* right along with him over the bridge, like looking for adventure, while the other one, Mosey, a black Lab who was more of a neurotic pussy, would stop at the edge of the bridge and freak out at the openness and the water rushing through in a little white-water quilt. She'd hunker back and bark like mad like at something evil there, like she was one of those Egyptian jackals who were like priests to the underworld, and she knew this was where Mum's soul floated away from the accident and her body at the crossing, crushed, and from the bridge out over the water. A day or so after she was killed, Simon came poking around with a broken hockey stick down at the site of the accident, where they spread new like blue chunky gravel at the crossing, and he found a fragment of the rearview mirror and a piece of the frame of her sunglasses. And then to confirm and like tie it all together, he had that dream where he was her and in the car that went from the top of the hill down to the tracks, timing it perfectly, crashing into the train hidden till the last second behind the big old stable barn beside the tracks. When the Jaws of Death pried open the car to get her body out, he was floating above the scene watching and listening, and then he-she drifted like with the wind, or like they were the wind, away down the tracks, away from the voices along the edge of the marsh, and then away from the marsh openness and out over the water.

At the crossing he looked up with his hand visored over his eyes like a squinty salute at the visored red light that didn't work for Mum, according to the official like denial version, and with the crossed boards with black lettering it was sort of like a skull and crossbones up there. He didn't really feel anything, he was so used to it, like this perpetual fact, and it was a long time ago, though time, he knew, like himself and everything else in the veil of maya world, wasn't really real, especially when it came to the soul, and soul things, like death, or knowing the like higher truth, or— As he moved to keep going, the red light blinked on bright, then right off again when he looked up at it, and he kind of freaked out for a second, stopped in his tracks, stepped back a bit, and it came on again, as the sun hit at just the right afternoon angle to refract through, like magnified from the back, like a signal from the other side, like welcome home, you're supposed to be here, you are welcome here, or like a signal hello from death he moved like a surfer in and out of a few times. Then like with his like marching orders slash confirmation he kept going and made his way up the hill, Mum's like luge-car launching chute, or like a ski jumper speeding down the ramp, timing it perfect—*bam!*—into the train—

The hill used to be so big as a kid, so hard on your bike to get up on the way home from school, you had to zigzag with like real exertion, back and forth, slower and slower, nearer and nearer the top, till you were almost stopped. Passing the

Hunters' driveway at the top of the hill, where you can first see the ocean sloshing around down to the right, and then dipping down along their like hillside domain, beneath their flat, perfect plateau lawn with its low little brick wall rim covered with ivy, he felt like they were there. They were such a solid family, like normal, nice to each other and with a home to return to, though don't kid yourself, he thought—in the ultimate inside, everybody doesn't get along. But you could always go over to their house, take a sugar cube out of the bowl on the kitchen table, though he usually just used to just pass by, like right by the corner of the house, cutting through the hedge, like on the way to the marsh, or later, like when he was eleven, to go get stoned down there. Mr. used to like bellow out your name and joke or like trip you, then went to AA and became like a totally different guy, all sensitive and tall.

The steep, straight driveway they shared between their houses was like a river with banks dividing their land. Mosey 2 saw him coming, came off the porch and stood, pretty fat, on the lawn with her ears up—but didn't come out to greet him, as he came up the home stretch, shushing leaves under the stripped trees, the hill going down on either side, more gently to the right, down through cleared childhood playland to the sea, past the road, and on the left, down steeper into the woods in a couple of long, tilted, leaf-carpeted steps to the railroad tracks. Mosey 2 wagged her tail like mad as he got closer and said something like *!Rulmp,* in a throaty little gulp-yelp of glee, like a yawn, but a yay in there, too, of summoned attachment at Simon's smell and master presence and like blessing touch over her head and ears, like water poured a few touch-thirsty times, and then she followed him and nudged at his hand for more, hey, *more.*

The house was empty and no one was there, he knew, but couldn't be totally sure till he'd been there for a while. He looked in the living room and it was like a set, perfectly set up, with Ginny's bright taste hitting you, and Mum's more like classic kind of crying through in the background, like the old hum of the old home. The front hall he turned back to was totally her, still, with the big open room white and the moldings gray-blue, the French doors to the porch and the tall paned window to the lawn with the sun pouring through, and the same-idea door to the terrace. Mum used to always have blue Pentel or Flair felt-tip pens at her desk, and she was always wondering where they went. The lawn was green still and long with dandelions, Dad.

Hello, he said dully low, pretty loud, in the hollow hall, in case someone was there, somewhere, like cleaning, like Gail, or Ginny got these whole crews in there sometimes. There was definitely no one home, and with the sun coming in, standing there in the time-stillness of the house he grew up in, in the middle of the late day, in later sort of lost life, amid like leftover childhood straining to get through, it felt like sorry unemployment and unassimilated adulthood and— He went to the piano in the corner by the door and, without sitting, played a first few notes, his fingers wider than he was used to on his little Yamaha keyboard. It sounded better, resounding surprisingly real inside the piano, and likewise filling the whole room he wore, in a way, like a house-sized helmet of music covering the life-sized stuff he was thinking/feeling. He hit the opening notes, like a slow, walk-away march, to "Lean on Me," thinking the words, and kept going as far as he knew, then did it again, and then sort of made it up from there, and went off on his own thing.

Half the hooks in the coat corridor were empty, but the bulletin board on the yellow way to the kitchen was chock-full of announcements and clippings and little things really Ginny, more like commercial-practical than personal. There was a mug in the sink, otherwise the kitchen was spotless and in perfect order like the rest of the house, except for Dad's workshop down in the cellar, which had its own kind of cluttered array, like the unconscious of the house, which was more like him, really, than order. There was pretty much food in the refrigerator, leftovers in Tupperware containers and tinfoil over bowls of little potluck mystery goodies. He didn't hear him coming, but the cat bumped like lovingly into his leg and stood there with him looking into the refrigerator, the lit shelves in there and what they had to offer. There was beer on the top shelf right, orange juice, pink grapefruit, and milk. Arctic mist *ahh*-ed out of the packed freezer. Out of all the choices, he just made some toast in the spotless toaster oven they must like empty out and polish every time. In the cabinet under the counter where it always was, the cat still with him, getting his head and tail and skinny little buttonhole butt in the way, was peanut butter, beside all the Campbell's and like baby peas. It was chunky, which he liked, and new, but they'd never notice, and at the bell, spilling crumbs, but how could you not, he made a pb & j, with mucho Smucker's raspberry jam from the shelf on the refrigerator door with all kinds of weird jams and mustards, also French's, and Dad's chutney, pickled watermelon rind, and like Liederkranz. Peanut butter on toast was great, like melted into it a little warm, and so he needed a big glass of milk, too, to wash it down, which did it for the milk, Dad—sorry. When he was done he rinsed the glass and like shook out the water and put it back, then wiped away the crumbs with his hand and sleeve onto the floor.

He went into the TV room and turned on the TV and the light beside him, on the rickety Chinese table with the cracked black lacquer, with gold people in gowns on it and little bridges in the background, that used to be in the living room with the whole like family set getting smaller and smaller, fitting underneath into one another like those dolls, though the smaller ones weren't there now, probably thrown away like so much other stuff. It was talk shows, soaps, the Senate on C-SPAN, with classical music playing over empty seats and people like milling around the chamber and no one at the podium. Court TV was some woman talking. CNN had refugees, VH1 was some bio, but MTV was rap with some pretty sexy black girls pumped up like the guys, in black bicycle shorts and black bras, but only a split second at a time, like strut-grind up, up. That black-and-white old-movie channel he was starting to kind of like when he got around someone's TV with cable had on a war movie, World War II in the South Pacific. The navy was everywhere once you were in it, like all the military, and war, too, once you realized it, we're like a total warrior culture, like the burning Armada prints over the bookshelves on the fireplace wall, all tilting a little from the spinning of the earth, Dad said, or the model of the *Constitution,* with the dust-thickened black thread rigging Dad made on his lap on a board in front of the TV, back when, like on school nights, his beer sending bubbles up its glass beside him, on display ever since high above the TV, on top of the bookshelves Dad also made back then. Witness came in, Hi, kitty, and jumped up onto the sofa and settled beside him, circling on the cushion and pumping down with his front paws, whyever they do that, like jungle nature, checking for snake holes, or pushing for the mother's nipple. Bombs missed the boat, just, kersplashed the water up around them like white palm tree negatives, upside down, of the ones tattered and tall, but small, onshore, and then the big mountain mushroom cloud of Bikini Atoll, while the Nips, like hornets, dive-bombed into battleships, after going, blank-faced, to their own funeral ceremonies, in silk bathrobes with wide silk belts and samurai swords, tea served by geisha girls with painted doll faces, bowing and walking away backward with little tiny steps under their kimonos dragging on the floor, turning and gliding away like they had bowls of water on their heads.

We've lost contact, sir, and Witness perked his head and

pointed his ears like radar when the bombs started banging again.

Dad came home when the news was just coming on, telling the top stories, and it was starting to get dark out. When he heard the car come in, Simon shut out the light, turned off the TV, and put the channel changer where it was on top of the TV on his way out, and went straight back to his room, past the kitchen, up the three steps by the stairs down to the cellar. He heard the front door open and rattle shut, and stood there listening. Without looking at himself in the big framed mirror over the Brown Thing, the old thick oak bureau inside the front door, with its three heavy stuck drawers, Dad looked through the mail, tossed the bills into the china plate to take into work, pay from there, part of his mystery of money not existing for his kids, but it never went away for him, for one minute of the forty years of family still ticking, pulsing out there, and here, within, his kids grown and thrown at various points in the great flux, the ever-present pressure ever present, even when dissolved, liquified warmly at night, every night, with all the bourbon-softened burdens of self and life. Forty years of family and this was a man who did his duty daily, off to work and back, like this, to his relative peace, an evening at home. He went up the stairs, and a middle one creaked, which Simon heard like a house-grunt hint, and knew Dad was going upstairs. A minute later the pipes sang, and there they were in their two opposite corners, upstairs and down, at opposite ends of the huge empty house.

Dad's funeral was held at St. John's in Manchester, where he and Ginny got married, on the way to Singing Beach. A small stone chapel with dark brown trim and a gravel walkway to the doorway, curved like a cartoon mouse's private entrance, it was usually open only in the summer months, but had heating, which came up through the metal floor grates dotted around the perimeter, puffing up your pant legs, breathing into the bells of women's dresses.

Dad never went to church (though he used to make a token paterfamilias appearance at the Catholic church with Mum and family on Christmas and Easter), as church is optional for WASPs, like a social gathering. So it seemed a little odd that his last worldly rite should take place in this unfamiliar little chapel, presided over by this guy no one knew, instead of outdoors somewhere, one of his places, like the garden at home, or even out on Singing Beach, just a five iron away behind the screen of trees like exposed nerves etched against the scar sky.

The casket sat raised in the center aisle up front, blocking and dwarfing the meager stage setting, the plain oak lectern to one side and the small sandstone altar behind. Lit candles stood in ascending rows on either side. Light from the lamps along the side walls petered out a foot away from the mounted sconces, so that each was a low-glowing globe in the general chapel gloom, as scarcely lit by the frosted white windows, patterned in miniature swirls, the perimeters rimmed with small leaded diamond panes, whose colors, barely illumined, all seemed the same dark tint.

Cars parked along the road and couples dressed in black came in looking late, looking around, nodded or whispered to others just arrived, still standing in the back, or looking back from their pews. Red dot flames flickered in their red glasses in the rear. Voices mingled softly like a formless, jumbled prayer, a quiet cocktail party transported, abbreviated by propriety and somber sadness, and swallowed in the dark open ark of the chapel, with its black-stained roof beams and rows of pews to seat, for this brief ferry transit, the survivors. The light fresh scent of lemony ammonia rose from the recently mopped linoleum floor in the warm dry air of the heating system and mingled with the arriving wafts of women's perfume, the irrepressible out-of-season mustiness, and a faint somber tinge of incense, the worn woody smell of the pews or something in the mingle suggesting the sweet dirt smell of rosewood ashes, like Mum, or cedar chips or sawdust, like Dad. Faceted glass cylinders of tallow yellow light hung by black chains from the ceiling over the single center aisle. The casket was black, bulky, and round like an overturned rowboat, perfect for Dad, large and seaworthy, for his further passage.

The church was nearly full, and the minister had peeked out his door twice by the time the first of the black limousines pulled up outside. The passenger door was opened by one of the stocky funeral parlor guys, who looked like a hit man, standing there with a solid, bought, solemn expression, blow-dried hair, hands behind his back as if he were handcuffed. Ginny's black shoes stuck out first, their game spike heels. Her ankles were swollen, like her spotty hand grasping the padded handle on the door, from the cortisone she took for her arthritis, and looked like they were wrapped with an Ace bandage under her stockings. She ducked out, face painted and wrecked by grief, followed by her two daughters, both tall and angular compared to her, and then, after a pause, like an afterthought, or a surprise, or begrudgingly, came her son, Arthur, who hadn't put in an appearance around here for years. The house they grew up in, in her first marriage—to a lanky, moneyed, beetle-browed drinker and tennis player and TV sports fan, a ranting complainer and bitter clever cynic when drunk—was just down the road from here. Arthur's thinned hair was frizzed, almost aglow, stunned, like it wasn't used to being washed and brushed. He looked like a dandelion, preblown. Both sisters wore a paper-white star: Phoebe in her leonine hair held back with a tortoiseshell comb over one ear, Elaine's pinned to the narrow lapel of her belted charcoal dress. Ginny, dry eyed and mean looking under her black veil, looked very small and frail and tired, if rugged, ready to fight or scramble like a goat up life's next rocky slope. She waited for Arthur, who took a last tug on his Camel non and flicked it not too far away, as if into an anarchist's stream of gasoline, then stepped over to her, hunched as if cold, cowled, just like his dad, and offered her his arm. They went in without waiting for the explosion, the other car, which pulled up presently. It was as if the two families, never really joined into one, now that Dad was dead, had divided back into the two original separate factions.

The first limo moved ahead and stopped, then slid away to go find a place to park or turn around, while the other pulled up to unload. Last arrivals trickled in as Red stepped out of the limo, followed by Anna, and then the brothers, dressed in dark jackets and Dad's ties. Simon's jacket, from his closet, from his past, was too small now, tight around the neck and shoulders, and the sleeves were an inch too short. The ties were Timmy's idea, out of necessity, since Simon didn't have one, and his one tie, the floral Liberty tie from his wedding the ushers wore also, was too festive. Paperwhites in their lapels matched Red's in hers. These were her idea; she cut them from Dad's crop down in the cellar and brought them around, room to room, upstairs and down, and gave them to everyone, along with a pearl-headed pin, while they were dressing. Ginny smiled thinly thanks-no-thanks and didn't wear hers. Red was like a man in her severe black suit, the long skirt hugging her narrow hips like a long black heart, tapering down to the ankles, where her two little shoes with thick heels stuck down like pegs to hold the heart up.

Ginny and her brood of three were just entering the chapel as the Curtises were unloading. Red led the way with her arm hooked in Simon's, followed by Timmy and Anna arm in arm. Arriving they had seen all the cars parked along either side of the road, but still felt like they were alone until they got inside the chapel and saw everyone there, like a surprise. Ginny and Arthur and Phoebe and Elaine waited inside the vestibule for

the Curtises. The congregation was quiet but not silent, just as
the chapel was dim but not dark, as the eyes adjusted, and the
moment ritually shuffled and rearranged, as the two families
entered in back, moved up the aisle in pairs, and filed into the
front two pews beside Dad. Ginny directed Arthur into the second pew, and Red, behind her, stooped forward to suggest he
join Ginny in the front row. He obeyed; he got up and sort of
hobbled sideways out, glancing wincingly at the others from
his pained perspective, and then moved sideways into the front
pew and settled with slumped shoulders beside his mother,
who looked straight ahead and ignored him and all the rest of
them.

On the other side of Dad in the front rows sat his sister and
brother and company: Aunt Meanie and Uncle Pete, Greg,
Uncle James and Aunt Nubs, and behind them in the second
row, Didi and Bear Junior and Didi's new husband, a Swedish
pilot who looked like a tennis pro.

The minister came out in his black pants and shirt and
white tab collar, no robe, followed by Mr. Hunter in a dark blue
suit, hair slicked back, his familiar tortoiseshell glasses, looking a little rattled and old, tall and gaunt and slow, like he just
recovered from an injury, as from a car crash—called life. In his
recovery he served as deacon at the Episcopal church in town,
the steepled, postcarded mother ship of this little summer
shell. Mr. Hunter wasn't Dad's best friend—Dad didn't have a
best friend—but he was a good friend, golf partner, and good
neighbor next door for over thirty years. For a while there was
the hope that maybe his new AA leaf would rub off on Dad, but
that didn't happen. They probably never talked about it.

The chapel was full of friends, not seen during the service
but collectively felt behind the family in the front rows, leading the seated and standing march into eternity, all connected
to Dad, which gave him a grave, commanding stature he didn't
have alive, a stature nobody had alive, because it was the power

of pure spirit, emotion, memory, death: the fraught omission, that conspicuous absence and pervasive powerful presence, numinous, like God.

The maternal, pear-shaped minister, his soft face pink, as shiny on top as his close-shaved cheeks, as if polished, fed the familiar farewell words to the congregation with an effeminately careful enunciation—

Oh God, our refuge and strength

—his maternal personality seeping into the solemnity of the ceremony, faintly disturbing the listeners as well as the transmission from on high, the benediction and ritual rote passage into the eternal tube.

Mr. Hunter read the Twenty-third Psalm. His voice caught a couple of times—

He maketh me to lie down in green pastures

—which he handled calmly by raising his head and looking benignly out over the congregation, who were entirely with him and lifted him back, and it was generally felt that this was the real heart of the service. Then the minister said Red would read, referring to her by her real name, Camilla. She slipped out from her place in the front row and cleared her throat at the lectern as she adjusted the microphone down. She read, without a glitch, a poem called "My Spirit Will Not Haunt the Mound," by Thomas Hardy, in an appropriately flat, but precious, sort of high-mass monotone. Returning to her seat she paused at the casket and touched it with one hand, kissed the fingertips of her other hand, and touched it with that hand too, then bowed her head, and crossed herself quickly.

The organ was a small surprise when it breathed its first notes. Hands reached for hymnals and leafed quickly for the page posted in black numerals on the wooden rack up on the left. They sang four verses of "Rock of Ages." After the hymn the congregation settled back into the pews with the rumbly, ruffled sound a sail makes when the boat comes about; it flaps wildly above in a momentary bout of contained chaos, then all at once the sail is full again and it is silent, or maybe laughs a little, and then is belly-full and silent. Next came the minister's personal message. He kept it brief. Without pretending to have known Dad, he praised his character—his well-known wit, intelligence, and kindness, his courtly manner and sense of duty, a true gentleman the likes of whom the world has very few examples remaining. And he indicated the show of love in attendance, testimony to a grand man, and mentioned, as well as the terrible sorrow, the sweet intimacy of grief. They should celebrate Dad's life, he suggested, as well as grieve his passing. No mention was made of the way he died.

The organ sounded again some rousing, somber, ancient first footsteps, the mourners shuffled and stood and sang, "Allelujah." The congregation settled again as if they were coming about again a final time—Dad's last sail home—and he was and he wasn't there. The body was blessed and entrusted to God, to dust, from whence it came. Reverend Wood smoothed his fulvous front, blessed those present, and withdrew, followed by Mr. Hunter. The service was over. The organ went into "Allelujah" again as two undertaker thugs moved in on the casket from either side. Two of Dad's friends came gravely up the aisle and, together with the Curtis brothers and Uncle James, they gripped the brass handles running along either side, lifted the casket from its mahogany cradle, and carried Dad out of the chapel.

Red stepped aside in the aisle to let Ginny and Arthur go first, then she and Anna followed at a royal distance, trailed by Aunt Melanie and Uncle Peter, then Elaine and Phoebe. Friends looked at them and smiled and cried. Some mouthed condolences, brief grief greetings, some set their mouths and brows in fixed expressions of sympathy, others were wrapped, faraway, in their own sadness. The next few rows filed out in order after them, until the remaining congregation collectively vetoed the wait and poured together into the middle aisle and swelled out slowly as one into the surprisingly bright, white-walled afternoon. On the walkway and the moist lawn beside the chapel there were hugs and handshakes, murmured conso-lations and hesitant good-byes, as there was no get-together afterward. He would have wanted it that way, everyone agreed. Besides, the burial was too far away, it didn't make sense.

Out the window beside his bed the trees were night black prison bars, and the sky behind was going away, coming through with red bled into the white in the one sun spot, brighter then gone, through the web of density, already dark in the high wall of the woods across the driveway he had looked out his window at all his life, and now here he was still. If you believe the soul is outside you, in a way, manifesting in every-thing it comes in contact with, and sees itself in, and lives in, like he knew, like inspiration, the anima out there and in here, both, together, as one, then this was one of the places his soul lived, and stayed, like Maine, too, and would always, even if he didn't even like the actual view, or like nonview, here, with the marsh blocked by the trees, not seen but known, looming there behind, with Mum and him the boy down there, and him the soul like suspended and embedded out there, right here, sepa-rate from everyone else, outside of time— Most of the trees in their straight-pant tallness stayed still, but a more slender one, near the middle, moved like its own sort of person metronome, left and right, shoulders tight, this black stripe, like with its own wind, and another one, smaller, beside it, moved, too, not in time, and its branches. He always had the feeling, seeing this as a kid, from upstairs in his room, going to bed in summer, and the side seasons, when it was still light, that out there in the woods was where night receded to during the day, and came out of at dusk, which was why it was darker, already, all day, and the seasons and nature and even, like, evil, the same thing, came out of these home woods, all woods, like a gas, or like this tall, like, ghost army, and that's why the cats liked to go in there, and him, too, back then at least. Now, though, he felt like no one was there, was the truth of it, nothing, and that made the soul a lonely place, not that he was lonely, him, but *it* was, maybe, who could blame it, and so he stopped looking into that particular void penetration, though he liked it, too, in a way, like longing, and turned on the TV on his bureau in there, the old Quasar black-and-white, as old as him almost, and still a clear picture, but no knob or reception for UHF, except for channel 38, which it was stuck on, but was all he wanted, anyway, for the Sox, who just died again, of course, in the play-offs, and the Bruins, whose season had already started. There was a coat hanger pulled open for an antenna, stuck in where the original one broke off, and it worked perfectly well, maybe better, if you thought about the transmitted waves being received in, like through a diamond-shaped basketball hoop, instead of just hitting or missing the like pencil regular antenna.

Out in the passage, he had the volume on low, he heard Dad cough and come walking into the kitchen, so he turned the volume down to nothing and sat on the end of his bed and waited there, listening. The house was a big box, with the kitchen the one jog out, its door at the end of the porch, with its pillars and railing and robin's egg ceiling. The window, over the sink opposite the door, looked out over the open back space, the garbage area roof, and the long like shoe box addition at the turn of the century, the back of the house, which wasn't heated or fixed up or even used, except for storage and childhood roaming, except for the first two rooms downstairs, reclaimed to this side for baby-sitters, which since Ginny moved in just over a year after Mum died was Simon's room. So you could see from the kitchen window over to Simon's window, right there to the right, if you leaned over the sink, and from Simon's room you could see the kitchen window, right there, if you stuck your head out the window, or pressed the side of your face up against a pane, and its light, at night. But so there they were, in rooms a right angle apart, right next to each other, out of the whole house, out of the whole world.

Dad put some green olives with those orange pimento plugs from a glass tube jar into a ribbed white dish, then fed the cat, in evidence underfoot, insisting in eights, then fed the dog, waiting mutely patient out on the porch by her bowl. Feeding the animals wasn't normally his task, but with Ginny away he had to do it. This time alone was like a taste of what life would be like if she died first, which they'd agreed wouldn't happen, and it was just as well, he thought now, because what an empty, pointless proposition that would be. He went with a glass out the passage, past the phone on the wall, past the portholed dining room door left always open, and through the end of the dining room, dusky dark now, to his liquor closet, narrow and tall and orange inside, and in the light from the front hall through the doorway right there, poured himself his first. He sipped some, standing there, and the welcome whiskey forked so fine, spread its fingers down the back of his throat in that soft first burn, part pleasure blending in, branding its greeting, welcome home, and he topped the glass back off, and carried it, belly-eye high, back to his business.

Simon sat there in the room getting dark as Dad went right past down the stairs to the basement workshop under him and under the kitchen, turned on the lights, his sausage finger to the wall switch button with mother-of-pearl, like a dime, inlaid where you push, and on came all the bare bulbs and scoop lights clamped all over the place, all hooked up together with extension cords into extension cords, stapled and held by bent nails into the walls and ceiling. His L-shaped stand-up workbench was in the kids' old playroom, right under Simon's room, where Simon now sat on the bed, and the older headquarters were deeper down into the earth, like the Bat Cave, two steps down into the cellar proper, under the kitchen, and reaching off in the cat-dark regions under the other rooms. The boat he didn't finish in Maine he left up there in the middle house, but he had the plans here, with the descending dimensions of the optional ribs he was making now, for support, because the hull, as it was, though certainly light enough to suit his purposes, even with the fiberglass layers to come, would be too flimsy, not rigid enough. He had a TV down here in his element and turned it on to half watch, and to have the presence there, to accompany him while he rounded the hours into one pleasant pass, stilling his humming placement, releasing both ways in time, making measurements and pencil marks on bone bare strips of wood, remembering things, thinking.

Dad had his half gallon jug of Early Times down there, so he didn't need to come upstairs, and didn't until after nine, when he cleared his throat, really close, at the top of the stairs, and said something. Simon turned down his TV because Jesus, he was right there at the top of the stairs outside his room. Dad walked away and Witness walked in a few seconds later, it was him he was talking to. He got a glass of ginger ale in the kitchen, and turned out the lights as he went out to the front hall and on upstairs. Dad always went to bed early, now that he was old, and after a little wait Simon went out to get something to eat, and then was free to watch TV, any channel and normal loudness, with the whole house between them, in their up- and downstairs opposite corners, and Dad's blotto sleep.

Simon heard, blended otherly in his dream, then registered in his waking consciousness, the muffled *Help!* yelp of the pipe banging off, and then the silence and sore, like, self again, sort of awake, morning, alone in the jar room, stirred like with this nervousness zipping around inside, he felt like he'd been washed up on a beach—and then the wave went away and left him lying there, awake in his old room, with the last bedsheet part of the receding wave still over him like shrink-wrapped, rumpled and smooth, and if he didn't move, the weird, next, better feeling stayed, that he was kind of suspended, and could almost tip up backward and like shoot headfirst out of the bed, and so to keep it, for like a minute, in that legless *whoah*-no zone, he didn't move. The window beside his bed starts lower than the bed, so he had a whole view out over the roof of the garbage area, the driveway, and the tall trees behind, in their tall, columned, evergreen interweave, washed in soft light with such clarity and attention to detail, and such stillness, like waiting out there in presto renewal, like totally morning. When he used to have to take a nap as a kid, up in his room upstairs, he'd look out into the tops of the trees, and more than once, till it became just part of looking out, he had this intense feeling of what freedom would be, and he imagined going out on the end of those upper branches and being out there where it became a bough, a boat, sprayed out, and sat, or like floated, lying there, like a Christmas tree ornament, or like a prince on a raft in the air, instead of trapped here in his room, age five or six, in his prison.

He was still in bed when Dad came downstairs and veered into the kitchen, so he just stayed there, he would never come back here, why would he. If he kept both ears off the pillow, he could hear the kitchen pretty well, he was surprised, he didn't think you could so well from out here around a few corners. Not distinctly, but just, and there wasn't much to hear, just Dad coughing a couple of times, some knocks, like of cupboard and counter, and the faucet running, and the toaster oven's tiny *ding!*

Dad didn't spend five minutes in the kitchen, then came

past and went back up to his room for a minute, then down, and was out the rattly front door, and started up his car with a catching cough, like him, and then three big throat-clearing *vrooms.* Craning past the kitchen, just over the yew hedgerow that needed a haircut pretty bad, Dad, he saw the back of Dad's car back up and stop, then slide forward out of sight, off to work. Years ago he could have retired already and gotten three-quarters pay for life, but he didn't know what else to do, because this was what he was, and who, but then last year he had to retire, no choice, and got half salary and benefits for life for just staying away. So now he went to his new volunteer job at the Vedder Foundation, which had all this money, and all these charities and environmental groups, and like a penance for being a Republican all his life, he helped figure out how to make more money, from the right investments, and who to give it all to, and what for. Simon felt like he should be getting paid, and a lot, for a job like that, he was sure there were other people there he was working with, doing the same thing, or way less, who were getting paid plenty. Ginny hooked him up with these people, she had him wrapped around her little finger, and so on the one hand he was this rich retired investment banker giving away his time and experience and work for free, and like giving away his island in Maine, but on the other hand he was still a real tightwad, worrying about money all the time, and not having enough, even though they'd go on these trips all the time, all around the world, and Ginny had everything new she wanted, and she loved new things, and spent like wild, even though she supposedly was this big Democrat.

Like Dad, he had an English muffin and some coffee, since the coffee was there, but he wasn't addicted to it like Dad, like the rest of the world, who had no idea how serious an addiction it was. That's where the real money was, in people's addictions, because as long as they're alive they keep paying you.

There was nothing to do and he hated this dead empty feel-

ing he got here like it lived here, and in him too— He went up
into Dad's bedroom and was surprised, a little, to see Dad's bed
unmade, on his side, because he'd never seen it unmade before,
except when Mum and Dad were in it and you went in there.

Mum? in the dark, or early morning, grainy gray, or maybe
moon blue light in the windows, and on the floor, and the
snowy corner on the bed.

What is it, Pooh-bear? as over there her wave curls up.

But when he thought about it he wasn't surprised, he
couldn't see Dad bending over naked, or after he's dressed,
pulling the sheet flat and smoothing it out and folding it over
the blanket and tucking it in. Dad left his razor on the side of
the sink, but put the shaving cream back in the medicine cabinet. He had Edge, like Timmy, like father like son, and he wondered if it was Ginny, or just like human nature, like genetic
evolution through advertising, that got him to change from the
regular white shaving cream he used to use, like Palmolive lime
or like Barbasol. Before that, when he was a kid, he used the
brush and soap and lathered it on, it looked so fun being a
grown-up. Simon shaved for the first time in a few days, so it
sort of hurt, and kept clogging the razor, so he had to rinse it a
lot, and then the precision around the mouth, and moving the
skin over not to nick the Adam's apple. He brushed his teeth
with Dad's green toothbrush, hard bristle, Dad, bad for your
gums, make them recede, and Crest, and stepped into the
shower he hadn't been in since he was a kid having a bath in
here for a treat. When he got the croup Mum brought a chair
into this bathroom, in the middle of the night, it was great, and
turned on the shower all the way hot, to steam up the room,
and sat him in the chair, it was great, even if it didn't work it
worked. The shower's walls and sliding door was this dimpled
frosted glass like ice, and Mum in her bath would hide her
heavy breasts with one arm, but not all the way, and not make
him leave right away, and her nipples were big and dark red

like lips. Wrapped in her towel she had her vaccination mark, this dimple, like in a mattress with the button gone, like an arrow went into her fat, for smallpox, and it stayed in, and farther back on her back she had a big mole, like Simon's on his elbow. He dried himself with the other towel Dad didn't use, and burr-dried his hair and put it back folded how it was before, almost—good enough.

Out in the bedroom with nothing on he saw himself sideways in the mirror, pretty big cock, check it out, and automatically pulled in his belly sticking out, he thought he didn't have one, really, but he did. Over in front of the closet mirrors, he opened the two side doors and shut them around himself in the little triangle room of mirrors, like he used to do, and there he was in a row getting smaller going away, his whole body he didn't see often like this, multiplied naked going off in the perspective distance beyond the looking glass, a hundred of him in different directions, and also the backside view of his head and body in diminishing repetition, and he flexed his torso and arms and shoulder slopes, like those guys do, forearms forward, look at that, definitely. His ass was white from no sun, but pretty nicely round, so with blurred eyes it looked like he had on a little bathing suit, except for the rusty nest, and the like big nose, drooping. Rusty Frog, he used to want his name to be. Seeing yourself naked like this from weird angles, and repeated, showed you in the most basic way you couldn't deny, multiplied, who you were, and it was a surprise, kind of enthralling, like idiot's like sensual-existential delight, and he thought of a woman seeing him or he could shave his whole body and be like one.

There wasn't really anything to do, so he went down to the rocks, just like he used to when there was nothing to do, or the marsh. Down at the Bigelows' pool, built into the rocks, he decided to do a painting from down there of out to the islands, and went back up the path to the house to see what he could find. His room was really two rooms, and in the outer room he knew there were maybe some paints, and he was right, in a box on top of the bookcase, but there weren't many colors, and half of them were dried up, no caps, but there was a watercolor kit there Red gave him once and it was still hardly used, but no brush. But Dad had plenty of those little cheapo brushes down in his cellar, and he found them after a while, after a wandering search, like when he was a kid, poking around down there among all the workshop tools and clamps and boxes spilled all over the place that spelled Dad, or like his unconscious. It felt dead down here in a way, the closed cellar stop in time, and he just wanted to get back up and outside to the living opposite, the wide open blue-eyed day. Dad had a good new Aquabee sketch pad, too, for some reason, for this reason, him, now, perfect for watercolors. On his way back down the path a car swept by at the bottom of the hill, lifting leaves, but didn't come up the driveway, and was gone, maybe a cop on his route.

He hadn't done watercolors for the longest time. It was different, it was nice the way it decided for itself, kind of, as it went into blends, bleeding, and the wash colors were all see-through suggestions of their solid selves, white showing through, and white, where you left it, was a color, too, it was, like, pervasive, it was like death, if you thought about it, there all the time, like the background of life life's made on, and there in every part of it, because life was flux through life, with death showing through the motions, whose time-limited colors, outside of time, like in art, were unlimited, which is why art thought it was eternal. It felt like a Sunday, except out of whose life, like that feeling as a kid you wish you could shoot ahead into the future and be yourself there, see what it's like, see what you're like—and *great,* here he was, like this.

He always felt like the ocean was different down here in Massachusetts than in Maine, even though Maine was like less than a hundred miles away over the same body of water, or two.

It was softer, if not in obvious color, quite, then its inner personality, what it held and did with the elements and their long-held secrets, the riddles of nature buried alive in there, ruthless, from here to the outer map edges of history, all its brave pathways, busy blue stripes, the endless penned horizons and people looking at them, dreaming about something somewhere else. The Atlantic is heavy. Mum used to say, about the Pacific, that its horizon seemed a little higher than the Atlantic. Or like they say, like the Mayans or whatever, the Pacific has no memory. Which, what a way to be, imagine. The Atlantic has like total recall.

This time of year, with the longer light and shorter days and whatever it was in the air— When he came out of the house, a dried leaf drove across the driveway like a little car, and it could have been funny, skidding, skittering like a crab, but instead he almost felt like crying. It was the saddest time of the year, like nostalgic, loss in every leaf and missing leaf, but beautiful, but beautiful more, maybe, to look at and get like the cinematic emotional sense of, stark and dark, than to be in under its motherless wet-blanket influence and wish you were somewhere else. Painting it now he was surprised how many houses there were out on Bakers Island, scattered under the lighthouse he looked out at all his life, and he wondered who they were, like all fishermen, and they must have a little harbor out there, with docks for their boats, or just moorings, or just regular people, like anywhere else, watching TV, they must have dishes, fat wives, bored kids leaving plastic toys all over the lawn island.

The two smokestacks over by Salem, like a couple of upright cigars, gave out gray plumes, thickening purply off to the side, even though supposedly they were antipollution. A late, long wind searched the coast and questioned the trees, stripped of their identity, twisting in the wind, and the twiggy, sifted answer was a long soft sigh like up to Canada. The waves, but in waves, made almost the same sound, but like in your mouth. It carried in the cold, overlooked him and called him home, it was chilly the whole time, but he kept at it, painting, anyway, clenched, his hands going hard, and he remembered the time, on a day like this, when Mum took them down here to take their picture together against the ocean on the edge of the wall, so it looked like they were in the back of a boat, but up high, with the waves sloshy gray behind in the black-and-white gray sea, and the wind whipping their hair in the longhair seventies she died at the end of, gone like that, and there was something there besides the wind, the wind was just a suggestion of it, which was why it was there, and the lament whispered away the waste of life sometimes stretching back so far, with so much missing, he couldn't stand it, and what it opened, and so he like corked himself, the way you can shut a thought, or at least he can, and the cold bottle body finally like popped him back home.

It must have been their theme this week because there was another World War movie on, in the Ardennes this time, with Messerschmitts groaning over in flocks and bombs whistling down and— He went in the kitchen and made a sandwich of leftover roast beef cut thick, eating a few chewy pieces in the process, and mayonnaise. Dad had it pretty good, with his roast beef and this whole setup for so long, but they spent so much and kept getting new things, as many as Ginny wanted, which was always more, and him, too, it was sick, the typical capital-ist sickness of materialism.

When Dad came home he did the same thing as the day before, and the charade went on, adjacent again, beginning with the ritual whiskey libation, with Simon listening, then the two TVs came on, like eyes opening, one above the other, in the near dark, separated just by the floor, which from below was ceiling. From outside, like to Witness or whoever, the audience woods, it was like the set of a stage, with the father in his basement workshop under the son in his bedroom directly above, and the father doesn't know the son is there, it's like classic. Dad picked up where he left off, and the problem was no easier of how to bend these strips he was measuring and making and going to glue together into ribs, though the problem was clearer, which was the greater part of the solution. Surely he wouldn't have to make a mold, that would be absurd, they were all different sizes, he might as well make a whole new boat. Measuring and cutting and sanding his strips was easy enough, though, so he kept going with that, and would resolve the difficulty, one way or another, as always, in due course, as it were. Simon wished he would pay attention to the show that was on, so he'd see how stupid it was and change the channel, so Simon could, too, and finally, forget it, he changed it himself, with the volume down. There was a documentary about the sixties, with Vietnam and hippies protesting, and he wanted to hear it, so he turned it up a little, it was Jimi Hendrix doing the national anthem over shots of napalm strafing rice paddies and bamboo villages with running little people and palm trees and hilly jungle countryside, like a game.

Dad coughed, and Simon turned the volume down, and heard him coming up the stairs, with his TV still on down there, and the light from the window down there a tilted trapezoid out on the ground in the dark under Simon's room, his blinking blue bleeding out. He went into the kitchen and got something, and went back downstairs again. Simon figured he just went into the kitchen and got something and went back downstairs again. He figured if he just went up, he wouldn't go up again, right away, so he went into the kitchen himself a minute later, like father like son, and, moving smoothly, grabbed a ginger ale and a bag of Fritos from the open corner shelf, and a couple of Milano Pepperidge Farm cookies from an open pack. They were like stiff glove fingers, he bit one in half, and always didn't like the chalky feel in his teeth of the first few bites of this kind of cookie, but they tasted good, he grabbed the whole pack, and he went back to his room, pausing at the top of the stairs to listen to Dad down there, his TV car chase, with screeches and a base guitar pulling it along, and his occasional little wood taps, and him like walking, and a cough.

The burial was in Brookline, where Dad grew up and his parents were buried in the family plot. About ten cars, all with their headlights on, followed the two limousines behind the hearse. They wound through quiet Manchester, led by a police car, which pulled over at the Y intersection in the center of town, blocking the incoming cars, so that the procession could proceed unbroken. A few people stood on the sidewalk and watched them pass. The flag on the green in front of the town hall was limp at half-mast. A stout old woman walking her dog stopped and crossed herself while her stubby dog strained ahead against the leash, avidly sniffing a yellow hydrant. Village houses, lined up like used books, familiar old volumes, discarded themselves, one after another, as they pulled past. Going down the hill out of town they snaked around a double-parked delivery van and slid along the homestretch of 127, past the field with the small red farm with the derelict greenhouse. A brown swayback horse stood grazing in the grass. Inside the limo Timmy sat back in the middle of the soft seat with his arm around Anna, his knees apart, her head resting on his shoulder. His face was poached around the eyes from crying. He stared straight ahead. Red sat on his other side, sunken in the plush burgundy leather like it was a man. She dreamily watched the landscape float past, her face long and faraway. Simon shared the opposing sort of sofa jump seat, taking up more than his half by sitting hulkily sideways. His shoes were his sneakers, flecked with coffee ice cream paint. His pants were Tee's, the belt who knows, his jacket his, his shirt and tie Dad's. He had loosened his tie, the small knot yanked to one side. He didn't look sad, or any blanker than usual. When they came to the turn to home by the Old Corner Inn, he pointed at it with his forefinger and his thumb up like a gun, aimed and lifted back with a whispered little *pshoo*. He glanced aside to see if he had any audience, smiled to himself smally. Another cop car was waiting on the side of 127 in the driveway of Brookwood School, where they all went, on the border of Beverly Farms, and it pulled out with the blue lights going and escorted them to 128, along the winding Grapevine Road, driveways with mailboxes and houses with fences, stone walls, a field, a church, along the curving corridor walled and sparsely roofed by late fall trees already all winter sticks. At 128 there was a state trooper waiting on the grass by the cloverleaf entrance ramp. Without turning on its lights it led the way, sticking to the right lane, through sparse traffic, commercial strips with commercial lease signs, exit signs for towns and roads, their childhood map with Mum, and Dad, low mirrored buildings surrounded by vast parking lots surrounded by woods, lots under development and unclaimed meadows, all glimpsed in passing from the tinted ultrasmooth silence of the padded interior.

Dad's commute, Timmy said. Red patted his hand, Anna tapped his tie, Dad's tie. They went past the Route 1 turnoff for Boston and Simon went,

Tseh, and when he saw he'd gotten their attention enough he added, This way's so much longer. These guys don't know what they're doing.

Yeah, but maybe it's easier this way, Timmy replied, with all these cars, and where we're going.

Simon looked through the thick glass partition to the front seat and the driver's area to see if he could see anything. Then he inspected the closed console behind him. He ran his fingers along the top edge, then poked at the middle of the cabinet

door in case it was a pop latch, and pulled with his bit finger-
nails stuck into the seam like a rock climber.

Liquor cabinet, he said.

Simon, Jesus, Timmy sighed.

Anna looked at him with her mouth set with something to
say, but didn't say it. Red opened her eyes and languidly closed
them again, feline.

'S locked. Simon shrugged. In the center of the partition was
a radio dial. He turned one knob and the needle moved. He
turned the other and to his surprise the radio came on, static,
loud, like they were inside a big fly. He turned it down all the
way, then graded it up again to a reasonable volume, but still
static. The numbers and the needle were illumined by an
orange bar glowing behind. Simon searched for a song but got
only static and talk.

Simon, come on, Timmy complained.

But Simon ignored him and pressed on, He realized it was
on AM, and found the button to switch it to FM. The static
vanished, and in the next centimeter was that old Three Dog
Night song: Jeremiah was—

He nixed it and moved on to the next, the Who. One of
those ones where Pete Townsend's arm goes around and around
in a big wheel hitting the guitar strings till his hand bleeds.

No, said Timmy.

'S like oldies.

The next one was heavy metal he didn't know and went
right through it. After an ad and then a hyper, chipper deejay
voice he cut off he stopped on a guitar with some bongos with
the drums. It was familiar and pretty good but when it sang it
was Billy Joel. To another emphatic no he didn't need he inched
ahead and got that Counting Crows song where the guy whines
that he really really really really really needs a

raincoat,

which Timmy liked, actually, but maybe for Simon hit too close to home, like his anthem of the pathetic loner life, so he kept going to a twangy slide guitar and a woman singing country.

Si, maybe right now's not the time for music, Red said huskily, low, like she had to clear her throat but didn't, her eyes still closed.

Maybe it depends on the music, he answered.

Anna stroked Timmy's collarbone and made a fish-kissy mouth up at him; Timmy's jaw remained as hard as his eyes were incensed. The next selection Simon came across came in clear and a little louder than the others. It was soft piano and yearning violin, pure delicate thought caught up in love's magic spell, slow with grief and attentive moment. In only a few phrases it delivered them aloft, together, in the suspended transportation of music. It was lovely. The hidden speakers were really good, clear and full, sourceless, and it lifted them partway out of themselves, by gradual persuasion, to a softer surface of mind in the air, out of this world, deeper into the heart, like crying, devastating and welcome and sweet while it lasts, just far and fast and light enough to follow inside, listening, nearing the holy spirit like breathing it, Saugus and cars out the tinted window, Santoro's parking lot and the tea pond through the trees behind, gulls slowly gyring in the music over the water. Chopin's Nocturne in E-flat, rearranged for violin and piano, the sonorous voice informed them after the final heartsteps stopped.

Artaud said people should play music instead of talking, Red said, suppressing a yawn that rose with her words and then yawning deliciously into her hand. Timmy nodded softly in agreement, his mouth a downward horseshoe of appraisal, like Dad's.

The voice promised next a piano concerto by Johann Sebastian Bach, and without an ad or news or any further ado, the strains came in like rational rain, Sensurround, like a second blessing. Red closed her eyes gently and kept them closed, her face a wan indoor moon in the filtered window light.

This was the way they used to go up skiing, and at 93, which swords up into New Hampshire, the limo slowed, as if a magnet to memory, and Simon said,

'S like we're going up to New Hampshire. But they slid past the exit. But took the next one, right there after the overpass, in to Boston.

I wouldn't mind going up there, Simon mused aloud. Get a little cabin.

You better go further than that, Timmy said. Anna said something soft and firm in his ear, and Red touched his thigh and fingertips without opening her eyes. He breathed in loudly through his nose, then his cheeks puffed out like Louis Armstrong.

What's your problem? Simon said. And then to make it like he didn't know what his problem was, he added, I'll go wherever I want.

Timmy didn't respond but stared straight ahead through Simon and the instant, and the car pulled along in its place, spaced behind the other limousine at the same ceremonial distance it rode behind the hearse. Behind them the other cars followed with their headlights on. Out the window the dead treescape of Massachusetts, cars and trucks; the slate buildings of Boston, ahead in the distance like the graveyard they were headed toward, nested in the leafless treetops.

Approaching Boston on the raised highway, which coursed like a river lifted on a monorail above the roofs and raw treed streets of Alston and Charlestown, the procession slowed to keep together. The traffic was light and fast. The other cars respected the string of lit headlights and mostly did not cut through them or cut them off. After merging with the flow from the Mystic River Bridge, they smoothly took the right turn above the Boston Garden, and after the fluid downhill S curves under the shadow of the road above, whose unseen traffic ran the other way, on a ribbon raised on green I-beam stanchions dotted with rivets like buttons, they entered the yellow-lit tunnel and momentarily emerged in the airy river ride of Storrow Drive. There were no boats on the Charles today. A small wind spilled silver flakes over the brown water. A few gulls floated along like dirty socks. Pigeons wheeled energetically up to the dirty MIT bridge in pairs, chests puffed—they were like shoes—wings carving the air with their graceful dual dihedrons, landed on the white-coated ledge, and strutted busily along, as if they were there to get right to work, to add to the layers of pigeon shit, graffiti, dated quaint political protests, and the Greek letters of fraternities. Past the dense layered pueblo of brick apartment buildings and the buildings of BU, the hidden football stadium and high-rise dorms, before the stately poise of Harvard across the river, the turquoise cupola standing out atop the white tower amid the twiggy banks of sycamores and similar brick buildings, they took the entrance to the Mass Pike in a smooth, long, slow circle pulling partially against gravity. They followed Ginny's car and the hearse, led by the state trooper, past the waiting horde of cars and through the second tollgate without stopping.

That's what I call service, Simon said, and nobody smiled. The cars behind them followed through the gate as well without stopping to pay, and then a few others popped on their headlights and tried to join the procession, so the tail of the snake was cut off at the tollbooth as in a trap.

Look, they're cheating, said Simon, but none of them looked back.

The Forest Hills Cemetery lay vast and groomed, brown and gray, behind the black wrought iron fence that lined the road, a long row of tall spears that ended at the stone block of the formal front gate, where the doors were swung open. The state trooper pulled over outside the cemetery beside a Brookline police cruiser that was waiting there. The two cops got out of their vehicles and conferred. The chunky state trooper wore dark shades and high black boots, like riding boots, pants tucked in like jodhpurs, a stripe down the side. He smiled repeatedly and nodded as he spoke to the Brookline cop, who wore his ceremonial dress uniform, navy blue, nicely pressed, two rows of brass buttons down the chest, black shoes spit-shined to a new polish. A pack of Marlboros lay on the dash of his cruiser. When the procession had passed into the cemetery and the state trooper left he pulled out a cigarette and smoked it sitting there in his cruiser with the dark shades on, as if he were one of the mourners. When the few stragglers from the funeral procession arrived with their headlights on he lowered his cigarette to wave them in, not because smoking was against regulations but out of respect. One car, a Nova without the headlights on, stopped and asked if this was where the Curtis funeral was. The guy didn't seem in the least bereaved, and when the cop asked him who he was, he identified himself as a reporter for the *Boston Herald*. The cop had never heard of him and so had no problem telling him the burial service was private.

The smooth, groomed hills and long lawns of the cemetery were covered with headstones in straight and curving rows that followed the contours of the land. Mostly simple thick stones, granite, gray and white marble, some laid flat, flush to the ground, old ones wafer thin and worn, some larger monuments like chess pieces raised on pedestals. Sepulchres bulged round like igloos under the ground, the arched doors to their vaulted underworlds framed in stone. Sparsely spread out at regular intervals, the nubile, denuded trees were surgically stripped of their extraneous lower branches to reveal the posing sculptural sexuality of each, limber birches and lithe tall elms, languorous long maples and hemlocks, sickly barked sycamores arching arm in arm above the named avenues, other lanes lined by thick columns of solid old oaks. A stand of firs, in perfect lines, like an overgrown Christmas tree farm, marked the far border of this quietly populated park, pleasantly rural and martial, rows of domino residents in their permanent dominion.

Between the high bloom of a leafless beech tree, to the left, its branches spread radiantly outward like an explosion, vaulted overhead with tracery as intricate as a stained-glass window's, and on the right the great-grandfatherly fullness of a spavined old chestnut tree, lay Dad's family plot, in the cathedral shade of each tree for half of each day, when the day had sun and the trees had shade. This day, though, this unreal state—blending piercing grief and bland disbelief, seemingly surrounded by a pervasive new freedom, oddly sweet on the surface, but maybe frightening on the flip side: a vast, quantum indifference, which could utterly subsume our puny human spirits—seemed oddly and airily separate from other days, from the rest of life, like skipping school, except in the grown-up world, all business, ancient in its ever-crumbling structure, its zillion used parts, the imponderable accumulation of civilization everywhere apparent, unavoidable, this life so fiercely felt, so fast forgotten, so intensely peopled, yet so empty, from the spinning temporal peripheries to the lively, madly mental core: and now the great missed lesson, like some terrible trick, lay here before them, both a keen presence and an absolute absence, in the form of a black casket.

Before the mourners had gathered at graveside, groups and pairs trickling down the grass slope from the cars parked along the newly paved cemetery drive, the undertakers worked swiftly to get Dad out of the hearse and onto the wide nylon straps stretched taut across the opening of the squarely, deeply dug grave, between the parallel aluminum pipes of the mechanism whose quiet electric motor would lower him in. A different, more appropriate minister was here for the burial, a childhood friend of Dad's from Maine and around here. His sister, whom

Dad had dated in his teens, salty summer kisses in Maine, arrived with him in his fake-wood-sided station wagon. He spoke to Ginny briefly, and asked those present to form a close semicircle before the grave. The family stood together, divided at Ginny into its two parts, the union proving now as tenuous and temporary as it had always seemed. Her face, screened in by a black veil she wasn't wearing before, was swollen and drained of expression. Beside her stood Red in her sunglasses, holding herself together at the elbows, beside the brothers, blank, flanked by Anna, visibly upset, who clung to Timmy, even more upset. Friends stood behind. Aunt Meanie and Uncle James and their spouses made the cusp on Ginny's side. Meanie looked devastated, like a clown whose face has melted into haggard caricature. James looked the same as ever, except older, leonine and stony, tear-filled pouches under his oddly naked eyes when he took off his glasses to wipe them on the lining of his jacket. He looked just like Dad.

Reverend Winslow said a concise prayer about burial, then blessed the body. Timmy was a basket case, for a moment, blubbering with his whole chest shaking until he sucked it in and gathered himself. Red grasped a white handkerchief in her black-gloved hand, and dabbed with it a few times up under her sunglasses, her mouth set downward in that Curtis trait like a badge of inherent dissatisfaction. Simon was dry-eyed, deadpan, impatient. He stuck his hands in his pockets, glowered into the dark well of the grave.

Reverend Winslow recited, again, the Twenty-third Psalm—

My cup runneth over

—then said the terse prayer of interment. The hit man hit the switch and the little motor purred and immediately sounded strained. Reverend Winslow paused in his prayer, since the body wasn't lowering into the grave as it was supposed to. The hit man turned the switch off and on and tried again, and shrugged to the other two who stepped over to see what was wrong. Beside the pile of dirt on the side of the grave the little motor whined an annoyed plea; a sea-sounding breeze lightly roared up in the trees. None of the undertakers knew what to do.

Reverend Winslow decided to continue the prayer, let them figure it out if they would. He paused at one point in the prayer, at the word *earth,* stooped to the pile of dirt, scooped up a handful, and dropped it onto the black enamel casket with a light scatter sound. He stepped back to his place and continued the prayer, and Simon stepped forward, to the surprise of those who noticed, which in a moment was everyone present. He cut between the crescent of people and the grave, and headed right for Reverend Winslow, who looked up startled behind his bifocals. Simon held up a hand, sort of like hello, don't mind me, and without stopping went past him toward the pile of dirt. It looked like he was going to get his own pile of dirt and toss it on Dad as well, but he went past the dirt and bent down by the undertakers, who, taken aback, stepped back. At the corner of the aluminum pipe, where the motor attached to the cable that was connected, in turn, to the straps, Simon deftly lifted back the small, wedge-shaped brake that was stuck in the ratchet wheel on the top end of the winch's wire spool, like an apostrophe that was keeping it from turning, and then he flipped on the motor the undertakers had been turning on and off. As Simon returned to his place to the brief applause equivalent of a few general murmurs, Reverend Winslow finished the prayer. The motor hummed quietly and the casket containing Dad lowered slowly into the earth. Red stepped forward and, first kissing it, tossed the paperwhite she'd been wearing into the grave, and then Timmy did the same with his, but without kissing it.

· · ·

Next night it rained, and with its light, scattering arrival and wind out the window, it was hard to hear down to Dad, but he could, just, in and out. There was a baseball play-off game on, though it was two teams he didn't care about. Dad watched it, too, so the volume was up enough, and they shook their head at the same time, like when a grounder went through the first baseman's legs and a guy on second came around and scored without sliding. The last innings Dad watched from up in his room in bed, and so now the TV eyes were wide apart, up and down, in the big head the house, in their diagonal opposite corners, floating in the dark, and looking out blue and blinking over the two of them, stretched out on their beds like lost guys on life rafts, lost but sort of living it up.

The manager came out to the mound and conferred with the beefy pitcher with the Fu Manchu. Simon and Dad both thought, Take the guy out, he's definitely had it. He decided to keep him in, and the next pitch was knocked into the upper deck in left center, a monster line drive still rising when it hit a fan, and they both thought, See, I told you. With Dad's schedule it was the late dinner plan for Simon, and he took one of the legs and attached breasts of chicken from the leftover plate in the refrigerator, thinking Dad would notice it, maybe, but not be sure, because there was still a wing left, and who knows what he remembered about his food, or anything in general, because he drank however much that night, as always, and who knows what it was like to be him, he might just think, Oh, I guess I ate it already, oh well, he'd have to think that.

This rain tore down the last leaves, except for some tenacious freaks holding on for dear life, even though they were already dead, and that was it for the foliage, and the next day was silver November, like suddenly, though October still, but sodden and stripped, with eel black trees, and their bony branches, like electrocuted, pointing off in all directions. The apple tree out on the lawn, foul of the first base rock, a haiku of girly pink blossoms for a week in the spring, sprinkled down to a circle apron beneath, now was like a witch's hand, twisted and gnarled, her face in the fist. After some oatmeal, which he learned to like, like by default, in the navy, or else it was the sick scrambled brain eggs, Simon decided, like by default, to walk into Manchester, maybe go to the beach. Mosey 2 went with him, tail high and whapping around, and Wit, too, tail up, too, unmoving, for the first part, down through the wet woods to the tracks, and right at the moment Simon was thinking they were both black like the trees, like home team uniforms, right for the day, Witness disappeared. On this one steep slope at the bottom of the hill Simon slipped on the slick wet leaves and caught his balance wheeling his arms back, like a sudden backstroke, one then the other, kicking one foot forward, and he's still up. Mosey, like dogs always do, knew the way, looking back now and then to make sure, or make sure Simon was still coming, and they followed the tracks, raised in places and cutting through little hills, to town. The skinny inlet behind the yacht club field was more mudflat than water, and the rowboats were overturned, different colors in the straw grass. He wore a jacket from his closet, from between high school and the navy, not exactly the high point in his life, but what was, and, like always, at least he was still painting, then and now, on his own path; he always knew that his day would come, that he'd be recognized and famous or whatever, so he was lucky in a way, because he could always move with a private confidence inside, that knowledge, no matter how grim it got sometimes, which it definitely did, a lot. His hands fit perfectly in the jacket pockets, with his elbows bent and the bottom snap button, but not the zipper, done up, and he thought he was the only person he knew, he bet, who no one ever told him what to do. The boats up on cradles in the marina yard on the inner harbor were separated into motorboats, on the left, going right up to the edge of the woods, and sailboats, the rest, crowded between the tracks and the closed corrugated buildings painted red. There was a rack of masts with fluttering name tags, and some of the boats were covered with those blue poly tarps tied down, some with old canvas tarps, and lots were covered with these white shrink-wrapped plastic tops he'd never seen before, up close, that were the new thing. They must fit it over the deck, as close as they can get the size, then go around it with a heat gun or something, shriveling the loose folds and seams and sucking the skin tight like over a frozen dessert. Going over the drawbridge section of the tracks going over the water between the harbor and the inner harbor, lined with houses crowded together like they were cold, Mosey 2 paused and looked down at the openness below. But when Simon turned and called her she sort of shrugged out of her preincarnation hesitation and came, like slinking a little along, bobbing her head in a weird, low, funny way, looking down and then forward, like she was wounded, or afraid she was about to be hit from above, and kept going to avoid it. Mosey was like Dad, not just getting old but already was old. Dad once said, like, Mosely, you and I are the only Republicans in this household, and it was true, including the cats, now down to one.

Where the tracks crossed the road coming out of town he got on the sidewalk, and Mosey stayed closer to him with cars and movement and town around. Passing Masconomo Park, where he used to play Little League, he looked over to the public landing, where along there they planted a tree, in a line with others, in honor of Mum, with a plaque from the Friends of Manchester Trees, whichever one it was, but there they were. It was right along here he wiped out on his racing bike in like seventh grade summer, coming back from the little party with Timmy's friends at Singing Beach, smoking pot, and he left there to not be with them anymore, and was going really fast, but you couldn't really tell how fast, in the dark, and really stoned, it was like, whoah, really zipping down the hill, com-

ing up to the fair glow, with the Ferris wheel and the Salt-and-
Pepper Shaker and the Moonwalk over the baseball diamond,
and all the lights and crowd noise and carnival music, and he
was singing that Bee Gees song to himself—

Lonely days

—when the side of his pedal touched and scraped along the
curb, and he wiped out, banging on the road, with those bright
spark bursts of impact exploding in his hitting head, behind
clenched eyes, scraping his leg and arm, and landed, stopped,
and opened his eyes right beside a hydrant he could have hit
with his head, he thought, looking at its side snout right there,
like sticking its hex bolt tongue out at him, when the bike
came crashing into him, however that happened, and, bleeding
like a war hero, like the statue of the guy right there across the
street, with the whole lit-up fair going on past it, he limped to
the phone booth in the liquor store parking lot by the tracks,
and liked seeing himself, like through a swollen eye, with
blood on his face, reflected like a ghost in the eerily lit phone
booth glass, he called home, and through the slow syrup of his
trauma drama, spoke slurred with a fat lip,
 TsimonMum.
 The beach was wide with low tide. The sand didn't sing anymore, since the storm right after Mum died, which was like her,
the like storm of the century, like not going gently. The big
houses set back from the beach seemed empty, and down at the
end a person walked with their dog below the big brick mansion
of Dad's old schoolboy friend, who was definitely gay, would say
how much you've grown, but had a wife now, where they would
always park and walk across his lawn and down the trellised,
rose-covered walk and wood stairs to the private end of the
beach. Winslow Homer did a pretty famous painting from
down there, where they used to spread their towels, of three

women in their old-fashioned dresses, or like dress bathing suits, dripping, coming out of the water, or drying themselves, or one her hair, with her head tipped, with no houses, like now, on the hump of Eagle Head in the background, the name of the painting, and there was a little dog in it too, playfully playing with the wave coming in, or with one of the girls. It had black ears and a black eye, maybe, like that dog in the Little Rascals, or maybe that was that dog. The dog with the person, an old man in a plaid cap, was as thin as him, with long legs and short hair the color of cinnamon, with white on his chest, and his stubby little handle tail and anal eye socket and big balls in their loose sack that bobbled as he walked. Down at the end of the beach there used to be a little sort of leaning cave that wasn't there anymore because the sand changed. The water was that tame Massachusetts, not always like this, but calm today, like he thought of it, and the little waves came curling shyly in, quietly spreading white foam that thinned to wider bubbles and then disappeared. No clouds no gulls no girls no money in his pocket, but he didn't need anything, right now, for this holding pattern, no big plans for now anyway, and anyway it was good to go home, in a way, even if there was nothing there but how it always felt, which was like a big hole.

That cool sonar sound reverberating underwater and ricocheting out into the dangerous depths, and the hatch doorways between sections of the sub all the guys passed through ducking and holding the I-beam lip over the opening and sort of swinging in, except for the one short fat one, who just stepped right on through, last of all, without ducking, and they made way, stepped aside and straightened as he passed, because he was the commanding officer. Then there was a big boom, like a big book was dropped on them, and the place shook and tilted and everybody grabbed the wall or sliding things, the alert alarm went off in whoops like a lunatic birdcall, like prehistoric, really loud. When Dad came home this time, Simon slipped into the dining room, catlike, instead of retreating back to his room, and watched from the shadows as Dad, after checking the mail, passed first the hall doorway, then the other one, into the kitchen.

Dad popped some chicken again, didn't know how to cook much else, and potatoes, quartered and slathered with oil, into the oven, and went upstairs to change into khakis, and Simon, stepping into the hall, heard him talking up there to Ginny on the phone, it must have been, or else himself, which he wouldn't put it past him. The smell hit Simon in the living room over under Dad's room, and filled the house downstairs before it was ready, with like the aroma of home, and Simon thought how cooking was one of those things other people were so used to in their domestic lives, like conversation and friends and vacations and money, but that he never really worked into his with much like social or gourmet priority, just in a basic way, like necessity, like Dad right now, who usually had like this built-in cook for a wife the whole time. He took it so for granted, like everything in his life, he had no idea how most people lived, and how he had it made here in his little kingdom he kept closed, like with a moat around it, with the bridge up, to any outsiders including family. Unless you like snuck in.

When he came downstairs Simon stayed right where he was in the living room without moving, like daring Dad to come in and see him, but he wouldn't, he knew it, and he didn't, he went right past the open door and turned, like you always do, at the bottom of the stairs, and went through the front hall and the coat corridor, with his deck shoes squelching, barely, their light little traction sounds on the white plastic marble tiles, like a flattened roomful gravestone of Mum. And standing there now in the dark he remembered, like he came there for a reason and this was it, Mum coming in there to see him the night before she died, he was lying on the couch listening to music in the dark, but the record had just finished, the stereo had just clicked those sad, last mechanical sounds when it turns off. The others were in the TV room watching TV, and she came in, and moonlifting some light from the hall on the side of her face and hair like a halo, she said softly,

What's the matter, sweetheart?

He didn't move, or even shrug, but just said,

Nothing.

And then she said something out of nowhere that later was like one of his key like clues, leading him to everything else. He couldn't remember how she started what she said, or how it had anything to do with him, but it was like she was trying to win him over, and it was like she'd gone through some big change, or wanted him to believe she had, like to a higher self or something, and she said from now on she was going to be like a free spirit.

Tseh, Simon tsehed in the dark, but softly, with hardly an edge, and he wondered what she meant, and asked her,

How?

You'll see, she said, sort of teasing, like I'm not gonna tell, it's for me to know and you to find out, and she smiled this serene enigma smile, like from another world, like she had a perfect plan in place, all worked out with the other world, and the next day, sure enough, she went there.

Next night after dinner Dad went into the TV room instead of down to the cellar, and Simon felt abandoned, in a weird way, but also free, in another, better way, in his room, to do whatever he wanted, meaning watch whichever channel. He didn't hear it, so he didn't know it, but they watched the same detective show, and changed the channel after the ads, when this thing came on about Canada, and they both switched to this one about a racing car driver who gets crippled in a crash in the first scene, it's incredible he lives, considering the totally crunching, end-over-end crash into the wall in a fireball, but it was sure to be slow going the rest of the way, because the drama was about his rehab, because he was also a drug addict, like on speed and willpower to live, against the odds, ever, to walk again, let alone drive again. The guy he met first in rehab was a big fat guy who had a high voice and was like this big Gentle Ben, and the first thing he said to him was,

How come you're so fat? If you were a drug addict, I mean, which Simon wondered, too, and their friendship, indoors at the clinic the whole time, began with him in a wheelchair, and they kept saying Denial ain't just a river in Egypt. Then his physical therapist, teaching him to walk again, hopefully, was a black guy in white pressed pants and bulging T-shirt, who used to be an Olympic boxer, who now considered every day he could think and walk in a pure gold medal experience, man. The racing car driver was a real Southern cracker, so he hated blacks on sight, on top of hating himself, deep inside, and refused to even talk to the guy, or look at him, at first, but of course by the end, after lots of scenes at the walking bars like,

Come on, man, you can do it! Do it, man! they ended up like welded together at the heart, and the guy walked, after hugging him, and both of them trying not to cry or make a big thing out of it, walked out of there, looking like a severe retard with his hands going spastically all over the place, his knees and feet pathetically caved and pointed in, but he walked out of there, man, and there were his wife and kids, keeping their distance till now, all dressed up by the car.

Dad cashed in early, and Simon went into the TV room to watch cable; he'd never come down. It was that Tom Cruise movie *Risky Business,* which was really stupid, but not that bad, actually, for such a typical formula. He was really young in it, and played this kid who— Simon heard, he thought, a sound out in the hall upstairs, and quickly turned off the TV, and then the light, when he heard it again, and went and opened the door halfway, the way Dad left it. Dad came creaking down the stairs and Simon saw his pale feet, barely, in the dark, descending, and at the naked knees he slid behind the door, between it and the shelves, and through the crack he could see Dad pass in the dark, across the narrow part of the hall before the coat corridor, and then heard his bottle bump against the shelf in his liquor closet, just across the way into the dining room. Oh so he couldn't sleep, and so he came down for a hit, like to hit him over the head and knock him into oblivion. Simon thought it was odd he didn't turn on the lights, that's what he'd do any other time, he'd come down with a towel around his waist and a lost moon look on his face without his glasses, looking older and like owly and lost, like his father, maybe sticking his head in the TV room doorway for a second, bewildered or blind, or blotto or all, with his mouth in a little o, brows elastically raised, like *oop,* you're in here, sorry to bother you, I'm just a cartoon character, tee-hee, out here tipsy-toeing around, then he'd go and get his hit, and maybe disguise it, or top it off with a trip to the kitchen for a fistful of like Planters peanuts, or cashews, then go back upstairs with his glass of ginger ale, like that's all he was down here for. Maybe he was just so wasted he was just going through the motions unconsciously, like sleepwalking, but at least he was walking, he'd seen him worse, there were all kinds and degrees and paternal variations of wasted. It was amazing how some alcoholics could function perfectly well in their lives, or so it seemed, with their pattern habits of work and life at home, and in the dreamworld in between sleep and infancy called drunk, every day, like an escape into your inner home hole, where everything's soft and motherly smooth and the same, like you, like music you like that repeats and stays good, and like lifting and safe. Simon knew all about it, that this was the way you slowly die, by killing yourself, first, every day, sweetly.

Dad went back upstairs in the dark, with the dark towel around his waist and his Buddha belly like slowly leading the blind way, and pulled his door shut, hard, like a curt comment down to Simon, but he knew it wasn't—or so what if it was? Simon shut the TV room door again, and turned on the light and the TV. Tom Cruise was driving this Porsche—

Whatever Dad was cooking was burning, and Simon thought of just going in and turning it off, but that would be a dead giveaway, so he had to think of some way to get him up from the cellar. When he smelled it Simon came out of the room with the cat following him happily thinking okay, feed me again, goody, and on the way into the kitchen he saw the smoke in there and was surprised a smoke alarm didn't go off—

He remembered there was this way, when they were kids, of making your own phone ring, by dialing a certain number and hanging up, but he couldn't remember what it was, and who knew if it still worked, even if he could remember it: 611, or 616, it definitely had a 6 in it that repeated, or maybe turned on itself, so like 9. Numbers to him always had their own personalities, sitting there packed into their little different shapes and number selves, some standing like on one leg, and so all the different number combinations, like in school, had other meanings first, to him, than just their numerical worth, and he used to have these number nightmares that were really intense, like where they were all swirling around in this big whirlpool, like taunting and ready to attack him, or the recurrent one, when he was really little, of them marching, getting higher, and when they got to ten it was going to explode, so he screamed and fought it and woke up all sweaty out in the light at the top of the stairs, with Mum holding him, talking to him, and the others standing there under him, in their pajamas, like a ring of angels. Red wore pj's, too, and from out there, some nights, they'd come out from their rooms to the top of the stairs and listen down to the TV room, with Mum and Dad talking, or not, or on and off, and they'd sit out there on the carpeting with their legs through the banister railing slats dangling down over the open. If they were going around up there they had to be really quiet, because Mum always could hear them, somehow, and she'd go like,

I can hear you up there, in this warning tone, get back to bed. Sometimes it was impossible, how could she, but they'd creep in almost stopped slow motion, and still she'd go,

I *mean* it, meaner.

He tried a few 6 numbers, hanging up each time, not really believing it would work, while the kitchen got smokier, and with Dad still burrowed away down there, oblivio, it came slowly out the passage like a fog bank, and then joking to himself he tried 666, and then like 966, and when he hung it up it scared him, it rang right in his ear, and then he thought fast, what if they were trying to get through and it was Ginny, and she said to Dad, who were you talking to, why was it just busy, and then on the second ring he realized it was him, hey, he did it, it worked, and he slid out from the smoke, coming past the top of the stairs seeing Dad's top of his head at the bottom coming up, so he definitely didn't see him. It only rang four times when Dad got to it, so it was a little odd, but maybe the person hung up, or probably Dad didn't think of that, because he had to deal with his little burning meal disaster, maybe pork chops or lamb chops like little shrunken flaming black tomahawks now. He opened the door to the porch and put the smoking baking pan on top of the doghouse, right there out on the porch, left the door open, and went back downstairs again. A little later, but in no hurry, after the smoke cleared, but not the burnt smell, he went back up and made a sandwich and brought it into the TV room, and after he finished eating it and was watching some highbrow pantry drama on *Masterpiece Theatre* with a pretty actress as the new maid, the phone rang again, and he picked it up in there, the phone on the corner table at the end of Mum's couch, and there was no one there again. Except this time it only rang twice, and there was no dial tone, no sound, nothing, like they were there listening at the other end but not saying anything when he said hello, and then again,

Hello? Hello?

It was Simon listening on the phone on the way into the kitchen.

Simon had walked through, and lingered in, and looked and poked around in, all the rooms in the house enough that they were like psychically marked, like the way a dog marks his territory by sniffing and pissing, but a person is more a dream animal, so you drift through places, taking them in, until. But so now that all the rooms were already played out, and made him feel kind of rotten, like slackly like homesick, going in them again, still he was sucked back, it was raining out again, and he wandered back into the back of the house—

Going to the bathroom posed a problem because he couldn't flush with Dad right down there under him, so that solved it, just don't flush, like people in droughts, like in California when they have to ration, and pissing was no problemo, you just aimed to the side of the bowl just above the water and let the bowl spread it silently down like pouring beer into a glass, or he purled a little bit at the edge of the water, on purpose, you hear that, Dad, like a dare, but Dad wasn't about to hear that in a million years. Baths he had once in a while during the day when the house was his, and sometimes he used Dad's shower, or once the other one upstairs, but there were no towels in there, so he just walked out wet, his footprints darkening the carpet, down the corridor and downstairs, and from then on he'd just have a bath in his own bathroom, right here. Soap he got, Coast, like blue marble, from the linen closet upstairs, one of like Mum's stations, and for shampoo he took Ginny's up in their shower, Dad would never notice that, he hardly had any hair.

Dad left a Time-Life Civil War book open on the radiator beside the toilet in Simon's bathroom, open to a picture of Abraham Lincoln looking seriously sleep-deprived and depressed, with dark deep eye sockets, and the longest expression in the history of the presidency. This meant Dad used this bathroom, sometimes, or used to, which made sense because it was closer to his workshop than the other downstairs one through the TV room, so Simon was on the lookout for him coming in here, at first, but it never happened, so he kind of forgot about it until this one time, beyond the blue-black TV zone of his room, he heard Dad coming up the stairs, and this time turn in this way toward him, so he turned off the TV fast, at the last second, and stood there, still, in the darkness, while Dad went into the bathroom, just through Simon's outer room, and clicked on the light. There was a pause. He couldn't be noticing, like, the ring around the bathtub, or even, like, the soap, but Simon thought for sure he was standing there with the old dead man in his hand looking down at the pee already in the toilet, and he was right, he was. But then he peed himself into it, thinking he must have neglected to flush it last time, my word, whenever that was, but there were always these little things, certainly more lately with Ginny gone, apparently she kept the domestic demons at bay, and then he flushed it, and in the crashing little gush of whirlpool applause, wiggled and like bowed and zipped up, and turned off the light and left, with their urines mixed together traveling the pipes to the septic, and Simon standing there in the dark in the next room, like a still statue of the lost son returned home in secret, listening with his head tilted a little to the side to hear, and his arms a little apart and hands ready, like an outlaw, ready to draw.

The food was getting low, at least in the refrigerator, though the cupboards were stacked, and the freezer was still full, though the really good goodies were gone; what were all those Ginny things in Ziploc bags, and all frosty and wrapped in tinfoil like body parts? He wished Dad would do a good shopping, Dad, and get some more stuff, like they could use some more ginger ale, or cookies, or milk, or munchies, like chips or Fritos or Pepperidge Farm, and maybe like another good roast beef, chicken, and some other real food food, like lots, Dad, though Dad would probably wreck it trying to cook it, and probably he'd just try and still wing it on what was still there till Ginny, like his mother, got back and took care of it. Staring into the sparer refrigerator now, Simon decided he didn't have much choice, so he took one of the three pieces of steak on the plate with the shepherd boy on it with a staff with a hook for their necks, left over from Mum and back then. It was gray, like a long dead tongue, but boy was it tender good steak, even cold, with the little slivers of fat like wax, it must have been a cut Ginny bought, because Dad just got your basic chewy sirloin special this week, and overcooked it in the oval old pan under the broiler. Maybe this was marinated before she left, or something, because it also had a kind of tangy taste, not taking over, but sort of in there, behind it, melting out, making it better. Good food was the greatest thing, especially when it like took you by surprise. He had to have another bite, at least, so he bit off just an inch off the bigger one of the two strips left. Wit wanted some, circling, leaning liquid eights around his legs, and coming up on his hind legs and touching with his front paw pads, like climbing or dancing with Simon's thigh, but without claws, until the very hook tips he couldn't keep in caught his pants, but not him, and ticked away, three two one, when Simon pushed him softly down, with a harder nudge when he wouldn't go,

No way, Wit, not this stuff, this is *mine*.

He made some Minute Rice, guessing at the water amount by looking, and in another pan some peas, from the big frozen bag of them, down now to the last few pellets, which he stuck back in the freezer, for the added psychopathology, like notice this, too, Dad, instead of just cooking them and throwing away the bag, the evidence. There was too much water in the rice, but so what, he drained it, and then drained the little off his plate, too, with the rice mound steaming, a little too moist and like stuck together, like Uncle Ben's, the rival, and by then the peas were ready, too, nothing like a good quick meal. Butter on both, and salt and pepper and ketchup on the rice mixed in, and some more ketchup, lots, on the side, for dipping bites, and he took it into the TV room, with Wit following him as if there were meat on the plate and he wanted some more love of it. And so, half jokingly, half blaming the cat, in his mind kind of liking the sort of menace, or whatever, of thinking of Dad looking in there and seeing only one piece left, and knowing there had been more before, he went back into the kitchen to get another piece of steak, telling Wit, with his finger, to stay down off the couch and away from his plate of food on the side table while he was gone. The one piece he'd already taken a bite from he took between thumb and forefinger and lifted like a sardine by its tail, over his face tipped back, like he was the cat, and took another bite, like biting off its head, and then, chewing it, gobbled the rest, and chewed it all roundly, in two parts, standing there in the open refrigerator, with one cheek bulged.

He was really starting to get cabin fever, though he did go wandering around outside whenever he felt like it, and it was only for a few more days, he could handle it easy. This tandem TV routine was working fine, and Dad was pretty deaf anyway, Simon's different little tests confirmed, so he could watch his own channel, if it was crucial, you just paid attention and turned it down if there seemed like a listening pause downstairs right under him, which actually was kind of a drag, though, because the TV wasn't within arm's reach, it was past the foot of the bed, so to change it, ever, he had to get up. Sometimes he went out of the room while the two TVs were on and went just out into the hall, like to test-stretch the situation, or into the kitchen, smooth-quick, to get something to eat, or a couple of times he went outside, turning off his TV, and from the porch went down the sneaker-silent steps to the driveway, and like a cat along the rhododendron edge and between the end of the bushes and the bike place and along the house past the garbage area to the window and glass double doors into Dad in there, frowning a little, frozen over his table, with a wooden bend at the waist, either puzzling over how to make some measurement, or whether to trust himself to cut it, or caught up in whatever scene on the TV or in his mind. He cleared his throat, which Simon could just hear through the glass, then put down the straight edge and went out of view, down the two steps into his cellar, as if he suddenly realized Simon was there, half hidden, standing back to one side in the light coming out, and instead of showing it on his face, or going over to Simon, or looking at him, was going, maybe, like someone in a movie might, with no giveaway expression, to like get a gun and come back and, still without showing that he knew, he'd act like he was doing something else, then just slowly like lift the gun, like it was the tool he was using, except turn at the last second and aim it over at him, and maybe saying one of those catchy little lines before blowing him away like, I don't like snoops, or something like that that kids would say at recess across the country, blowing each other away, and comedians and ads would pick it up and inject it into the mainstream of language and popular culture like it was already there, like, Go ahead, make my day.

But the only barrel Dad was lifting, pointing it right in his mouth, was the whiskey jug, standing in the paint closet, like a confessional, or urinal, where it lived on the shelf. Why didn't he just take it out with him and have it right there with him on his work table, Simon wondered, kind of annoyed at his pathetic little deceit, even with himself, even though there was nobody there with him, he thought. He went around on the

back patch of driveway to the lawn and ocean and garden side
of the house and down the little hill against the house, beneath
the sticky lilacs, where the window looked right in on Dad,
right there, close, instead of across the room, and he liked it,
because he was a little above Dad, right there, like looking in
on his life, and he had no idea. His glasses slipped down his
nose as he drew these long curves using string like a compass,
and each time he made one he paused and looked at it, sort of
stumped, with his lips trumpeted out, like it was wrong, but
would have to do, and in fact would be fine, and then, setting it
up and looking away at the TV for a minute, he made another
one. His pants were falling down, but he wore them that way,
with a belt, and didn't tug them up, even though, watching
him the whole time, you kept wanting him to. His shirt
bloomed out, almost untucked, to button capacity, and bumped
like a hard balloon against the edge of the table when he
reached across for the last part of each curve, and then moved
away, and then a little while later, doing the same motion,
bumped up against it again. He lost his pencil during a pause,
and looked around and couldn't find it, mumbling, like, I'll be
damned, while it was stuck on his ear with the arm of his
glasses the whole time, he was used to this, and he solved the
problem years ago by putting a couple of nails in the wall, like
every few feet, all around the room, and the lower cellar workshop, too, and put a pencil on every pair, so there were pencils,
whittled down, like little works of art, on their two nails, all
around the room, every few feet, and when he lost one, like
now, he just grabbed another one. His expression was the same
as if someone were there, and what he did, so there wasn't much
to see that was secret, except this absorption, and sometimes he
stuck out his lower lip, glossy, for a moment, not sure of what
he was doing, or not quite satisfied, or deciding it wasn't quite
right, but perhaps good enough, and he coughed into the air
out of the back of his throat, and then sort of gaspy, again, into

the top of his fist, like the microphone melted into his mouth, and so the sound was lost. He was drawing these curves right onto the workbench, and he numbered each one.

Simon went and got this video camera he saw before, rooting around, that Red left there, in the top drawer of the Brown Thing, in the front hall, one of those good new ones with the little viewer that sticks out to the side. He brought it back to where he was watching, and wondering if it'd work in the dark, but think of that Rodney King video, that was in the dark, he shot Dad still doing what he was doing before. It was slow, like in terms of drama, and he was tempted to tap on the window and record Dad's response, but he refrained. There was a moon getting full, coming in and out from behind the silver baggy clouds over the water, and the water down through the black bony trees was more silver than the clouds, where the moonlight spilled over it, or more white, actually, than silver, and if this came out on the video it could look pretty cool, except it would have to be way enlarged, like movie screen size, or maybe he could get Red to make it into some stills and make a painting from one. He tried moving the camera a little bit, like avant-garde, streaking the light on the water, but it didn't look like it would look any good, like a lot of those abstract expressionist paintings he felt like were pretty bad. He liked doing abstract stuff more when he was younger, but they were more geometric, or like geomorphic, not just a mess of paint. Those were more pure imagination, and he'd do them more, or all the time, if he could, or so he told himself, but he had to sell them, and people liked landscapes and seascapes, like their view, or at least some scene somewhere, or so he thought. He turned the camera to the house, and it looked like a dark lined page, seeing it from so close, so he moved back to the edge of the lawn, getting most of it in the viewer, but there wasn't much to it, just like this big blue ghost box, like a big TV. Heading back, the back way, he saw the cellar light was off, guess Dad went to bed, Night, Dad. He went back to the front of the house and stood in the middle of the lawn, waiting for Dad maybe to come through the front hall and up the stairs, since the light was still on, and sure enough, in a little bit, here comes the judge, too small to make him out in the viewer, or when he moved closer to the terrace and up onto it, you could, just, in the lit window of the door out to the terrace, in the middle of the dark shot. Dad had a glass of ginger ale, and as he shut off the light on the front hall table, to go upstairs, the moon came out from behind a cloud again, and lit the night blue and bright, Simon included, centrally standing there, lit, in the middle of the terrace, another standing dare for Dad to see, and he didn't move on purpose, to be seen or not in the bettor's adrenaline thrill of heartbeat and moment, the like dire confrontation, at last, with Dad, as he walked toward him in the dark, but nothing happened, so he must have not looked up, or just not outside, or just not noticed Simon, wouldn't be the first time in his life, that was his like paternal role, not noticing Simon, and that was Simon's like major why, like why Simon was Simon. He went back onto the lawn and waited, with the camera rolling, for the light to come on upstairs, which it did, after longer than you'd think, what was he doing, the light in the upper right-hand corner window, like an advent calendar of the house, and only the window to Mum and Dad's room open and lit. The bathroom light came on and Simon got his upper half profile, like Alfred Hitchcock, miniature in the viewer, but clear and perfect, as he stood there peeing, then he withdrew, and the light went off. Then the other light went off, and that was it, Night, Dad.

The weekend was a drag coming up, because Dad would probably be there the whole time, he lived there, after all, and Saturday woke a little later than the other days, and there he was, outside, after his usual quickie breakfast, and he passed by Simon, under his window, going between the driveway hedge and the garbage area, over to the corner lawn mower room, with its own outside door with a brass doorknob gone green on the flange, but not the knob, and got out the big-wheeled wheelbarrow, more like a deep cart, and pushed it, with a rake in for the ride, around the corner of the back of the house, to go rake, and do Dad in the garden. From inside the dining room, out the tall French windows, standing just to the side of the sun streaming in to a gridded parallelogram over the black-and-white linoleum tiles, like it slid off them and was elongating away, Simon made sure where he was out there, past the leg of lawn, like a chubby scarecrow somehow freed, but still standing there, holding his stick he'd been stuck on all this time, and cleaning up the area he'd been looking at all that time, dying to clean it up but hadn't been able to, and went into the kitchen and wondered what to eat.

There were still some eggs in their slots on the door, so he made toast from Dad's long polka-dotted pack of Wonder bread, accordioned down now to a few pieces left, muffins long gone, and some eggs fried up fast on the flat Teflon pan that was scratched and a little shredded on the surface from forks, like with bacon, or from washing too hard, and the yolks broke, the first one when he cracked it down out of the shell, the other one when he tried to flip it, so he mixed them all up, half scrambled like what-do-they-call-it, and in the open part of the pan put a few of the five roast potatoes still left in a bowl, and cut them into slices to fry, with the side of the spatula cutting, probably, into the Teflon, him, too, a little, as he did it. He poured a little oil over them and they like crackled like mad, popping little pinpricks of oil spattered out, but it fried it fast, and the eggs were ready already. He turned off the flame, but before taking the food out of the pan, he ran, sort of sliding with his long straight-legged walk-run strides, back to the window in the dining room, to see the picture of Dad in his garden now, standing there with the rake resting like a hockey stick in his hand, looking down toward the ocean waving up at him through the stripped trees at the bottom of the hill, or maybe a bird went by carrying some memory shred streaming behind it like a banner, and now he was lost in the rippled window riddle of its passage, trying to find the beginning pieces of what ended up like this, right here now, whole but lost, like history on a hill in old New England, amid leaves and loam, here and vanished, with nothing left but a man there to wonder and wade through the end of the golden season, brown paper leaves like so many numinous messages spread around, crumpled, and falling, a few, through the still air.

The first bite Simon took was potato, with his fingers burn-touching the tips, and his tongue, but he chewed it, *hah,* like a dog, openmouthed, followed with some yolk, yum, with his fork, and he decided to have it like Russian style, right out of the frying pan, and poured the ketchup on the ridge where the potato went into crispy egg, and salt and pepper all over, and took it by the handle into his room and watched some computer-animation cartoon that looked more human than real cartoons, but also faker, but at least they got rid of those jerky movements the guys used to move with when they first started to have them look like that. The pan, cooled a bit, was still too hot to put right onto his lap, so he got under the covers and laid it on top of the blanket, on his lap, and the warmth came through his pants and it got hot, but not too, it felt nice, like more than a cat and flatter.

He used to really love cartoons but none of the ones he watched were still on, except like Bugs Bunny, and Porky Pig he didn't love, but it was still on, and same with those Looney Tunes ones that kind of bugged him but you'd still watch, like Betty Boop. Road Runner he really liked, *meep-meep,* with his Acme dynamite, and the plunger thing that came with it to set it off, and Acme everything, and after school, Speed Racer, and those okay ones like Deputy Dawg, with that fat rooster who talked really *slow*, in a Southern *drawl*, and those two who punched in, like with hour cards, at the beginning, carrying lunch boxes, like they were showing up for work, which they were, but first, meeting on the way, they went,

Mornin', Sam,

Mornin', Ralph, calm and normal, like they were still kind of asleep and this was the morning routine, and then the whistle went off, reaching rubberly in its scream, and they instantly went into high-speed action trying to kill each other, all these crazy cartoon ways, all day, and then when one of them was about to get killed, no way out of it, the whistle would go off again, and they'd stop in midair, like Road Runner off the cliff, and Wyle E. Coyote, and head off, slow, together, back home with their lunch boxes again, after another tiring day's work. The Road Runner, though, could look around with his lightning-quick head movements, in the extended second he noticed he'd run off the cliff, and turn around and, before he fell, shoot safely back to the edge of the cliff before he fell, *meep-meep*, but Wyle E. Coyote always fell, into a little puff of dust at the bottom of the cliff. He always wanted, back then, to go out west, to the desert, and like flat mesas and big cactuses holding their arms up, like stick 'em up, and the mountains sugarcoated on top with snow, and horses and stuff; he still would, maybe pretty soon.

He heard the door in from the terrace to the front hall shut with its metal storm door clatter, and moved the pan, done, and took the few steps to the TV to turn it down. He stood there listening, but heard nothing, until a minute later the toilet in the TV room bathroom flushed in the far walls, and then Dad went back outside with the same storm door sound rattling shut. Good, he was gone again, and cartoons would be over pretty soon and whatever was on next would be on before the World Series game this afternoon. The shows in between sucked, still kids' shows, not like cartoons, which are for everyone, like dreams, so he got up, and after washing the frying pan, good enough, and sticking it back under the sink, still wet, but too bad, it would dry down there as well as anywhere, he went outside onto the porch, and looking around, sneaking, like his own little cartoon adventure, went around the house the way he went last night, and the way Dad had gone earlier, maybe that was why, with the wheelbarrow, and when he got to the open part after the house, still under the trees, before the driveway goes down in its S curve, pretty hairy in the winter driving, like for the different mothers driving the car pool, he slipped into the woods on the other side of the road from Dad and went as parallel to him as he could, waist deep down the hill, hiding behind trees, going like *plink plink* on tiptoes, or like sliding from tree to tree, the cartoon character getting closer.

Dad looked up from his raking, like he might doing anything, abstracted, stopping and standing there in the inner sift of his, like, rotating states of Dad washing through his head, like wind colored with images, with his glasses on, like goggles for seeing lost and found things of the past, but this time it was here, it was something near, it was Simon. The leaves shushed and stopped, and Dad looked around and didn't see the dog, and didn't think much of it, but something in him wondered, also, a little, and waited, and had an antenna still out, on alert, when he started raking again, and kicked a rock in the half grass-rooty dirt, wondering if it was maybe like a little star stone that would move and come out, and he could throw away, or the tip of a bigger one, or of like the huge time immemorial iceberg ledge of the whole hill. Simon stayed behind the tree and stuck his head out slowly, as if being seen that way would be less than faster, but also not to be a sudden movement, and he watched Dad for a pretty long time, and Dad didn't see him, or even look over his way, but just kept on raking and sort of mooning off. He was calm, standing there, but dumb and soft,

like a cow, Simon thought, and Simon was calm, too, but like a
cat, with the hidden advantage and quickness ready, and the sly
quick eye hidden, except to its, like, coiled and crafty patient
self. It smelled like touch football out, the matted leaves covering the ground smelled a little like vinegar over the top half of
North America. The decades used to seem like whole eras, each
distinct, stretched out with characters and characteristics they
spell out for you at the end of them, in like *People* magazine
and *Time,* but now years were getting so fast, piling up into
the others, blending and gone like nothing, you might as well
do nothing, and seeing how the nineties were whipping by,
too, with seventies fashion back in fashion, which was a joke,
like sideburns and long hair again, and girls' hair parted in
the middle, but not much else to stand it out, really, except
like bell-bottoms on the girls, with like some tummy showing,
and pointed collars, and nothing different, really, from before,
he felt like he was not just getting old, but also kind of numb,
and also old enough to die, if he thought this, because thinking controlled everything, even though you couldn't control
your thoughts, or yes you could, which was not at all the cosmic comfort of being folded back into the sleep you came from
he pretended or thought he thought it was, or should be, or
could be, especially if you believed it, but, more like, he felt
like crying, but that would be like a champagne cork popping off the top of his head, or so holding it in he felt like
cracking his own tight jaw, or like burning down the house, or
like burning down Dad, or like sneaking up on him with a
shovel, because here it was with them, exactly like in this situation, with no one else there except the two of them, at home,
abandoned, and they were both alone, they weren't together,
and thinking himself into a flushing like whirlpool funnel of
life and time tunnel time, but clear and cool in the center of
it, he felt like everything had passed him by, and it so wasn't
fair, and he hated it when this feeling crept up on him and

whooshed in him like he was surrounded and overwhelmed by it, or so then he like surrounded it and so it was in him, like it was him, the home feeling of himself he always returned to, when it came down to it, instead of, like, home sweet home, or some solid self, or something with love and someone else there, instead of just him, and this long loss, and what do I do all the time, except, like always, just keep going, and don't worry about it.

He didn't bother to sneak going back, he just walked in the open, over the old leaves of home, ha, without even looking back to see if Dad saw him, and though he felt the possible impossible, an aimed tension bull's-eye on his back, he knew he didn't see him, because Dad never would. The driveway was dry and black, wet, still, under leaves, outlining them, and brown pine needles clumped together along the edge behind the back of the house. The cat sat there on the porch at the top of the stairs, like a bookend, or a little Halloween idol, knowing all the bad things, where the top pumpkin would be, one on each stair in a row by age, when they used to carve them and stick candles inside, one in each, bringing the inner demons alive, and when the flicker of light moved inside the eyes, the faces shot scary looks around the stairs, and the sharp shadows would leap like wing spokes of night, sending out sharp sort of scary messages. Simon could be like a kid, like himself the kid, and himself himself, at the same time, sometimes, like now, when it clicked that way in the perception and fertile like feel. Candy corns he loved eating, the three layers, top white first, like a little tooth you chipped off, soft, then the yellow little butt bottom, then the orange *mm*-middle, were mixed in with candies in wrappers, like jawbreakers and Tootsie Rolls and Tootsie Roll Pops and Bazooka bubble gum and Mary Janes and Squirrel Nut Zippers, whyever they were named that, in the big bowl the mail was left in on the Brown Thing, in the front hall, just inside the front door from the porch, where Mum and Dad and you and the world came in and went out into the world, and the cats waited patiently, like ancient Egypt, for as long as it took for someone to come let them in or out.

The World Series game still wasn't on yet, but there was a football game on, and they kept completing passes, both teams, like it was practice against the second string, or touch football, except the receivers got really clocked a few times, but always got up and jogged, like rubbery, with their chin strap undone, shaking their head, back to the huddle and the high fives and ass taps, and sometimes they'd knock like the foreheads of their helmets together, or thump their chests, and kids all across the country would do the same in their games, like the wacky custom spike dances after touchdowns. One guy didn't get up, but stayed down on his stomach, face mask down, pounding the AstroTurf with both hands, and not moving his legs, and the trainers came out in their shorts and white socks pulled up, and knelt down on one knee and talked to him, like praying, for a long time, before touching his leg to see if it worked, and slowly flexing the knee up, and they showed the replay, in slow motion, at the key crunch part, again and again, slowing it to stutter stops, and when the leg got bent the wrong way, freeze-frame— There it is, Dick.

That's not the way your knee's supposed to bend, said Dick, and the other goes,

That hurts.

Dad came back in, down in the cellar, and did a few soft-sounding, methodical things down there, and then came up the creaky stairs, past Simon, and went into the kitchen to make lunch. He looked into the refrigerator, waiting for something to jump out at him, then when nothing did, got some bread and lettuce from the white middle of the head, left down in the left drawer with its Saran wrap veil mussed by Simon, and mayo and mustard, unwrapped a piece of American cheese, took the jar of raspberry jam from the door, not much left, and combined them all, layered, into one of his custom Dad sandwiches, and cracked a Ballantine ale, and even though he was alone, after sip number one, bubbling down his work-ready throat, poured it into a glass against the side, keeping the head down to a trim half inch. He cut the sandwich in half, diagonally, into two triangles, and rinsed the knife and left it in the sink, which Simon heard, and took his lunch into the TV room, and chose the baseball, just beginning, over the football, ticking down to halftime. When halftime came, Simon switched the channel to the baseball, too, but couldn't really get into it, but kept watching, like Dad, after polishing off his sandwich and ale in no time flat. It was a pitching duel, great, a lot of hoopla but no action, just lots of foul balls and watched balls and whiffs, with car and beer ads every five minutes. Two guys walked in a row, and then advanced on a sacrifice fly. Only one down, with men on second and third, and the meat of the order up, but the next two guys got out, first on a grounder the guy held on to for a second to hold the runners, then a strikeout, and the pitcher, with a greasy, droopy mustache and curly long hair, pulled down tight his nasty old cap he superstitiously refused to wash or replace, and, enlarging his eyes, puffed out his cheeks in relief as he trotted off the mound, and Dad turned off the tube to a shrinking rectangle, unblooming fast to a last flash point that blinked off, and went out through the coat corridor, where Simon heard him coming, his shoes quietly squelching their little deck traction, and passing rhythmically into the kitchen, where he put the plate and glass in the dishwasher, and then the knife, and got another Ballantine ale, cracked it, and took it down the stairs, like a knocking, walking drumbeat, you couldn't miss him, and turned on the TV down there, where it was the football station, which he left, and so Simon, glad, hearing the cheering, switched over.

Simon went to take a leak in his bathroom, did it against the side, just like Dad just now with his ale into the glass, purling the gold into swirling bubbles that came together white in their quiet congregation, bigger and less of them in the pee. Dad changed the channel back to the baseball, and Simon started to flush and realized, and stopped before it went, but it went *shhh,* and gulped the stop with a little bang, and Dad heard either that or the cheering of the football game through the floor or the stairwell air, and he stopped and stood and listened, then shut off his TV, curious, and heard the TV up in Simon's room, directly above him, though he couldn't tell what it was, his hearing wasn't too hot, but he definitely heard something, he was sure, pretty sure, as he headed up the stairs to check this curiosity or vague danger. Simon heard him coming, and hurried, silently, into his room, turned off the TV, and quickly smoothed out his sheets, good enough, and without hesitation went over to the closet, which had no door, and went in and through, up behind the clothes in there on hangers, touched the ones moving to stop them, and froze there, with his back against the wall, looking out. It was a deep enough closet so there was room enough, just, for the clothes, mostly jackets and shirts and a parka he didn't know was here, not to bulge out much with him standing back there, and he was in the dark, and his legs, too, though they showed, and his feet in their sneakers among ruffled other shoes, and a lacrosse stick head whose shaft slipped to the side and tapped against the wall, barely, and Simon grabbed it, as Dad came into the room, and held the taped handle with his left hand in the corner, like he was ready to play, or go like charging out at Dad with it, if he had to—*Haaah!*—not really, but you know, maybe, actually, you never know.

Dad paused at the doorway and stepped into the room where Simon couldn't see him, because the closet was in the far corner, and though the room was small, he could only see straight out, but he could hear him breathe a big pause, and he stood

there, standing there in the room for a little while, looking
around and wondering at the stillness. The TV was off, but still
warm, and he could have touched it, but didn't think of it,
maybe because he didn't believe, anymore, there was anybody
there, or anything to find, but it was just him, or some other
sound of the house than he thought, though the pillow on the
bed was dimpled, still, from Simon's head, but he didn't notice.
But he did stay there for a little while, lingering, like the room
had a spell, or presence, for him, hidden in it, which it definitely did, and he moved over closer to Simon, to the middle of
the not very big room, where Simon, staring straight out, could
see him looking, bent over a little, right at him, he thought at
first, frozen, with his heart clapped, clogged, in his throat, but
he wasn't, he was looking at the table past him, at the picture of
Mum in the green leather frame with the gold date from his
wedding to Ginny on it, in the late bleak sunlight shooting in,
in one like spotlight shaft, filling the corner and closet front,
and Mum's face, with the tenuous gold. Mum's big face on
Burnt Island beach, smiling, with her sunglasses on top of her
head, the beach and water and Dad in the background, his back
turned, with one hand in his back pocket, like Mick Jagger, out
of the picture almost, or wanting to be, but in it, like him, like
it or not.

That was a real close call, but Simon felt like, okay, that was
the one time, and so now he wouldn't get caught, and he'd be
careful from here on in, but he'd made it through the test, and
felt like he had broken through something, so that now he was
free to do more what he wanted, and to be, like, out over Dad
more, or playing the line between them more, for fun and just
to do it. That night he watched Dad make dinner, and eat it, in
the kitchen, from out on the porch, where he would have been a
sitting duck, standing out there in the open, though in the
dark, but in the light from the door, actually, at one point,
when he was about to sit down and eat, to let the cat out, and as

he stepped to the door, Simon stepped back and froze, relaxed, against the house, between the black green shutters, while the door, with its nine panes in the top half, inched open, wide enough for the cat's skull, and skillful Witness threaded out, with his tail straight up, curled at the tip and tapping into Simon's pant leg as he rubbed by in a body-stroke greeting, then went on his way out into the night shift, just beginning its nocturnal dream progression, here on the lined flat porch, where it would also end, when it was light out, at the door, in a patient wait, ready to be let in, to be fed. Dad had no expression most of the time he was alone, just like his face at rest with his mouth downturned, a little jowly, and eyes pouched and a little sadly slanted under his glasses, and when he talked to Ginny on the phone the next night, Simon saw, through the porthole of the dining room door, his face lit up and all animated, and he moved his left hand around as he explained a story. He hung up, and, heading back downstairs, came right toward Simon, who stepped back a bit, but not aside, and watched and like challenged Dad, again, to look straight ahead and see him, his face a circle portrait in the porthole window, back a bit, like out of focus, or deeper into dark water, in ice, dim and out of focus, but there, lit enough to be seen, not moving away, as Dad walked toward him with his head down, still in the conversation, then right near, where he turned left to go down to the cellar, he looked up, his glasses and face were pink, two feet and less from Simon's, right there behind the glass, framed in the circle, and for that second it seemed like he saw him, but he didn't register anything, and slid past and was past. As he went down the stairs, Simon slid out through the door, hinged both ways, and it made a cracking creak that blended in with Dad's creaks going down the stairs, and from the top he saw him descending the last part, foreshortened, like his shoulders were compressing into his feet, and at the bottom he turned.

Back in their respective places with their two TVs on, on

one station, with Dad ten feet away, down, looking through his *WoodenBoat* magazine on the workbench, not paying attention, Simon sitting above him on his bed in the dark with his sneakers on. Dad went to bed, as usual, pretty early, and Simon fell asleep, too, before the news, with his clothes on, and the TV still on. When he woke up his clothes were twisted and sweaty, and he felt out of joint in that way, out of time out of place. He thought he heard something. Maybe that's what woke him. He shut off the TV and watched his vision blotch out, spots clutch-climbing across. The moon was out, outside, the night had that blue glow, like from his TV. He heard a solid knock under him, down in Dad's workshop, followed by a stumble and tumble of things, like wood or a couple of boxes on the floor, knocked by someone who didn't know where they were going in the dark.

This shot him wide awake, not worried but alert as an animal on alert, and without thinking he was out of his room and at the top of the stairs, listening down. If it was Dad the lights would be on in the hall, and down there, unless something was weird, like he was sleepwalking, or really drunk, which was probably what it was. It was quiet, and then there was a dragging sound, and something fell with a bang, surrounded by a little clatter, and it was quiet again, in a pause to get his bearings, if it was even Dad, or whoever was down there, maybe somebody breaking in stumbling around. There was another movement and in its sound Simon moved down the stairs. He could see a lot in the room, in the moonlight coming in the window. He was surprised to see a flashlight beam bouncing its ball up the wall and lancing over toward him, then down on the floor like it didn't know where it was going. He didn't say anything, or move, but just stood there, like a warrior, poised at the bottom of the stairs, trying to figure out if this was even Dad or not, so it was scary suddenly. The guy, whoever, stopped, like he knew Simon was there. He could have shined the light at him. Was he trying to be tricky, or was he just wasted? The dark figure approached behind the flashlight, and it was like sudden combat, heightened and hairy. The guy breathed through his nose, sounding familiar, but actually not like Dad at all, and moved in a kind of slow lurch right toward Simon, who stood up straight as the flashlight lifted away and, he kind of knew it was coming, suddenly swung and hit him.

Through all this snow and nothing else around, a long column of people, like soldiers, but people, in two rows, wearing black and formal clothes, pushed along up this steep slope, and at the front was Simon, and who he was with, leading the way up this structure, like a radio tower built into the mountainside. He had to get them all there safe to the funeral, and he knew how to do it, so he was glad he was in the lead, and in charge, but he had to explain, but couldn't, because he had to climb with his hands and his feet the metal X's of the structure, which for some reason kept him from being able to talk right then, and everybody crowding in was asking him questions, and automatically blaming him, or accusing him, or ready to, he could tell, so it was this building pressure, but he knew he knew what he was doing, and would get them all there safe, and then he'd be able to explain, and then everything would be okay, so he wasn't worrying, now, but still there was this intense pressure, and all these people he had to deliver, but he was glad to, and would, if everyone would just shut up and leave him alone for a minute.

They found Dad dead the next day around noon, lying on the floor at the bottom of the stairs down to his workshop. Ginny called him at work after he didn't call to wake her good morning, my dear, like he usually did, every morning she was gone, and she got no answer at home, and when he still wasn't at work by eleven she called Gail and asked her, trying not to sound too worried, to go over to the house and check it out. Gail found him and called the police, saying he was passed out, facedown, and they should send an ambulance. The ambulance was there in ten minutes, and the ambulance guy knew he was dead right away, and shook his head at his partner and Gail, standing there hugging herself, watching as he touched Dad on the side of the neck, then under the jaw, and then the wrist of his arm bent the wrong way. The partner called the cops on the phone on the way into the kitchen, which is when Simon woke up and heard him, but not what he was saying, or who it was, and then in a little bit, hearing voices out there still, Simon saw the cop car arrive, outside his bedside window, with two guys in it, who got out.

The cops knew it was for the ambulance guy to pronounce him Dead, and by this time Simon was wide awake, but still in bed, listening hard down, wondering what was happening, and deciding what to do. They found him a few minutes later when they started to go through the rooms, and he pretended he was asleep, and they woke him.

Wha-a-a—lifting his sleepy head, squinty, slow.

Who are you? said the senior cop with a cap on.

Simon, he croaked, and the cop went on,

What are you doing here? And Simon looked at him with his puffy face pulled in, like at the impertinence, like who's this guy, and said with a cranky shrug,

I live here, and sleep-crusty and deadpan dull, but kind of aggressive, added,

What are *you* doing here?

PART TWO

My brother, like a bird, in his annual spring migration up to Maine, appeared in New York at the other end of my buzzer, as usual, needing a place to stay. I fed him, a lot, and told him I wished he'd called in advance. He said forget it, he'd just leave that night, and he left.

I can picture it all: He takes the bus up, settles into the cold summer house. Painters show up, he tells them to leave. Then he's told by the fatty caretaker that Dad wants him to leave. He eats food left on the shelves from the summer before. He paints, he sleeps. He goes off to different places on the island and makes paintings. He's in his element.

People show up and trouble begins. Timmy is testy. Then Dad arrives, and tells Simon to leave. They have a tense confrontation. Simon pretty much ducks him for the rest of the summer. Once everyone's gone, after the summer, it's peaceful again. When it gets too cold in the fall he has to leave. He gets an apartment in Boston, but needs a place to stay until it's available. He asks Dad if he can stay at home in Manchester until it's available. Dad says no. Simon goes anyway.

That's it in a nutshell. In more telling detail: first, going up to Maine in the spring after he left me in New York, after the Mexican restaurant:

High tide, nice, in the big tidal pond like a lagoon beside the highway, for a minute, just past Portland, the first real coastal feel, he always liked it right here, the water right up to the grass edge and trees reaching out over the water, the black low railroad bridge on pilings about a mile across the water, leading its straight line straight into trees, houses hidden under their roofs in the bright first green billows across the water, spread out like blue corduroy with the breeze. The sun was up there full blast now, making royal morning from the water up to the sky, pouring in this side of the bus onto his lap. Puffed clouds were coming up from behind, but would they catch up? Doubt it. He opened his pack of orange cheddar peanut butter crackers, don't mind if I do, and devoured them with the o.j. they give you, too, the orange snack pack.

They took the Brunswick exit and cruised up the commercial strip, like the fifties still, past Miss B's, still there, where Dad would stop and they'd get truckers' specials, just the boys. The music for a quarter, flipping selections like pages of a book inside the glass, country pink and rock-and-roll green and purple, and the road like a river turned and curved and followed the river, brown like dark beer, foamy below the little falls. After Brunswick it was the coastal route and towns with seagulls. Brick Bath clustered on the hillside, cubist roofs to the riverfront, the Bath Iron Works with the huge crane and battleships with white numbers, enormous, like the river here, closer to the ocean. In all his time in the navy Simon didn't go in a boat once, except this skiff he sort of stole, or just like used one day, from a beach with prickly balls like Christmas tree ornaments everywhere, in Spain, Gibraltar. His car in Cuba he got for a hundred bucks, no windshield, so he wore goggles. Gitmo, they called Guantánamo.

At the next river, next town, Wiscasset, where there was always traffic in the summer, with a traffic cop standing there causing it, sending flotillas of ice cream cones safely across the street, now there was this sleek new wider bridge stretching ahead like the neck of a goose in flight, low, smooth cement, like it was licked there. On the right, rotting in the water, the old listing schooner Mum and Dad had their honeymoon bet on, had two half masts left. When they were just married they bet whether the masts would still be standing when the first one of them died. Mum lost.

Scout gulls swept in to lead the way for a while, then peeled off. He liked them when he first saw them, like at a dump after not seeing them for a while, but mostly Simon didn't really like gulls. Like with people, he didn't put them in paintings, except maybe once in a while, one standing on the rocks, or on a roof, like a live weathervane. Cormorants were pretty cool, though, like wet cats, or little vampires, with their wings out to dry. Ospreys, though, were the coolest, cruising around like discount eagles; he always kind of felt like he was one. Their big stick nests set up in the best places, those hooked beaks and claws for fish.

At Damariscotta they got off Route 1 and went through the little town, pausing, after the harbor waterfall at the bottom of the hill for a breath before ascending toward the white church at the top with three arrows through its black heart weathervane, and the hilly loop back to Route 1, past fields, and the white farm ice cream place where, with Mum, they saw a rainbow over the far field against an overgrowing thunderhead, and then two, and then, like a joke, or in case you didn't believe in God, a third rainbow, all at the same time. And the little motel with little cottages with lilacs between them, where they stayed when they came to visit Timmy at Camp Kiev. Mum had hers, and they had their own, and smoked pot in a toilet paper tube with a tinfoil bowl, palm the back, like in the pre-bong days, and Mum came in after, they were tense and stoned, but she didn't say anything, luckily she didn't notice. After the parents' day dinner at Camp Kiev, barbecued chicken and corn on the cob, and the play with Indians, and somehow angels, starring Henry Kissinger's son, they launched all these paper boats out into the lake with candles in them lit. They flickered and kept going off in their own drift like a little city spreading out to little points of flame, each with a little reflection tail under it, like gold feathers melted into the black stoned yawn. It was really buggy, and all the families.

The next stretch, right after Moody's Diner, always made him think of Alaska, with the trees scrubbier, the little like tundra swath under the power lines. Then after the flower place that started out as a little stand, when they were newlyweds, and now was this big place with greenhouses, the houses of Thomaston, like littler versions of Manchester, with clapboards and dark green shutters, or black, and widow's walks, but fancier styles, some of them, or trying to be, like with cupolas or pillars, sort of Southern, with porches on lawns back from the rows of elms, gone now from disease from beetles, wrecking the town, with gaping sky in a glaring strip over Maine Street, like it lost all its teeth, the stumps removed but the bumps still showing, and the little consolation oaks they planted, instead of the graceful arms of the interlaced canopy cave that used to be there to pass through like a great green cathedral. The prison always kind of gripped him, or now he just noticed it, like looking at the guys loading laundry at the loading dock, and the coiled razor wire along the top of the yard walls between guard towers, he always imagined a baseball diamond in there, and they were really good because they had so much time to practice. The prison store he always noticed, too, with wood crafts in the window, but had never been in, you always passed through Thomaston because it was the last town before the ferry.

The upper right two window shades were always pulled down in the Montpelier House on the hill straight ahead, he always noticed because they were this beautiful robin's egg turquoise, he wondered if they were made that color, or probably they faded to that, but if they did, then from what? It was like American history right there, with the monster cement factory industrial wasteland, like the next era moving in, behind the museum house where George Washington slept. The long diagonal conveyor belt ramp that came out of the bottomless pit and up to the cement monolith building, like the Soviet Union, wasn't moving, but dust rose in clouds from the work below. The road ran between deep quarry drops, and the grass and leaves along the side were always dusty and blighted, it was like this raw patch of rape of the earth.

If they didn't make the ferry after sitting there for ten minutes back there . . . but he could tell they would, this guy was like the ferry himself, he did this every day. Rockland was a pretty depressing town, but you were there. Left at the light and there were the same few people walking the sidewalks like it was any decade, take your pick, even the thirties, except the cars, these skinny guys with serious haircuts and fat girls with no expression. They were poor like all of Maine and then the summer people came breezing in, but Simon knew this was what the world was like, these people, because he was more like one of them, in their same like marginal reality. No summer people around yet, it was better like this.

The ferry was there unloading. Simon loped down the paved slope painted with numbered slots for cars like a big hopscotch game, cars lined up with the drivers in them, ready, half of them pickups filled with stuff.

The house in Maine was cold. He went from room to room, like a breeze that let itself in the screen door, and opened a window to blow and flick out a couple of dead flies lying on their backs like professional wrestlers on the sill. Mum and Dad's room had the similar beds with curved wood headboards and pale bedspreads and a rug between them, and the similar bureaus across from each other, with mirrors on top, so you could see your back in diminishing repetition, like with the closet mirrors in their bedroom in Manchester. The window seats under the three bay windows bulging out, looking over the dock and past, like in three panorama panels of the whole Thorofare, had dark blue cushions, same as downstairs, and also the cushions in the wicker furniture with their knobby feet like balls of yarn. The curtains were pale blue faded flowers, and the walls were pale blue, with white windows and trim and doors. The floors of the different rooms were painted various shades of gray, and in here was the lightest gray, almost white. The mussel shell on the bureau had the colors of the room swirled in it like sky, and on the faded blue back the colors of all the rooms on their side of the house, which was all pure Mum.

Red had the whole stained-wood middle house to herself, upstairs, except for guests. Her room, like all the bedrooms except Mum and Dad's, had the roof-slanted ceiling over one of the beds, and dormer windows punched through. A book of some Russian poet woman, Anna Someone-ovna, was on one of the bureaus. The bedspreads were on the beds but without the folds under the pillows. The doors, like a lot of the doors in the house, didn't close all the way, because the house was kind of falling down, Dad, on its pilings and piles of rocks in the water, like slowly slipping to its knees. The door with panes to the balcony was stuck, and, lifting a little, he unstuck and opened it. The middle balcony over the dock sloped down and outward a little and was covered with canvas painted white with oxidized green dots around the edges from the copper nails that bled through. A power boat that definitely didn't live here purred by, up the middle of the Thorofare, with a powerful rooster tail whooshing up behind it. Over at the ferry landing there wasn't a soul. Across the sky a jet nib scored its white equals-sign tail, which disappeared fast behind it, except for the inch that went with it. The first green of the few deciduous trees, interspersed in pockets and fringed in places along in front of the whole solid, dark, serrated evergreen bank across the Thorofare, was lighter green and fresh-looking, like lettuce. A gull slid by and looked over at Simon as it passed. Another came curving down from over the roof behind him to join the other one and fly along with it. They went over the ferry landing and past Brown's and kept going.

In Dad's shop downstairs it looked like not a whole winter but maybe a few days had passed without someone in there using it, except it was pretty dusty on the surfaces, but it was always sawdusty in there. They used to have a Ping-Pong table in here and a bad stereo and it was like the butt room. There were dents in the pine boxed around the beam overhead, where the windows bulged out to the dock, with their window seats under the balcony, from hitting it with the edge of the paddle when you missed a shot, and there were still some butt burn marks around the benches and on the floor, like little craters painted over with the deck gray. The table saw had a cardboard box on it and a dust-covered boat model, built only on one side and open lengthwise down the middle, like a cross section, so you could see all the ribs and how it was built. One wall of the room, whose other side was the shingled wall of the passage outside to the dock from the stone stairs, was one long like workbench table, stand-up height, with scoop lights clamped in place above it and their wires nailed in with those little like wicket staples for nailing wires in. This wall was filled with all the tools he used on nails, and also on nails, all around the walls, were pencils, and pencils missing, just like in his other workshop. Over the winter everything in here froze, like everything in the whole house. This whole place was his cellar in Manchester exactly transposed to Maine, above ground here, or more like above water. At high tide the water came right up almost to the floorboards and you could hear it slapping and lapping under there.

Out in the passage between the houses there was a breeze, in the breezeway, and a pickup rumbled by at the top of the steps, red. The tide was going out or coming in, whichever it was, and Simon felt like same with him. Inside he had this one head, still arriving, like waking up fresh and innocent from a nap, and you're a man's age out your solemn eyes or sadness in the mirror. It was pleasant out here in the open and the like lucid that came in through him, like he was a medium for it, we all are, but he was aware of it, and attuned to it, like an expert at it, and that's why he went out in it and painted it, like an animal, one with it, and putting it back, like giving it back through his brush tips, tender skillful touches onto the canvas, his second skin, the skin of the world. He went to the places he painted and painted them there, but then took them back and finished them up in his room and the room beside it, where he did most of his painting and mostly lived, like a little apartment within this whole rambling three-part house standing on all its wobbly stilt front legs in the water, exposed like shins at low tide.

He ate what was there. Spaghetti and a jar of sauce with tuna from its little can mixed in. Rice and a rice pilaf mix and potato sticks. Even a few of the baby foods, which were actually really good little treats, just puréed fruit. He'd take his plate of food up to the balcony and eat it there, and then get back to the paintings he left last fall, or maybe snooze a little, and maybe like beat off, and then go into a dream, while a few flies, then a few more, all like doing push-ups together, feasted through their hairy little probiscis snouts on the leftover smears.

He opened the middle, wider window and dropped out some dead flies, and in came another he tried to catch, too, but it was all supercharged like from another hyper world outside, traversing the room in loud, long circuits, like it was on a helicopter mission, and had the figure-eight repetition route all programmed in. Finally, one of the times it came back, they go for light, he got it against the window, too, using the curtain to trap it in. He lay back down on Mum's bed and decided to do a painting of in here, with the bureaus with the mirrors, and between them the windows with the curtains in between with light in the folds, and outside out the windows, in three parts, the docks, the boats, the Thorofare, with the trees of Vinalhaven across, with a little sky in there, and the few houses, though maybe out the windows wouldn't be that detailed, you had to wait and see, but knowing him, like Mr. Detail, it probably would have all of it packed in the three windows, we'll see. He set up an easel in there at the foot of the beds and started right in on one of his new canvases. He never penciled in drawings anymore like he used to, but just started right in and it quickly took over all by itself, it was one of the fun parts, like effortless, like all you do is watch it happen, and get to go along for the ride like from the inside. He used his teeth and tasted paint and it marked the plastic cap without getting it open, so he needed pliers to get this little crusted old tube of ultramarine open. And also he needed a knife or screwdriver to scrape some of these other tubes, and the crusted palette, and to pry out the metal inner seal under the screw-on cap of the turp, so he went down to Dad's workshop. It felt moist and cavey in there so he opened the door to let air come in the screen door. And as he passed through upstairs he left the two doors to the bathroom bridging the middle house to the other house open. And that night he opened the window in his room and propped it with a stick he stirred gesso with, until the mosquitoes came in. And so like that, by degrees and days, the house gradually opened its eyes and its home consciousness to the surrounding traveling sea airs and the warmer island perfumes of greening spring and the living spirit of Simon the inhabitant, as he happily enough lost the linear and found, and sort of softened, and filled in, with his lovelike flotation capacity and gentleness, the seam between so-called self, with its normal illusory sensory and like mental experience, nonstop, and that other area, between the ache, where time is out, and dreams and like death and all the shadow elements of the unreal get a play vote and a safe say, like a place to stay, in you, without fear of impossibility and automatic cancellation, and in that home zone loneliness was scattered like sunlight on water into fuel for art, since loneliness is like the art it arrives in, impervious to life, and they come together in beauty, so it's as accepted and familiar and almost invisible as you are in the soul's mirror, and much more sacred, since where did this come from, down the ages, if you think about it. The answer is nature, which is God, and like they say, the way is one but many are the paths, like art, one of the highest.

The day after the funeral and burial, just after nine in the morning, Simon was arrested. Two cop cars came, a Manchester police cruiser and a state police cruiser. Three officers came up the porch steps and one, Chief Raddick, knocked on the front door. Timmy and Anna were in the kitchen with Bennie having breakfast, breakfast number two for the little guy. Timmy opened the kitchen door and spoke across the porch.

Can I help you?

The cops looked at one another and walked over to him, clomping loudly and dwarfing the porch. The state trooper's heels knocked a louder and more menacing slow beat than the others' shoes. Anna stood beside Timmy in the doorway. The rest of the house was still asleep.

Hi, Captain Raddick, Timmy said as they neared.

Hello, Chief Raddick answered cautiously, no catch of recognition softening the ruddy facts of his face. Chief Raddick had a son Timmy's age and had coached Little League when Timmy played. Timmy had played on the Beavers; Chief Raddick—Captain Raddick then—had coached the Acorns.

Timmy, Timmy clarified, Timmy Curtis, and held out his hand to shake.

Ah yes, said Chief Raddick, nodding. I—I'm very sorry about your father and everything.

Thanks. So . . . what's up?

Is Simon here?

Simon? Yeah—why?

I ah, I'm here—we're here—because we have a warrant for his arrest.

Simon? Are you serious? Anna touched him on the shoulder.

In connection with the possible murder of—Richard Cary Curtis. He looked down and breathed out—there, he'd said it.

Timmy couldn't believe this was happening; but at the same time it didn't surprise him one bit. Anna spoke up firmly.

May I see the warrant, please? She stepped forward amid the men. I'm an attorney, she added.

Yes, of course, said Chief Raddick, and he withdrew the warrant from the inside pocket of his coat and handed it to her.

She unfolded it and glanced over it quickly. She noted the name of the judge on the bottom; the seat of the court: City of Salem, County of Essex, Commonwealth of Massachusetts; and the charge reckoned: murder in the second degree. She handed the document back to the officer and said,

Wait a moment, please, and withdrew into the kitchen, closing the door against Timmy's semiprotest, pulling him with her.

I'm taking the baby into the other room. I'll make some calls for a lawyer. Take them in to Simon, but ask them to wait in the next room, and *you* go in and wake him up and tell him they're here to arrest him. Timmy listened with his head bowed, like he was listening to something in the next room.

Bennie, in his seat, banged at the table with a spoon like a windup doll.

Tell him to get dressed and go with them without any protest, she went on, but tell him not to say a *word* to them, *nothing,* except that he wants an attorney, and that he won't say anything else until he has an attorney with him. He gets one phone call, he should ask for it, he should call here in an hour. Okay? She gripped Timmy by the shoulders. He looked dazed, hurt, but nodded.

Don't worry, she said, everything'll work out. Now I'm taking Bennie out of here and then you can let them in and go get Simon.

Maybe I should go with him, Timmy suggested.

She lifted Bennie out of his plastic seat and plastic bib. I don't think they'll let you, honey . . . and I don't see any point . . . There's really nothing you can do right now. Except to tell Simon not to incriminate himself, not to say a *fucking word.* She leaned over, holding Bennie on her hip, kissed Timmy a quick connubial snout kiss, and whisked the baby out of the room. Anna clerked for a judge in Chicago her first year out of law school, so she knew about criminal procedure.

Timmy let the cops in and did just what Anna said. He led them through the kitchen and back to Simon's room and asked them to wait in the next room while he went in and woke him. Simon was awake sitting up in bed. He knew the cops were here, you could see it on his face, you could see one of the cop cars from his window. His expression was sort of sickly scared, but also wiseass know-it-all, like he was used to this and ready to make trouble, of the special mental Simon sort, for anyone who tried to invade his sphere. Mum used to call him Rascal. She also used to call him Blister. Timmy took his expression personally, and felt like fuck you, felt like leaving the room and leaving him to his own sorry fate. But he did what Anna said, though he couldn't bring himself to be entirely blunt about it.

He told Simon they were here to take him with them. Simon opened his mouth incredulous, like it was so ridiculous. Timmy told him Anna said he should just go along with them without any trouble.

They can't take me in, Simon said with an annoyed expression like when somebody turns on the light when you're sleeping.

Simon, they're here, yes they can. His voice got softer with these last words and keened to a pleading urgency. They're here right outside your room right now.

For three days the whole house had been like a crime scene—it *was* a crime scene—with detectives poking all over the place, looking under every cup and thimble, dusting for fingerprints, searching everywhere for anything. The cellar where they'd found Dad, and the adjacent rooms, including Simon's room, had been taped off, off limits, while they took photographs and measurements and made diagrams, just like Dad down there, but a whole team of them with their beer bellies, like he didn't die but multiplied. Both nights after they were gone Simon had stepped over the tape barrier and had a good look around to see what was so top secret. They'd turned the place totally upside down, including his room. You wondered how they could make sense of anything with the mess they'd made, or what they thought they were looking for. They looked around the rest of the house, too, but that was more cursory, like they didn't believe they'd find anything out there, except up in Dad's room, but that was a little touchy and tentative because it was Ginny's, too. After they finished and took down the tape and left for good, Ginny got Gail, who got someone else with a big pickup to clean up down in the cellar, clear everything out and get rid of it all. The truck had like wooden fence walls in the back to hold loads of junk. It backed in right under Simon's window, and out of it came two guys who went picking through Dad's stuff, taking all the good tools and nails and stuff, it was a total free-for-all. Simon tried to stop them saying that all was good stuff and they couldn't have it, it was *his.* They should just take like scraps and garbage and get out of there. Gail, upstairs cleaning the rest of the house, came down when one of the guys went up to get her. She kind of protested to Simon, but he ignored her, and when she persisted he told her levelly to butt out and mind her own business. She got all upset and went upstairs to tell Ginny, who was shut up in her room on the phone, in the bath, in bed, whatever she was doing up there. Ginny came down in her bathrobe, bullshit, and from the top of the cellar stairs she roared down at Simon in this weird hoarse voice that didn't seem like it could come out of her, like *The Exorcist,* deep and all quavery,

Simon, you get out of that basement right now or I'll call the police!

Which was a joke, Simon thought, since a whole squadron of them had just been there for the last few days.

These guys are taking all this perfectly good stuff, Simon said back at her pretty sharply. He felt like he was being reasonable, and felt like just flipping her the bird and saying, Sorry, Ginny, vacation's over, move over. With no makeup on she looked scary, but he wasn't scared of her. He never liked her for one second of the whole time she was married to Dad. At least he wouldn't have to pretend anymore now, not that he ever did before.

Now that the cops were here again, and this time to get him, Simon felt like he'd been tricked. All he had to do was relax and not think and he'd see the way out of this, or like through it, no sweat, they couldn't do anything to him, what could they really do?

Simon, Jesus, this isn't some joke, Timmy blurted, louder than he meant to, and he finished softer so the guys in the next room wouldn't hear. Simon, listen, you don't understand, they're not just here to question you, they have a *warrant,* he whispered hard, for your *arrest*—for *murder!*

Simon's little smile stayed glued there, but kind of froze, and his face fell around it, and it was like the room froze, too, in shock at the word, and what a second ago was a strange like smirk now blanked out in this sudden stupefaction and blunt real fear. Timmy stepped toward him to snap him out of it.

Simon, listen. Anna said you should just go with them without any hassles, but don't say *anything,* except that you want a lawyer. She's already getting you one on the phone. When they give you your one call, call here in about an hour and we'll have a lawyer by then.

Simon wasn't about to take Anna's advice, or Timmy's either, just because she was all bossy jumping into action, Miss Lawyer suddenly taking over like this was her situation, when really it was none of her business, it was his, just him and only him, and whatever would happen would happen. He'd been here for days dealing with these guys already and she had nothing to do with it. He'd already talked to them plenty, he didn't need her or anyone for that, and still didn't.

Timmy left him and, closing the door behind him, told the cops lurking outside the next room that Simon was getting dressed and would be right out. Timmy stood there with them, crowded on the little carpeted landing by the window looking out at the back patch of lawn and the lilac hedge and the glittering strip of water beyond, the sun pouring in on their synthetic uniforms, their hairy hands. Simon came out after a minute dressed in the same thing he wore the day before—after the funeral and burial—and the day before that and the day before that. Timmy met him in the outer room and said,

Do you want to brush your teeth?

Why? Simon said and breathed his evil effluvium in a silent *haaah* into Timmy's face. So I don't give my bad breath to the guys interrogating me for murder? He stepped toward the officers like here I am, and then slipped sort of slyly aside into the bathroom right there and took a long leak, drilling into the toilet water while the four men outside the open door listened to the purl, and then he flushed it like hi, Dad, bye. He came out and turned to the cops and said,

Okay, I'm ready, like they were old friends come to pick him up. Let me just grab my coat. He went bumping past them, tight squeeze sideways, into the coat passage to the front hall. He still, by lifelong habit, hung his coat on the lower hooks lined up on one side at kids' height. Dad's parka was still there on his higher hook, opposite. The cops hesitated behind him at the entrance to the kitchen, the way they'd come in.

C'mon, Simon said to them, let's go if we're going, and moved through the light hall to the front door, with them trailing like his entourage.

Along with Chief Raddick and the other Manchester cop was the same chubby state trooper from the day before. He had escorted them not only to the burial, but back home from the burial as well. What seemed like the treatment like for eminent citizens now looked like they were keeping tabs on a murder suspect. Out on the driveway the guy said to Simon,

Come with me, and he reached back and fumbled with the handcuffs on the back of his belt.

I'll go with these guys, Simon said, and headed over to the Manchester cruiser and his two fellow townsmen. The state trooper came after him huskily, as if he was on the other team in street hockey, out there on the driveway right where they used to play it, but Chief Raddick raised his hands, palms pushing peace, like a ref, which also was practically the case, *let it be,* and the state trooper didn't like it and began to object, but then didn't bother. Simon got in the backseat, separated from the two up front by a steel grid partition, not exactly the limo this time. The hardware on the cruiser's dashboard was impressive.

Simon looked with interest at the radar gun, like something you could shoot tennis balls out of, propped in its holster holder under the digital readout screen, which was turned off. The younger officer drove, and Chief Raddick turned in the passenger seat and said, Now I'm going to read you your rights, son, as they pulled over toward the Hunters' and turned and smoothly went down the steep driveway, followed quite closely by the state trooper.

Timmy and Anna watched from the front door. The rest of the house was asleep still. Anna swiveled softly, rocking the baby side to side.

Do you think he could have really done it? she asked.

Timmy didn't answer but gazed with a pained brow as the police cars slid down the hill past the sloping patch of cleared woods, all dead leaves, where the Space Trolley used to be, the two wires it ran along extended as tightly as possible but still drooping gracefully like phone wires, like a bird's flight, between the two trees at either end.

The painters came one day when it was cold, and he was still sleeping under lots of blankets when they tramped in talking loudly and dropping tarps and boxes of cans of paint on the floor downstairs, then going off up the stone stairs to get more stuff, their voices half foreign-sounding and chewy, going away, and then in a minute coming back, their volume slowly going up again until they were back in the house below him. The screen door slapped shut so many times it seemed like they were doing it on purpose, joking, or like they knew he was up there and wanted to wake and bug him. He pulled on his pants and shirt from yesterday and the days before that, piled on the other bed with other stuff, and went and stood at the top of the stairs.

He smelled cigarette smoke, then saw some puff out, bluish. There were three or four of them. One of them laughed, and it rasped out of control into a cough that went on and on, wetly stuck in his throat and sloppily deeper, trying to catch and get it out like it was alive in there. They went into the living room and he couldn't hear what they were saying, except loud above the rest,

I doubt *that*!

followed by laughter of all of them. In this and their chopped, swallowed cadences murmuring, and in their more than mere presence, unseen down there, he felt their disdain for the absent summer people who weren't even real inhabitants of the house, just rich owners who could afford to let the house just sit there most of the gray year and have it spruced up, along with their boats, for those prime few vacation weeks of high blue summer.

Boots clomped on the stairs, and a head rose up with long dark hair falling onto a jean jacket, then a Bud belt buckle, and then when he turned at the top, a red face, and red hands hanging as if dripping, and Simon didn't move, but the guy saw Simon's feet and reared back with a surprised face.

Jesus Christ scared me. Didn't know anyone was up here.

Yeah I live here, Simon said.

Well, said the guy stopped on the landing where the stairs turned under the slant of roof. Nice place to live.

Like bitten by what the guy said, Simon kind of clenched without showing anything. He wasn't awake all the way, and felt sort of padded in the head like with that watery layer under your skull, but clear out the eyes. People shouldn't be allowed to wake you up, like in some tribes they always let the sleeping sleep, because they're with the ancestors.

Guess we're gonna do some painting for you, the guy added when barefoot Simon didn't move or like welcome him up.

I don't think so, Simon said defiantly.

The guy shrugged his square shoulders. He was tall and skinny with long arms sticking out his sleeves and those big red hands. Simon had seen him before all his life. He had a bad pizza face and not quite a beard, but not quite not. Like shaving would be a raw meat massacre, so he didn't till he had to.

Eh Vic, he called downstairs but straight at Simon. Got someone up here says we ain't workin'.

No, just, Simon muttered, I didn't know. I mean, like what room are you painting?

Guy shrugs. Upstairs rooms.

Well I don't know, I mean, I'm up here working.

Well jeez. Victor meanwhile clomped up the stairs.

Ho, he greeted. We got a problem heah?

Simon thought this guy died a long time ago from something. Maybe it was his brother. Victor was big and bearded with a belly. His sleeves were torn off and he had a complicated sort of botched tattoo like a nasty bruise. His boots were unlaced so his thick calves could fit in.

No, said Simon. Just I'm living here. He didn't know if he was backing down, or what, but he just stood there. And I didn't know about this.

Well hell, Victor said. We're all set to go.

Wool what are you painting?

Upstairs all ovah.

Wool weren't you supposed to come like in the spring?

Not that I ever heard of. Just got the call to do the job last week.

Are you doing the other side too?

The two guys looked at each other.

Other side of what? You mean outside?

The other side of the *house,* Simon said, over there, nodding and jerking his thumb over his shoulder. He easily got frustrated trying to communicate with people.

Not that I know of. They exchanged glances again and Simon could tell they were thinking something about him. Guess I oughta call Doreen, straighten this right out.

Why, is Doreen who called you? Simon asked like he was trying to be helpful now. Doreen was the fat cleaning lady, like the Gail up here, who got the house ready at the beginning of the summer, with her husband, and closed it up after. He'd had sort of tense encounters with her at both ends of the season, with her arriving to do work and saying, Oh I didn't know you were here, Simon, and him saying, Yeah, well, I am.

This guy Victor was part tree part pumpkin, part like lineman and big part big slob, and the other guy could pass, no problem, for an axe murderer, but it was the mention of Doreen that rattled him, ready to retreat. Not that she was tough or anything, but she reported to Dad about the house. Victor stomped slowly back down the stairs and went to the phone to call her. Simon noticed he already knew right where the phone was. These guys probably party in all the houses like a big free-for-all when the summer people are gone. Simon withdrew into his room as the other guy went like a Slinky Gumby junky down the stairs after Victor.

Simon pulled on his purple sale fake Nikes, gathered brushes and paints from the bureau tops and the painting he was working on from last year, plus a new one he liked of just water, wiggly wavy, and took them over into the middle house into Red's room. He went out on the balcony where the sun was coming through whitely and it was warmer out. There was no chair out there so he went back inside and tried to pull the bent bamboo chair with the cushion out, but it didn't fit, even sideways like turning it, and the cushion fell out, and so fuck it, he put it back and went and looked for another one. In the far room, the sort of guest room, there was a wooden chair and he brought that out and sat on it, tipping back on the back two legs, with his neck and the back of his big head against the shingles and his feet up on the middle board, bending then adjusting with a little slip and slide forward to the top of the railing.

It was white out with calm fog that would burn off, and so

was actually quite bright already. The ferry was still there, the engine not turned on yet, so it was like seven. These guys got up early, lobstermen or not, like they had to, like the navy. There was no sound of lobster boats, or sign of any activity, except the one he could see at the mooring in the soft doughnut hole around him limited. They had already long gone out, were already off in the fog around other islands. The one at the mooring, like all of them, seemed stern with their square cabins like heads, and the bow almost a right angle like an axe blade. Simon could feel their hatred of summer people like it was written on their forehead, on their stern, and blaring out the radio, and like the engine grumbling the whole time was the person, black comments coming out of the pipe stack with the hinged lid like a puppet jawing quick puff quips and long loud streamer curses when they rev and go, with one guy inside lifting things around, and the one standing erect with slicker overalls on behind the wheel. He never painted them.

The ferry engine came on so it was seven-thirty, they warmed it up for half an hour. He could see the guy up in the bridge move behind the tinted green glass. Donald Fisk, the captain who used to be their caretaker, until he was caught ripping off liquor and food in the fall. Had a retarded kid, Puppy, who worked as a boat boy at the Casino and used to catch the boats and tie them up and greet everyone by name, he knew all the names of the cattle boats that came through, and their captains, and he'd row out and visit them. He'd sleep overnight in his sleeping bag in different people's boats, at their moorings, and one year he went away somewhere. Donald Fisk dressed like Dad and had this daughter, too, who was pretty cute, really cute, actually, who went to the island school and now college, she was this little like island-fresh preppie but island girl, and so she's at the ferry landing in Rockland and Jamie Wyeth sees her in the parking lot and talks to her because she's so cute, and next thing you know she models for him now.

Someone was in his side of the house here, he heard, and Doreen appeared in the door dark. Simon, I didn't know you were here, she said, not very friendly, resuming their dialogue of just this from last and other years. She didn't open the screen door, so it was like one of them was in prison speaking through the partition. He glanced back at her without moving from his seat pose, propped back. Her face was puffed from sleep and she was already fat so for that second it seemed like she was fat just from sleep.

Well I am, Simon answered flatly.

Your father didn't tell me you were coming, she added, putting a finer point on it. Her painted fingernail zing-zwinged softly on the screen.

Simon, half turned to her, made a sarcastic sort of half smile.

Did you tell Victor and his guys to leave?

I didn't know they were coming, is all he replied.

Well they're here, she said, and they're going to work.

Good for them, Simon said, shrugging slackly and blinking blithe calm that came out more seething and way stiffer than he meant.

Does your father know you're here? She pronounced it like *lather.*

Eyes lidded still, he gave her the sarcastic half smile again, but this time with a wincy little pinch in his face, and a set sort of side nod to end the dialogue, for this time around, this round.

Manchester was same old everyday Manchester, like proof in the world to Simon that everything was the same as it always was, and would stay that way, and not that he was worried, anyway, but he'd be fine, this would blow over like everything else. And also now that Dad was dead everything had a different flavor, like lighter, like the air was easier to breathe, and better to move through, like in a bubble, metaphysically growing and bending, like purely subtle to the supple cosmos.

They pulled in behind the white cinder-block police station between another cruiser and a black new Ford Bronco jacked up a little on chunky wheels. These guys loved their vehicles, and the guns, too, were a big part of their beefy macho code and like honcho brotherhood of toughness, they thought, even in softie little podunk Manchester. The Bronco had a Manchester Hornets bumper sticker, and one for Jasper Sporting Goods, Simon remembered those, a striped bass jumping on one side like a basketball player, and a concentric target on the other, and when they got out, after Chief Raddick told him, through the wire mesh, he could get out, to which he thought, well, obviously, he noticed a baby seat in the backseat of the Bronco. The state trooper pulled in after them and parked abruptly on the other side of the cruiser. As he shut his door solid *chunk,* like pissed, after a little pause inside like a woman checking her makeup, Simon thought, a guy called from the door, up the few steps to the police station entrance, to Chief Raddick, saying So-and-so was on the phone, and he hustled inside to get it, nodding to the rookie to take care of Simon, which just meant take him inside. From back here you could see the back of the library, where Simon used to go with Mum, sometimes just him, just to be with her even though it was the library, like a different church, the church of the mind, people whispering, follow her in the soft sound, foot clops echoing, maybe some murmuring, wait for her or follow her while she went into the books and picked some out, with the crinkly clear plastic covers and a white note inside it saying

DO NOT TAKE
PLASTIC-COVERED BOOKS
TO THE BEACH

though Mum would, if she felt like it, just like she'd steal flowers from in front of houses at night in Maine on a walk after dinner to put in vases at home, or if Dad said no about money or buying something, she'd do it anyway if it's what she wanted, too bad for him, like the last car she bought and died in.

The rookie reached over to usher Simon, but without touching him, and said, Step right this w—as the burly state trooper asshole stepped between them with his big boot in front of Simon, and Simon managed, in the slightest change of expression, opening his mouth and like laze-glazing his eyes, looking right at him with blatant derision, with a hint of a little wobble of the head, like when a table is lightly knocked and the vase on it settles back in place, to tick the guy off more, and like one-up the stakes and tension in the sudden little power-trip standoff. The rookie stood there between the parked cars and didn't say or do anything, as Simon and the guy froze for a second, standing staring at each other like dogs about to fight. Simon's laissez looseness, like lubed in there somehow between his eyes and mask and the tight human knot of his body, said to the guy's hateful glare and dumb rock presence, I'm like water to you, or like you're like oily water off my duck's back, you stupid asshole, you can't touch me. Simon knew guys like him galore from the navy and he hated them like anything, but also kind of liked being fuck-you tough against them in his own like part street part steel part like Taoist passive watery way. It was like a confrontation, who would crack and back down first, and Simon knew he wouldn't, and defiantly and with a glimmer of glee almost, looked right in the guy's bulging frog eyes. There was a red strap mark on his forehead from his hat, and his buzz cut, shaved on the sides, stood straight up, flattop, like a brush, like it was made by the hat with like shock treatment. They were about the same age but totally different types, except in the alpha, totally different like life paths, and Simon hated the guy, and vice versa. He could zen out and be tough at the same time in this animal-personal territorial warrior staring contest, he could stand there however long it took to outlook this fat fuck in his fascist uniform, and it was like the guy knew it, and so he gave in, acting like he wasn't, and spoke.

You can get your hometown pussy-ass sweetheart treatment from these guys, and I hope you enjoy it, because as far as I'm concerned, maggot, you killed your father and I'm gonna get you.

Oh, I'm shaking, Simon said, as if this guy were Timmy.

Tough guy, huh?

Tougher than you.

Yeah we'll see how tough you are.

You've got nothing on me.

Like he was some crook on TV. Simon rolled his head back in a weird gesture, both defiant and dismissive, slo-mo.

The rookie right there behind them opened his mouth to speak, or step in and stop them, stop all this, but he didn't do anything, didn't say anything, though he definitely felt what they were doing and saying was way out of hand and, especially out of the captain's sight, procedurally really wrong.

Yeah, where were you that night, then?

Wouldn't you like to know.

I already do know.

Yeah, I was right there, right?

You're admitting to me you were there, then?

I thought you already knew.

Now the rookie stepped over closer and almost spoke, but only like cleared his throat. They both looked at him like who the fuck are you, twirp, and then looked back at each other.

Problems with your father?

Like you wouldn't be*lie-ie-eve.* Simon stretched out the word like a taunt. It was like their tension receded into each of them and was gone for a second and they were just talking now, schizo-phrenically suddenly friendly almost, but with the viciousness still right there behind, ready to slam back in again, maybe worse, like breaking into a physical fight.

Angry with your father?

The guy thought he was being such the psychology interrogator now and Simon let him think it, fucking doofus. He breathed a silent syllable out his nose like a soft little laugh-puff.

Not anymore.

At this the guy glared and bore down on him like schizo vicious again, nasty petty rodent eyes narrowing over his pin-toothed little rat mouth that opened its simian overbite and kept it there, oafishly agape, till his greaseball voice slid out of it like a snake,

I hate scumbags like you.

Simon let it wash over with a lazy, blithe, half-mast, you-can't-touch-me slow blink. The rookie made a scuffed sidestep motion, but still stayed aside, like a timid referee. Both totally ignored him, and the big goon sneered,

You're going to fry, you little fuck, and I'm going to see to it.

You're too stupid to catch me.

How'd you get the cut on your eye, asshole?

Tseh, Simon sort of sneered back, half smirk half smile half ha.

Yeah, shaving with a blunt *in*-strument. Simon squinted and like lifted his chin.

And thinking he was being clever again, since he was onto something, or so he thought, and so he was, the guy softened, or pretended to, and said, like straight conversation, man to man, even a little you-and-me,

And what blunt instrument might that be?

Dint find it? Simon blew a soft little *peh* puff of derision, and was about to add something but didn't.

What? the state trooper asked almost coyly.

How many guys you need?

You mean we missed something?

Could be . . . with blunt mystery leading the big dumb shit on.

Dub . . .

You wouldn't want to give me a hint.

Simon shrugged slow why not, or like he could care less, so maybe.

Where else should we look?

Simon shrugged again and smiled outright, like he liked toying with this guy, and then it disappeared and he was right back deadpan again.

Is it hidden somewhere?

Simon looked at the rookie still right there listening, like who the fuck are you again, are you still here, kid, then back at the trooper, sort of pursed like he was about to speak, or maybe whistle, or like spit at him.

Go ahead, tell me, the guy said, and it was like such a flat-footed, flat-out challenge, Simon couldn't resist, or didn't see why he should.

Maybe if you ex-*tend* your *range* a little, might shed a little *light* on the situation, and with that the door to the station sucked open and Chief Raddick spoke, just loud enough across the small parking lot,

Is there a problem?

The rookie and Simon looked at him and the doofus looked with all his carnivorous hate again right at Simon, like now was the moment, from this moment on, motherfucker, he'd get him. Without looking over at Chief Raddick he moved to his left toward his car, still eyeballing Simon, and a slimy little smile wormed up the sides of his lipless lips before he took his head away, ducked into his car, and, macho man mean-ass, shut the door as hard as he could.

Simon looked at the rookie and gave him a little nod sideways, well let's go then.

· · ·

Doreen was fat and direct and had a loud voice like everyone up there, but she wasn't tough. She was a big softie. She hated dealing with Simon in this way, having to confront him and tell him this or that. She just wanted to do her job. Her husband stayed out of it, though she wished he wouldn't, but he kept saying, I'm staying out of it, raising his hands like a stickup, like ultimately he was doing her a favor. She called Dad and Ginny, right that day, and got their machine. Ginny called back in the bloated, kick-back tube time between dinner and bed. Ginny translated everything to and from Dad, standing right there, instead of just handing him over, and then at the end of the conversation he took the phone and spoke, briefly, for himself.

Doreen, he half yelled, as if he had to because she was a Mainer and on an island off the coast, you tell Simon for me please to get out of that house and call me immediately. Thank you.

Next morning she showed up at the same time as the day before to tell Simon. He wasn't in Red's room, where she first looked, though a lot of his stuff was, and a mattress was gone from one of the beds. He had dragged the mattress across to the cat room, where it just fit on the floor, with just enough room to open the door and fit through and get in and out, but not even close for Doreen the Door. She knocked and pushed the door against the mattress on the floor and stuck her head in at a slant, and seeing Simon in the sleep smell, squeezed further in.

Simon, I have a message for you from your father. She had this memorized and breathed to remember the rest. He said you're to get out of the house and call immediately.

Tsyeh right, said Simon, more at Dad than at her, turning in bed so the sheet came away a little, which made her nervous, but she looked.

That's all I have to say, she went on, this is none of my business. This last was her husband's input, and it helped her clear herself, and get out of there.

The cat room was called the cat room because it had no real use and there almost always used to be a cat in there, sleeping all day or standing lookout by the upright little window looking out at the little field and fieldy life beside the stairs and the people passing up and down, Mr. Winslow's falling-apart wooden dinghy planted with flowers by Mrs. Winslow in memory of Mum, and then of Mr. Winslow, maybe another cat out there, there used to be five, all black and differently tailored bits of white, moving through the tall grass, forget-me-nots, in the shifting shade of the swishing trees, or discreetly entering or already orientally in there or the other shady cool cat station across the way, down in the corner of the laundry room. Simon lay on his front looking out the window like a cat. The mattress was as thick as the baseboard space between the floor and the bottom of the window, so it was like a custom fit, right snug in there, and his chin was on a level with the sill two inches away. The morning was out there live like a movie—though not much happening. He pushed open the window and let in the sound and little chill. He could hear the painters on and off in the other part of the house but barely. His sleep had been like a safe ride on this raft he kept returning to between rolly dreams, and it was the perfect place to be, except that there was this like hollow tall column room under the mattress like a long wide chimney connecting to the earth he knew he had to go into, when this safe part was over, by lifting the mattress like a lid, and just get in there, he'd be inside, and outside would be everyone else, floating around in their regular lives, looking in, and the difference was that they were in outer space, basically, lost, and he was in this inner space, kind of trapped. So he stayed on the surface, and after he woke, and Doreen, like another part of the dream, left, he stayed there longer, looking out the window, open, with that cat feeling, he at least knew how to relax, and be almost like a plant, be in the moment and let time pass into its slowest pure syrup pace and place in him, until it vanished, other people could rush off in their lives and never have this, but he had this advantage, which was the spiritual animal, or like animus, that could stop everything, seep into the lucid, and, for however long, like live there, heightened or half not there, which was the height of it.

Places have personalities too, and deeper like souls, and sentient days like this one. There was no boat in the water, and Dad's car was somewhere, but not right up on the street, so he walked, and this was the world's way, this time for the morning to go into him. No life in the village houses like gifts along the mowed field going up the hill and past the church at the top of the hill. The real island part of the island began in a whiff of fir sweetness draped between the architecture of trees, like all these little balconies and deep rooms and parapets on either side of the road, and actual human houses interspersed on one side, keeping their like neighbor distances apart, rooty little dirt driveways between them, grass between the tire paths kept dirt every day by cars that weren't there now but were off somewhere at work. A cat sat in a window and looked at him. He gave it a little nod up to see if it would nod back, like he used to to his cat, who would. It didn't even blink.

This was the one road out island, until it forked and went around the island back to itself. Little stones in the dirt edge crunched lightly underfoot where he cut the corner and took the road to the left. After a few houses with small porches and parked trucks and mini barn sheds, a real barn in a mown field, it was only trees, dead ones over a wetland low spot, and the road dipped up and down again. Through thinned trees on the right the green glass of Southern Harbor had sky blue up the middle. Young birches, like girls made out of long arms, stood together on the upper woods side of a thick meadow slope, dotted with Queen Anne's lace and daisies and clumps of whatever those purply blue flowers were, like long knuckles, not lupin. The slender birches were white and lovely with black eyes and mouths, and their swivelly leaves shimmered like price tags, stopped and started again like cheering. The grass was still wet, green hair, standing straight up, stiffer, right beside the road. The tips like wheat had a little weight. Pale airmail blue butterflies fell around the flowers and rose up again, jittery, like they were just learning to fly, they were all over the place. The sky in the open around the road was baby blue, too, at the bottom, and bright day hung high, with fog still in some of the trees, but not for long. His shadow slid before him, slanted off to the right. Everything was money to Dad, even though he like never talked about it, and like a broken record his favorite word, *responsibility,* kept coming at Simon, like haunting him, like the voice of God, out of the Dad in him he wanted to like exorcise, and kind of could, but if the guy weren't like totally pickled from alcohol, like his brain in a jar, preserved, and just reserved Boston mentality, but could value like wider in the world, like some people, like his own son, for one, who got his whatever from somewhere, not him, maybe Mum, or actually maybe him, like flipped in spite of him—like he was an artist trapped in a banker's body—he wouldn't think Simon was just playing hooky his whole life. But then he would be like a totally different person, it would be like asking him to grow wings or antennas or wear a dress, or like show his love, or like have some. We'd all like to be doing our hobbies all the time, is what Dad said once to Simon about being an artist, and that kept going around in his head, but Simon knew how to shut out anything, when it got to be too much, or even before that, in the way you just go blank and like rise up in your unconscious, that invisible powerhouse animal, and like apart in your consciousness, like you're a little taller and more diffuse, above and around your walking body, and even the like subtle body of your feelings, sensory contact, and the world of the immediate moment, so like part null cloud now, and more spirit, like pure witness, like in meditation, or painting, or guys in war, or when you have sex.

Where the road crested and rode back down the other side of the hill, curving at the bottom like a tail away, Simon cut over in the direction of his shadow into the bowl meadow at the base of Ames' Nob, before the layers of growth began with bay. Ames' Nob was the one mini mountain on the island, with a view all ways from the round rock nub top, over trees to the far reaches of the island and Vinalhaven, fitting into it like the same island with the Thorofare cutting its wide river course between them. The path through the meadow was there, but not yet used, or much, so the long grass fell over it, wet, and darkened his pants with cool swipes he didn't notice after the first few. It was like a safari going up here, as you passed through a different zone of growth every hundred feet of altitude, instead of every thousand, like on a real mountain, as you cut across the hill and up the same path from childhood that seemed so long back then, so far. Crooked sumacs like flagged canes with their furry skin and milky blood were first out of the field. It smelled good and green in here, sweet. Bay bushes covered the bottom like a broad skirt, their dark shiny leaves. And everywhere else, stretching off, the massive army of ferns, their banners draped all over the hillside, still growing, they were great, like the first like primal plant humans came from, like think of the in-curling little fiddleheads when they first come out, totally fetal, and when they get bigger, like now, their form and all their gestures, with all their leafy flag arms out, are like totally human, look at them.

Silver alders were next, like lots of tall shins, now we're into the trees, the dappled shade, their lively leaves like birch leaves, but even more shimmery, maybe these were poplars, like falling coins. Then over into the great spruce rooms, all tall shade with shafts to the rusty silent soft floor with roots, needles, the dirt path and creaky branches off in there listening to him pass, and the high trilly tweaks of chickadees, or whatever they were, singing back and forth between silent pregnant pauses in nature. Then the billy goat scramble up the last part, with your hands and careful foot placement on the gray rock cracks like crumbled stairs. On top, hidden in the rock till you find it, the little brass Geological Survey marker, like a coin long gone dark green, showing the directions of the compass, north a little left of where you think, like it wants to point not magnetic north, and not true north, but at the Camden Hills across the water, where the eye goes, to their smoky clay blue repose, the lovely long woman lying there. Hi, Mum!

Toward the Thorofare the overachieving sun was at about ten o'clock high, and that was about the time, and from up here you could get the roundness of the morning's peak hour rising up to take its full breadth and scope of light and fresh stillness, before letting it fall and reach away into the ragged rest of the running day. Houses he didn't expect he could see from up here he could see, at least their tops or backs or roofs in the painter's middle distances. The water tower, like nested in the trees on the other hill, looked like a soup can with the label removed. The ladder went up its side and curved over at the top. He moved over to the middle hump of hilltop rock and noticed, not to the left, where the path line came across the meadow from the road, but straight ahead, past the bay bushes and the ferns, where the hill went further down to the road at the bottom, another path cutting straight up he'd never seen before. He moved over a little more so he could line it up and look right down it through the sumacs. It looked like Africa, or like the sumacs were walking up the hill like at night, each wobbly stick one a step that stayed. He'd definitely do some paintings up here.

· · ·

They *arrested Simon?* Red couldn't believe it. Her mouth dropped open and she looked around, almost twitching, as if searching for her next line. Then it came to her:

I'm calling my lawyer, she said, and strode into the TV room. Anna sat by the phone with a yellow legal pad on her lap.

My God, Red said by way of a greeting, rolling her eyes as she picked up the phone and rapidly punched out a number.

Seymour, it's Red, call me back as soon as you get this, it's an emergency. My brother has just been arrested—they think he murdered my father. He's down at the police station right now. We need a lawyer *pronto.* I'm in Massachusetts. The number is 617-555-1968. Bye.

After she hung up she breathed, staring, glazed, out the window, and added to her faint ghost reflection, *Fuck.* Then, What, hon? to Anna, who'd moved aside while Red was speaking to make room for her on the couch.

The area code is 508, Anna said.

Oh, right, they changed it. She picked up the phone, hit redial, and left the number again.

Anna spoke to her in a composed lawyer voice, her equipoise belied by the *w* for worry and wife on her brow.

Red, I've already arranged for a lawyer for Simon.

Oh—good, sweetie, thanks, Red said, distracted.

He's already on his way to the police station right now from Boston.

Oh, that's great . . . Red didn't seem too interested. She looked at Anna and through her.

What I mean is, Anna persisted, pulling the cap of her pen on and off, he already has representation, so you don't have to—

Okay . . . but, y'know—you call your people, I'll call mine, Red answered with a quick sigh that offended Anna—which she noticed, and tried to ameliorate by adding, Don't you think?

Anna felt Red was being condescending and dismissive, and her tone tightened.

Yes, I think that's fine, but don't *you* think we should discuss this and coordinate—

Oh, I'm sure we'll have plenty of time for all that.

Red left the room, met sad eyes with Timmy, and they hugged. Standing out in the hall still, looking out the window over the lawn, listening upstairs for any signs of Bennie, he half heard their exchange. Heartened, he decided to go in and comfort Anna, which he regretted right away, as she immediately started laying into him about Red, and *you Curtises . . .*

Red decided to make a real dinner. She drove her rental to Cooper's to get food, stopping off at Singing Beach on the way home, even though it was dark. She looked at the ocean without getting out of the car, and could just make out the white wool of the breaking waves. Neil Diamond was on the radio, and she actually thought he was pretty great. Passing the police station in the middle of town she cried, and sort of combined it with prayer; and her day's offering emanated from her hands, the blue Le Creuset pot, the warm yellow kitchen: the good smells of food cooking filled the house with a pungency so delicious it was as if the house itself were famished.

They sat around the kitchen table as if they were still kids half their size; the table shrank.

So when are you guys going back into Boston? Red, at the end of the table, asked Elaine.

Well tonight we were going to go—she glanced at the others with her cigarette wristily poised to make sure they'd finished eating so she could light it—but Mom's flight's at eight-thirty tomorrow morning, so we're going to spend the night and give her a ride in.

Ginny's leaving? Red said.

She didn't tell you? Elaine blew smoke to the side, waving and wishing it away.

Ginny's leaving? Timmy repeated. Where's she going?

Um, she's going out to California, to Sally's—and to be near her mom. Apparently her mom took all this really hard.

Well we better talk to her and tell her what's happening with Simon, Anna asserted. Right?

She already knows, Phoebe said.

She already knows? Timmy frowned. How? She hasn't been out of her room all day.

Phone, Phoebe suggested, looking as uncomfortable as she felt.

Elaine, too, felt this disclosure cast her in a suspicious light. She didn't know her mother hadn't talked to the Curtises all day. She crushed out her butt on the side of her plate and rose to clear it from the table.

The way the Whaler skims over the water and rocks up and down a little, and the wind fits your face, tears pull out the sides of your eyes. Around Iron Point, past the Pingrees' big house up there like a wedding cake, white, the Thorofare goes along, still wide, into the spread train of the sun glittering bright morning, now, as Simon went into it, a little chilly with just his T-shirt on, filled with wind, rounded out from his back, the sleeves flapping like little winglets, before it narrows into the Little Thorofare, straight ahead, to the left of Babbidge, with its fir trees all crammed together like a crowd of people barely fitting on the island, and to the right it opens up into open bay, the far blue meat of Isle au Haut in the background like another, flatter Camden Hill traveled way over there, like Blue Hill, another bump on the rim of the bay behind Burnt Island, right there straight ahead, not far, at the end of the Little Thorofare. And right there on the right, you passed every time on the way to Burnt Island, and the way back, like the pilgrimage, the little lighthouse Goose Rock that sticks out of the water, like a sparkplug. Or like a priest looking over Mum's sea grave, between Babbidge and the other little island, where they scattered Mum's ashes. Simon, tossing his handful when it was his turn, got a little bit of it in his eye, when a little puff of dust of her like ghosted up back in the wind, fast, in his face, as the other little pieces all fell into the water, right in his face, and he like *pp*-spat it out, and it watered for a while, in there, Mum's last physical contact with him, not the sweetest touch ever, while Dad after his handful, after Timmy did his, dumped the brown paper bag, lined inside with plastic, upside down, to tap and shake out the last bits and little smoke. Then he dipped it in the water, to get her last dust, and poured it out. From here Burnt Island was right there, and from Burnt Island you could see this spot, past the seal rocks in the Little Thorofare you had to go around that went under at high tide, like seals themselves that lounged there in the sun at low tide, and Dad a long time ago said he was going to put a plaque with Mum's name and dates on the rocks to the left of the dock coming up the ramp where you could see the spot, her grave, but of course he never did it, just like it took a couple of years for him to go get the ashes from the cremator in Salem, where they used to burn witches at the stake, so they could finally spread them here where she wanted.

The little meadow at the top of the ramp was fresh green lush grass, not that long yet, but getting there, and soaking the sunlight in its pocket of peace, some daisies dotted in there. Deep in the trees was the hush of the woods, skirted by the path that cut along through spiky ankle sprays of juniper, overgrown, the gray-blue hard little berries not there yet that gin came from, whoever figured that one out, maybe the Indians, probably the Brits, addicts'll try anything. The smooth stones are sorted by size on the beach by the sifting and slow tossing of the tides that made them, and will forever, till the world ends, or global warming starts new beaches again inland. The water was close now, full bowl high tide, the beach sort of breasty and shorter. Beyond the cove curve of the beach the little house sits up there, back in the shade of its trees like under the visor of a cap, or the skirts of the women standing together. Their talk was in whispers over the island, mornings were mothers gone to the stores in the shelves of the trees. They all seemed like they were holding something, because they were, together like a chorus, a whole standing brace of the deceased with their skirts lifted, showing in, and their layers lifted, arms out, like busy with banners and flags. Walking along the beach he scanned for flint, you sometimes found chips, or once in a while a whole arrowhead. Simon was really good at finding them, like his grandfather, who he kind of looked like, too, especially this one baby picture smiling wide, and his grandfather, old and mean, but not for the moment, with the same lip-smooth grin, like senile greedy glee. The trees spoke to him, like some tall wall private prayer, an ancient invitation invocation, and he heard them, roger, I read you, and he saw them standing in their standing almost glory, this tableau of trees, generals or women like widows, and so he decided to paint them from the beach, and stopped right on the hump of the *m,* between the two sort of harbor halves of the cove, and set up his easel right there, sticking the legs into the stones, then putting a stone under one to get it just level, and solid. He undid and opened his wooden little suitcase of paints and scraped off the palette board with a stone with an edge, like man the tool user. He squirted out more paint, like forest green and the ultramarine and the white, which was getting down there, than he usually did, like he was hungry, he guessed this was one of those days, then good, when he worked fast and maybe did a lot.

The trees he did fast like they told him just what to do, while the light was still fresh morning topping the tips, and he did sky above bold blue, but just a cerulean stripe, and down to the beach, with a little of beach chunked in, and the water too, but just the edge of the cove. The little house up there, his house now, he was home, and it felt like it. But the fir trees were most of the painting, walled in soft light and their own shadows, with their layers of female he kept feeling, like scarves or slips, moving a little in the wind, layers of loss, disguised, but losing their disguise, of Mum.

It came out good, and in about two hours he was doing the finishing touches, yes and no, and started to get into that color contrast business where they touched, which he could do any-time better, actually, which was just as well, because the light was different now, higher near noon, or past, just, and he went on to the other canvas he brought too, make another. Which he did. In a while his stomach gnarled a curly little knot of noise, and another, like a pet in there, hungry. *Girl.* The stirry sift in the trees was steady, like water, it was everywhere, the medium of the other world among us.

At the arraignment in Salem there was a long wait for the judge to come out. Simon asked to go to the bathroom, and was accompanied by this skinny-ass court guard with a raspy, whis-pery voice to the regular men's room out in the hall, used by courtroom observers and the press, who all stared at Simon as he passed.

Three men in coats and ties stood at the tall urinals in the men's room staring through the tiles like old cracked yellow teeth in front of their faces. As if choreographed, two of them pulled down, one after the other, on the chrome handles, mak-ing little booms followed by the waterfall flushes, and as they slid to the sinks to wash their hands, they both noticed Simon coming into the bathroom. They were both journalists. One of them played it kind of cool, but both stared at him, and the more blatant guy blurted out,

Simon! How are you holding up?

Simon looked at the guy like there was no way in the world he was going to answer him, but that didn't stop the guy from going on.

How do you think the trial's going? Do you think you'll get off?

Simon didn't say anything and just walked over to the wall of urinals where this big guy was letting a long one fly, like he'd been stabbed at the bottom of his gut and it was just leaking and leaking out, like why they called it taking a leak. The guys pulled paper towels noisily out of the dispenser and dried their hands, then still stood there, like lingering.

I believe you gentlemen have finished your business, the big guy said in his calm threatening baritone without looking around. Why don't you let the man pee in peace?

The two guys looked at each other and tried to act like they weren't like stalking and gawking at Simon. They left.

Some people just don't know how to behave, Pete said to Simon without looking over at him.

I know who you are, Simon said.

And I know who you are.

You're working for the prosecution getting evidence against me. Pete had finished peeing and now was standing there shaking it. He shrugged like so what, then Simon realized oh, he was zipping up, or maybe the shrug was like both.

I finished doing that, Pete didn't mind telling him, and didn't get anything incriminating.

That's cuz there wasn't anything incriminating.

If there was, I would've found it.

They were talking like two spies meeting, looking straight ahead. Simon liked this guy even though he was against him. He felt like he wasn't against him really.

You like doing that? Simon said it more like a question of real interest than as a challenge or whatever.

It's a job. Pete faced Simon three urinals over. Some of us

have jobs. His accent was working class, pretty Mass., kind of tough, but smoothed off by the world.

And some of us are artists. Simon looked at the guy and it was more like a kindred meeting than some alpha face-off in the men's room where one might like pee on the other's shoes.

We're both good at what we do, Pete said, rinsing his hands. We're both outsiders and we're both poor.

At least I'm not putting people away.

I don't put people away.

Pete tugged down two pieces of paper towel for each large hand and bunched them together and threw them away without seeming to really dry his hands.

I work for defense attorneys. I save guys like you's asses. I'm just working the other side now because I owed someone a favor.

Who?

The Rockland police chief.

You're from Maine?

I'm from East Boston. But now I live in Maine.

You don't look like you're from Maine. Simon sort of smiled. Or yeah, you kinda do. Those glasses.

Pete's glasses were tinted brown. He smiled at Simon's comment, one of his front teeth was a little chipped and darker than the other, as he reached for his back pocket and removed a card from the bulky contents of his wallet, stuffed fat like a tortilla. He slipped the card onto the surface beside the sink and said,

If you need any help.

Then he left.

Up in the little robin's egg room off his room, the window open to the balcony over the water, the harbor breeze lightly banging rowboats together and clinking wire stays against a metal mast, Simon did some minuscule, like phobic, ministrations on this painting of the White Islands from last year, whose seaweed, underwater, was captivating him, it was like hair underwater, and much lighter than you'd think, like almost mustard ocher sometimes, also reddish rusty, like Mum's original hair, and his, if you really looked at it right where it came out. He felt like he almost shouldn't touch the painting right now because he wasn't in the right head, like in the lucid, like always, usually, and maybe he'd wreck it, but he knew he wouldn't, and that that feeling came from not being in the element enough, painting, since Timmy got here. People absorb and suck you away from yourself, from art, and it made him feel kind of terrible.

Timmy, meanwhile, over in his room, was gripped by Simon and his unwanted prevalence. All he wanted was to come up here and relax, be with Anna and relax, which they could both definitely use, and be with Bennie, his first time up here, and instead it was like everything was infected, invaded, by Simon. In spite of what they said, he was eating their food and hanging around him, around them, just, like, *staying there,* even though he acted like he didn't want to be there. He was weird. He did his little wobbly head thing or arm exercises in the middle of while you were talking to him, and he interrupted you all the time, cut you off and complained about Dad obsessively, and about anyone they talked about, he didn't brush his teeth and had really bad breath, didn't wash and smelled, and he had that annoying, bemused, snipped little smile, like he was so right, when you talked, or when he was making some opposite, totally out-there point, thinking he was so right, when really he didn't know what he was talking about, and couldn't speak in coherent sentences, but kept stopping and stumbling and chopping up what he started to say. The way he wobbled his head and shook his shoulders out of nowhere like some sleazy dancer was really strange and drove him crazy. This was Timmy's favorite place in the world, all year he looked forward to coming up, but instead of a vacation, what he got up here was Simon, and dealing with Simon, which was the last thing he wanted to do, he grew up and got married and started his own family so that he wouldn't have to stay stuck in the old one—but here it still was: here Simon still was. He had enough trouble as it was being married. He had enough trouble as it was just being himself.

Anna came back from her run all red like she was mad. But she wasn't, she felt light and clear. She could see how knotted Timmy was, sitting bent on the window seat, with one foot pulled up, clipping his toenails, and went over, and when he looked up at her and tried to smile, but couldn't quite, she kissed him on his sunburned forehead. Out the window it was sublimely calm and reflective out over the water. The houses across the Thorofare had soft gold faces. The done day had lost its strength, its breath, and stood still in its lovely last light. She'd had a nice run up at the golf course, and felt happy, expanded, keenly aware of how beautiful it was out, especially coming off such a stressful year in that sleep-deprived time warp you live in, upside down and inside out, in a baby's first year, added to the regular numbing sensual barrage of living in the city, and she wanted to tip Timmy toward this awareness of this beauty and actual peace, as he so often did with her.

Timmy used to write poetry, and the pieces he made now, boxed sculptural assemblages, had the delicate touch, the surreal eye and ephemeral sadness, the distinct details and emotional permanence, of poetry. One early, literal one seemed good in conception, but looked like a horror movie prop when he made it. It was of an eyeball with lips instead of eyelids, because what he sees he wants to say at the same time; and also, for the artist, seeing is eating. He kept this sort of creature symbol in his studio like a pet, or a plant, moving it around. It was titled *The Artist*.

Anna got up and went to take a shower, while Timmy went to go check on the little guy. He glanced in at Simon, as he passed his room, where Simon stood in front of his mirror, and his eye fell, as it did every time he passed now, amid the mess in there, on Simon's radio, which was also a tape player. Simon took off the buffalo T-shirt he was wearing and put on a plaid green and black button-down shirt, tucked it in in the mirror, then pulled it untucked. Then he tucked it in again.

Timmy had blamed their baby-sitter for taking cassettes from the living room downstairs. Heather cried, denied taking them, but looked down guiltily, and was very quiet the next day. Simon knew all about the missing tapes, but said nothing. That night, looking for some good music when the folkways show came on the radio, after the reggae, Timmy poked in Simon's things and found the missing cassettes. When he confronted him, Simon got aggressive:

What are you doing going in my things?

Before it really began there was a lot of whispery quibbling between the lawyers for both sides, standing up at the judge's bench, the judge listening and nodding yes and no and speaking in a regular voice. One thing Simon heard his guys keep saying was the phrase the right to a speedy trial, the right to a speedy trial, and he pictured a speedy trial, like with everybody on speed rushing around in fast motion and like speaking really fast—

The judge heard both sides and without ceremony—it seemed like he'd already made up his mind—looking over his papers, declared,

It is this court's decision, after due consideration, that the defendant, Simon Cary Curtis, be released from the custody of the state upon payment of seven hundred and fifty thousand dollars bail.

He cleared his throat and continued that a further condition was that he shall remain physically confined, for the duration of the trial, to a single residence, to be determined by the court, and his confinement to said residence will be insured by use of an electronic bracelet, which he will wear on his person at all times during this period, so that his movements and whereabouts can and will be monitored by law enforcement officials. I have to wear a bracelet? Simon leaned over to Will Deery, the junior of his two lawyers, tipped back in his seat. Looks that way. And so like I'm under house arrest the whole time? Yeah, this is great. Simon didn't seem to think so. Hey, at least you're out of jail, right? This is great. Simon didn't answer. He glanced back at Red and Timmy and them, and saw they were happy for him, so he automatically made like he wasn't happy at all, which in fact he wasn't. He was just the same as he always was. There was same old him safe inside the tube of self, and there was everything and everybody else out there, outside him, which didn't touch him any more, now, than it ever did. He wondered how he'd get his clothes and sketches, back at the prison, where he'd spent the past week, not unhappily, in a pretty good couple of rooms, TV, food, separated from everyone else. You couldn't trust those guys back there for two seconds. Especially since he was like famous now. He knew his stuff would disappear.

My sketchbooks back at the jail, Simon said to Will Deery, who never really listened.

Don't worry, you don't have to go back there! You're out on bail. This is *great,* he said, sounding like Tony the Tiger, without moving a muscle on his face.

So I'm free now, right? So I can like, go out for lunch?

The siblings stood by, watched by the wall of reporters standing behind and still in their seats, wondering if Simon was going to join them. Simon stepped over to the railing with a big grin he tried to suppress, but couldn't, and when he spoke it broke out all the way.

Red reached over and gave him a kiss and hug that held on

longer than he liked because it kept going deeper. He didn't push her away, but kind of put a lid on it inside, and waited till she let go.

Hanks, he said softly and was surprised he was suddenly so welling all up, like a hot wall of what, so he turned away, teary, so no one could see it.

Simon didn't know that Red put up the bail money. He just thought it was one of those things they'd kind of work out later, like credit or whatever from when he got his money from Dad's will when he got off, and he also thought it wasn't really real money you put up for bail, but like a bond, which was like an IOU or whatever, and you got it all back after the trial, so really it was like nothing. You just had to show you had it, like for security, but you didn't really have to give it over, unless you were someone who didn't have it, like if you were poor, like most criminals who get caught, and then you stayed in jail.

Nor did Simon realize Red was paying for his defense. He sort of knew, but Timmy said she could write it off, and Simon knew she was like incorporated, so her money wasn't really hers, like legally, personally, or she could spend money she didn't have, like any amount, because it was all business, like investments with her environmentally conscious broker, Randy, and her environmentally conscious portfolio, her accountant and her managers and her agents, her lawyers, producers, and other investment guys, different partners in little things, some club, an animal rescue place, a hemp farm, hemp clothes, this African furniture import scheme that never seemed to get off the ground, and then real estate, like her house in L.A. and her place in New York, some land in Montana . . .

When you got that rich it was all just a matter of them all figuring it out, rearranging, forking some over, putting most of it away. Plus Timmy said they'd asked Mum's sisters, who were both loaded, married money, and could always come up with any amount, no sweat, and even if they said no, or no they didn't have it, they definitely did. There was no way they wouldn't come through for their dead sister's son, it was their blood, their family, they had to, they definitely would, if it came to that. Everywhere he looked, when it was family, he was surrounded by money, so it was not a problem, and soon he'd have his own bundle, too, once he got off, and he could sue the state, for like millions, for wrongful arrest, or like violation of his civil rights. And on top of all that, his paintings would sell now for tons, for the rest of his life, like he always knew would happen. And who knew what other sweet deals he could make out of this whole thing, like a book deal, movie rights, go to video, whatever else, like on the Internet, however you cashed in on that, no one really knew yet, it was so new, he sure didn't, he definitely was not like a cyber guy, he'd never even been on a computer, except when Red showed him once. It was his story. He wasn't stupid, he knew what a huge phenomenon this trial was, and that all the publicity was like seriously wasted world-wide advertising, just screaming for products to make money on. He always knew his wave would come along, and now all he had to do was ride it.

Reporters rushed out into the crowded hall to hunch over their cellulars and get their stories in fast, first, or to tell them on the spot, off the cuff, into the cameras, professionally managing not to squint into the bright lights and black eyes of handheld and shoulder-holstered cameras. Zwirner, his lawyer, pushed in front of Simon, like blocking for him, had his briefcase up in front of him like a shield, his head ducked like he might get hurt, but Simon walked smoothly with his shoulders in their usual round muscled hunch, and looked around impassively at the swarm around him. People yelled questions and called for one another to get out of the way. He squinted from the bright lights above the TV cameras, held up his hand, and noticed a lot of the people in the pack were women, or at least some of them. He wondered if those lights were *kliegs*.

. . .

For the third time they were going out to see friends, and for the third time, without saying anything, Simon emerged as they were making sure poor Heather was all set with Bennie, and were about to head out the door. Timmy opened his eyes wide in eloquent exasperation as they headed up the stone stairs, the front edges scored with finger-sized claw marks from the quarry drill, but didn't say anything to Simon, as he and Anna had agreed was the best way to handle him, at least for now, to minimize the tension and hassle, because he wasn't going to go away, and wasn't going to change. The other night they had gone to a friend's on the other side of the island, and though Simon wasn't invited, he just came sort of mutely along, following them to their car like a dog, Timmy thought, or, as Anna said later, like a child.

Now they were going to the Stoltzes', just on the other side of the village, so they were walking, and Timmy had the feeling, even more, now, that Simon was like a dog, and felt like going, *Go home!* Simon's presence kept the other two from talking, and as he and Timmy both wore sneakers, the only sound as they moved, three abreast, like outlaws through the sleepy tiny downtown, was the steady clop of Anna's heels. The fountain's little lion heads spat arc spouts on either side, like pissing into the little pools. Above the granite block retaining wall, continuous lawn sloped up to the houses, and in one of them, between gauzy white curtains, a TV could be seen going. Simon commented to Anna on the white, handpainted peace sign on the green barn door of the Watermans' storage shed ahead.

That used to be there, like when we were growing up, and then when they painted the building, someone painted it there again.

She knows, Timmy said testily. She was here then too.

As, in fact, everyone at the Stoltzes' was there, then, too.

Timmy's lifelong friends up here Anna had also known always, and so they became the core friends of their marriage. Simon, two years older than Timmy, knew these people, too, but wasn't exactly friends with them, used to spurn them as like typical rich kids, but now was almost eager to be among them, he'd known them all his life, too, and they weren't so bad, some of them. Timmy wished he'd stay away—but what could he say?

The Stoltzses were a large family of large, dark-haired, dark-browed sisters and one boy, Stephen, who was Timmy's age and Timmy's friend. The Stoltzses were big partiers, their parties were famous enough on the island that the word *Stoltzing* was used by some summer people, and some islanders, too, to mean *partying.* Their house was the perfect party house. The parents used to have rollicking parties all the time, too, and during their teens, the kids would have their party going on upstairs, with pot and rock and roll and people's dogs and plenty of beer and chips and stuff, while the parents had theirs going on downstairs, in coats and ties, khaki and red yachting pants, navy blue blazers, and the pink and green, the sounds of the two parties blended together on the wraparound balconies outside. The house was on the water, over the water, actually, on pilings, and looked like a huge old galleon, like the *Mutiny on the Bounty,* run up on shore, and propped up to stay. The elaborate woodwork of the window trim and the balconies was intricately painted purple and custard yellow, and in lesser lines and end dots, red, which sounds like a garish dessert, but against the great brown shingle hull of the house it looked good, unusual, appropriately festive, especially compared to the other massive, more austere houses lining both shores of the Thorofare.

The Stoltz father, who made chocolate Easter bunnies, and whose nickname, therefore, was Easter Bunny, had died a few years before, and now the family and the house seemed haunted by his absence, and the lingering, deep-drinking partying now seemed duties of lingering grief, like a long, boisterous wake without end. Easter Bunny was a good-natured and gregarious man, if something of an eccentric, whose appearance on Maine Street outside the tiny post office in an unbuttoned but belted trench coat, with bare legs sticking down to hairless ankles, sockless loafers, might make you wonder, if you didn't know him—and then still. One windless August afternoon he went out, without mentioning it to anyone, for a spin in his squarish old mahogany cabin cruiser, its name pieces of his kids' names put together. The boat's trim was painted the same colors as the house. It was spotted, from afar, off Iron Point, chasing its white tail of wake in a slow circle, and when a lobster boat got there, there was Easter Bunny crumpled on the deck.

Stephen Stoltz was a big friendly guy, like his father, and greeted them loudly, like his father, from the depths of the upper deck, and hit some gong he had up there, as they crossed the lawn from the stony dirt driveway, where a number of cars with local and out-of-state plates were parked. His grinning head popped out, beaming, between the American flag flying from an angled pole off the house's balcony stern and a row of nautical flags festively draped in droops along the railing, and beside him appeared the pretty, curly-haired head of Katherine, who was often there and in fact rented her ground floor space for her gallery from Steve, who owned that house.

There were about a dozen people there. Music was on, not loud. Everyone stood a few steps from the bar, as if the long ship room had been tipped, and Simon, who didn't drink, drifted to the back to look around, stepped out on the balcony, but it was buggy, so in a minute he came back in. Timmy was talking away, smiling and animated, to his two best friends, smiling his winning white smile as he nodded and kept talking. Each of them held a bottle of Heineken, and the short one, wearing tennis shoes and a frayed sailboat belt, carefully picked and peeled the label off his. Anna and her friends had white wine in plastic cups. Simon checked out the stereo, and looked over the selections out on the table, and the long rows of tapes on the rack on the wall, and below them the rows of CDs. In the cabinet below he noticed a whole home video library, and then saw the TV and VCR in their built-in slots. He could live for a couple of years off how much just this stuff right here was worth.

Anna left in like an hour with no objection from Timmy, and to be nice she told Simon she was heading back if he wanted to go with her and her friend Lucy, who hadn't seen Bennie yet, but he said no thanks, he was staying. The people were a little more lubed up now and were nicer and warmer, and it rubbed off on Simon, stoned before he got here, as they smiled away and asked him how his painting was going. Timmy, he noticed, was looking at Katherine, and was drinking booze, now, from a glass, now that Anna was gone, like whiskey or dark rum on the rocks. He was talking to his friend Merrill, who was his best man when they got married up here, two summers ago, and who Simon owed a hundred and fifty bucks to, so he steered clear of him. Merrill had bought a captain's clock, he called it, for Timmy, from him and all the ushers, and Simon never paid him for it, and got a letter, later, in New Orleans, from a lawyer in Boston threatening him with legal action—*tsheh*—if he didn't pay up, he couldn't believe it. He ignored it, of course, and last summer when he saw him Merrill didn't say anything, so he felt like it had slid, but still he stayed away from him anyway. What an asshole, getting a lawyer on him for that, it wasn't a legal matter, it was family-and-friends personal. Timmy nodded as Merrill spoke on, gesturing with his hand and the cigarette in it, but he was looking over at Katherine, holding a Bud, talking to that guy Guy, who was supposedly an artist now, too. Simon was sure Timmy had a fling with her, and not that long ago. Simon kept looking at Katherine, too, but not for her, but because Timmy, and something about her maybe kind of reminded him of Mum.

Steven had fireworks and a little cannon set up out on the balcony aiming out over the water. Simon thought he was too drunk and was going to blow his hand off, or somebody's face. They kept like stooping and stupidly looking down into the cannon, laughing and laughing. Simon saw this guy in the navy once fucking around with parade artillery, drunk like that just, get his hand and up to his elbow spattered to smithereens, chunks all over the wall, and the guy laughed harder, stumbling around, holding up his gushing new stump, until guys grabbed him and he passed out.

Bob Marley was playing now twice as loud as before, and some of them were singing along the part that repeated like a chant, like they'd never grow up, or at least not out of their time slot in pop history. Some islander people showed up, twice as fat as the summer people, who weren't so skinny themselves, except Merrill, who was a real like alcoholic string bean. They carried their own cartons of tallboys, and when Steven told them to help themselves to the bar or anything they wanted, or at least feel free to put their beers in the fridge, one of them said thanks for all of them, and they plunked their six-packs on the railing beside them. It was that guy Victor, the painter. He nodded solemnly to Simon, and Simon nodded back. He probably got to paint this place, too, and charged a ton for all that trim. His sleeves were torn off, like they didn't fit his big arms, but the bugs didn't seem to bother him, or any of the islanders.

I used to play golf with you, Simon said to one of them he remembered. The guy and his brother used to use the same clubs, and they had a driver that was bright red. The guy had a bushy beard now, apple cheeks.

You a Curtis? he asked.

Yep, Simon admitted.

I 'membah, the guy said.

And your brother, too, right? Simon said.

Yeahp. He gulped down like half his beer in one suck, like a bear. He blew his cookie, he added and glared right at Simon, his head tipped forward for drunken focus. Simon snapped a bottle cap whirring like a flying saucer out over the water, it curved back and landed on the rocks. He didn't know if he meant his brother killed himself, or went crazy, but didn't ask.

Okay okay okay, Steven laughed. *Get back!* He was ready to fire away.

Timmy came outside with the others for the action. He had that glazed look like Dad, and really red eyes. Then Katherine came out, too, by herself; Simon thought she had left. She was drunk, too, but also, with her light curls like rope unraveled, and a soft, more relaxed expression, looked prettier, but she wasn't Simon's style. She leaned against the railing beside Timmy with her breasts like propped between her upper arms, and she leaned also against Timmy, who said something to her that made her laugh and tilt her hair and head against his in kind of a laugh excuse to lean against him a little more.

The first one was a dud, and everyone whooped and clapped and laughed.

That's okay, that's okay, said Steven. That was only a test. Only a test. He bent down and lit a match, then quickly shook it out. Please stand by.

A smash of glass breaking down on the rocks from a bottle somebody dropped got some laughs, and Steven down in his crouch doing what he was doing grinned at that. He slid the cardboard box to the side and then lit a fat fuse that sparkled then seemed to go out, but then *thwoomp,* the thing shot out somewhere into the darkness, and burst too close to the water, but so with the reflection other half, it looked whole.

Booo, everyone went. *Sssss.*

Wait, wait, Steven said. Now we have the trajectory. Now we're all set, Houston.

The next one went twice as high and burst brightly into a surprisingly wide orange wheel, whose spokes sizzled at the ends before it sagged as a whole, as it faded, and you could see little streamer puffs of smoke drifting sideways from the expiring tendrils, and a few of the larger, faster falling embers made it to the water. Cheers and whistles and more whoops for this one, and, *Yeah!*

All *right!*

Excellent!

Encore!

Then they started judging them, like the Olympics, with numbers, and then trying to name them, which was funny at first but fizzled out after,

The Crazy Daisy! And,

The Wicked Hangover,

and so Steven read off their names after each one, and everyone laughed at that, even though most of them weren't funny. The last ones had booms, after that beat of initial hesitation when you brace yourself like a kid. Katherine had her elbow up on Timmy's shoulder. She fed Timmy a drag of her cigarette, and he followed it like a fish with his lips puckered, not finished yet, when she took it away, and they both laughed. Simon watching from the other side of Steven figured she'd fucked like half the guys here.

Steven cleared people back while he started to dismantle the launcher, then decided to just leave it, and brought the box inside. Timmy, in the movement, stepped back and bumped onto a bench, which he then stood up on, and with one hand up on a rafter, he stepped a long step across to the railing, and giving Katherine his beer for a second, sat himself down there. Simon shook his head, he was so stupid, he was so drunk, he could easily fall off and crack his head open on the rocks, and so, ignoring Katherine, like she wasn't even there, Simon went over to him and grabbed him by the biceps with a hard little jerk on contact, like he was jokingly pushing and pulling him back at the same time.

Jesus Christ, Timmy blurted out, and looked at him *ugh* with disbelief in one eye and disgust in the other. What Simon saw was drunkenness and how hooded and slurred his eyes were, and then how he stumbled when he got down from the railing.

What's wrong with you, Simon? Katherine stepped in, lifting her chin and like her breasts defiantly.

What's wrong with *me*? He turned to her and looked down like he always did with people. *Honh,* he scoffed breathily, like a laugh. What are you talking about?

Why don't you ever say hello to me? She stepped forward and didn't seem at all drunk. You always act like you don't even know me, you just walk by like I'm not even there. She tilted her head back and her lips stuck out as she considered her charges and what else to express. What did I ever do to you?

Simon frowned and bit his lip in a nervous little smile as Timmy watched.

You act like I did something wrong to you, she persisted. Did I offend you somehow? Tell me, because I resent it. Katherine glanced at Timmy like they'd talked about this.

This took Simon by surprise and he shrugged and like bobbled his head like someone from India. He often sensed people were mad at him, but most of the time no one ever said anything, unless it was an argument, which was different from this, out of nowhere. Anna, when they had that thing about food last year, accused him head-on, but that was about something, at least. He felt like Timmy got them to do this for him, and he felt like really shoving him now.

Look at me, Katherine said less aggressively now, but not letting him off the hook. Simon looked at her and said,

You don't say hello to me either.

Okay, mister, hello. She held out her hand for him to shake. He looked at it, two rings, the red palm, then at her face, to see her angle in this, which seemed straight friendly, or ready to be, but not quite yet, and then at Timmy, weirdly glowering, like he was like acid-memorizing the scene through his hurt eyes.

From now on we'll say hello, okay? she persisted, still holding her hand out. Come on, shake.

Simon smiled nervously on one side and went, Tseh.

Come on, what's wrong? Are you scared of me?

Tseh.

I'm not scared of you.

Simon wished she'd cut it out.

Are you a snob in there? Do you hate me?

He didn't, but he did think she charged for sales tax, and then kept it herself, on top of her rip-off percentage. She kept reminding him of Mum, even though she didn't really look like her at all; but *something* . . .

Come on Simon, Jesus, Timmy said. What's wrong with you?

Simon looked at him levelly through lowered brows.

Just shake her hand. He shook his head.

Simon shook her hand, as if humoring them, and was surprised at her strong grip, but nicely soft, and how she held on still a little longer after he raised their grip up and down like, *There,* and that little longer was replayed, and her good grip, soft but strong, in his head later, in bed, stretched over into unmistakable physical meaning, he didn't know what, y'know, because he didn't like her especially, and didn't think she was so attractive, but he'd fuck her, but not really, though he polished her off quickly enough right now, no problem, pleasure actually's all mine, a little spurt into the sheet.

I'm going home, Simon said to Timmy, and ignoring Katherine again, as if she weren't there, if you want to go back.

People back inside were leaving. Timmy looked at Simon like disgusted, and Simon saw Dad in him, the lush, unmistakable. Katherine said something lightly to him and he said,

No, I'm staying here.

Simon shrugged and rubberly shrugged his mouth with slow eyes blinking and staying down, like it's your life, your marriage and wife waiting back there with your baby.

When Simon got back he looked in the lit window from outside by the box. Anna was in there with Lucy, so he walked silently out to the end of the dock and sat on the bench out there for a while. Night and the water was hard to paint, but he should try it again one of these days, one of these nights.

Rumors flew. One ricocheting around for a few weeks was that the defense was going to get the charges dismissed. Different explanations were floated for how they would accomplish this. No witnesses, not enough evidence, tainted evidence. There was no crime committed: the father, in fact, committed suicide. A third, unknown person did it.

The Internet was saying the wife had him killed. Or there was one from the supermarket tabloids that Simon liked: the dead first wife did it. Mum.

One story revealed and confirmed that for a while during the initial investigation they thought maybe Timmy did it. Timmy thought back now over the questioning, and realized how in some ways they had tried to lull and catch him off guard. They repeated the same questions over and over. They painted Simon in different colors and shades of innocence and guilt, to see Timmy's different reactions. He and Anna talked about every new development with a kind of morbid fascination. But this shifted to something strange and dire and sickening when it was suddenly about Timmy. Part of the story, of course, included Anna—the wife was a lawyer, she helped him plan it, to get the inheritance, and pin it on Simon! From that point on they decided to stop paying attention to the media. It had become an obsession. The press itself had become obsessed.

Zwirner had warned them how outrageous the slinging would become. He should know—he was behind a lot of it. But of course they couldn't ignore the media, so they decided to be more selective. They agreed to stop reading the tabloids. But on the subway and sidewalks all over New York the new developments, and even relatively buried stories, leapt out at them. Their selective press ban didn't last a week. It didn't even really last a day.

Simon was staying out in Manchester, alone some of the time, or with Timmy, or Red. He charged food at Cooper's, and they delivered it. The *Globe* and the *Herald American* were delivered, and he watched the evening news every evening, over like a Stouffer's, or one of his creations, like crumbled hamburger mixed in with Minute Rice and tons of A.1. Twice a week he got xeroxed press clippings from all around the country FedExed from Red's publicity people. Usually they were the exact same UPI articles, or like Reuters, or copied from whichever bigger city paper, or sometimes there were these curious little lies, like totally out of left field, on computer printout sheets labeled LexisNexis on the bottom. Or like the one claiming Ginny did it, and they had the guy she hired in their pocket. This was from the *Star*. These stories always came last in the press kit, as Simon liked to call it, taking a page from Red's book, and were always the best.

Will Deery called once in a while, but never really said anything. Simon didn't ask a single question, just listened carefully as his lawyers told him only so much, and no more. This, and the way, a few times, they sort of stopped each other from saying more, told him more than they did.

They told him from the start that they'd get him off. Around this time, this guy Father Ryan came by to see him, and asked him a few questions about his life before all this, but mostly they chatted about the Red Sox, and why they always take a dive at the end of the season. Simon kind of liked this guy. He was more like a Buddhist than Father Anyone, except like crossed with a baseball broadcaster or a retired coach, with his Mass. accent, but smart, and like middle class normal. And slow, as in calm. They sat in the kitchen and had coffee, and Simon pulled out some cookies. Simon watched, like amused, as this old guy's fingertips of his spread hands came together and apart again, one finger after the other, like in a wave, like an underwater plant in a wave, as he spoke, and he nodded single nods very slowly now and then, when Simon spoke, in sync with the fingers. He liked the guy, and thought after he left, in kind of a kindred way, That guy's a snake. Zwirner said he was his legal and moral adviser, and an old friend. Red later told him he was a Jesuit and also a lawyer. So that made him like a double snake, Simon was right. But like snake in a good way.

The thing that got him most about his lawyers was that they never once, the whole time, asked him what happened. He kept waiting for them to, and they never did. The whole time.

One day, out of the dull repetition, it was like suddenly the show began. Zwirner sprang into action with a dramatic speech, accusing the police of having gathered evidence illegally. He had gotten a fresh haircut for this performance, just a trim, and he looked sharp. He wore a pinstripe suit, a light blue shirt with white collar, and a berry red tie with paisley blue eyes. And he had a silk kerchief in his breast pocket, the same color as the tie, folded with three corners sticking up. His chest was puffed as he paced. He prodded a rigid forefinger on the table in front of Simon as he drove home his main point. He was playing to the camera. He was talking about the flashlight.

While Zwirner, afterward, always in a rush, packed papers into his burgundy briefcase, and Will Deery stepped to the railing for a word with the family, which a bunch of reporters artlessly, craningly, attempted to overhear, Simon, unattended, turned, and for the first time really faced the camera. People were pushing to get out of the courtroom, and most didn't notice that he had turned, though some noticed and pointed, others saw and stopped to watch. It was like Simon was looking past them, or through them, which he was. He was looking at the camera, and the impersonal collective contained in its black open eye. He had no discernible expression or feeling or attitude, except he seemed remote or calm or untouched or indifferent. Except that he kept looking, imparting his like implacable presence in a long, mute introduction, like, Simon, live, kids, here I am, until Will Deery saw him, and quickly, deftly, put a hand on his shoulder to turn him away, and the busty woman court officer standing by gestured for Simon to follow her. He hesitated, as he turned away, long enough to do a smooth, strange sort of farewell curtsy gesture. He slid his hand slowly through the air across his chest, palm down, at a perfect level, like a backhand in tennis, or a slow-motion sideways karate chop. His expression was a little weird, like stoned, slack eyes, what else is new, and his lips were pressed and a little folded in like when you pretend you have no teeth, and when it was replayed everywhere on the news and like on FOX shows, sometimes in slow motion, he seemed like he was underwater.

Simon was looking right at the camera when he did this, so everyone assumed he was doing it to the camera, and everyone watching, which maybe was true. But what nobody noticed, because they couldn't see him, was the man sitting calmly in his place beside the camera, in the second to last row, patiently waiting while the benches and the room emptied out. Some people were standing, waiting out the rush, to get a look at Simon as he got up to go. Immobile in the midst of the bustle sat an old priest, in black vestment and white tab collar, pink and brown spotty hands folded on his lap. It was that guy Father Ryan.

Timmy had this memory of Mum and Simon. They were in the parking lot at Middlesex outside Simon's dorm. They were dropping him off there for the first time in the fall of his fresh-man year. Timmy helped carry junk up the three flights, past other families and new kids doing the same thing. The parents greeted each other like they knew each other. When everything was up and Mum had met Simon's adviser, she started to unpack and set up his room, but Simon stopped her.

I'll do it Mum, he said. It's my room.

Down in the parking lot in the car before she started the engine to leave, Mum paused at the wheel like she'd forgotten, or was just remembering, something. Timmy looked at her while she tried to figure it out. It looked important and he didn't know how to help her. She bit her lower lip, and for a confused moment it looked like she was making a joke face, except without any joke in sight, just this distortion, and Timmy was about to nervously laugh with her, help that way, when her chin puckered and her lower lip, still bit, quivered, and glancing apologetically at him with stitched eyebrows, she started to cry. That was in the fall of 1978, not hard to figure out. Because that winter, at the wheel of that same car, right after Christmas vacation, she died.

And an even worse one like that happened just before Mum died. After a hockey game at Middlesex, Simon went off to get changed without stopping to see her. He didn't even think about it, but when he called home a couple of days later to ask for some money, and he said, Hi, Mum, it's Simon, she said,

Who? Why should I talk to you if you won't even talk to me, when I drive all the way to see you? And she hung up. And that was the last time he talked to her.

The courtroom was packed. Zwirner stood and said the charges should be dropped.

I submit, therefore, that a *corpus delicti* ruling by the court will find that the charge of second degree murder cannot stand because there is no proof that a murder occurred. The evidence simply does not add up. We know that a man died—but we don't know how. We look at his body, and we don't know. The evidence, logically considered, does not point to murder. Thus an appropriately rendered *corpus delicti* ruling by the court will find that the charges against the defendant are substantively unwarranted and inappropriate, and therefore should be dropped entirely and immediately.

In the crush of the crowd afterward in the corridor outside the courtroom, reporters rushed out between the opposing walls of cameras and glaring lights, and jostled to the phones or huddled over cellulars, yelling, or crouched, backs to the wall, over laptops, getting the news in as quickly as possible, repeating the phrase "corpus delicti, corpus delicti," so production assistants could look it up, producers could run it by legal experts, and their assistants could look it up . . .

The little guy woke like an alarm clock at exactly four-thirty in the morning, crying in the monitor on their bedside table. Usually they switched off days, but up here Timmy took the early shift, happily. It was always hard to get up in that first tremendous exertion out of the heavy drug- and dream-lovely power of unfinished sleep, but you got used to it, and it was always, oddly, easier to get up when you had a hangover. The bottle was ready downstairs, and once he got it in, it was like meditation, except a little wired, like part of his self was missing, but so meditation not of the self but in the action of his life, with the baby and beside it. Now that Bennie was on food, too, there was that whole messy game. Ben was so awake and happy to see him and be up—Mr. Smiley!—and to get another mouthful of purée and spit it out and laugh at that, and shake his head away as Timmy caught the spat purée with a deft, quick spoon, like Mum, and sent it right back in again.

The tide was high, the waters lapped the floorboards under the house, and stopped, when a lobster boat, groaning by, left its smooth wake sliding in under the silky still surface, bobbing the boats at their moorings, the rowboats tied at the dock bobbling against each other, and then gulping, sloshing, under the house. The silence was visual, and therefore spiritual, but also actual, and the actual light came up lightly out of the stillness out the window over the water and the watery reach of the waking world. The dark bank across seeped up into single trees with dresses down to their ankles and knees, and the blue white light of the public landing, with its fading candle reflection, went off when he wasn't looking. Bennie settled with little sounds into his bottle. Timmy went off somewhere in his mind, and when he came back the windows on the gray-shingle huge house right across the water were all glaring scarlet like the house was full of fire, like every morning when it wasn't cloudy, and it stayed that way for ten minutes, bright, while the pale boy blue sky, tinged light girl pink above the torn top edges of the dark trees, sort of drifted and lifted softly over the streaky water, still slow and silver-dark with night's lingering last sexy satin look.

When Timmy creaked down the stairs, a sharp-beaked dream bird tapped twice the bone and dried bloody dome on the inside curve, his skull, and the second one woke Simon from the good grip like an accomplice, and stayed with him, a stray hint, with its cracking sound and blinky face, as he obediently rose and went out the screen door at the foot of his bed and peed a strong arc off the balcony into the full tide swelled right up to the house below with a purling, smacky fountain trickle. Timmy, preparing in the kitchen, didn't hear or see it out the living room window he and gurgly Bennie settled in front of, with the bubbleless bottle, after the messy orange eat. Simon got the ribbed bedspread from the other bed, wrapped it over his head like a nomad, and went back out and sat on the wet chair, moved the wet spot over, then sat as still as the kingly invisible spell. The changes were happening slyly slowly, so you couldn't see them, except compared to how it was a minute ago, except for the boat breaking the rule and opening the crack the day would spill out of and fill with colorful motion and mind. It got brighter, higher up, and was chilly, but worth it, except for the no-see-ums, getting his ankles and feet and face. His arms were wrapped in, so he couldn't shoo them, and tried not to mind, but that put them more in his mind, until he forgot them, enough, for the house across the Thorofare, box full of fire, and another, farther over, glinting brighter, but only in half the windows, the other ones black.

In an inspired introductory mixed metaphor, a writer for *The New Yorker* described Simon's gesture as like that of an umpire slowly indicating "safe"; but also, possibly, as it was one-handed, a variant of "out"—combining both, yin and yang, in a smooth, grounded sort of tai chi move. Why this gesture caught the attention and imagination of the media and, through the media, the public at large, the way it did, became part of the discussion of its meaning or meaninglessness. Why Simon, and this story, became such a big deal was not discussed.

This video clip of Simon went out into the world and proliferated with a life of its own, with totally like psychic megalomedia wings. It was played again and again during that first week, and then almost like an intro or Pavlovian signal, to mark the mode and reentice interest, it was used to spearhead other reports or filler footage of the trial, throughout its duration, and afterward it became like its own symbol of whatever people wanted, or just of itself, along with the other one at the end, foisted together into the pantheon of image language like of global society, our new like digital monoculture. Simon, or actually Pete, for him, tried to copyright it, but the footage wasn't his, and it was already out there, like atomized and sprinkled down and recrystallized in people's heads.

• • •

Y'know, Dad's really pissed at you.

What do I care?

Anna was gone, and now it was just the boys again.

Well you should care.

Well I don't.

Simon softened his voice to like his reclusive remove, to show how mellow he was, but it came off as annoying menace to Timmy, who heard the hard edge in there, barely, clenchingly buffered, and saw for the millionth time how impenetrable and impossible Simon was, and the way he sort of wobbled his head back and forth as he said it, like his neck was rubber, or the joint was loose, like a few screws upstairs, and with his eyes drowsily lidded, drove Timmy crazy.

Well that's good, because he's coming tomorrow, Timmy added, and left the room, stubbing his toe on the threshold on the way out, which he never would have if Simon weren't here and aggravating him, and it hurt, and he felt like punching the wall when he walked away. He hated how Simon was like this lurking presence, like an unwanted resident guest problem in the house, who acted, he thought, like he was so independent and unobtrusive, but really was as dependent as a child, and very much, too much, there, but also he hated how he poisoned the air and things with Dad for him, too, and before Dad was even here, it was hard enough with him anyway, and this was his one or two times seeing him all year, and he wasn't going to live much longer, the way he drank, and was aging, fast, and this was the first time he was going to see Bennie.

This encounter was more by chance, like by surprise, than the others, which was maybe why they were more direct with each other than usual. Timmy was making his little housings, and cutting and sanding corners down in Dad's workshop, while Heather watched, literally, the baby sleeping, when he needed something flat and heavy to place over the frame backs when he glued them, so he went on a search, beginning in the middle house kitchen, full of tools, and the pantry closets crammed with boxes of junk, but what he really wanted was like a low table, so he expanded the search to rooms upstairs, where, after the bathroom, all nicely prepared like a bed-and-breakfast by Doreen, under Ginny, so different than Mum, with little hotel shampoo and conditioner bottles in a basket on the shelf over the toilet, and the guest room with its handsome pine closet whose stand-up like coffin doors were stuck shut, he creaked open the door of the little next room, and was surprised to find it completely dark, except in a second for the little red light beside amber like clock radio digital numbers, which turned out to be the VCR, when the TV, with a sort of electronic *boing,* popped on from a point in the middle of the screen, and there, a few feet away in the dark, in the glow, ensconced in the bent bamboo and cushion chair, was Sir Simon, a bowl of pistachio nuts in his lap, grinning like the moon, holding the channel changer like a secret weapon. The shade was pulled down, the curtains were drawn, and it was like noon on a beautiful day out there in full swing.

What are you doing in here? Timmy asked, annoyed.

Nothing, was Simon's first response, followed by, Watching a movie. What are you doing in here?

I'm looking for—he started to explain and then stopped, and started in on Simon, I can't believe you're sitting in here in the dark on this beautiful day, like Mum with them in the TV room during the day making them go outside.

I'm watching a movie, he snapped back, big deal. So what if it's day or night, what's the difference?

You lounge around here like you own the place, without a care in the world, with your art as the big excuse for everything, and you don't even do it very much.

To—*each*—his—*own,* he pronounced complaisantly.

The VCR was on freeze-frame, Katharine Hepburn as a young woman in a burgundy belted dress, stepping, sort of stooping, her mouth stuck open like a fish, into a fancy elevator, hand-tinted gold in clumsy colorization, which Timmy liked, but not right now.

Yeah but this isn't your *own,* Timmy shot back, that's the problem. You act like it is and just hang around like you have all the time in the world—

I do.

Yeah, well, everyone else doesn't. I work hard all year, with never enough time to do what I want, and I take care of the baby, which you have no idea how hard it is—

Boo-hoo for you.

You're such a jerk. Timmy's eyes quivered with plosive anger, his nostrils flared, which kind of amused Simon, the guy could barely contain himself, let alone pick his words, and spit them out, which he half didn't even want to bother. Some people have responsibilities—he cut himself off and was about to just leave, but came out with, You act like a teenager and you're thirty-one years old and still can't take care of yourself, even though you don't think of anyone else but yourself—

Thirty-two, Simon corrected him. He pushed Katharine Hepburn fast-forward into the elevator and jerkily up, f-fwd, and stopped her with her mouth compressed and her arms crossed with her fingers showing, in the middle of tapping impatiently.

Why can't you take anything seriously? Timmy demanded.

What's there to be so serious about? He cracked a pistachio shell in his molars, and spat the two halves, like it was one of his teeth, broken, into his hand, then dropped them onto the floor, adding to the loose pile there, and munched the nut.

You think you're so responsible, but you're a drunk just as bad as Dad.

You can be like that, but one of these days you're going to

slide too far and it'll be too late and nobody'll be able to help you or want to— Timmy was definitely one for dramatic pronouncements and doomsday scenarios; but Simon did call him and the rest of the family, every winter, out of money and about to be evicted, or worse, pleading misery, cornered and repentant, with vows not to gamble anymore, or get in these self-torture situations, if he could just get some money to get out of this, just this once, this one last time . . .

Simon looked at him, and having gotten his lick in, didn't say anything, waiting for him to feel finished and go. He pushed f-fwd again in another quick spurt, and then another. Timmy shook his head.

One of these days you're going to be sorry.

Yeah, like when? Simon broke open another pistachio with his fingertips and, with his canine, fanged out the salty green meat.

Like tomorrow.

Oo-*ooo*, like big threat. He cracked another in his teeth, and couldn't resist,

Why tomorrow?

Dad's coming tomorrow. Timmy held the door by the knob and pumped it, waiting to leave, but still stayed.

Good for him. Simon's habitual blank expression, even in the dark, didn't fool Timmy.

Y'know, Dad's really pissed at you.

What do I care?

Well you should care.

Well I don't.

The next court appearance was a motion for a change of venue. Nobody expected this to go through, though it was the defense's duty, as a matter of course—almost a ritual, really, in highly publicized cases—to file the motion. So it was quite a surprise, a collective gasp popped into a flurry of excitement in the courtroom, when the judge, considering the matter over lunch, decided to wash his hands of it. He came back after the break and announced that he agreed with the counsel for the defense that the unusual degree of media attention, especially saturated in this home area, would make it practically impossible to find a panel of jurors who did not already have opinions one way or the other in the case. The prosecution, he pointed out, gave no persuasive argument or protestation against this point, nor sufficient assurance that a fair trial could be, or indeed should be, held here in the county seat.

Accordingly, I hereby remand the furtherance and authority in this matter of the Commonwealth of Massachusetts versus Simon Cary Curtis to the jurisdiction of the Massachusetts Superior Court, County of Suffolk. *This* court is hereby dismissed. He smacked the gavel, and hurriedly bailed out of his paneled roost without so much as looking up. And with that crack of the gavel, the usual courtroom sense of plodding, deliberate inevitability had suddenly been shattered, and a dramatic zing of uncertainty and wild possibility ricocheted around the room, out the doors and onto the airwaves, and all the technomagical means of infotainment dispersal.

While the courtroom cleared, Simon sat still at his place, facing forward. Again when it was time to go he turned to the emptying room and the camera. This time he made no gesture and showed no expression. But he felt a sort of engulfing surge of power-pleasure, like going into his blood, when he saw the guy he hoped he'd see, sitting quietly in the back near the camera. Right where the priest was sitting before sat that guy Pete, the detective. The like one person outside of jail Simon had met during this whole thing who he really liked and actually, like, trusted. Pete, sitting there as big as two people in his open overcoat, had on glasses tinted brown so you couldn't quite see his eyes. He wore a suit and tie, and sat with his knees apart and his big hands on his big knees.

Simon knew that the right things happened in their own certain ways, the like cosmic unseen organic order, and he had that sure, safe, like ball feeling of feeling contained on the unthrown inside. He didn't know the facts yet, but he didn't need to know to know. He just knew there was an inside, like there's a backside to everything, whatever it was here, maybe it was, like, his life up to now, who knew, but he was part of it, obviously, or hopefully, a big part, as much as he was of the evident outside front side. What he learned later no one else knew, except the people involved, and their few satellite knowers, like wives and whoever each person told everything to, that this change in venue happened not because of the defense counsel's brilliantly cogent and unassailable persuasiveness in arguing for one, but because a decision was made, for certain inside reasons, way above all their heads. Zwirner took smug credit for the move, like he was Mr. High Tight Insider, but actually he didn't really even know why it happened.

Though they let him think it was his doing, in fact it wasn't the deft power play he made above the provincial little prosecutor's head, and behind, Zwirner thought, the judge's cowled back. It was because of a maneuver made from the top. Simon, later, picturing it, pictured that Plexiglas game from the seventies, like 3-D checkers, with red and blue marbles, except instead of checkers it was like 3-D chess here, with each of the floors a floor of a building, and the players were the people in their coats and ties, like penguins, each playing their walking little chess game parts on their different ice-slippery floors, but really they were just pawns in the overall game. What Zwirner saw here began with a call from Miles Weld.

Miles Weld told him what he'd already told him, that the probate stuff was going through without any problems; then he suggested they have lunch. Zwirner said sure.

They met at a glibly nautical brass rail place off Commonwealth Avenue, full of round tables with square tablecloths as white and nicely pressed as the shirts of the waiters and waitresses. They arrived in the winter noon from opposite directions thirty seconds apart, pumped hands standing by the bar, and were shown to a corner table in the back. Miles Weld's brother owned the restaurant, which was called the Islander. He was never there, as he lived in Bermuda half the year, Nantucket the other half.

Both ordered drinks, and smiled in moist complicity as they clinked glasses to a nod and a wink. Miles got right to the point.

My brother was wondering if you'd thought about trying your case here in town.

Miles's other brother was the governor.

Well I'd certainly *like* to. Zwirner smiled. But it's not exactly in my hands, which soft meat flowers he opened, palms upward.

Yeah, no, right, Miles agreed. But one of his guys—y'know Greg Gregory?—was wondering if that little plaid prosecutor might not be secretly relieved if he got this thing off his laptop. Zwirner smiled at the plaid. His smiles always disappeared quickly. Laptop nearly lifted another. On the third day of pretrial hearings, the first day the Court TV camera was there, the little guy had tried to show his—his what? His colors, his sportiness, his only other suit, his individuality, his *unlikeliness?*—by sporting a plaid suit. Not laughably loud, but not, say, madras, and not exactly pinstripes. Green and yellow plaid, with a plaid vest inside!

Well, I'll motion for a C of V. . . Zwirner shrugged. This, of course, was routine anyway. Zwirner considered. Not so much what Miles Weld was saying, as where it was coming from, and why.

I mean, the guy would probably run for cover first chance he got, don't you think?

Possibly, but it's not up to him. It's Paretsky. He'd kill to keep this thing.

Paretsky was the county DA, the guy's boss, who'd held that position for as long as either of these guys could remember. The only reason they knew him was because he kept running for higher office—and losing.

Paretsky? Miles finished his scotch and lifted the glass and a finger to the waitress with a brief light brightening of his face. Paretsky's sitting fat.

Yeah but on this . . .

Miles put it another way:

Paretsky's a Republican. Small shrug, small smile.

Essex County was heavily Republican, Zwirner of course knew. But this was not precisely Miles Weld's point. But it was all he said about it. He shifted the conversation into neutral: they rued the sad demise of the Bruins, the Celtics, the Garden, then questioned recent Red Sox trades, and marveled at this past season's particularly spectacular fall dive.

Down on the rocks, as the waves purled in, spacing out, neither in the painting nor quite in the world, he wasn't any age, or if one, then his younger, undefeated, self, watching the bay, he wondered those kid things, like if teeth would float if you flicked them out, gently out, like little halfhearted mussel shell boats, or there were long green snakes as wide as the wave riding sideways inside the waves and onto the rocks as the waves crashed over them and crushed them into white foam. The sky was white, and the sort of notch marks on the water for wind wavelets were the same, like little chipped wings, as the dark green and blacky blue marks he made to fill the boughs, to make the trees, in the same way that the ocean has the same salinity, supposedly, as human tears.

The island had that ancient and also fresh integrity of natural beauty, you could smell it, it became part of you, and he was lucky he had it in him, like from birth, of all places on earth, so many were wrecked, or not beautiful to start with, just ho-hum, or worse. The amazing thing was how the spirit of place here stood up to the social climate crawling all over it, or it just stood as itself, untouched, because it didn't care, like Simon. June was the best month, not only because of the freshest green and the coolness, still, and how crisply beautiful and sometimes foggy it was, but also, more so, because there was no element, yet, of the intrusion the island and Simon both ignored, rocks both, but now the people were coming, and their money and drinking values they wore around them like auras of bad karma, even though they were familiar okay people in some ways, who didn't know any better, who greeted Simon and bought his paintings at the art show, or from Katherine's, or right from him, or commissions of their places with their views, and the island took down its dimensions and passed more into the present, at least to them who owned it and took over for a month, while the islanders and the twelve-faced island lay low, working and waiting, you could see the takeover happening now by day, as the full ferry unloaded the heads and cars of all the people coming to stay in the way, walk obliviously in the middle of the road on Maine Street, driving the islanders, driving, crazy, and go out in boats and buzz around the Thorofare, crisscross the bay, the day, and among them, Dad.

When they got the change of venue, Simon's lawyers acted like it was this big battle victory on their sure way to winning the whole thing, but Simon didn't see why it was such a big deal, and nobody explained it to him, or said a word about it after the fact in court. They set a date for the trial to begin in Boston on April 8. This happened on Simon's birthday, but Simon didn't tell anyone this and nobody knew. Except Timmy, after not saying much at the railing, said happy birthday with a sympathetic little shrug. This gave Simon a little like flush of surprising emotion through his hidden emotional headquarters and upper body to his fingertips and lips, even, weird, but he didn't say anything and was pretty sure it didn't show.

But he was wrong. Timmy totally noticed. One of the things he told Anna at pillowtop that night was that he'd said happy birthday to Simon and he like blushed and jellied his eyes and jutted his jaw like he was going to lose it.

This will be over soon, Anna patted his Tummy. It's moving remarkably quickly, even for a trial of this kind of notoriety. I wonder why.

This was the thought and question of the senior partner to whom she reported at work. The firm was a large, reputable midtown firm that did mostly corporate law. Anna was in the fledgling litigation division. The head of this department, her boss and taskmaster, was the one she called the day the police came to arrest Simon. His name was Richard Dell. Out of law school he had worked as an assistant district attorney in Manhattan, and secretly wished—or not so secretly, Anna knew because he told her so, more than once—he had become a defense attorney. Get in the ring. He knew those guys—it was a very small club, the big boys—and he knew right away who to recommend to deal with the situation up in Boston.

He called Leonard Maynes Finch and talked to Maldwin Finch, since Robbie Maynes was in court. Finch talked to Maynes an hour later and it turned out Maynes was not in court, but had just been on the horn with Mel Laszlo in New York. Mel Laszlo was calling for Sid Kornfeld, who represented Red Curtis, who was looking for top representation for her brother, who had just been arrested for the murder of their father. This was a sweet and curious convergence. These guys, of course, knew right away what a gold-mine godsend this was. They didn't waste a second. They talked to Jack Renner in Boston, and his first response was to whistle one windy, long descending note of exclamation. Finch and Maynes laughed on their separate lines in opposite corner offices, and Finch's laugh rasped into a cough he couldn't stop, so he covered the mouthpiece and coughed it out. Jack Renner said he'd send Jack Zwirner out right away out to the Manchester police station—Manchester-by-the-*Sea,* he stressed, which evinced further laughter—Oh-*ho!*—the *Sea* in their semicoded parlance meaning *money*—and they took it from there.

Renner, of course, knew Greg Gregory. Knew him well, from growing up, from Harvard and Harvard Law, and all the years in the gilded trenches since. Their wives were friends, and their kids skied and smoked pot together. A number of times Renner had represented—and in most cases saved their ass, or at least served them well—people Gregory had sent his way.

When Greg Gregory called Jack Renner, Renner was as cagey as Gregory. These guys loved this.

Jack, Greg Gregory.

Gregory, was all Renner said, and waited. Both could feel the other smiling, and neither smiled easily, nor often. Though the sight of the other made both men smile; and thus, in the extrapolation, their kids slept with each other on ski vacations.

In a last-minute move, Simon went off the island the day Dad was coming, and Dad was there at the ferry landing in Rockland waiting to get on the return boat. Simon thought he wouldn't be there till the afternoon boat, knowing him, but kept an eye out for him in case, and there he was, with his pregnant belly in his light blue shirt, with his belt rounded under it, over by the ticket house, standing beside his one duffel bag, and Ginny, with a handkerchief on her head, and sunglasses, like a disguise, and her one duffel bag. They left a whole set of clothes, and everything they needed, there, and whatever else they needed they sent up UPS, in as many boxes as it took, however much it cost, so it would all just be there. Simon wondered why their car wasn't in line, them in it, and since it was crowded, fig-

ured they didn't have a reservation because you couldn't just call
and make one anymore, you had to get one by mail, or in person, and so they just went, thinking it wouldn't be crowded,
which is just the kind of thing Dad would roll his eyes at and
give them shit for, but if it happened to him, it just happened,
so what, no one knew, life went on. They were so oblivious,
they'd never see him, even if he walked right up to them, but he
waited and walked off, not with the first eager people out of the
gate, up the ramp, but with the stragglers, with boxes and big
bags, no big rush, up the side, when the cars and trucks started
going off, lifting the ferry up a little more, each one that went
off, sort of hiding behind one long one pulling slowly up at
walking speed, and walked straight, without looking, over to
the right, to the little red hut snack bar, with its two umbrel-
laed picnic tables, and behind it, to the marina parking lot,
where he paused to watch them, behind a yacht up on its cradle,
the boat's fiberglass bottom sanded in circular sander marks,
ready to be painted or patched or whatever, but it better be
sanded better first. Dad was gone now, but Ginny still stood
there reading the paper. Someone came crunching over, suddenly right there, from the side, but it wasn't Dad, it was an old
Mainer with green pants and shirt and red suspenders, vivid X
on, or like *off,* his back, carrying an old wooden open type tool-
box. He looked at Simon with no expression on his flinty face,
he had these clear blue beautiful eyes like cracked marbles.
Simon moved over to the grassy embankment where the fence
went up to the road, where cars were leaving, and Dad came out
of the ticket house with an apple juice from the machine and
glugged it down, standing on the middle stair, like mid-air, and
Simon thought he must have a hangover. His hair was getting
pretty white, and his head and arms were pretty brown already.
That's the *guy.* Simon wondered where the dog was, he wouldn't
leave him in the car for when they took it over next ferry, or yes
he would, windows open a crack, dog'll be fine.

Dad carried both their bags onto the ferry when it started loading, and Ginny, behind him, going sick-person slower, carried her shoulder bag and her newspaper with her finger keeping her place, and Simon headed up the hill, not really rushing, but in long strides, across and up the sidewalk, up the side of the parking lot hill, as they disappeared into the cabin.

He wondered as he walked up Maine Street, Rockland, where it was pretty hot, wow, if this ever happened to other people, or just him, but sometimes, like right now, he remembered a dream and knew it was from like five years ago, it was incredible. Like he had those little white curlies he saw that no one else saw, but they were really there, like little sperms swimming, like on your field of vision, like on a movie screen sometimes, those little heat swirls from the heat of the projector's bulb, swimming in their quick little whirlpool turns and disappearing, like little *c*s and *s*s, his initials in his field of vision, that he put, sort of hidden, in his paintings, sometimes, or he had these little ones he did recently, and was still touching up, that were just of them.

The buildings on either side of Maine Street were all the same height, with stores on the street level, brick with granite, or just granite, or boards, painted, or chipping, or totally worn out, like driftwood, windows sort of severe, with nothing behind them, a lot of them, like faces he passed on the sidewalk, some soft tourists mixed in, and the cars all seemed to be looking out of their lives at you, or looking for something that wasn't there, cruising slow, or revving and jerking fast past. In the deli there were more flies than anyone else seemed to notice, and he looked at the plates of what other people were eating—

He took a newspaper from Bangor someone left on the next table. They were talking about the depletion of the Georges Banks, and how all the cod and haddock were gone because they'd been fished out. In another one, about the Decline in Lobsters, they blamed it on guys coming up from Massachusetts and stealing them. And in another, nurses said nurses were coming down from Canada and stealing their jobs here.

There was another article in the paper about a guy who stole seventy-five hundred dollars' worth of lobsters in a truck from a guy who owed him that much money, while the guy was delivering the lobsters to a party given by Stephen King. The judge, when the guy said he owed it to him and wouldn't pay up, said that's too bad, but you can't take the law into your own hands, and stealing is a crime, even if you've been stolen from, even if you're stealing from the person who stole from you. But what about if you stole back what they stole from you? Simon wondered. It was like that time with his cousin Stuart and Roger Clemens, the judge told Simon sorry, betting's illegal in Massachusetts, so Simon had to pay him the rent, even though Stuart lost the bet, whether Roger Clemens would win twenty games, Simon was right, he did it, so Stuart owed him. Stephen King, who was like the King of Maine, couldn't be reached for comment, but a spokesman said he heard about it and thought it was funny, it was like his characters intruding on his real life. The pastrami sandwich was pretty good and greasy, and Simon wondered if they got all their lobsters, finally, at Stephen King's party. And the story didn't explain how the guy stole the lobsters—how'd he actually do it?—like with a gun, or sneaking up and taking the truck at a gas station, while the guy was paying and getting cigarettes or like taking a pee, or what, because it's not like you can sort of just take seventy-five hundred dollars' worth of lobsters and like rush off with them under your coat—

There was a phone by the bathroom, and with the change from paying he called Mal and said he was around, and could he maybe come over and look at that barn. Mal was this guy he knew from down in New Orleans, who, weirdly, had a summer place here. Mal was married to Janice and they had a boy and a girl, Mike and Penny, who were a couple of brats when they were together, which was almost always, but apart they were all right. Mal used to be an artist. Simon had been to their place the summer before, but didn't really notice the barn. Their house was on a back side street of Rockland, over past the one light where you come into town on Route 1. There were a bunch of houses like it on the street, pretty beat, between trees and lawns. One of the houses across the street from them was like kids' central for kids in the area, and though it wasn't officially a school or camp or day care, it was like that, with a swing set with chain swings, and a jungle gym and milk crates out back where kids played all day, all summer, spraying one another with the hose and screaming in Maine accents, while this real fatty with stretch pants over her fatness lumbered around like an elephant with slow heavy here-she-comes movements, telling them to stop that right now, the kids squealing and peeling off around her a hundred miles an hour.

Mal answered the phone, and said in his deceptively friendly Southern accent he was just out the door, but Jan would be there in her studio in the back, if he just gave a holler if he came over. It was a little bit of a hike to get there, but not bad, and with all the cars going by, with their windows up or down, radios on, spilling out, and all the activity and houses and people, it was like Civilization. It was hot over here like the heat wave over the whole country, everywhere but out on the water. A delivery truck stopped at the light with a whole string of cars behind it had an old-fashioned picture painted on the side of it of a girl in a bonnet, and under it it said,

LITTLE DEBBIE

HAS A TREAT FOR YOU

The lush trees among the old houses and lining the street going back from the coastal road were like summer profusions in front and behind and around him, and Simon, safe, wondered and could picture what it was like here in the winter, with loaves of snow hatted on the houses, and icicles like bangs, like fangs, and ice on the drooping telephone wires, and high continuous snowman snowbanks, frozen solid, and drifts like long-buried ghosts sculpted by the chiseling wind, so wicked no one's around, it's so fucking cold and desolate and black-and-white world, for weeks under time, when suddenly, one day, like unexpected forgiveness, a blue day arrives, brightness bursting everywhere, like a blessing, a reminder and return of color and the wide world beyond your winter, hibernating self.

The hydrant outside the kids' house was painted purple and other colored stripes, but otherwise there was no sign or sound of the kids, but then, sure enough, up the street, coming the other way, he saw them, in a long, wobbly battalion line, on bikes, behind the fat woman, in the lead, in this custom like fiberglass tricycle, like a pedal boat, with an antenna bending back and boinging around, waving its blaze orange pennant attached to the top. One of the kids had a horn with a rubber ball he squeezed frenetically every time the girl with a bell on her handlebars zinged back at him. Except for the two girls who set their bikes carefully aslant on their stands, the other kids all let their bikes fall to the ground and crash into each other on the grass in front of the porch. Three of the boys had crew cuts and freckly sunburned noses, and half the girls were already fat. They scrambled noisily up the porch steps and inside, followed sedately by the two careful girls, one tall and one squat, with identical feathered haircuts.

Mal and Janice's house, across the street a little farther on, had a bench on the semiporch, and on the bench sat a mar-malade cat, who stared right at Simon as he stepped silently up the steps and knocked, not too loud, on the door, then looked in with his hands cupped against the glass like a swimming mask. Inside he could see some toys tipped over at the bottom of the stairs and a pair of shoes on the second stair. The cat languidly waved its tail as Simon knocked again, and then opened the door and went in. It smelled like dead food, and it reminded him of going over to a friend's house for the night as a kid and wanting to go home.

'Lo, he called out not too loud. Janice?

There was no sound and nobody home, it seemed sure. He moved past the room with the TV with the couch in front of it to the kitchen, where he looked again at the story about the Georges Bank on the front page of the paper on the kitchen table beside a glass and an ashtray with three bent butts in it. He heard a soft, sandy scraping sound, like slippers, and was sort of startled as he looked up by,

Oh my God! a startled Janice, really startled, clamping her hand to her heart. Simon, she shook her head, what are you doing here? She pushed a strand of hair behind her ear and composed herself, breathing. I mean, hello, but you scared me half to death. She stood in the doorway like it was his house and she was waiting for him to invite her in, then collected herself further, pulled a butt out of a pack from her pocket, lit it, and sat down, offering Simon a seat, too, and something to drink.

Juice, Simon said, if you have any, would be good.

So have you been up for long? she said into the refrigerator, its light refrigerator roar and hoar.

Yeah for like a month over on North Haven. I called a little while ago and talked to Mal, did he tell you?

No, she sucked on her cig, no he didn't. She sounded a little annoyed at Mal, or at Simon, but, Oh well, she shrugged it off, you know Mal.

Actually Simon didn't know Mal that well. He felt like Mal didn't really like him, and avoided him, wouldn't really give him the time of day, and then he could turn around and be really nice, like when he was drinking. Janice was the one he was more friends with now, and their friend Clyde, who he met them through. Clyde lived back in the other slave quarters across from Simon's first place in New Orleans, his first year there, he got through a friend of Red's who wrote for magazines and was from down there.

Yeah I told him, like I told him back in like May, and he said, Simon paused, like clogged, and started again. He said I could maybe, like, stay back in your barn. The humming refrigerator suddenly stopped, and the room stepped into mid-morning silence, streaked with her layered clouds of smoke, and him there with her there with her hair up. Simon liked her enough, and she liked him, he knew, but she wasn't his style, though kind of pretty, but sort of a retread, like a little chunky and over the hill, and married, to Mal, with Penny and Mike. They had a time, one time, when she was sort of drunk, and started stroking his back, and then started kissing him, but it stopped, and they talked about it, or she did, all serious, the next time he saw her, at a cookout a week later at Clyde's. She came over to him, after avoiding him, and said, all serious, they had to talk, and she said to Mal she was going to see Simon's paintings, and they went up to his place, a little messy that day, and she did all the talking, and Simon sort of shrugged and said okay, whatever. He was glad, anyway.

Yeah sure, I guess, said Janice, sort of frowning. So you've been out at your family's place?

Yeah, till now, but now my father's here and doesn't want me out there.

She nodded understandingly, but sort of seeming to wonder.

I mean, I wouldn't be here all the time, or even that much, Simon went on. Just to have a place to get away from my father, part of the time, and just be away from there, like a backup.

Right, she stabbed her butt out. Well I don't see why not, and wound the string of hair that kept coming out back behind her ear again, if Mal doesn't mind it's fine with me. She looked him right in the eye: I guess.

I won't be any trouble, he said sweetly.

Oh, I know that, Simon, she put her hand on his on the table, and for those few seconds he froze. That's not what I'm concerned about. It's just—she breathed out a big sigh, waving the smoke away, but only whirling it—you know.

Well like I say, I won't be any trouble, Simon replied.

Well, maybe we should go out and take a look, she said, getting up, so you can see what you're getting yourself into.

They went out the back door and across the pretty big lawn to the brown barn with vertical planks chewed dark by rot at the bottoms, hidden, kind of, in the tall grass that caused it, like bad teeth hiding in an overgrown beard. The lawn had a croquet set set up way wrong, and mallets and balls were left lying there where they died, poisoned, or quit.

I'm good at croquet, Simon said, flipping a blue ball with his foot toward a wicket and hitting it with a clink.

Well good. She was warming to the idea of him here, he was glad. Maybe you can show the kids a thing or two. Mal's not too into it. Simon could just see him, playing holding his beer. Mal was definitely a drinker, Southern style.

Yeah I will, Simon said, a little lift of enthusiasm in there. Do you play too?

I guess, she shrugged, and pushed and kicked the stuck door open with her Tretorn toe. She had on shorts to her knees, which was far enough up, and from the side her face looked kind of mad, like tired of life, but inside, in the dark where he could barely see her at first, she was her regular friendly self.

So this is the place, she said. They were in a sort of side shed room with a low slanted roof, attached to the main big room of the barn by an open doorway with no door. In here were some rusted tools, like clippers and an old saw with big teeth, on nails on the wall, and the lawn mower in the corner like the animal that lived in there, that seemed to say, What are you doing here? The one window, four dirty panes that wouldn't open, showed muted tree green through the glass darkly. Janice stood there and shrugged.

This is good, Simon said brightly, moving to the doorway to the dark barn proper. This is all I need. Janice laughed a little and said,

We have a fold-up cot kind of thing we can stick in here, and I guess a table and a light and whatever—she shrugged—a chair. It's not much, Simon.

No, this is good, he said, and meant it, pretty much.

For the bathroom you'll have to use the bathroom in the house. He nodded assent. And you could paint in the barn. The big doors open, if you can get them open, and we don't use it for anything except our suitcases and stuff.

She tried, in the near dark, and then Simon tugged on the nonsliding door, and on the second showoff exertion pulled it screeching open in two jerks, sending flakes of dust and rust particles raining down in the light let in, into their hair, and they closed their eyes and *pffspat*, moted air swirling. It was a big, open, empty barn, and Simon liked it right away, like it was his.

Yeah this is great, he said, sounding more flat than enthused, but meaning more enthused. I could set up in here and paint, definitely. Or maybe like sleep in this part, too.

Whatever, she shrugged, and smiled.

As they walked back to the house he asked her, So where are Mike and Penny—and Mal?

Penny and Mike are at this day camp they go to in Camden. Mal took them, and then's off doing things, who knows?

As they crossed the croquet course she pointed out her studio off the kitchen, and showed him when they got inside. She was working on this pretty big canvas of a turtle shell she had there on the table. Pushpinned on the wall were lots of drawings of it, and what it turned into. The shape went away and the pattern took over, like overgrown. Simon thought she was a pretty good artist, but definitely more like the 1990s, whereas he was more like timeless classic.

Walking back to town he felt a huge hole of relief, though he didn't really feel anything to be relieved from, that he knew of, except just Dad, but fuck him, he couldn't tell him what to do. Back in town he went back to the deli to use the phone. He called the house, see if Timmy was there, and after three *rrr*atchety rings Timmy answered.

Hi, I'm over in Rockland.

Simon?

No, *Dad.*

Well Jesus, Simon, most people when they call on the phone say who it is at the beginning of the conversation.

I think you know who I am.

Now I do.

You always do.

Simon, I'm feeding the baby. Is there something—

Is Dad there?

Yup, he came on the first ferry. Did you take the ferry over? You must have seen him. Simon didn't acknowledge. Did you see him? No reply to that, either, but instead,

Did he say anything?

Yeah, he said hello. Listen, Simon, I have to go—but could you do me a favor?

What.

Get me some formula for the baby. They sell it at any drug-store or grocery store or supermarket. The stuff they sell here's like all sugar syrup, really old in rusted cans—

Sorry, I don't have any money.

I'll pay you back, Simon, I need it.

I said I don't have any money, Simon said, and hung up.

The Monday before that pretty grim Christmas, the scheduling judge for the Massachusetts Superior Court issued his ruling as to where the trial would occur, the date on which proceedings would begin (or resume), and the judge who would preside. The trial would be held at the Leverett A. Saltonstall Building in Boston, county of Suffolk, in three weeks' time, on the twelfth of January, the Honorable Judge Lawrence O. Word presiding. Leverett A. Saltonstall was Pa's—Dad's father's—best friend. He worked for him for two decades. Right-hand man. They bought their houses in Maine at the same time . . .

The scheduling judge's decision to schedule so soon the resumption of pretrial proceedings was unusual. It was as if everyone wanted to keep the plot moving nicely along. It was agreed, for instance, with no disagreement from any quarter, that the change of venue would constitute a change of venue only: that there was no reason to start discovery and evidentiary motions all over again. Instead, this shift to a new location, new court, and new judge was to be, in effect, only an interruption in the pretrial proceedings, already well under way. And of course it was a significant upgrade to an appropriately grand stage.

The new prosecutor assigned to the case was Assistant District Attorney Sandra Gorman. They called her Sandy, which was the color of her hair. She had a lot of trial experience, and a very impressive conviction rate. Though not in murder trials. She had never tried a murder case before. Her field was sex crimes: rape. Some said that this, automatically, no matter how good she was in rape cases, made her the underdog here, simply because this was a murder case, and all the laws, nuances, and courtroom tactics were different. Some said these factors were just the same, whether rape or murder, and that her high conviction record for rape in fact put her at an advantage, or at least showed her superior skill, since rape convictions—until she came along—were notoriously difficult to win.

Simon learned about her, or more like just looked at the pictures of her, in an article about her in *Boston Magazine.* Red read another profile, sent by her people, from the *American Lawyer.* Anna saw the same piece, devoured it twice, and gave it to Timmy. It sat on his bedside table, and he read a little more each night, or started to, or started again, but couldn't concentrate, and each night fell asleep before much of a person could form in his mind beyond the picture of Sandy Gorman in a gold-buttoned lady lawyer suit, by now very familiar to him, standing guard at the beginning of her story and the gate to his shaky slumber.

Sandy Gorman did not look like some jaded prosecutor of violent sex crimes. She looked more like a suburban mom, with a little hint of former Playboy bunny. She seemed so normal, friendly, and familiar—the girl next door who had been an A-student goodie-goodie and went on to be first in her class at law school. This wholesome appearance, no doubt, accounted, to some degree, for her success with juries—they intuitively saw she's clearly on the right side, and must be right. She always did her homework thoroughly, always worked hard, and always believed in what was good and right. Simon, by available contrast, never really did his homework or worked hard, then or since, and always lived by his own rules—which amounted to a patent lack of them.

The first time Simon saw Sandra Gorman was the first day of court in Boston. He didn't see her at all as this like dire nemesis who might put him away for life. Or possibly take away his life—he didn't yet know about the governor's capital punishment bill currently snaking its way under the rug in committee. His impression of her was more one of almost amusement, made more so by the relief it masked, and its like molten flipside, fear. *Her?* Tseh! No problem. If anything, he kind of liked her. In that totally unlikely way of completely different types, but still, there it is.

Nothing really happened this first day in the new courtroom, but it felt to all present like a momentous event. The first flight of press representatives were there in their suits in the front rows, surrounding the Curtis contingent, their cameras and cameramen out in the halls, their location vans, like big toys, stacked on the street and the sidewalk outside the courthouse. The courtroom was packed. Zwirner wore a shiny green tie and had a haircut, though not short. The locks in back still curled raffishly over his collar. Sandy Gorman wore a smart beige suit almost like a man's. She was kind of chunky, but still had pretty good legs, from the knees down, which was all her outfit let you see.

Simon was led out of a side door by a requisitely thick court officer with a deluxe standard-issue handlebar mustache. Will Deery followed close behind. Though he had refused before, taking it off and stuffing it in his pocket when they tried to make him wear one, Simon now wore a tie, one of Timmy's. And his jacket, which Red got for him and gave to Will Deery to put on Simon, fit nicely. Not like the one he wore before, which looked like a bad fit from a thrift store, or like he stole it.

Simon looked straight at Sandy Gorman with a bland, calm, like anomie-in-the-eyes expression, as he walked right toward her where she sat at her table, with her knees together, lookng back at him. Her associate beside her, a trim black guy in glasses, gold rims with like tortoiseshell straws on the arms, was busy with papers, or pretending to be. The tabloids said this first encounter was charged with dramatic tension, but actually it was dull and routine, with barely any confrontation or emotion in sight.

The judge came out after ten minutes, announced by the bailiff,

All rise.

He was bald and round, maybe sixty, moist eyes with pouches under his glasses that looked like they grew there, from magnification or some sad greenhouse effect. He wore a navy blue tie and white shirt under his black robe, and a no-

nonsense expression, as he surveyed the courtroom and spoke clearly and deliberately, his voice a little gravelly, into the microphone supported on its bent neck before him. The courtroom was all ears. He named the case, the place, the courtroom, and the date, and invited the lawyers for both sides up to his bench. They conferred up there for fifteen minutes. The audience became restless. This was not the show they bargained for. But this prologue pretty well presaged what lay ahead. In the end, nothing noticeable was accomplished. This was a Monday afternoon. The proceedings would resume on Thursday.

On Thursday the prosecution and the defense both submitted motions to the court. The prosecution moved that the television camera be removed from the courtroom. Sandy Gorman ardently pitched her hopes.

Zwirner in his turn stood and concisely, point by point, refuted them. Clearly he saw this one coming. No judge in the country had yet banned a television camera from a courtroom since they had first been introduced eight years ago, he began, and for good reason: the public's fundamental right to know, the principle of full disclosure of all facts and facets of any public trial, which derives from the public's right to attend and observe trials. This established right and time-honored tradition, whose roots found their historical source between, in essence, these very walls, in the old New England courthouses, like this one, which were designed with their large galleries— which he indicated with a docent's sweep of the arm—to accommodate the citizenry—he gestured grandly with both hands—whose vested right it was, and *still is,* to attend and observe any and all trials: an essential freedom and bedrock guarantee of our open and fair judicial system.

Zwirner was visibly pleased with his performance. He basked and gloated in the afterglow, looking around the room and taking it all in: the collective admiration and incontestable comprehension, as he saw it, in the traduced, attentive faces, the rapt eyes, the cold camera—before sitting himself down. The papers and the TV news were impressed as well, and for the first time they focused on him, his lawyerly skills and accomplishments. Before this, attention had gone to Red, to Simon, a bit to Dad, and in the past week, to Sandra Gorman. Sandy Gorman, everywhere you looked. Now it was his turn. Now they remembered his big cases, his impressive list of victories. The BU foreign exchange student who bashed his girlfriend's brains in with a hammer as she slept one night in her parents' Medford home. The radon-contaminated Charlestown elementary school . . .

The first few days of pretrial in Boston were forgettably redundant. The only excitement was the rush of the press and onlookers before and after court to get a glimpse of Red as she came and went with Timmy and Anna, the Springers trailing behind like extras. Questions showered over them. Only Will Deery, leading the way, spoke through the verbal fusillade.

Let us through, please, let us through.

Dad's car, which was actually Ginny's, and he left his Massachusetts station wagon in Manchester, was on the ferry with Simon. No dog, only groceries and other bought things in the backseat. Ginny had a compass stuck on her dashboard, because she was so lost, but it would only help her get like more lost, but on the ferry it seemed in its right place, as it moved a little in its fluid floating way, keeping its horizon integrity, like a trick, the way it slides around according to its own true north, like Simon.

No sign of Dad on Maine Street back on North Haven, but his car was there, not where Simon left it, but closer to Dad's walkway down, so Dad had used it, Timmy had his own car on the island now. Simon walked by smoothly and looked down there and saw Ginny's head in her kitchen window over the sink, and their upstairs door was open. Coming down the stairs he was ready to see Dad at the bottom, or coming out of the middle house, but he didn't, and inside Timmy shot a *Shhh* at him for letting the door slap shut, and standing in the kitchen they continued their conversation from the phone.

So did Dad say anything about me?

I thought you didn't care what Dad thought.

I don't I'm just wondering.

Well, yeah, he asked if you were here, and I told him yes.

Why'd you say that?

Because it's true.

I wasn't here.

Well how was I supposed to know? Anyway, he meant were you staying here, and the answer is yes.

Did he say anything else?

Yeah lots.

About me, I mean.

Yeah, he asked how long you've been here, and I told him all of June.

I can't believe you said that. Simon cut sharply away and looked into the dining room, where the baby's meal was splattered on his tray, on his chair, and on the table at the far end by the windows, the sun-splashy day out there among the boats. Why'd you say that?

Because he asked me, Simon. Timmy resumed rinsing and putting bowls and glasses into the dishwasher. I'm not going to lie for you.

Thanks a lot, Simon said, bluntly acid, and left, cutting right past him, and went up the stairs three at a time, stretching long steps up, too loud for Timmy, who froze in aggravation, but didn't hear Bennie waking. Simon knocked around a couple of times, moving things around up there, and Timmy wanted to go up and tell him to shut up, but didn't want to make it worse, and so didn't.

Simon, up in his room, didn't quite know what to do now, so

first he started to pack some clothes, and then started to pack painting things, but then didn't, because just because Dad wanted him to go didn't mean he was going to go. So he went out onto the balcony to sit and think and whatever, not think, and there was Dad's head below in the slot where you could see down, between the side edge of the balcony and the overhang bulge of the windows of Mum and Dad's bedroom sticking out. Keeping his eyes on him, Simon silently moved the chair and slid over to the far side of the balcony, where you couldn't see from down on the dock, and sat back, tilting up on the two back legs, and rested his head against the sill and screen of the open window to Bennie's room, not three feet above the baby's head in the crib in his slipping sleep. Ten minutes later, hearing fitful chips and bleats on the monitor, Timmy checked on him and saw the back of Simon's head right there above the crib like a target, a framed portrait from behind, and he shook his head and would have laughed if he had a witness or an audience.

The door downstairs clapped shut, even though Timmy had undone the spring the day he arrived, and Timmy closed his eyes, to regroup his patience, and opened them to see Bennie still sound asleep, his chubby cheek and squished mouth mashed into the flat mattress, and Dad padded in downstairs, in the inaugural first of his restless rounds in and out of doors all day, all summer.

Timmy? he bellowed with zero baby modulation in his voice.

Timmy, surrounded by his life, these guys in his family, shook his head slow, out of patience, and headed out of the room to respond softly down the stairs, but Dad clapped back outdoors, and he let him go. Timmy went into his room, where the beds were pushed together and unmade, and went to the middle window and looked down at the box where Dad had some tools and stuff spread out, like pieces of evidence, and then Dad's arms appeared, putting down a couple more things, then withdrew. Through the side window was Simon, sitting there where he couldn't see Dad, and Dad couldn't see Simon watching Timmy look down at Dad. The door slapped shut again, and Timmy went downstairs to tell Dad what he'd already told him, please be quiet in the morning, and the afternoons also, the baby was sleeping.

Ah, there you are, said Dad genially.

Dad, the door, Timmy began as he saw what he knew from the slap, that Dad had hooked up the spring again. I undid the spring on purpose so the door wouldn't slam.

My apologies, my boy, Dad replied. I thought the house was falling into sad disrepair.

No, but Dad, if you could keep it down, Timmy said softly. Not just the door but everything—he nodded upstairs—he wakes up really easily.

Why certainly. He moved past Timmy mumbling, Of course, of course . . . Timmy followed him into the living room. You won't hear a trace of me again, he reiterated as he inspected, lips pursed, the selection of last summer's magazines. Timmy knew this wasn't true—but what can you do?

We have the flower boxes arriving this afternoon sometime, I'm told, he informed Timmy as he knelt with one knee on the cushioned window seat, knocking and screeching open the side window onto the dock, the drop to rocky sort of beach, or shallow water, or, depending on the tide, water right there, close up, gulping under the house on its surprisingly skinny front leg piles.

Dad stood and rubbed his ruddy hands together, surveying the baby play area, the room, and Timmy felt like he was being critical, like always, even though he made no expression of disapproval, said nothing about the disarray, said nothing period. He padded out of there, and Timmy followed him and caught the door from banging shut behind him, and undid the spring again. Then he set to work making pads for the door, out of cut strips of kitchen sponge, to keep it quiet. He was gluing them in place because he couldn't hammer now, and he couldn't find, and didn't want to search anymore among the mess in Simon's room, Simon's rooms, for his staple gun, which would have been perfect, because it depressed him even to look at the mess, every time he passed by the open doorway, let alone go through it, bit by bit, like detritus after someone's death, or worse: this was his life, so he stopped right after he started, and went for the old Elmer's. When he went out on the balcony first, to ask Simon if he could use his staple gun, he was gone.

Dad continued to go back and forth, with things, sometimes only carrying out a single item at a time, like a screwdriver, or even only a screw, or a few, in his plump fist, but continued steadily, in and out of the symmetrical mate door across the breezeway dock passage from Timmy, into his workshop in the middle house, sometimes staying inside longer, sometimes bouncing right back out and lingering by the box, considering. At first Timmy kept thinking of things to say.

Tenderness came, as ever, indirectly, in hidden hints he had to look for and find, but that were there, they were there, sometimes, after, as when Dad passed the doorway Timmy was working on carrying an orange heavy duty extension cord, loosely coiled, and the way he carried it, with his pants falling down, where they always were, he looked like a cowboy,

Pardon me, m'boy, placing his hand, meaty, on his shoulder where Tim crouched, and he felt it, fairly gentle and heartbreaking, like no understanding after a disagreement, or liberated frustration, or transcendental sex . . .

Bennie started crying, but it was about time, so fine, he headed up, and in there there was Simon's head again, in the open window right behind the screen like a framed portrait of how he was, facing the other way, and slipped down half out of the picture, unmoving, and apparently unperturbed by the crying, two feet away from him, which had escalated, that fast, into a fire alarm scream. Bennie's eyes were little slits in his big bald head, he was screaming like a banshee, and when Timmy picked him up he stopped crying as soon as he could catch his breath and return to breathing baby sanity, panting, quick little inhale sips, from the effort of wailing. Dad appeared in a surprise appearance in the doorway, as Timmy ogled and tickled Bennie's belly with his forehead and hair while he changed him on the bureau top spread with a towel. Dad watched, bemused, with his hands folded behind his back, and Timmy waited for him to notice Simon in his direct line of vision, but he didn't, and as he stepped farther into the room and over to Timmy's side, still didn't, his hands clasped behind his back, observing, so that Simon could easily hear him when he said,

The first grandson. Clearly moved and wanting to say more, but not knowing what to say, he added an expectable, easy: Wonderful, m'boy.

This wasn't the first time he'd seen him, but it was the first time he'd come expressly to see him, and really paid attention and said something like this, more than passing like bubble comments that pop and are gone, and now, just looking, looking like a big baby himself, the grandfather, he teared up and swiped his tears with his forefinger and thumb under his glasses, which of course really got Timmy and made him cry, too, except after, but for right now he was just really glad, and gladdened still further when Dad added, coughing, to clear his choked emotion,

I suppose a grandfather should hold his little heir apparent, which Simon definitely heard and registered and filed away as further evidence for future reference and like retribution. If I may, that is, as Timmy finished taping his living bundle. May I?

Yeah, of course, here. Timmy handed him over, delighted Dad had at least shown some interest. Dad's reactions to emotional matters worked on the buried-deep/delayed-reaction system, often never making it out, but sometimes coming later.

Sometimes after one reaction he'd come back later with another, more considered, or finally arrived, like *this just in.*

Heavy little fella, he held him not unlike a football and jostled him a few times like he must have Timmy—right?—and Timmy took this in hungrily, for some reason as perplexed as he was pleased, and then of course in the afterglow or like falling ash sadness after Dad left the room without seeing Simon, right there the whole time, and creaked down the speaking stairs, and lo the door was silent success, or maybe held still open by the needlepointed brick doorstop Mum made of the spark plug lighthouse Goose Rock, as if she knew, like embroidering her own gravestone.

Simon took this scene in whole through the hole in the back of his head, and Timmy, in a moment of lightness between them, from his side, at least, leaned over and tapped with a fingernail fillip, and zinged, the screen, and Simon, with a delayed reaction, turned slowly, deadpan, and looked at Timmy with that bothered-brother, level-lidded, flat expression that reminded him, exactly, except without the blood, of the time, the year after Mum died, when they both kept wrecking cars and boats, going back and forth as if taking turns, switching off in their shared destruction and self-destruction duties, or competition, when Simon woke, Timmy thought he was dead, yelling his name and shaking his shoulder through the open car window, after getting out, after demanding to be let out, but kept hostage, but then getting out quickly when Simon skidded to a stop, not killing them, just, before the wall curve around Smelly Beach cove, after a hell ride through town, weaving and leaping over the drunken racecourse home. From the hill across the cove, crying in the purple dark, he watched the skewed headlight beams lance and jerk around the cove road, lurching and speeding up on the other side, before the final metal crash and crunch of glass; the engine went off, and the lights stayed on, and Timmy ran like around a walled track in a dream, in a burst of terror burst further into terror, hearing, loudly, his heaving breath, and when he got there, the little Rabbit that had skid-hopped sideways, twice, through the lit dogleg of downtown, then bounded, lucky, like with invisible ricochets, the rest of the way, was crushed into a hydrant and a tree where the road turned up the hill, but Simon didn't, and the windshield was smashed with a spiderweb head mark, and he was in there, heaped over the steering wheel and the dash, dead.

Simon! Simon! Timmy shook his shoulders and screamed at him, *Simon! Simon!*

And Simon didn't move, until released by his melodramatic long-delayed reaction, slowly, like a cadaver, he tipped a little back and lifted his head like a horror movie, his face all black with blood, and he leadenly turned it and opened his eyes with that deadly dead expression, flat and unhorrified, like he was used to this, and in a tone like a drone, annoyed, like Timmy had needlessly, thoughtlessly, woken him,

N*what,* Timmy?

Out of the dullness on the fifth day of court in Boston came a little excitement. The judge sedately announced his ruling that the camera was banned from the courtroom for the remainder of the trial.

It was an unexpected ruling, and seemed to take everyone by surprise, including a visibly delighted Sandy Gorman, who, three days before, had argued succinctly—some said too succinctly—for its removal. Due to the unusual degree of publicity already generated by this case, she had reasoned, the presence of the camera in the courtroom, and the access it afforded, would only serve as a high-powered distraction, and an unnecessary, unwelcome conduit for general entertainment. The court of law was not, and should not be, a stage for entertainment. The public's right to know was not sufficient cause to jeopardize a fair and impartial trial. This was a trial, not a show.

No one really believed the judge would rule to ban the camera from the courtroom. This, of course, meant headline news, top story on the tube. The news organizations huddled and pooled their appallingly powerful legal talent to challenge the ruling, along with Zwirner and associates, in an appeal. The hearing before the Court of Appeals, in keeping with the unusual expediency of this case, was scheduled for just two days after Judge Word's ruling. In the meantime, the television camera was removed, and henceforth banned, from the courtroom.

It was at this time that Simon began drawing in court. The day after they removed the TV camera from the courtroom, a clutch of sketch artists appeared, like a drawing class on a field trip, with their large pads and colored pencils and chalks, and their distinctly unprofessional attire. They sat in the near part of the jury box, empty until now, in the first two rows. To many there it was like the old days. It instantly felt right. It just seemed, regardless of the legal and libertarian principles involved, that this, after all, was the way it should be. The stenographer, with his strange, archaic skill, was no longer a lone, redundant anachronism, joined now by his prestidigitational peers. One result was that, magically, the hype inside the courtroom was noticeably toned down. As if the trial had changed overnight from a slick professional event to a more hands-on, and maybe more exciting, college championship.

The artists calmly, quietly, made their drawings, seemingly oblivious to, and at the same time nicely in sync with, the slow pace and inane content of the proceedings—or just not that interested, this was just a job, to which they were grateful, but not thrilled, to return after a long work stoppage/hiatus they never expected to end. Some worked fast, all worked efficiently, each at his and her own pace, roughing in the figures, then refining, shading, filling in the colors, the faces, and the backgrounds.

Simon paid more attention to them than he did to what was going on in the hearing. He liked these people, the same way he liked the guards in prison, and regular like working-class people anywhere, in theory anyway. They had their place in the system, but had themselves more. They weren't like the self-important lawyers, or the drooling bloodhound reporters, or even that strange stenographer guy, sitting erect and attentive, and like weaving away on his weird little typewriter. The regular clothes the sketch artists had on were like shirts and sweaters and whatever, pants, or like sneakers. This one woman in her forties with short hair wore a faded Red Sox cap. A fat black guy had on a Cape Cod windbreaker. Real like Boston citizens. These were his kind of people, even if they weren't people he'd really be friends with. They were normal, real people, and artists, so maybe less than normal, who were drawing. He felt like if these people were his jury, he'd be all set. They wouldn't even have to have a trial. They'd just draw and automatically agree with him, by like artistic telepathic affinity, and let him go.

During a twenty-minute afternoon recess Simon went over to see them. His lawyers and the prosecutors were gone for the break. They had followed the judge through the door behind his bench to confer in camera about whatever they'd been arguing about. Red went out to have a butt, and Timmy and the Springers went with her. Many of the press corps headed for the doors the moment the recess was announced. Others followed after Red went out, though they didn't directly hound her, except by looking, but let her be, on a tight visual leash, puffing away at her habitual corner place past the elevators. The view was the bumpy gray wall of the adjacent building, and a piece of street, below to one side, where people ticked past on the zebra-striped section of crosswalk. Sometimes pigeons, enlarged and near, puffed to keep warm, huddled and strutted back and forth on the ledge right outside the window, and through the glass you could hear their faint pleasant purring coos, closer and more intimate than the occasional honking car out there, the sweep and noise of traffic, the quotidian beat of commerce in the dread philistine Boston afternoon.

Nobody told him he had to stay in his seat, and everyone else was getting up, so Simon, trying to look casual and walk like inconspicuous-smooth, went over to the sketch artists, to look at what they were doing. They didn't seem surprised at his appearance, and kept on drawing. This interlude was a chance for them to catch up, fill in and finish pictures, be ready to do new ones. The one with the Red Sox cap folded a sheet over the top to start a fresh page and said to Simon,

Stay still, which he did, while she scratched out his hasty close-up likeness, because that's what he was doing anyway, and he kind of liked her. No way was she his type, but there was that unsuspecting uppy little spark.

That was on Friday. The next Monday Simon brought in his own pad and a couple of pencils. His lawyers had tried to get him, before, to carry a yellow legal pad, and even a law book, like them, and like jot things down during the trial, for pure show, to make it look like he was taking notes, like to tell them any insights and discuss strategy later. As if. The reality, if you can ever say what reality is, was that they never talked to him about squat. They never asked him what he thought, so he never told them. It would have been like a pure charade, and he told them forget it. No way was he going to play along like that, like some idiot. It would look so stupid. They were lucky they got him in a coat and tie, and that was from Red saying it was her one condition for paying for his defense. But that was as far as it went. Why should he let these guys tell him what to do? But when he saw the sketch artists, and borrowed some paper and a charcoal pencil from the woman to do his own sketches, Zwirner thought this would be a nice touch. And so

Simon walked into the courtroom the following Thursday carrying a big new Aquabee pad under his arm, opened it up and got to work drawing, like the other artists, as soon as he sat down. Finally he had something to do in there, instead of just sit there.

Timmy made it to most of these pretrial hearings. It was a slow time of year at work, and his boss was more sympathetic and flexible than Timmy thought he'd be. It was the power of star power coming through. Maybe sympathy, too, and understanding. Plus there was some work in New England Timmy could take care of while he was up there, packing and shipping for two private collections, and for the Boston museum they were trying to move in on, the Museum of Fine Arts. They had shipped and helped hang a traveling show there from New York, and now, especially with Timmy's help up there, they were hoping to get more work from them, maybe open an office in Boston. Timmy liked being up there. It was home turf, he had friends, and it was different being there now that he was grown up. He stayed with a friend from college or with friends from Maine, usually for a few days in a row, stayed up late with them drinking beer and watching cable, then drove back through frozen Connecticut in the middle of the radio night. Those drives those times were lonely out there, but lovely also, and serene, secure, with the insularity and extensity both, his coiled spirit sprung in a leap of release, cowled in the safety of a moving target, the feeling of freedom for now, like the music and the headlights filling the dark passage with open imagination and a renewed sense of possibility, as memory layered in seamlessly with fantasy as liquid and fresh as daily reality, and so much more promising! These late-night drives from all different times in his life were all connected to one another, like they were all part of the same one long late-night drive, this dependable respite and deep source of himself penetrating like a highway through all the mixed-up, loosely chaptered layers of lonely time and scant self and the world's endless, genius imagination you're a little fucking gnat speck part of—or do you create—like some philosophers actually believe!—the whole thing, *reality,* in your head? Sometimes you just had to stop what you were doing, or were supposed to be doing, and go for a while in the opposite direction, or just out and away and into some inner-outer zone of release and renewal, or else fall into the sad, artless ease of familiar, unconscious repetition, and worse. The problem, though, was when what you were doing most of the time was more like these psychic vacation excursions than what you were supposed to be doing. Though who's to say what you were really supposed to be doing? Your wife! Or how about if what you thought you were supposed to be doing was the wrong thing, like neurotic or delusional, or just misguided, or was in fact in the same quicksand category of feckless aesthetic degenerate as the escapist, supposedly regenerate, alternative? Timmy's best thoughts, like these, spun themselves out of that intimate, late-night, abstract tissue, way lighter than words, too exquisitely ethereal to be actually worded and said out loud; and too often, as on these expiatory nocturnal New England sallies, when Anna wasn't there to do it for him, the existential ramble unleashed in his head devolved in spirals of damnation into a swirling, lurid catalogue of his failures and weaknesses as a man, as a husband, as a father, as a brother, as a friend, as an artist . . .

The story was a monster, and the trial hadn't even begun yet. If there was any wavering of interest before on the national level, it was gone now with the judge's ruling to ban the camera from the court. This fixed the proceedings for good in the fore of the national news front, as a *Times* op-ed piece put it— or, as it seemed to Timmy, on the forehead of the national consciousness.

Oh, *that's* what "in camera" means, Timmy said after Anna

straightened out a point. She flipped through a magazine as he spoke.

I was wondering why they said that. Like they go defend-*ant* for *defendant*. Like *in camera* instead of *on camera*, I thought they were saying, like some people say waiting *on* line instead of *in* line. Like people from the Midwest say *on line* for waiting in line, like they say *roof*, like *woof*, for *roof*. Or like they call a grocery bag a sack. Or that's people out west, like Colorado over, I swear, however that happened. Except it was wrong either way, the arguments weren't on camera or in camera, they didn't even happen in front of us.

Anna smiled a sweetie smile, and kept reading.

Red went to a few of the pretrial hearings in Boston. She had a mysterious knack for picking the days when big things happened. She'd call the day before from L.A. and breeze in and then breeze out again at the end of the day, saying she'd love to have dinner but she had to catch the shuttle down to New York. Timmy wished he could take the shuttle back and forth, but those days were past. He had enough trouble paying for his gas and road food going back and forth in the coughing red Escort. But at least he had his music.

I'm delighted, delighted, Dad said, over his shoulder, trailing off, as if to himself, but to Timmy, back in with Bennie, as he headed, having bid his good evening, out the entry and the wounded wing screen door. His tools were in, the day was done, and before going over to the wifely warm cloud of dinner aroma and the soft auras of light vectors spreading furnitureward in pools from lamp shades and up the wood walls of the living room, to settle in with his book and a drink, he headed into the middle house one last time for the first golden head start swill, and in the gloom at the bottom of the stairs, about to turn into his workshop, he met, like a scare, Simon Cary, sliding silently down. They nearly collided, but stopped face-to-face.

I heard you were here, Dad's chin drew in and his mouth pulled down at the sides.

And I heard you were here, Simon said back.

There was a tense pause, making the dimness gelid, and then Dad rolled his eyes and shook his head with a soft sigh and a tired sort of self-shrug, and turned and went, his head bowed like a turtle, into his workshop. Simon stood there, still, for a second, as if appalled and abandoned and turned to stone, his hand held out as if for a hand, to show the surrounding shell of house what Dad was like. He wondered what Dad was doing in there right this second, and listened, but heard nothing but the house, like breathing in its darker depths, where it stayed cool and moist and no one seemed to go but him and Dad, it was like that place in him with Dad's eyes on him, but fuck him. In his workshop Dad stood there frozen, frowning, as if looking down at his distorted, dark, fish-eye reflection in the dead mute TV screen Simon brought back down to its uneven place on the old wood stove that hadn't had a fire in it for thirty years, since Dad took the pipe out and asked someone to patch the hole in the wall, and the good fellow put a paper plate over it with a wire sort of globe, like the lines of a basketball, attached to the back, to hold it in there. His lips pressed out in thought as if about to blow a bubble, he looked to the open doorway to see that Simon wasn't there. But Simon was there, and from his angle Simon could see, on the far bench, that Black & Decker belt sander he had to use, soon, to smooth the edges, and the corners especially, of his recent frames. Kind of copying Timmy, he was using driftwood for frames, and it looked pretty cool, and even better if you sanded some of the gray off, however much came. Not cutesy like arts-and-craftsy, but just the right frame, for some of them, if he got the right-size piece of wood for the right-size painting, not round like driftwood branches, but flat little weathered lumber strips. A person walked by on the dock out the window, which prompted Dad to move to the shelf, where a pair of brass faucets lay gifted in their box, the spigots sticking out like nostrils, and as the approaching footsteps resounded hollow in the passage, Simon slid into the person passing like a scapegoat slipstream out past the open door and Dad and the green screen door, it was a tall skinny kid with big feet in big basketball sneakers like boots on him. He looked over at Simon, startled, with his mouth in a guilty little teen *o,* and said sort of hi, and took off up the stairs, three at a time, with his oversized T-shirt luffing, up and away.

Simon went over into Timmy, who was, what else, feeding the baby viridian mush with the little white-coated spoon. Timmy looked like he was in no mood, and Simon thought it was alcoholic.

Dad wants to see you, Timmy said without turning.

No he doesn't, Simon said again.

Yes he does, Timmy snapped. I just saw him.

So did I. Simon stepped noiselessly behind him to the window, and Timmy felt like Simon was this caged animal acting smooth and self-contained, but really was trapped like in impotent rage.

What did he say?

Nothing. The water stretched its surface reflections in crazy morphing shapes.

Nothing?

Grinning Bennie banged and spattered and spat and grinned.

Yup.

Fanlight rays came up, shifting lighter green shafts from the greener deep god, and the way the water waved, with its inner spindles like wiggly smooth, it was like it was him.

Snow flew like a real winter over those weeks. First it fell, slow motion, out the windows and in the sleepless ocean sky, onto the architecture and over the laws and the land, exhaustively treed with a trillion twigs between similar towns, composed, detailed New England compositions, as far as history's busy hands had reached. The next day the snow rested calmly over fields, loaved on cars, limned along branches and windowsills, tufts and Nike signs on ledges and abutments, unbuttoned in morning falls, puffs, then bloomed off roofs in swirling dresses, powdery, powerful wishes rising up, gusting, vague velleities sucked away into the colorless air. Disposable days busily imagined themselves into being, gathering, conjuring, and teetering headlong into oblivion. Plows scraped along, lifting great white wings, long waves curling off the revealed black roads, orange lights rotating, tossing flashes and luminous spirals into the black-and-white polka-dotted night. City shovels noisily scraped sidewalks, chipped away at liable ice. Overcoats and parkas came off and collapsed indoors, hung up, empty, boots wept in corners, by doors, and everyone talked about the snow. And everyone talked about the trial.

He's guilty.

He's crazy.

He'll get off.

He'll never get off.

It seemed reasonable that the fact of the bowl's absence the day Dad was found dead should be allowed into the record. But it also seemed technically logical that if there was no actual evidence—no bowl—then it couldn't be allowed as evidence. There was legal precedent supporting both interpretations.

The Captain Simon Curtis story got full archival treatment by a *Globe* columnist, who researched the subject, he disclosed at the beginning of his lengthy weekend article, at the Massachusetts Historical Society, the Boston Athenaeum, and the Boston Public Library, as well as the Smithsonian and some obscure Internet sources. Captain Simon Cary Curtis was involved in the China trade, where he made his fortune importing spices, tea, china, and other wares, exchanged primarily for furs he obtained in the Pacific Northwest, in exchange for rum, textiles, and soap manufactured in New England. He was also reputed to have been involved in the lucrative opium trade, opprobrious only in historical hindsight, like the slave trade, in which he was also said to have been busy, although there were no documents extant to support this. At one time he owned a sugar plantation in Barbados. And there were rumors, in his day, circulating in Brahmin Boston, that he had illegitimate children, by a slave mistress at his plantation—what amounted to a second, secret family.

Simon had heard stories about this guy growing up, but he personally wasn't into like ancestor worship of a bunch of hypocritical Puritans, so he never knew the details. But he liked these stories about Captain Simon Cary Curtis, and always identified with his namesake forebear, the maverick captain. This bit about opium he'd never heard, but it made sense and fitted right in with his vague picture of the guy, and he liked it. He definitely liked the guy going off around the world doing whatever he wanted and he was glad that now everybody knew about him. Simon knew he wasn't named after him for nothing. These things all fit into place over time. Maybe this guy was more than just like his antecedent ancestor. Maybe it was more direct of a like a personal continuation, like same-name reincarnation. Simon knew there was more to these things than anyone could say or see. Simon knew like intuitively how things worked inside and outside of time, like the real nature of history, the saga of the soul, and the like oversoul. You never knew with these deep old connections and heredity and stories passed down with their own lives somehow separate from any one person or people or time. It wasn't just stories and coincidence with this Simon Cary character. He had a definite feeling about all this now that it came up. Like he was him.

Simon woke to the full wide movie screen of summer lettuce
canopy, the big old maple's many supple money hands suspended and waving lightly diaphanous green, on the outer layers, darker inside, like inside a big shredded umbrella, open
over him and letting in, through torn spots, the sky and soft
breeze—he could look at the leaves like this all day.

He bowled the red croquet ball through the thick grass
toward the blue ball in the middle of the lawn and hit it with a
solid, satisfying, ceramic click. The lawn definitely needed to
be cut and he decided to be helpful and do it, maybe if he did
that and other handyman type things around they'd knock it
off the one-fifty for the room. Three hundred for July and
August wasn't bad, though he didn't have it right now, and
July was already going, but she said whenever you can, and he
bet they'd take a painting at the end of the summer, if he did
one, say, of the barn with the tree with the swing, which he was
thinking about doing anyway so maybe he'd do two, like one
like tester quickie for them, and another one to sell it. In the
dark in the barn the lawn mower was caught against an uneven
stack of flowerpots with a plastic sack of something stuck in the
top one and overlapping out like a rasta's hat, the way they look
like there's a dead cat in there in the pouch, and the last wheel
of the lawn mower knocked them over in a toppling tower, and
the top ones crashed and cracked and broke all over the place.
Janice's window was open so she heard but didn't see what it
was, but could guess and shook her head with a little smile.
Out in the sheer daylight he couldn't get the lawn mower
started. After a lot of hard pulls he checked the gas, and it was
empty, stupid, so he went back in the barn to look around for
the gas. His eyes slowly adapted to the dark and he could
slowly see how disorganized it was in there, like someone's
unconscious, and he saw the light and turned it on, but it
hardly made any difference, a barn bulb hanging up there, not

at all bright. There was a rope coming down, too, in the open, with a knot at the bottom, and he stood up on the knot with his feet together, holding the rope, and started to pull and swing back and forth . . .

He couldn't find the gas, and knowing Mal there probably wasn't any. His cot wasn't bad, pretty new, with a good foam-rubber little mattress layer built into the tight canvas sag, and white caps on the bottoms of the aluminum legs. He lay down and felt a suggestion like of sex, and sort of ticklish strength, when he touched, which he knew was always enough, and so, first on his back, and then on his side, with the old spit and polish, yanked and stroked, just so, an ass just right with the skirt lifted from behind, at a bar, like anonymous, she wants it, pushes against him, and right when he goes way in and up against the like cushion of her ass he came into his other hand with a heroin rush through his whole body, and then after a minute, when he came enough out of the drowse, he licked it, and it tasted almost gross, but not quite, not bitter and like yellow, like when he had too much coffee, and he swallowed it, it was good for you, protein, and like fresh from the source, when he heard right then a noise of someone, and then a crow behind that, going, *Raw!* like a person. He sat and wiped his hand on his pants and zipped up smoothly fast like he wasn't doing anything, and Janice's voice and his name came near, and there she was, in the creak and crack of the door, darkened by the daylight behind.

Do you know where the gas is to the lawn mower? Simon said quickly in kind of a slur she could understand because she was used to him, and southern, but a lot of people wouldn't. *Raw!* the crow croaked again outside, pretty close. He felt sort of oozy loose from coming still and she stepped toward him out of the shape in the door, a real person, a real woman, and he was afraid for a second she was going to touch him, if she saw, or like kneel down and suck him. *Rock-rock!* But she didn't see, or maybe she did, but she didn't touch him, she was just coming out to see him, so far.

Oh I don't know exactly, but there's a can out here some-where. Unless Mal took it to the boat, she said in a normal voice with Mal in it. Maybe she did see or could tell and wanted to whatever, but her voice wouldn't tell, and when he got up for them to go look there was a definite like boner bulge still in his pants, and he never wore underwear, so it was right there, like outlined, if she saw it, and she did she did, but didn't do any-thing, just softly said, like it had some other sort of ulterior meaning,

Simon, you don't have to mow the lawn.

No, it's okay, I want to, he went past her into the open barn half darkness. She found the gas can over under a coil heap of hose in the corner past the sliding door, as Simon, in his corner, kick-swept aside some of the broken shards of flowerpot. Out in the sun, covered, as they emerged, by a bulky, slow-sailing cloud like a huge Beethoven head of cauliflower, he poured the gas into the lawn mower, but it wouldn't pour right, even though the opening was open, letting out the fumes and the air in, he could feel the sloshy weight of plenty in there.

There's a spout in there inside out, Janice said, and Simon unscrewed it, got it sticking out right, and poured it, glug-ging, into the mower, then started her up first rip, almost, but it coughed off, but stayed on when he revved and eased it on the second pull. He let it idle and seethe blue smoke while he trot-ted around the lawn in a show of sprightly energy, picking up the wickets and the two stakes. He started in with a mohawk stripe right up the middle over to the house, like a path for Jan-ice, like the green carpet treatment, who stood squinting, smoking, by the barn, ignoring the cat weaving, leaning against her calves and shins.

The wind shimmered over the longhair grass in wind over

the world in delicate miniature, as he marched in rows and mowed around the edges, eating it up toward the middle. In the shade of the tree with the swing the grass was richer and thicker, and still a little wet, with silvery beads of water up under those spider tent thingies, making them white, and the mower moaned, too full, too thick to cut, and he lifted the front to not stall, and went through the thicker stuff like that, slower, like eating. The mower trundling along with him, holding the handlebar and helping the go gear go, and the summer sweet smell of the cut grass and the greening of his sneaker toes as he marched along, all brought him right back to him as a kid and the lawn in Manchester he had to mow most of the time. They'd play whiffle for hours with the elaborate, evolved house rules of which bush and drainpipe was foul, past where was fair, and out on the fly was a homer, till it was dark. They played you could pick the guy off running by throwing the ball at him and hit him, if you could. Simon had this excellent rising fastball, and a wicked bender that was a little wilder.

When he finished mowing the lawn, this was his plan, he set up the croquet course right, using the whole lawn. He was a real sharpshooter and liked being poison and going around at the end like a shark, getting everyone and winning. When the kids got home he got a game going, though they didn't want to play, and refused unless Janice played, too. Janice was wearing sandals, so they decided to make it the Barefoot Sweepstakes and Mike said,

No, it's the Barefoot *International* Sweepstakes.

Simon explained the right rules, though he could tell they didn't get all of it, and showed them how to hold the mallet and swing it smoothly forward, like a pendulum between your legs, but Mikey continued to do it his way, golf style, or more like an axe. The balls clacked and bounded around the lawn while they warmed up, watched by the tabby cat on the back step, and then Simon made them shoot for the stake for colors, but Mike, and Penny, too, refused to give up their red and black, and so Simon said,

Okay, fine, then we'll shoot for the order we go in, which they did, and Simon, blue, got closest and got to go last. Janice stubbed her shot and they wouldn't let her take it again so she, green, had to go first.

Fine with me, she said, lighting up, and slid her Bic lighter into her hip pocket of her shorts with her middle fingertip. I'm glad to go first as in all things.

Yeah we'll see, Simon said, when we all hit you. Mikey could have hit her, sitting there, a sitting duck, but he went past her, like he had his own better strategy. Then Penny hit the first wicket and got caught in the second and wanted to go again, even though she was wicketed, because she had another shot, she thought, from going through the first wicket.

Yeah, but you can't, Simon said, because you're stuck in a wicket, so you have to miss a turn.

But I have another shot, cuz I went through that one, she said again in her sweet little accent, more Southern honey now and manipulative.

Sorry, Simon said, too bad, and stepped right up and hit her through with his ball, and then sent her not too far past the corner wicket, not out of kindness, but where he could get her again after he went through it. Then he hit Janice, and looking like he was thwacking himself on the bare foot, standing on his ball, sent her out, perfect placement, past the far middle wicket for when he went through there. Then he hit Mike and sent him farther out, past the next corner wicket, to wait for him there.

This is no fun, Mikey whined, you're killing us.

On the following Tuesday, as he'd indicated, Judge Word issued his ruling. The courtroom was charged with expectancy,

as if the outcome and drama of this first real face-off would pre-
figure and determine the course and outcome of the whole trial.

He spoke coolly, deliberately, as if reading a fortune cookie
fortune, into the silver egg of his microphone bent on its stem
toward his downturned mouth.

It is my ruling that this court shall allow into evidence all
relevant testimony submitted to the court in reference to the
alleged china serving platter or bowl said to have been missing
from its usual place on the bureau in the front hall of the Curtis
home . . .

At the afternoon session there were suddenly twice as many
sketch artists in the jury box. Though he'd slacked off on his
own drawing in court, lately, after the first little spurt, Simon
got his Aquabee pad from the closet where they let him keep it,
off the room where he ate lunch, and waited for the court officer
every day before going into the courtroom, and he got back to
work, if you could call this work, which for Simon it wasn't,
and it was if anything was. The closet didn't have a shelf in it,
only a bar across for hangers, so he left it on the floor in there.
The afternoon, back to normal, was one long, sluggish delay,
with lots of little delays in between. Nothing happened but the
lawyers up there at the bench arguing, at times talking so you
could half hear them, sometimes joking around, it looked like,
sometimes leaning in and whispering heatedly. Simon drew
them standing there in their few different poses. He drew the
empty prosecutor's table, the high windows with the blinds
pulled up, and the imbricate bare branches like veins, claw tips,
outside one. He drew the judge's head with his bifocals down on
his nose like a beak and his lips pursed together like a woman
librarian, or, Simon thought after he drew it, another beak that
got chopped off, like a nose from an old statue, for being, like,
such a beak.

When the lawyers returned to their tables the day was done,
the gray out the windows gone deeply blue one minute, violet

the next. Zwirner, looking very pleased with himself, chattered quietly and quickly as he put some papers into his briefcase and clicked it shut, while Will Deery, nodding and listening to him assistantly, stuck a stack of documents in a brown accordion folder. Simon tried to listen in, but as it often happened with Zwirner, he spoke cagily quick and low volume, so he could only pick up bits and pieces, which were nothing different, nothing good. Simon felt more comfortable speaking to Will Deery than to Zwirner, which was just as well because Zwirner never seemed to want to talk to Simon either.

We're gonna make a statement out in the corridor, Will Deery told him, then we've got a couple of cars in the alley out back for the quick getaway.

Stick with us, don't say anything, Zwirner added without looking at Simon. He buttoned his suit jacket as he bustled past. Let's go.

Red and Timmy and Anna and the Springers waited in their row for the lawyers and Simon, as they'd been instructed. Reporters jostled for position along the aisle and fired and lobbed questions as the Curtis entourage passed, heads bowed, faces somber, tried, glazed. The lawyers and Simon led the way. In the oak-paneled entry space to the courtroom between double doors they paused to gather themselves. Zwirner spoke like a coach during a break in a game.

That night back in the TV room in Manchester, like the old days, kind of, the Curtises saw themselves on the eleven o'clock news coming out of the courtroom with the crowd all around them. They had dinner, tortellini and salad on plates on their laps in front of the TV, because *The African Queen* was on AMC and Red really wanted to see it. She sat on the sofa closest to the TV and talked during the whole thing, telling stories about what happened behind the scenes during the production, interrupting herself, Oh, wait, wait, when a certain scene or moment came—the waterfall, the locust swarm—and she'd say whole

speeches and sections of dialogue verbatim along with the
movie with the exact intonations and gestures, Katharine Hepburn rolling her eyes and Humphrey Bogart weirdly baring his
upper teeth.

The news came on after, and there they were coming out of
the double doors into America's living room.

Tshah! Simon blurted out when he first saw himself like
skulking between Will Deery and Zwirner. It wasn't the first
time he'd seen himself on TV, but this time had the punch of
a real scene, and the others were there for him to react to.
Zwirner made his fumbling little speech as Simon behind him
looked slowly around the room like a loose cannon. Behind him
was Red in her dark oval shades, and Timmy and Anna hidden
back there, in and out of view. The next clip showed the little
scuffle outside the elevator, but you couldn't see what happened—only that it was crowded and hard for them to get
through, and before Simon grabbed the guy's wrist it cut away
back to the reporter guy talking out on the courtroom steps,
people behind looking toward the camera, light traffic headlights flowing by behind them. The reporter said that the judge
had made a significant ruling on the admissibility of some evidence, which legal experts suggested was in the defense's favor.

Why don't they tell what the ruling was? Timmy asked out
loud.

Keep it simple, Red answered from her position closer to the
TV, at the same time that Anna, beside her, said, Because, huns,
the proper explanation would take longer than they have time
for in those few sound-bite seconds. They have to be selective.

Yeah but then they go on later about like André the seal in
Boston Harbor or a skunk in someones's garbage—

Viewers like their human interest stories, Simon chipped in,
just like they like their murder story and then a little politics
and the sports and the weather. A little shocked, no one
responded. They're programmed to have their same little news

meal every night, he went on, like the same menu, but different things, but same portions, each night at exactly the same time.

Still no one said anything. Timmy was livid and appalled. Simon, spouting off like that, Mr. Carefree Know-It-All Defend*ant* Celebrity now.

They need their fix, he concluded, TV's a total addiction.

As Red cleaned up the dishes in the kitchen, Simon sat at the table and Timmy stood on a chair, opened the paned cabinet, and lifted out one of the china serving dishes. He held it there in the air.

This is the one Sandy and Gail were talking about, he said. It was the platter they used for roast beef and turkey for formal meals out in the dining room.

Yeah that or the other one, Simon pointed to the rounder mate inside the cabinet, leaning up against the wall, held upright by the little strip of wood on the shelf put there just for that.

Red headed out of the kitchen and paused in the passage across from the phone, where she took from the upper shelf a green bowl they always had but never used.

This is the one you meant, she said to Timmy. You mixed it up in your mind with the bowl that was out there. The sides of the bowl she held were large ceramic leaves, the veins like veins on a human hand.

I know, I didn't mean *that* one.

No I know, she replied, what I mean is you combined two different bowls in your mind.

They agreed that the missing bowl was definitely a bowl, and that it was strange and typical how people could be so certain when they were so wrong.

It's pure emotional: Timmy's theme. Standing again on the chair, he put the bowl back in with its blue family. He moved the chair over and lifted another bowl out of the next cabinet. It was like this one, he said. Same vintage or whatever, same type, like Ming, but different shape, and gold rim.

A lot like that one, Red laughed. Like exactly like that one: like that's it.

Timmy put the bowl back, got a beer from the fridge, cracked it, and sat down at the table.

You shouldn't drink, Simon said. You're an alcoholic just like Dad. You think you're not but you are.

Timmy didn't look back at Simon, but stared through the table in a spell of heated self-control, concentrating on not responding and not getting mad, which he was, totally, but he kept it in, or kept trying to. A cigarette, he felt like, would be really good right about now.

What about, he said, changing the subject—or rather staying on the subject and veering around Simon—Ginny? First she just disappears without a word, and now she's taken sides against us. What's her problem?

Nothing new, Red said, blowing mini ripples across her tea reflection, fingers bonily cupping the mug.

It's true, Timmy agreed. It's like she was always against us, and now she has a reason, a cause, whatever.

Yeah, now it's *offi*cial, Simon joined in, strangely stressing the *fish.* Timmy realized at this instant that Simon was stoned. He had that smile, the overly glad grin, his eyes were red and had that glaze and gleam.

Before going to bed they watched Letterman together, same siblings and same seating arrangement as Sundays twenty-five, thirty years ago, watching Ed Sullivan in the evening after dinner with their treats and a spoon, do not spill, ginger ale and ice cream sodas, Mum and Dad.

Dave had a new hair deal he joked about, curly but short, the bangs cut straight across but jagged. Julia Roberts was on. Red knew her, they were in that cowgirl movie *Durango* together, with Susan Sarandon and Tim Robbins—when those two met and first got together—him acting like Jimmy Stewart, earnest, tall, effectual sheriff, almost a goofball, good guy, bending the rules in the end and letting the girls, bawdy barmaid hookers turned vigilantes, go, to help catch—

Dave looks like that guy on the cover of *Mad* magazine, Simon said.

Alfred E. Neuman, Timmy, in Dad's place, piped in, legs crossed, like Dad. Simon sat on the TV side of the same couch, where Red was before.

Her hair looks good, at least, Red croaked, lowering her magazine for a sec to reveal her head slumped into her shoulders where she lay on the other couch, as on a stretcher at the end of some devastation, feet where Mum sat, leafing through magazines.

Is David Letterman mean like he seems? Timmy asked her.

No, he's perfectly nice, she murmled, except he takes your hand and won't let go of it.

Red had been on Letterman five or six times, once in a really short dress he kept commenting on, the way he keeps going back to something from before when he doesn't know what else to say, or to cut off the flatness of what's being said, especially when it's a babe, which Red officially was. Though she'd said a few things about it, like how nervous and pretty grumpy but also really nice Dave was in real person, beyond that she acted like she did with most of her work and her life—she kept it mostly to herself and didn't say much.

Red didn't tell Simon because she didn't want it to go to his head, but the week he got arrested and it was all over the national news, she learned from a writer at Letterman, a friend who was an old boyfriend and who since married a friend of hers he went out with right after her—they overlapped a bit, in fact, but Red forgave them—that they had a joke about Simon they wanted to use that wasn't very nice. They had a number of them, and at least one was going to make it into the monologue. The head writer and Marty, the producer over on the side with his Evian water, really wanted to have the joke in the monologue—the story was huge news and totally ripe for picking, an itchy scab just hanging out there—but Dave refused to scratch. Not because he thought the joke was in bad taste, but because it involved someone he knew, sort of, and liked. He couldn't, or didn't say why, but he refused, even though they had it on the cue cards. Red suspected the main joke was the old boyfriend's, this sweet but bitter sweetheart Ray, a real drinker, bye, Ray. He called, but wouldn't tell her what the one joke was, or any of the others.

Later, though, when Simon's personality began to weirdly emerge and in a subtle pervasive way started taking over the trial and the players and the overall story—it wasn't so much about Red anymore, definitely wasn't about Dad, and no longer really seemed to be about murder, or death—and everyone in the country and who knows who beyond was talking about Simon the shaman versus Simon the psycho, then Dave had a change of heart, and felt the whole circus was ripe for ridicule, Red or no Red, and he let 'em rip without restraint—just without mentioning her. Though even then his vicious heart wasn't really in it, just his glibber muscle, that acid slaphappy reflex, like a tongue that snapped flies out of the cultural conversation, and, cynical sandman, spat the crunchy mean little laugh proteins back out over the millions of still-awake sleepyheads. To his credit, Dave tried to contact Red when he decided to go ahead with the jokes, but she was out of the country. Her people said they'd give her the message, and they did, she got it, but didn't bother to call him back. The old boyfriend Ray also sent her a cryptic e-mail, part warning part greeting part poem. Simon saw every show around this time and didn't mind the jokes. He thought they were pretty funny, some of them, and he came out looking pretty good, actually. This was his time in the pop realm and he sort of liked it, though he knew it would pass and go away, but also that it never would go away. This kind of saturation lasted your whole life because the minds it went into were all alive at the same time and so you'd only die with them. The chorus of eyes and minds behind you sense but never see, except in a glint glimpse, of the like magnitude of the multitude. Millions blinking off the end of a generation like fireflies or candle flames, lights in city buildings late at night, going out gradually, one after another, unnoticed, but steadily, till they're all out, except for a couple of floors lit solid, and it's the black flight block sleep of unpiloted thought building amazing emotional images out of layered loss before dawn, when, blushing gray into colors seeping up, the city rawly awakens, another batch of daily lives unleashed, another reeling century of avid, sold civilization—

After the pathetic news, this tabloidy movie star show was on, and after talking to Richard Gere in a tux for about two seconds, or more like chasing him with the camera and questions while he went, sort of smiling and blinking, from some lobby and ducked into a waiting limo, it was Red, sitting in a deep couch in some paintingless Sheetrock living room with cushions and the empty gazillionaire afternoon beach in the background out the plate glass. She looked thin, but not glamorous thin, like she thought, with her legs crossed and her arms crossed on her lap, lifting to speak, but more like gaunt and shriveled from within, like a dried apple, though she wasn't there yet, and a Baltimore Orioles cap with her hair up in it, except for some careful casual squiggles down on either side, more on one side.

They asked her why her name was Red, like they always did, and she said it was better than green, which she'd been saying since she was like six, and then gave the rest of the same old answer,

My hair's red, and then reached up for evidence, but *oops,* there was nothing there but the strands, which she twirled in her fingers.

Your hair's blond, said the guy with poufed blond hair as dyed as hers. We all know that.

Yeah, but it's really red, she said, sounding just like Mum.

They cut to an ad and Simon went and got some more Super Chunks, the last row, and a glass of Janice and Mal's pink lemonade in a pitcher on the top shelf of the refrigerator. Red he thought for sure was in New York; who knows when that show was taped? There was always this barrier between him and whoever, and when he wanted like to call them, he couldn't, and sometimes it lasted for days, easily, without talking to anyone, and sometimes weeks, or all winter, pretty much.

Is Red Curtis there?

Who is calling, please? A foreign accent, he couldn't tell a man or a woman or what country. Eastern Europe or like Russian.

Her brother.

There was a muffled pause, then sounds in the room of life, and after a long time a few footsteps came near, and Red said,

Hello? a little annoyed.

Hi Red, it's Simon.

Hi, Si. Her singsongy sweetness bugged him.

Hi. He didn't know what else to say. How're you doing?

I'm doing fine, then she spoke to someone in the room half a voice away. He pictured her in the room she was just in on TV, except night. Sorry, she came back. I'm doing well. What's up?

I don't know, I'm just calling.

Are you in Maine?

Yup.

How is it, who's up there?

Well it's good, right now I'm over in Rockland at my friends', where I'm renting a room like in their barn.

Why are you there? She said something to the person in the room again and quickly came back. Why not North Haven, sweetie?

Well, I was there, but Dad kicked me out. He punched on the TV again and put the sound on mute.

Why? There were squiggles of sound in the background on the line flying crazily around. He had that sunken feeling of: there's so much energy everywhere in the world, how do you match up to it?

Beats me. Doesn't want me there.

What did you do?

Nothing. He just wants it all for himself.

Oh, Simon, I'm sorry.

Yeah, well, I wouldn't really want to be there with the guy anyway if he's like that.

Did you have a fight about something?

Nope, he just told me to leave.

Oh Si, I'm sorry.

Her saying that again gave him a surprise like rise of crying, constricting behind where you gulp, and tears pushed close, and he froze and didn't say anything, except a little,

'Hanks.

Are you okay? she said into the silence and the faraway squiggles of sound, like his sperm curlies he sees all the time in the air. He kind of coughed and answered,

Yeah I'm fine, fast, in one run-on word like Chinese, then changed the subject. I just saw you on TV.

Oh, she fake laughed. What did you think?

I don't know, that show's pretty stupid.

Yeah it is.

But you were good.

Thanks, sweetie.

Again there was a pause that this time sounded the end, which he filled with,

So are you coming up to Maine sometime?

Why should I? she shot back, and this volley sort of echoed between them over another pause neither of them filled this time. Later it kept coming back, like a personal pinch that wouldn't go away, and he said back to her in his head, a bunch of times,

Same reason you do every year and have all your life.

Listen, sweetie, I should go, they're roasting a pig or something out back, and a man's voice swimming by, or waiting right there, said,

A *producer*, and laughed, and Red signed off with,

I really should go, but thanks for calling.

Kay.

Bubbeye.

Bye.

He stepped out into the wet lawn in his bare feet, to go back to the barn, and through the pall of night out there and right here he felt the pull of winter, always there in Maine, lying low in the cool corners, the indigo shadows, and in the blue-black sky, partly cloudy, partly starry, tonight, a kind of rising and falling depth, like a threat, for some reason, this great night radiance, sad and supple and reaching as the dying-for-love soul of a motherless boy-man.

He was set up under the trees to paint the barn and a funny thing happened that never happened to him before. While he was looking the barn into a seen thing, with its old guy personality sagging there, like it died there, but not quite, like it could make it on its crumbling last legs through the end of the century, and as he painted it into its lagging, lovely self, like an old, swayback horse, he kept seeing where he was, too, right then, under the tree with the swing, as he saw it from his place in the barn, and how he would paint it, and so by the side of the barn, where it was just some bushes to the fence, he stuck it in, two paintings in one, so instead of just seeing the barn and painting that, it was like the barn was seeing him back and including that in itself, except without him there, just the swing, empty. And the weird thing was it was easier to do the tree and swing than the barn part he was looking right at. It was like it was being seen through him, and all he had to do was paint it, without thinking or deciding anything, just do it. Painting was always by itself, in a way, like this, but not like this where he didn't even see what it was he was painting, except as it came out in the painting, and it came out great. This deep, luscious shade, like you could go in there, instead of the dark barn, and go deeper that way into the sweepy cool of another world.

He thought they were coming home in a couple of days, but there was Janice in the metal touch sound of the back screen door clicking open and shutting, but only her. She came over to him and said hi and lit a cig.

How's it going out here, Simon?

Okay.

He glanced up but didn't really look at her. She sat on the board seat of the swing and smoked, getting a grip in the pauses between drags. How's it going for you.

Not so great, she admitted. Mal got tanked over the weekend and last night started getting nasty when I asked him to have dinner with his family if you please, which was why we were here on this little vacation after all? She flicked her butt hard with her thumb, tossing off the ash in an arc. And the cabin wasn't so great itself. There was this creaky ol' hand pump that splashed into the sink instead of running water.

He nodded but made no comment.

So Mal's still at the lake cabin with the kids. Simon didn't say anything. I just had to get away. I mean Mal, when he gets like that, she sighed, and those kids sometimes, too, I'm sorry.

He's an alcoholic, Simon said. That's bad news.

Yeah, I guess, she sighed. I took the car and left them there with a note without one, but there are lots of cars and folks at the other cabins if anything happens. Tomorrow I'll go back and get them . . .

Not I guess, Simon insisted, he *is*. It's like my father. You just have to see that that's what the person is. Everything else falls under that.

Janice skidded her sandals in the dirt patch under the swing and came to a stop.

I'm glad you're here, Simon—but I thought you were out on the island now.

Yeah, no, my father's still there, so, he gripped his teeth together, closing the statement, and his jaw muscles bulged off his cheekbones like a horse.

So you've been having a hard time with your father?

Not a hard time, Simon spat back. Just he's a jerk.

Why, what happened? She pressed her hands and knees and feet together.

Well first he doesn't want me there before he got there, even though the house is sitting there empty, and it's the most beautiful time of year—

I know this part, she put in gently.

And then now that the house is open, because with his new rules there's a time when it's open and a time when it closes, or that's what he thinks—Simon's eyes leapt around. But so now when he's there he tells me to leave.

But I mean, I guess, what's the *larger* story? she asked. It seems like you have a lot of animosity towards him, not just from this, right?

Tchya, he splurted, 'hat's for sure.

But why, Simon? What's it all about?

Simon breathed like a bull out his nose.

Okay, you want to hear the whole thing? He said it fiercely, like a threat, but it didn't faze her, and she replied,

Yessure, okay.

Okay, Simon sighed, exasperated but working himself up to

it. First of all he's been a drunk all my life and like a total space-man instead of a father. And then after my mother died it really went downhill.

That was what, she asked, gently Southern again, about ten years ago?

Fifteen. And he killed her.

What?

Yeah, he killed her.

I thought she got hit by a train in her car.

Yeah, well, that's what happened, but there's more to it.

What do you mean?

Simon looked at her straight with his shoulders going slack, but his eyes unusual.

Look, I know some things nobody else knows or wants to know.

He picked at the crimped ferrule of his paintbrush and scraped away a scab of dried orange paint, while Janice peered at him, worried, holding on tight to the two ropes of the swing like she might turn into a little girl, or take off straight up. She felt a warp of reason and pain blend and bend the moment.

Like what?

Okay, you wanna know?

Well yes. She wasn't sure she wanted to know, but went ahead and said yes, and added, It sounds like something you need to talk about.

Okay, my father?

He breathed in and let out a derisive *pphunh.* He pulled a tight odd smile.

Okay, when my mother died? I know for a fact she couldn't stand it anymore with him, and told him if he didn't stop drinking she'd kill herself—

You mean she did it on purpose.

Yup, and he knew she was going to do it because of him, and

didn't stop her, but by not doing anything he like dared her to go ahead and do it.

Wow, Simon. Really?

Yup. He picked at a zit bump, not really a zit yet, on his neck under his ear.

That's horrible. She said it like *whore.*

Hi know. He gave it a squeeze and winced. But that's just what he's like, he just goes right along in his track no matter what anyone else thinks. He's totally selfish, like a spoiled little kid.

But Simon. She didn't want to pry in such a delicate, combustible place, but it was either say something, or not, and so she did. If she killed herself, then isn't she the one who did it, not him?

Nope, it's him, Simon said, flatly acid. But that's probbly just how he rationalizes it, too, letting himself totally off the hook and feeling all sorry for himself—

Wow, Simon. She didn't know what to think or say, but for the moment was caught up in this constricted zone of someone else's roiled emotions, different from your average situation. The sun slipped out from behind a puffy pillow island and, like God appearing, or happiness arriving, lit the yard he was painting, and lit the painting. What a terrible thing to carry around inside you.

Hi know, he breathed. But that's not all. His face went set like exertion on the wane. I have lots more on him too.

She didn't want to ask, and didn't, but shut the flow of the Simon stuff, and brought it back to the more normal here and now with,

But so you're heading back out to the island, what, her intonation a careful friendly question, not pushy, tomorrow or the next day?

Yeah, well, if it's okay.

Whatever you want's fine, Simon, really, I'm just wondering because tomorrow I'm going back to pick up Mal and the kids.

Really, you're driving all the way back up there? Simon stood with his legs way apart to get down to just the right level on his canvas, starting in on that again.

It's only two hours—she got up, setting the swing into slow motion—and it's a beautiful drive.

Yeah, I like driving, said Simon, who hardly ever drove. It's like thinking.

The fatherly way is forward, onward, and the ferry plowed its way ahead like a whale reined in by its wake, with Simon, its third eye, standing at his place on the balcony. A man with skinny legs and shorts to his knees and a yellow slicker and a purple cap stood up at the bow chain with his son, Simon thought at first, wearing a hood, but it turned into his wife with shaved legs, the way she stood and shifted and faced him, sideways at attention, her face hidden in the hood.

It was chilly up there, but you stayed up on the balcony. Maybe he'd make a fire when he got home, he thought almost on purpose against Dad, because they hadn't had a fire there for years, like legally, since Dad took the stovepipe away and laid down the law, no more fires, after the one time there was a chimney fire, but Simon had had fires in there plenty of times since then, he knew where the pipe was, in the back of the sail locker, behind old oars with leather tacked around their middles for the oarlocks, and all you had to do was stick the piece of pipe in between the stove and the wall and it worked fine. There was no danger of another chimney fire and burning the house down, like Dad was paranoid about, because it wasn't a real chimney fire, before, from buildup in the chimney, but just soot right there inside the elbow of the black pipe going into the wall, that caught and smoldered and backed up into the room, filling it densely, fast, with coughy smoke, and it seemed like a big disaster, so the alarm in the middle of the island went off, and the old fire engine came, and all the island guys, like in a dream, lined up along the fence along the street at the top of the stairs, waiting to spring into action if they had to, but only a couple of them came down inside and took care of the problem, by pulling out the pipe with pink towels around it like potholders, and bringing it, smoking like a big bent cannon, outside onto the dock, and knocking the burning crust out from inside, over the railing into the water, where it hissed with steam and sank in slaggy chunks. Eric Hooper held a hand mirror in the opening in the black hole in the wall to check up the chimney, and it was fine, no smoke no fire, hardly any buildup, just a little square of blue sky, like a mini postcard, in his hand.

There against the ferry balcony railing was Eric's and also Simon's cousin (his cousin's kid) Bear. He was only like fifteen, sullen, but still with the good goofiness of a kid.

Hey, Bear, Simon said.

Hi, said Bear in a pretty deep Mainer voice that seemed older than his string bean body and his furry little light-colored caterpillar mustache.

A woman came up the stairs, her curly head, then her body, then her daughter in a Patagonia pullover and braces and her curly hair in a loose ponytail. Simon, at the railing, glanced at them, but also sort of past them, as they passed behind him to go to the bench. The daughter was cute and noticed and liked it that Simon noticed her, she looked down with her long lashes.

Bear slouched at the railing, sea sights ticking by in his eyes. Simon spoke to him,

So are you going to the school on the island these days, or back in Massachusetts?

Here this year, his rs more like hs—Heah this ye-ah.

So is that like going against your mother, or . . .

That woman could argue the sky beam blue—he rolled his

eyes—but yuh, she 'greed—he rolled his eyes again—'s long as
I go to *college*—

Then he said what he wanted to tell Simon the whole time. I
went, y'know, and checked out your brother's village out on
Burnt Island after that storm last October.

The hurricane you mean?

Well it didn't hit here really a real hurricane, but it sure was
one wicked storm.

We got one down in New Orleans last year shut the city
down without power and flooded streets for like four days.
Roofs ripped off and cars and dogs flying through the air—

Cars?

Practically. Floating . . .

Flying dogs.

Yup. Simon looked back at the girl biting her fingernail.
Ever see one?

Bear bit at his lip and kicked his heel with his heavy construction boot, way frayed through the cuff in the back from
being too long and like, teenager.

Well, we got hit pretty bad, and I went out to Burnt Island
to check your brother's little village, I told him, and what a hell
of a storm it was for *it,* if you think about it, maybe times *ten*!
He spat spray as he got excited. But I'll tell you, that little village was still standing, even the wharf with them little sticks
sticking into the rocks.

Mmnh, was all Simon had to say to that. He hadn't actually
seen Timmy's village, and actually didn't really care if he ever
did.

Bear looked at Simon like he had a question to ask him he
didn't want to ask. Simon thought maybe he was imagining it
and looked over his shoulder at the girl again, and she saw him,
but acted like she didn't and kept talking to her mother, who
nodded slowly, reading her magazine.

So you must be some pissed off 'bout Burnt Island, Bear

said, and Simon looked over at him, thought for a second, and said,

What do you mean? He thought he meant the cabin. They're not going to wreck the house anymore, he said. It's—

I know that, Bear blurted. It was us was gonna do it!

Simon shrugged and sort of scowled, like, *What, then?*

I'm talking about they're giving the island away.

That's what you said last summer Bear, Simon said softly with a little sneer.

Well that's cuz it was true then, too. They just hadn't done it yet.

I don't think so.

You don't know? It's *true.* Bear pleaded as if it were him on the line. They already did it. You don't *know??* Gave it to the town of North Haven, for *free!*

How do you know?

Because I *know!* he gasped. I was right there the whole time it's been happening, right along with my dad.

They already did it? Simon made a face with a skeptical mouth, squinting the sun dots bouncing on the water into molten sparkles.

Ask my pa!

Simon looked at him like, you don't know.

I swear! You'll see.

Simon didn't believe Bear while they were talking, but he kind of did, and after Bear went below, he knew it was true. Coming around the anchorage into the landing Simon saw the figure of Dad in his light blue work shirt and long shorts pass into the dark underpass, and he wondered why the middle living room window was open.

Over a week later Simon saw Bear and his father, Bear, down at the Landin' gettin' a burger, and little Bear, taller than his father, but skinnier by half, talked about Burnt Island, and Big

Bear said yup, it was all true, those fucking assholes. The afternoon ferry was unloading right then and Dad was on it, getting off, and drove right past them in Ginny's Acura, with her beside him in big Jackie O sunglasses and a handkerchief on her head, without either of them noticing him.

The next day Simon woke to the knocking again, like Dad had never left. Sometimes in his dreams Mum had never died and she'd be there, just like her regular self, and in other dreams it was like she was dead but she was back for just a little while, like a day or a weekend or just a couple of hours, like the one he just had right now. She was happy to see him, but was like all business, rushing around cleaning up and making phone calls and writing things down, because she had only this little time. But she was happy to see him and gave him a big hug and wouldn't let go, and so he didn't either, and he woke up to Dad, the opposite, down there knocking *wake up, go away and stay away* in annoying knock language. Simon pulled on his pants and shirt and went through the bathroom and the middle house and out the other bathroom and up Dad's ramp to the street, not stopping or making a sound as he came outside, and saw the door to Dad's upstairs open, with Ginny in there somewhere doing whatever she did all day indoors, she never went outside. The back to Dad's station wagon was open, and in there with a couple of full garbage bags was the old cobbler's bench Ma, Dad's mother, used to have for a coffee table between the wicker couch and the window seats. It was the coolest old table with cubby boxes like a little building, little drawers on one side, and the middle work-worn wood worn concave smooth like an old stair, but deeper, from pounding, and a hard leather surface on the other side pulled tight and nailed in there like one of those ancient Irish boats, coracles, they used to make with skins and tar, almost like the rowboats Dad made, actually, and now Dad was throwing it away, just throwing it out, it was so typical, and for some reason this got Simon more like inflamed than the whole Burnt Island thing, though not really, really that was it, but it seemed that way in the immediate impact, how it hit him. He pulled it out of the back of the car and carried it like a little coffin down the stone stairs and went right into the middle house with it to Dad in there, surprised, but not really, by his abrupt entrance.

Simon.

Are you throwing this away?

I didn't know you were here.

I can't believe you're throwing this away.

When did you arrive?

You're throwing this away?

Dad looked down at what he was doing, lining up strips of wood on a long piece of wax paper to glue them together with this totally toxic butterscotch gunk. The boat out in the passage was getting there, covered with the stuff, and looked like a big caramel dessert. He hated being put in the position all the time where he was opposed by Simon, and in turn had to oppose him back, when really, much of the time, he didn't want to oppose him, but the problem was, he just didn't know how to deal with him, and really, in the end, would simply rather not.

I love this thing, Simon said, holding the cobbler's bench just inside the doorway with his feet apart and his head cocked to one side, Dad with his belly up against the table, fresh little splash splats of resin on his shirt. I'll take it if you're throwing it away.

Dad breathed measured composure, looking down through his glasses like the problem was clearly laid out there on the table—if only.

If you want it, it's yours, but you will have to take it away with you, not leave it here.

Okay but I'm just going to leave it in here for now, he stepped toward the door.

You are not leaving it here.

Not *here,* I mean out here behind the curtain.

The curtain was gone on this side of the house, but the open closet by the door to outside was storage mostly for Dad's overflow, or old leftover stuff, like a tiller and an old canvas golf bag, collapsed, like some old golfer's sock, the two old club shafts the golfer skeleton.

So long as it doesn't stay here, Dad looked back to the strips of wood that never talked back—though the boat was experiencing some difficulties, actually, though nothing insurmountable. The boat, indeed, was almost done.

Simon stuck the cobbler's bench on the floor by some boat cushions with Mum's Magic Marker writing on them, CURTIS, hi Mum, look what Dad's trying to pull now, and put the cushions on top of it, half hiding the thing. Going out and up the stairs to the street, even though he won, he had this feeling of total outrage, still, that Dad was throwing it away. He threw away tons of junk from their rooms and from the back of the house in Manchester in this big purge, part of Ginny's whole like plastic purge, there and in the houses up here, suddenly all the ship-print wastebaskets turned into plastic like canisters, the Mum Merimekko curtains were replaced with cutesy bed-and-breakfast floral prints or whatever, and without telling anyone, and it was like a massacre of their past when they found out, and it took years to find out what was missing, still they didn't know the extent of it, like old photo albums with all the pictures in them, files full of drawings and paintings, their whole childhood . . . The cobbler's bench, sitting there in the closet, half hidden, wasn't safe from Dad, he knew, and he went beeline to Dad, still drip-painting sticky resin syrup over his strips of wood stuck together, laminated pretty lamely, like making a big hockey stick blade, except fat as a ski boot and kind of wacky. This was the bow? There was a pad of small white notepaper on the table, and Simon took a little whittled-down nub Dad pencil, and wrote in his roundish, clear, seventh-grade handwriting:

I give this table
to Simon and now
its hereby his.

He gave it to Dad and said,
Here, sign this.
What's the meaning of this? Dad glanced at the note.
Nothing, just proof.
Proof.
Just that you're giving it to me, I want to make sure.
Don't be ridiculous, but he signed it, sort of scratched his linear signature, and put the pad on the table. Simon tore it off the pad and went out with it, feeling like now he won, and went in to show Timmy, who didn't know what he was talking about, till he explained the whole thing, twice, including Burnt Island and the will—how really it was left to them, the grandchildren—all spun together, by sort of overflow mistake, and his only reaction was,

Simon, you're crazy. He was reading a magazine and didn't want to even look up and get sucked in, but did, he couldn't help it, because he couldn't believe this, though yes he could. So what's that for? he asked.

Proof, Simon said.

Proof of what, Simon? Timmy shook his head. That's pathetic.

Proof he gave it to me and it's mine.

Proof to who?

Proof to me.

But what for? he half laughed. In case you forget later?

Legal.

What, in case you go to court?

Yup.

What, you're going to take Dad to court?

Maybe.

Why?

Sue him.

Sue him? For what?

Lots of things. You'll see.

Like what?

Like this, he flapped the paper.

You're going to sue him for a table he gave you?

Yeah, maybe. If he tries to take it or throw it away.

You're going to sue him for a table he just gave you.

Yup, and for other things.

Like what?

Mum's lawsuit and Ma's will, but those are just part of it.

Part of what?

Burnt Island.

Simon, you're crazy.

That's what you think, Simon said with his gathered incrimination going back into him. But if anything happens I have this, you'll see.

He folded the paper and put it in his pocket and went back outside, knowing he was right, and wanting, in a tense, almost muscular way, to prove it, crush something and break out of this little island head trap, whose tricky like rusted springs and deadly clamp were permanent properties of his whole lifelong life. It was much more than just this one little thing, it was everything, and he felt it closing in on Dad, the source, and even culminating in Timmy, too, just then, the way he just dismissed it, and him, he was an idiot. Out in the passage he looked at Dad's boat and felt like every square inch of it was Dad, kind of botched just like him. Out by the box there was the man himself, inside the window, and he stepped away out of view as Simon went toward him, then came back again as

Simon got there, so they were facing each other with the window between them, the bottom half all the way open, like a fraction, empty below, except filled with Dad's belly, inside, and though there was double glass between their double nominator heads, face-to-face, with Dad a little higher, inside, Simon could see and hear him perfectly when he said, all like quavery, Simon you're rude and impertinent, and I don't want you around here, and with that he began to close the window, but Simon reached up and stopped it with a firm grip and stiff arm.

Oh, no you don't, he said, don't try and shut me out. And holding the window open, with Dad standing there, wax Dad, he felt like he had to say something more, so he said, I know what you do in there. Even though it was still whole high day out, and Dad didn't drink in the day, Simon knew Dad knew what he was talking about. Now that he'd started, and he felt like Dad started it, anyway, he felt like this was it, he let her rip.

You think you can have your own private little world in there where you can hide from the world and drink and do your little things, but you can't get away from me.

Dad stood there, a little above him, without moving, looking back at him through the glass with a serious, contorted brow expression. He still had his hand on the top of the window, and Simon, stiff-arm, kept his on the bottom, keeping it open in case Dad tried to push down. They looked into the trouble in each other's eyes, and Dad started to turn away, and Simon, not very loud, but hard and clear, commanded,

Don't walk away from me, and Dad, for some reason, obeyed, after a little hesitation, and stepped back in view and stood there. He stuck his hands deep in his pockets, looking down, and asked,

What's wrong with you, Simon? more mildly, a real question, than arguing back.

You're what's wrong with me, without missing a beat. You, and you know perfectly why.

I'm sure I don't know what you're talking about. Dad, though uncomfortable, visibly perturbed, seemed ready to hear him out.

I'm sure you do. Simon looked at him brutally, like he was ripping through him and seeing all the worst stuff. Dad remained glued to the spot, waiting for him to go on. You know, but I'll tell you, because you're such in denial, you don't even know what you know, but I do, and you know it—

Simon—

Like okay, he tilted his head and stuck out his index finger like a gun, number one. Like Ma's will, for one.

Simon, please—

That money I never got, and the stocks everyone else got. And the money from Mum's lawsuit, which you never should have settled for so little, anyway, I know why you—

I've told you many times, I gave you that money, and a lot more, the many times you asked me for money, and I sent you a full accounting—

Well I talked to the lawyer, and he said that money was ours, all of it, not just the little bit you gave out, but you're keeping it to leave to us in your will, to make it look like you're leaving money to us, when really it's already mine.

This is preposterous—

Yeah, sure, and I know why you settled out of court. You knew they'd find out.

I don't have to lis—

I know you killed Mum.

This really stunned Dad, and Simon read that as direct incriminating proof. A kid with stringy long hair and his painter's cap on backward walked by with stooped shoulders and looked at them as he passed. Dad's disconsolate horseshoe mouth tightened as if on a drawstring. Simon saw the expression as snobby, like an English butler, like up the butt, rather than the leonine contortion of terrible distress it was.

Why don't you go back where you came from? he said and tried to lower the glass guillotine between them, but Simon held it up, and so he walked away into the recesses of his day-dark workshop.

Yeah, go ahead and walk away, Simon said to the air, and answered him later a hundred times,

This *is* where I come from.

He forgot, in the heat of his attack, to include Burnt Island in his charges. But Dad knew what he'd done, and it was unbelievable to Simon that he'd go ahead and give it away, and not even say anything, unbelievable, but he could believe it, that's what was so fucked, that's what Dad was like. He went in to tell Timmy, but he wasn't in there, so he went upstairs and found him.

Shhhh. He was just putting the baby down. The baby's perfect little legs rested together like restaurant breads in a napkin nested in a basket. Timmy had on a T-shirt with sleeves to the elbow, and hadn't shaved. He wouldn't look at Simon.

I just want to tell you something serious I know you want to know.

Simon, please whisper, at least, Timmy said, more almost intimate than the usual annoyed, and so Simon did whisper.

So I just talked to Dad, okay, and Dad just—he held on for a second, letting his breath and his words calm down and catch up with him, as Timmy gestured with his head outta here, and so they filed like a ritual out onto the balcony. Pope Simon the Pissed could have cared less if Dad the father were down there, below, but anyway he wasn't. Brother Timmy looked a little ragged out in the daylight, like he'd definitely been drinking last night, but he was in an okay mood, squinting with his forearms resting on the railing, his hands hanging limp, one with a freshly lit cigarette with a string of smoke going up that squiggled when his thumb flicked the filter a few quick, light, unconscious times in a row.

Y'know it's true they're giving away Burnt Island, Simon said, deciding without deciding to go with that, and keep the Dad confrontation to himself.

That's what you said last year. Timmy's face was tipped back, his eyes closed to the wan sun deciding between white day and sunny noon, maybe soon.

Yeah wool they already did it. Simon sat on his side of the balcony leaning back in his chair.

Timmy tasted this info, tainted, no doubt, by Simon's distortion disease, and though he didn't believe it, he didn't like it. He opened his eyes to see a normal family down on the far dock lift canvas bags, a cooler, and a picnic basket into an Aquasport.

How do you know? Silky blue smoke strands disappeared upward. The day was calm.

Cuz I talked to Bear. Simon's big inside source.

Bear, or—which Bear?

Both.

They gave it to the town of North Haven, and the town accepted it, and it's done.

Simon's jaw muscles bulged, and he shook his head, blazing. Timmy didn't react to the news, but to Simon, and his reaction was to close his eyes again, and soak in the semi-sun. He took one good last tug and flicked his butt out in a propellered arc down to the water, where it hiss-kissed when it touched. If this was true, which he doubted, siding with Simon against it made it more acceptable, weirdly, not as a fact or act he could easily accept, but as something he'd want to just let be, if fighting it, or whatever, meant siding with Simon.

Mum used to call Simon Blister when he was a little kid, and you had to wonder if it wasn't her death or any one thing that happened or could change, but that he was just born like that, and this was just how he was and ended up. Sometimes he seemed fine, if a little weird, or kinda scary, eccentric but original, and truly an artist, in the classic cliché of the artist who can't get along with people, and so society, and so is a penniless loner drifter loafer who doesn't wash or work or talk to others, much, and the only thing he knows how to do to connect, outside himself and in, is paint. But at other times you looked at him with his bloodshot eyes, a little hollow in their sockets, and their strange or vacant expression, like he's blurred and totally shot inside, like his yolk broke, and the strange little body movements, and the nowhere pattern of his life, lost in the compulsion ride, perpetual repetition, completely alone, and he seemed seriously troubled, like truly mentally ill. Just thinking about him, your brother, like this was painful, let alone dealing with him, let alone siding with him on Burnt Island. Timmy wasn't thinking about Burnt Island, but about Simon, when Simon said sharply,

So what do you *think*? The front two wheelied legs of his chair banged down like punctuation.

I don't know, Timmy said in a dismissive mumble, like another language, the sullen mumble language of disconsolate teenagers.

You're just like Dad, Simon spat back, you don't want to face anything.

Timmy looked at Simon, his loaded, lidded expression, and, shaking his head a little as he got up, tugged open the stuck screen door and went inside.

Yeah, see? Simon said after him. Just walk away, just like him.

And then, right behind Simon's head, the baby inside, as if it were a baby inside him, began to cry and cry, and he couldn't stand it, and so he got up and left the balcony, too. Inside, at the corridor, he crossed paths with Timmy to the rescue, and in his quiet, blue, almost pleasant mood, in spite of Simon, he turned his head to Simon, as he passed, and softly said,

Boo.

· · ·

Of all the stories Pete heard about Simon during his inquiries, sketching in the family and guessing at their relationships, the first one Steven told him stood out. It was typical, classic Simon. In its few strokes it spoke volumes. Steven convinced himself, with Pete's gentle prodding, that telling this story wasn't a breach of his friendship with Simon, since it happened two summers ago, not the previous one in question. And besides, this story was out there on the gossip mill, it wasn't a secret. Timmy had told it to Steven and some other friends, drinking and peeing at night around a big beach fire, soon after it happened.

A friend of Ginny's, some old lady who lived over in Rockport, saw a painting of Simon's on Ginny's wall, and loved it, and wanted one. It was of the Camden Hills, from across the water. Her house was on the coast it depicted, a touch of white in the painting. Ginny told Simon her friend wanted a painting like it, and would commission him to make one. She gave Simon her number, but he didn't call her.

Calling people was something Simon couldn't do. It was one of his problems in life. Even if his life depended on it—which, in a very real way, it *did*—he couldn't do it. Sometimes, after all kinds of agonies and putting it off till way past the zero hour, when he was totally down and out and backed up against the wall of himself, the walls of dire circumstance closing in, he'd work himself up to making the call. But those times were the exceptions. And often it'd be too late. Mostly, usually, he just stuck with himself and whatever came his way or crossed his path.

Anyway, Simon didn't call the woman, and Dad and Ginny couldn't understand why. Supposedly this was how Simon wanted to make a living, and here he was just throwing an opportunity away. There were other examples of the same behavior. They were baffled and frustrated, and annoyed. Ginny and Dad both reminded Simon, but nothing happened. This went on for two years. Finally one day the woman appeared in front of Simon, up in his rooms, when she was visiting Ginny. She told him she'd like to commission him to do a painting like the one Ginny had.

Okay, Simon said. Six hundred dollars.

He got a check for four hundred up front. This was toward the end of the summer. After Labor Day she called him and asked how the painting was going.

Fine, he said, and said he'd get it over to her soon. Actually he hadn't started it yet, but he figured he could whip it off in no time, no sweat. He left in the fall, however, without delivery, and the next spring she called, right after Memorial Day, however she knew he was there, and he said,

Oh yeah, I have it, though of course he didn't. He asked her if she could send him the other two hundred, he could really use it. A check arrived three days later in a baby blue envelope with her address printed on it.

In June, up there alone, he didn't answer the phone, so he wouldn't have to talk to her, or anyone else for that matter. He didn't like answering the phone, anyway, any more than he liked calling, unless he knew someone was calling and knew who it was. He could tell it was her sometimes when it rang into oblivion. Then one night around eight, still light, the water out the windows calm and no one around, she got him. He thought it was going to be John Cabot, who he saw the other day and who'd have some pot.

Yeah, sorry, I still have it here, but I'll give it to you soon, he said and hung up the phone. About a week later she got him again, on the phone, and said she would be out on North Haven the next day and would come by and pick up the painting.

Okay fine, Simon said. Great, he added, upbeat.

When the woman came the next day he gave her the painting, and she gushed over it and said how wonderful it was, she knew just where she was going to put it, and she made a joke like she had begun to think she might never see it. The thing was, the painting he gave her was Ginny's. He took it off the wall in their dining room the day before, blew dust off the top of the frame, then sort of cleaned it, once over, like with his finger, licked. He made a quick sketch of the painting on a blank canvas he had, almost the same size, which he didn't usually do, he just painted it right on, but this was so he could paint the painting again, like in the next week, before Ginny and Dad got up there. He also had a photo of the painting from before, so he could copy it no problem.

He thought, from Timmy, that Dad was coming up after the Fourth, like the fifth or sixth, but actually, surprise surprise, they showed up on July 1, which Simon thought was still June, but he didn't keep track of the days, especially up here. Simon thought, Oh well, so what, she won't ever notice, she's such a space.

But the first thing Ginny noticed when she walked into the house was that the painting was missing. She thought she'd been robbed, which she had. Steven didn't know how Ginny pinned it on Simon—whether he admitted it, or if she called her friend and then confronted him, or got Dad to, or what. But the truth came out, and Dad was bullshit. Ginny was, too. Dad blew up at Simon and told him to leave his house immediately, and that he was not to return, he was no longer welcome or allowed there, he was no longer his son, and he didn't want to see him around again.

So Simon stayed out at John Cabot's, part of the time, while JC was gone during the week, which actually was great for Simon, while it lasted, nice little A-frame cabin, like a barny boathouse in a field, right by the water, in Southern Harbor, really quiet and nice. He also camped out on Burnt Island, which he always did as a last resort, or sometimes just for like a retreat treat. That summer before he did the same thing he did this past summer, he snuck back, when he felt like it, to get things like food, or just be there, and he appeared and stuck around, like now he was allowed to, when someone else in the family, usually Timmy, or Timmy and family, showed up for however long, it was kind of clear for him, then, though he had to be like skittish on his toes, ready to sort of disappear if Dad came around the corner. You could usually hear him coming because you knew his padded tread, with his rubber-soled deck shoes, and he'd let the screen door slam, and he'd cough or like that, somehow announce himself as he came in. Dad saw Simon some of those times in the summer just past, and didn't say anything, or even talk to Simon toward the end of the summer, like everything was normal, or he was semi-forgiven for now.

But so two summers ago Dad stayed bullshit all summer. They'd both veer away if they saw each other in town, and Simon had to be extra careful not to get caught when he was at the house. One day—this was the second half of the story Steven told Pete that time—Ginny was over in the kids' side of the house, getting it ready for someone coming, one of her daughters or Timmy and Anna. Simon was in his room, getting some stuff or maybe touching up a painting by the window, when he heard her coming, too late to leave, so he got under the bed. She came into the room and started changing the bed-sheets, and she saw Simon's sneaker under the bed. When she reached down to get it she saw his hand, then him.

Simon, my God, she said, horrified, blanched. What are you doing under there?

Hiding from you, he answered.

All you have to do is walk and listen to the talk of the trees, smell the subtle cinnamon in the sweet grass while birds practice their music, same few notes over and over, but like variations on a morning theme, or for painting it's just like wind on the water. Simon took his easel, all folded up in itself, and his outdoors kit, and a bag with a bag of pretzels, some beef jerky,

and a big bottle of Sprite, and headed out, his birthright migration route, over the water to Burnt Island, past Mum, in the
Whaler. Someone had the design idea of making the insides of
Whalers the turquoise color of swimming pools, but for some
reason Dad, who was color blind, painted the inside of theirs
yellow, which was now chipping off in places, especially along
the gunwales, and in the bow where you stepped on and off,
and where your feet went under the steering wheel when you
drove, because it wasn't the right kind of paint, and he didn't
use any primer. It was like a map of a country exploded all over
the boat, the different little states and town spots stood out
with a mesmeric lift off the background yellow.

Instead of setting up on Burnt Island he went in kind of a
protest move over to the beach on Calderwood's, across the
water from Burnt Island, which you usually looked at, and
instead, this time, looked at Burnt Island from there, and realized this was why he was here, to look at Burnt Island, like with
a final burning gaze, one last good time, before it was gone,
even though it already was, and really never would be, and
paint it that way, in the like purgatory of the ever-present.

Luckily for us the sun moves slower than we can see, because
otherwise we'd stand around all day watching the changes and
never get anything done, which was how Simon lived, actually,
but for a painter painting on the site you almost do see it move,
and you have to paint around that, anticipate and ignore and
leave certain things, like decide on the shadows for yourself a
little ahead of time, let reality meet them. The island looked
bigger from here than he thought of it as. You could see past
the little house, hidden brown in the trees, the next beach they
never went to, except walking over it, and a pretty long rocky
stretch, with trees coming right down to the rocky like road, to
the point with the osprey's nest on top of the dead tree, where it
turned to the open bay on that side, looking over to Deer Isle
and Stonington. His grandfather bought the island in the thir-

ties for two thousand dollars, and everyone said what do you want an island for, and now it was worth a million dollars Dad just gave away. The middle stretch of woods had a whole gray section going back in of dead fallens, some still standing, lots tipped over. Some tree disease must have wiped them out, but that was just as natural as if they were alive and well, just like fire was natural, or flood or earthquake and death. Nature was these things and all the crazy unseen interconnected processes of life feeding life, not just what you hiked through or what people thought of as nature, like the Discovery Channel in Madagascar—which actually is incredible—Nature was not nice, was the truth of it, and Simon lived closer to nature, in a way, than to people, he was nature, as much as nature was, and definitely more than most people were, except for like Aborigines, or African tribesmen, or how Indians, or really all mankind, used to be.

The jagged treeline he painted faster than he usually did, like it was angry, like a torn crown, and when he looked at it later, like in a few days, and whenever after that, it was incredible how much it looked like fire, except dark, like the negative. And the weird thing was, and he didn't think it was a coincidence, and he didn't think of it now, but how green and orange were the only colors, the only words in his life he mixed up sometimes, when he was talking, he never knew why, it must have been something from when he was learning to speak, or learning colors, or maybe this, now, was why.

The rocks were slanted here at the end of the beach where he was set up, and it made it a little awkward to paint. He had to stand above the easel, farther away from it than he was used to, and with one leg forward, one leg back, to balance, he had to hold his arm straight out to reach the canvas. The tide came in and he had to move up the anchor twice, to keep the boat from banging, and the third time he had to move the easel, it was now in the water, and decided, instead of moving it, to stick it right in the boat, why not, to keep the same angle to the island he was painting, and standing up in it he continued, with the water going up to the sky every once in a while. The boat kept knocking against the rock, so he took in the anchor, pushed off, and floated in the bare little wind straight toward Burnt Island. A gull pumped easy m's above the uneven continuous w of the treeline, then on across the Little Thorofare, and looked down at him skeptically as it went across his bow. Like the horse knows the way, the boat drifted into the painting, going a little left, which was good, right toward the beach and the dock. The house, the cabin, more than halfway across, was less hidden in the trees, now, and the black windows were like dark sunglasses. Simon, done enough, skulled the last little way to the dock, doing it like Dad would, flipping the oar, angled against the stern, standing like a Venetian gondolier, sending out with each thrust two little whirlpools, like sunken tops, spinning away from either side of the oar's blade.

High tide was the best time, by far, on the beach, with the neat curve and the brimful water right there making it narrow as a road, and as gray and smooth, but slanted, and the slight breast swell of the smooth stones, where the first cove scallop overlapped the second half, bent back toward the house and the path up there through the trees, over the meadow with the uneven steps up the rocks.

Inside the cabin were the tar paper and leftover wood and a five gallon container of white paint from the fix-up effort last summer that never quite got finished. In the kitchen the last furniture was crammed in one half the room, stacked high like kindling for a bonfire, and under the sink with no faucets and no pipes was the plastic gas can for the chain saw, though the chain saw was back at home in the sail locker. The other rooms were empty, fixed up as far as it got. He never quite got to it, but he could totally see himself painting in here, this view out the window he'd painted plenty of times, one of the like classic views of his psyche, looking over the beach and up the Little Thorofare to Mum, and past, and all kinds of paintings from all over the island and the bay, finished in here, his studio, his home on earth, it fit perfectly, like his whole life had been leading up to this, and then, rising in him, like losing your temper or mind, the ugly opposite reared its Dad-head—

He can think he can—

The long light coming through the trees in glints, and over the meadow hillside in stretched-out strips, alternating with long shadow stripes, wider in the dry grass, full, at the edges, of goldenrod, was really fall already, it was sad, but it was great, and the full-cheeked clouds the longing light came through closed over it, like a curtain closing, before sunset, taking the best personality of the colors of the day out before the play was finished, and the last scene of the day was like an empty house. The cool huge shadow room of the forest was all tall stillness, with slender black column trees starting to shift and tell and sift the spell of night. Branches creaked like skeptical comments, and stopped. The water below, and spread across, was pearly gray, calm enough to reflect the other island down, a sailboat anchored like in its crook. The far drone of an engine, either a lobster boat or a little plane, riding along the rim of dusk, was the only sound, except crickets, that stopped for a second for a quick breath, or to confer and readjust their violin legs and bows, and then kept going, live, in concert. It was chilly on the edge of the season, with the sun gone, and Simon did a handstand on a flattish driftwood log on the back of the beach, it pumped you up and got you warm in no time, like a jump shot of adrenaline. There was a lot of driftwood collected over in here by the tide, and he didn't want to go home where more of them were now, for the big weekend, so after chucking a few rocks way out there, then skimming some and counting how many times it skipped, the circle-touches, like someone running away, someone small, shrinking as he goes, feathering off to the last dot, he decided to make a fire and stay here for a while longer, or maybe even the night, or go get some food and stuff and come back out here for a few days, till people cleared out back there. So he went back up to the little house to get matches, hopefully, and found a box of Ohio Blue Tips (with the warning on the box, Dad's fatherhood motto, KEEP AWAY FROM CHILDREN) on the shelf over the nice old enameled propane stove, and he grabbed the can of gas, for instant like mega-kindling. Out the window, above the tangled pile of furniture, the wall of firs across the little back clearing was lit at the top, for a moment, by a golden blush of sun coming out, and the color green and the laden cones and the light was so saturated it was incredible, like honey golden, and the spire tops of the trees on the other side of the house made these soldier shadows, lined up different heights, up the wall of these trees, so there was like a little shadow self tree inside each of the trees, and in there in the whole wall of shadow he noticed the rectangular shadow of the house, as if drawn in, a little darker, and more solid, barely there, but there definitely, especially once you saw it. As he stepped out of the house the glow of this light was incredible, again hitting the house and filling the meadow like with the glowing golden honey light, highlighting a monarch butterfly and a couple of white moths like fluttering pieces of paper and a couple of electric green-blue mini helicopter dragonflies, wings like of cellophane clicking away, then with a sudden whir, cutting right over the roof behind him and through the room shade of the two big firs in front of the house, a bird with a white tail like a deer dipped and reared up to stop on the short grass of the path, like a landing strip, and as it did that he saw the yellow bright under the wings flash like a silk lining, it was a flicker, and when it stood there and jerked its head to look around, he saw the red spot on the back of its head, and as it started to peck at the ground for ants, the little gray-brown body jumped a little sideways a couple of times, showing the V-neck black chevron stripe on its chest, and when it stepped he could see the black polka dots all over its belly, and then noticed they were all over the body. Flickers were incredible birds, and he thought this was like his grandfather coming down to see him and say something definite again with his presence, and the little bird standing there, looking around, even looked like a little old man, a little bit, or, actually, as he kept watching, a lot. It looked right at him, and then another one came flying in and stopped on the landing strip path, too, closer up to the house and Simon, and he thought Mum, right away, hi Mum. She would definitely come down as a bird, like at her mother's funeral a couple of years after Mum died she came as a squirrel, came right in from outside, the light green spring day in the open side door, and hopped up on the altar railing and walked halfway in to get a better view, stood there for a while on its two hind feet, tail twitching, watched for a while, then turned around and scurried away along the railing, hopped down, and went out the door, back outside, and then driving home, after coming along by the marsh, just before the tracks where Mum was killed, there was a dead squirrel lying on the road, which was pretty incredible, or, more like, a little too obvious, Mum. Dad stopped the car and got out and picked it up by the fluffy tail and tossed it through the high fringe weeds down into the marsh. Mum used to slow the car along there to look for egrets, and stop if there was one, or point out a great blue heron, and, coming in the other way, she'd stop above the beach and point out the kingfisher, swooping in dips, wings tucked in for a split second each time, then rising again, then dipping again, like a telephone wire, across the cove, and it would stop right near them, on the wall at the back of Smelly Beach, and pose, with its perky posture and its tufted warrior head like one of those crested Roman soldier helmets. And so now, when he got back down to the beach and was gathering driftwood, when a belted kingfisher came flying across and landed on the end branch of the same log where he stood on his hands, he realized what he knew anyway, that these weren't just birds, okay, they were his mother and his grandfather, and there was a major message here. And so then when he heard the shrill, broken whistle of the osprey, like desperate morse code, harsh, high, hash marks of sound in the air, he wasn't surprised, and looked up and around, to find it, and when it came pumping over the trees, carrying a fish in one claw, and it turned its hooked head to look sharply behind it, and dipped down like it was ducking, he thought it was very cool, but like kinda too much, too. But then—and he'd never seen one before, here or ever, actually, close enough up to really see it—like a hang glider soaring in, it was so massive he couldn't believe it, this colossal bald eagle, unmistakable, majestic, with its white head and fat, huge wingspan, appeared overhead, magnificent, really close, and came veering down, chasing the osprey! trying to take its fish, and he thought that not only was this incredible, it was unbelievable, it was one of those times when the dimensions of reality shift and a message comes down through the seam from the mystic other side. The osprey didn't try to get away, but kept darting down, or to one side, with a sort of flutter, when the eagle cut at it, with its beaky Beckett head, and since it was so much smaller, it was quicker, and like elusive, without having to really dart, or duck, or worry, much, but so, more than the actual battle, but the fact of it, and the force and father power of that eagle presence, was what was really something. It was awesome. They kept at it, going behind the trees, then emerging again, over the water, for like five minutes, then went over behind the trees again, not to return, though Simon heard the high squeaky like hinge calls of the osprey, like ten minutes later, over in the direction of its nest, so maybe it won, or just, the eagle went away. There's another Burnt Island, off another part of North Haven, and the weird thing, he realized, was that's where the eagle's nest is. He didn't puzzle over what this meant, like a literal message, any more than you puzzle over what a song means, or a painting, though some people did just that, but if you got it, you got it, but still, he wondered, with wide open knowing wonder, and felt immense in spirit, and felt like he was definitely called on, like a chosen witness, and to do whatever, whatever the message was, he was the medium that received it, the only audience, and he carried it now, like infused with this really strong feeling, like of destiny, that he had to do something, and significant, like nature and the mystic, where they meet, the human, and he knew he could, and would, because he always had that feeling for himself, anyway, like a shaman, and now it was just enhanced, like a certain special time had come, and he felt now like he always knew, and didn't think about that, but just felt this chosen centeredness, like an Indian or a cat, sitting there calm as the water out there, as the night spread out over it in gradual nocturnal permission granted, sneaking and stealing and streaking colors from the day into going gray, and then buggy dark blue and black, as the fire got going, sending up flocks of sparks, at first, like flies, then settled its sticks into embers, its embers into a good hot eye of orange, pulsing bones, with flickering wings and blue feathers and the orange madder leaps of fire eating upward, fast, with darting tongues, as he fed the fire sticks, and crackling, sappy branches, like arms, and drier driftwood legs, the bigger logs, each addition and poke sending more sparks swarming spaceward. Big sort of loaf wreaths of black, dried seaweed floughed onto the fire, smoked thick, for a moment, as they crackled and caught fire fast, like hair. There was a whole supply of the stuff washed up and packed together, dry, with the driftwood, like a salad nest bed under it, so he kept stoking with that, and more wood, till the fire got big, and pretty wide, going as high as him, and he stood there with the long stick he used for a poker, staring into the faces in the fire, and like cities crumbling, war and the shifting shapes, like thought, and where we came from, with his head tipped to one side, his frozen like raging moon expression lit by the leaps, transfixed and far away, like layered off in time and in the mystic power and place, the shamaning shaman, with sort of a scary, psycho edge, if anyone was there to see him, like when he sat, with his hair dented, ninth grade, his tie loose, crooked, on the couch in the TV room in Manchester, the afternoon after Mum's funeral, while people around him talked and passed into the bathroom, or back out into the front hall and living room and dining room, where the bar was, and all the other people were, more than had ever been in the house before, like in a dream, everyone they knew, but this was no dream, but more unreal, and he sat there, slumped, rumpled, on the couch, staring into the flame of a Bic lighter he held, he turned the flame way up and kept lighting it, again and again, holding it down as long as he could with his thumb burning, but still doing it, that was part of it, no tears, Ma, staring like that into the flame.

Red arrived, golden-tanned, after three weeks away in Australia, on the day discovery concluded with a smart Hollywood crack of the gavel. She stood with the rest of the rustling room and said,

Lunch on me, as the grinning lawyers approached with their decreasingly reticent client lurking behind in shadowy tow. Red gave him a peck at the railing, then a punch, when he didn't respond, which elicited a crumpled half smile on one side of his mouth.

In the elevator Simon said to Red,

You don't look very tan for like, South Pacific.

I only like a little bit of sun, she enunciated, being sort of someone else, Brit or older and elegant, her single nod downward holding her blink shortly shut. They plowed through the crowd and the cameras. In the first of the two cabs they took in

tandem, both brown and white and round like an old pair of
saddle shoes, Simon asked her,
     So did you spend time with the Aborigines?
     You should be one, she replied, they're just like you.
     I know, he said, Dreamtime . . .
     They drove in graceless stops and starts through the semi-
sunny noon, between the common's black trees and rows of
brick town houses like old volumes holding the city's proud,
brittle history, the bigger buildings taller legal tomes, formal
and formidable, leading in textbook smooth architectural alternation to the venerable grande-dame masterpiece, the Ritz.
     You're staying here? Simon *tsed*, not totally disapprovingly.
     Why not? Red shrugged. The production pays for it.
     Simon had the solid sense when he was with Red, when she
included him, that his life was his own original independent
production that would get off the ground one day and pay for
itself like tons of times over, once it got up there, like her, into
recognition, and he just had to be patient and wait it out,
which was his strength, his stubbornness, and so he did just
that, and now here it all came.
     They walked in under the green scalloped awning guarded
by the little guy in braided livery like one of the flying monkeys
in *The Wizard of Oz*. This hushed expensive opulence everywhere inside, like a palace, so clean and peaceful, so close to the
regular rushing, dirty world right outside, like anyone could
have this if they just figured out a way in.
     A seal-headed guy in shiny shoes drooped toward them and
smiled eerily, clasping his bony, death-white hands together.
     The Curtis party for lunch, Red said, and Timmy and Simon
felt like that's what it was like with her there sometimes:
     Party, Simon spat sideways to Timmy.
     When it was just them, it was just them. Timmy felt like
explaining this to Anna, but it would bother her. He looked
back and lingered at the entrance to wait for her approaching

now from the other cab with the two lawyers and someone else, a woman in a red overcoat. They were laughing. When it was just them it was just them, but when Red was there it was the Curtis party. Who gave her a lifetime pass to life and the world at large? She did. Everyone did.

Tch. No prices on the menu, Simon said when they were seated. The round table had a square white tablecloth, smooth pressed linen like the napkins, which were folded into bishop's miters at each place.

You get whatever you want, Si, Red kind of cooed.

What, like my last meal?

No, she bit back fast but held it. How about like your first meal in your new life? Just the kind of thing Mum would say.

Sounds good to me. He didn't oppose Red the way he did Timmy.

Sounds good to me, too, said Zwirner. Who asked him? He smirked like the truly smirky guy he was. They listened to the specials and ordered.

I'll get that, too, Will Deery said to the waiter after Timmy ordered the prime rib.

Sounds good to me, too, Zwirner said again, big grin, and added on a Heineken. When it came he poured it against the back of the tilted glass, like Dad, and Simon labeled him an alcoholic as he quaffed, like an ad, the German prepee and half-inch head. When the waiter came with Red's Campari and soda, Timmy pointed to the beer with his chin and said,

I'll have one of those, too, please.

While they waited for the food Zwirner took over and told them about what was coming up next—jury selection. The judge had decided that the questioning of potential jurors would take place in a conference room closed to the general public. Members of the press could attend and observe in rotating group shifts, four at a time, an hour each. They would object to this ruling, but if they filed with the Court of Appeals

to have it overturned, they would lose. The judge would announce his ruling after lunch.

So is this good for us?

In terms of getting the jury we want, it doesn't make much
of a difference. But in terms of the overall balance of power in
the trial as a whole, it's definitely in our favor, because it'll further pit the press against the judge, which automatically pits
him with us.

So the press is against us?

Yes and no. They're just like the people out there personi-
fied, except worse. They may each have their own opinions one
way or the other that probably won't change, but what matters
most is that they sell papers or get good ratings, so whether or
not they're with us, they're with us. We're the assignment, and
it's a hot one, and they want to keep it hot. And that's definitely
to our advantage. We'll play them along for all they're worth—
and they're worth a lot.

But the jury.

The jury isn't separate from the press. The press is our way
to the jury—one way, outside of court. Of course what happens
inside the courtroom is the main event for the jury, and that's
mostly where we get them. They'll be sequestered, and they'll
be ordered not to read the paper or watch TV or listen to the
radio, but they'll know what gets into the press, we know
that—if not from secretly reading the paper or watching TV or
listening to radio themselves, then from their husbands or
wives or whatever. But that's for us to orchestrate, and we'll
deal with it as it comes. I just want to remind you and stress
that you, none of you, should speak to the press or to anyone
but yourselves and us about what's going on. They're total scor-
pion scavengers, these guys, they're like piranhas—Red knows;
right, Red?

Roger that.

And they'll do anything to get to you and get a story. So

really beware, and don't say anything, I'll handle the press, and we'll be fine. Right, Simon?

Simon gave him a tight little notch of a nod up that was as much in defiance as in agreement.

He'll be a good boy, Red grabbed and gripped Simon's forearm, tight inside his jacket sleeve, a little short, bermed against the silver forks Simon felt like stealing like half the things in this place.

They ate and gobbled around eating. When it slowed and dessert was on its way from menu imagination to the table, Zwirner introduced Deb Sullivan, again. He had introduced her when they first sat down, saying their names around the table even though she knew already who everyone was. Now he explained her presence.

Sully here's a jury consultant, best in the business, knows Boston and its citizenry like it's one big family—her family. Knows what they're going to think before they're even chosen for jury duty. Sully.

She had really red lipstick and tons of blush to match her scary red outfit. She had her color chart done some years ago at the same time she was first going out on her own as a jury consultant, after a good decade as a defense attorney, well respected for her streetwise forthrightness—she was known as one tough broad—while still remaining every bit, or so she imagined, the lovely lady. The color red came up the big winner on her chart, and she adopted it like the new uniform for her new life.

When Zwirner gave her the floor now, she addressed the whole table with an inclusive, smiling, sweeping glance, and at the same time gripped, beside her, Simon's forearm, as Red, on his other side, had done before. She spoke in a brash, friendly, neighborhood accent, like a beloved local politician, which someday she wanted to be—maybe soon, like after this trial . . .

Simon here is in good hands with Jack, let me just say first, as I'm sure you already know.

Simon felt like pulling his arm away but also sort of liked it being touched by her. This lady was weird in her Hollywood or, like, Halloween costume and so sure of herself. But there was something about her like in a cheap waitress townie almost hooker way he kind of liked, too. She was busty. She was like a loud girl grown up. She was like a big lollipop licking herself and liking it. And like, those big buttons.

My job—and if I don't mind saying so myself, you're in good hands with me, too—is to direct and assist in jury selection. She pronounced *jury joory*, Jewry. *Joory* selection is very important, obviously, because it's the *joory* that ultimately decides the outcome of a trial. It's our very important job, therefore, to determine the individual and overall makeup of the *joory*.

Desserts arrived, afloat, and descended—fruit for Red, and Anna, chocolate cake for the boys—but didn't distract from the main entertainment.

During lunch the wind closed the clouds and now it was colder out. The bulky gray batting sagged heavily with snow or rain, and before it came crashing or drifting lightly, whitely, down, the brown city seemed to lift its chest and, spurred by the wind and the subtle rising animal sense of emergency, to speed up all surface activity with a scurrying, homeward urgency.

Nice sky, Simon said out on the sidewalk as Red emerged from inside. Timmy and Anna squirreled off in their puffy parkas toward Exeter Street and their connubial constrictions. Zwirner and Deb Sullivan, coconspirator birds of a feather, coats flapping around their knees, walked together toward the common and Will Deery, who stood at the corner of Commonwealth Avenue frozen in a *Seig Heil* salute to catch a cab. Red looked after them with a savvy squint behind her shades as she responded to Simon:

There's a Greek play called *The Clouds*. It's a satire of

Socrates, for being off in his head all the time—off in the clouds.

Yeah, but he was right.

Red still watched the others diminish down the street, flapping like sailboats, toward the living statue of Will Deery, proudly hailing, and beyond him the darkened figure of Emerson, seated, larger than life, on his pedestal inside the common, enthroned among the bare trees with his books, eternally contemplating the traffic signal a block away, the eternal ebb and flow of human commerce and desire.

Yes, but they killed him for being so right, she added absently, and in the same remote, abstracted tone, I wonder if he's fucking her?

Simon's face brightened a little with surprise.

That's what people do, she sighed, then, expanding minutely with new life, I mean I know what I see, y'know what I mean? She was doing a voice, but whose? Humphrey Bogart? W. C. Fields? One of the Three Stooges? Maybe it was just a voice.

What I wonder is not if, but when—right now, or is it a thing of the past? What do you think, Scooter?

Mum used to call him Scooter. No one had called him that for a long time, except Red once in a while. As a kid he was reluctant to do what Mum said unless it was something he wanted to do. Which was how he became so reluctant to participate in life according to life's parental rules and dictates. She had to tell him a number of times to do things, and to push him sometimes she'd say, Go on, *scoot,* and then to soften, or just because she had to say it so often, she'd call him Scooter. She also called him Blister sometimes, starting when he was a baby. There was no way to cover that one with a Band-Aid, and she didn't even try, because she didn't even notice, because she was too mad to notice, those times it came out.

At the corner Will Deery leaned in the open door of a cab

but didn't get in. He shut the door, and the cab containing Mr. and Mrs. Timothy Curtis turned and sped up Boylston Street back toward Simon and Red. Another stopped and Will Deery opened the door and held it as the other two got in. Red, watching them, said,

I'll find out, and as Timmy and Anna passed, and dispiritedly waved, Simon felt like, she's just like me.

Deb Sullivan in her red outfit sat that afternoon in court for her first time at the defense table as a proud temporary member of the team. Even her briefcase, parked beside Zwirner's between them, was red. Simon's chair on the left was scootched over along with the other two guys', to make room for her, so he was sitting now half off the table, with his legs out, like slab-thighed apart. When she stood to make a motion Simon looked at her, then looked back at Red with the slightest poker nod and sly, unpressed smile, and turned back away with a slo-mo, blithe blink that stayed shut before slowly opening, to show himself and the world watching how calm and cool he was. The motion Deb Sullivan made was beside the point. The session ended in fifteen minutes after a brief huddle up at the bench that broke into laughter, like all they did was tell jokes up there, before breaking up for the afternoon.

Simon didn't have a ride back to Manchester, since Timmy and Anna were going back to New York. Logistical plans were still being worked out. He was being confined by order of the court to the house in Manchester and vicinity when he wasn't in court. They still hadn't put the electronic bracelet on him yet, but no one seemed to care. The rules of his house arrest were still being hammered out. Like could he drive Dad's car downtown to get food, or could he go to the beach or whatever.

Red told him in the elevator with the others and Miss Busty Red Joory Adviser that he could come back to the Ritz with her and she'd send him back to Manchester in her car. Her car was a limo on call, paid for by the production. In the cab approaching the Ritz she leaned up to the opening in the unscarred Plexiglas confessional partition and told the driver to keep going. She'd decided to take Simon shopping for some decent clothes.

Practice wearing them for when the jury gets here, she said. The lurid jury expert had gone on about the importance of appearance and projecting a certain image, something Red knew a thing or two about.

Simon shrugged *sure,* figuring he could probably pick up a few things that he could wear normally later, if they weren't too dress-up. One thing he learned in the navy was how to dress sharp, though he never did, he didn't have the money or any reason to. Like he learned the length of his pant legs was twenty-nine and a half inseam, and he could take any pair of pants to a tailor or cleaners with a guy back there, and have them make a perfect fit, maybe a cuff, like an inch. They also taught you to spit-shine your shoes, but he didn't have shoes now you could polish, just sneakers, or like those canvas kind with rubber from the discount bin. Dad, he remembered, once told him when he was in the army they made everyone clean their guns with their toothbrushes, and when someone asked what they were supposed to brush their teeth with, the sergeant or whatever was like,

That's why God gave you a forefinger, private!

At Brooks Brothers he felt like a kid again, with Mum trying to dress him up then, too, to be like Dad. The guy dealing with them was a faggy pink-faced guy in his fifties with a fresh-clipped silver mustache and sideburns and less silver hair combed about two seconds ago. If you made a Noah's ark of all the different types of people in the world, this guy got to go as his type to a T.

How can I help you, sir?

Simon would hardly look at the guy, let alone answer him. Red took over and the floorwalker readily adopted the refractive obsequiousness that addressed the male customer through the female. Another effete fellow emerged from a mahogany warren with a yellow tape ribbon around his neck and began to measure Simon.

I know what I am, Simon said. I'm twenty-nine and a half inseam and thirty-three waist.

Thank you, sir. Nevertheless, if we can just . . . Lift your arms, please . . . The guy had an odd accent plus the fey like lisp. He measured Simon's neck and arms and even his wrists. Simon felt like this was the time in the movie where they'd have just music and a montage of all different shots of getting measured and trying on different things, like wasn't life a blast now, with this shopping spree, shuffling all these new possible identities and possibilities. Or like when a person or a couple moves into an apartment in a movie, they get to work in their music montage burst of new life enthusiasm, fixing the place up and painting it in their paint-spattered work clothes that are so obviously spattered by the people in wardrobe, not by real work, and at the end of the sequence the job's done and they have Chinese take-out in white boxes spread out on the floor and a bottle of wine by candlelight, ready after this scene for the next part, where, if it's life, things start to fall apart.

The only other person in the men's suit department with them, after an old crone like a crane creakily left with a dark blue Brooks Brothers bag weighing him down, was a guy definitely checking him out in the mirror who Simon felt like he knew, maybe, or if not him, then definitely his type. Some days you saw things through the same prism or from the same perspective, like the lens for the day, maybe put in place in a dream the night before, and for Simon now it was like this sense of people types. Not everybody fit into one, but some people were like archetype captains of their set, it was amazing, wherever you went it was like, oh, there's that kind of guy . . .

This guy, though, was wearing a turban, even though he was

standard-issue preppie, written all over his boyish, milk-fed face, like he was taken right off the racks here, the world head-quarters for the formal uniforms of preppiedom, along with L.L.Bean, the *cazh* (casual). The guy's name was probably Chip, and he imagined he was really cool, or like way out there, with his stupid rag-head wrap like a taxi driver. He was harmless enough, but when he looked over at them, acting like he didn't recognize them, or care, Simon kind of hated him, and all his type, and felt like flattening him, like cracking his nose with a head butt, but he just ignored the guy, like he could anything, anytime, anywhere, this was one of his great skills, after all, except right now it gave him a little like less-than-skillful stiff-ness in his movements and bearing.

Please relax your shoulders, sir, the soft tailor said, softly touching him with two fingers only, but Simon didn't loosen but just leveled a look at the guy. Turned with one foot tiptoe to see from behind, Red was trying on a pinstripe jacket over in the corner mirrors. She had the sleeves rolled up and the collar up. For her the jacket was a dress.

The turban guy had danger radar the wrong way, Simon felt like, because he came over right where they were, and hovered and watched, like wasn't this fun, especially now, with him in on it, too. Simon gave him a grave direct look, but the guy, instead of going away, reached for one of the jackets on the rack right there in the middle of them, and said, like fake-ingratiatingly to the guy measuring,

May I? and took a tweed, even though it was obviously way too big, and tried it on. With his tongue poking in his cheek like a jawbreaker he mugged in self-amusement, with his hands lost up the sleeves, like he just shrank. He rolled up the sleeves, like Red. Simon continued to ignore him.

What do you think? Red came gliding into the reflected frame wrapped, hugging herself, hands deep in the pinstripe pockets.

'S good, said Simon. Get it.

Looks nice, the turban guy piped in, stepping over and wrapping himself in the same way as Red in his oversized jacket.

Simon was ready to tell the guy to get lost, but to his surprise Red was nice to the guy, from her first glance his way. Instead of minding that he was butting in like this, it was more like she liked it and welcomed the private audience, or liked him, and now could improvise more playfully with him there. Red often came to life like that, or responded with a fresh energy and a brightened face, to some outsider sticking their nose into the family, or whatever group she was stuck with.

Knock 'em dead, the guy said, smiling and familiar like he knew her more than just spotting her, but like really knew her, and she knew him, too, and Simon thought for a wait-a-second second they really did know each other, and that was why. The guy saw Simon looking at him long and added,

Oh, sorry—but his grin didn't subside in the slightest, and it wasn't till later that Simon realized the totally sarcastic, like wiseass, way he meant the *Knock 'em dead.*

The last glance of sun forked through the branches and vertical tree trunks, backed, dark, into the hillside, whose lower lit bowl flattened to a long lawn filled with people standing in groups holding drinks in plastic cups and talking in that collective party hum that sounded, if you closed your eyes, or looked away, like a soft, pervasive roar, way more powerful than it seemed when you were standing in it, part of it. The crowd, with the oldsters in coats and ties, swelled twice as thick around the two bar tables covered with plastic paper tablecloths, bottles and cups and plates of sliced lemons and limes. Igloo ice chests filled with ice cubes stood open like little white coffins on either side of the bartenders, who kept the drinks coming, while the other two guys kept them stocked and

dropped beers in clinking pairs and threes into the rowboat
filled with water and iceberg chunks of ice. Also on the crew
hired for the party were teenagers parking cars out on the road,
and two standing there along the walk in, pointing the way
like scarecrows.

The house was up on a hill, and the party was down on the
lawn at the bottom of the hill. A lot of people on North Haven
had a lot of money, and the host here sank more than usual into
his place, so that it showed, in a refined, subtle ostentation, in
every groomed inch of landscape: the flower garden first, in
rows, the various species labeled on stakes, as you passed on the
winding boardwalk toward the house, and a big vegetable garden, half hidden beside the perfectly painted gray planar house,
with its large plate-glass windows and opposing pairs of sliding
glass breezeway doors that slid easily open and shut, leading
you to the narrow path on the other side, trickling down the
steep hillside, through the rock garden pockets of terraced
flower beds and spreading sprays of juniper, alternating with
rocks fitted snugly into stone wall edges, curving and straight,
and packed into the ground in layered steps, and jutting crags
of ledge that made the whole hill underneath show like tough
tumor toes wearing through the rough wool life layer. The long
lawn filled with people was lined past the far end zone by the
tall regiment of gold-hatted firs in their long evening gowns,
and beyond the sideline opposite the bar and food tables at the
bottom of the amber hill a tawny meadow spread soft-haired
over leonine contours beyond the bright, linear lawn, reaching
down to the unseen beach. At that outer corner edge of the
lawn, as anally groomed as a golf course, was a pond so planned,
with its kidney shape and one willow and lush side salad of
reeds on the far bank, that it looked like one of those plastic
pond homes with a plastic palm tree for a pet turtle, and the
water was tinted a scary, unnatural green, which conversation
cleared up was a nontoxic antibacterial additive they put in the

water to make it safely swimmable for the little kids. But the result looked so artificial that the rest of the meticulous landscaping, too, seemed part of the same Fantasy Island spread, the tiki torches lined up on tall stakes around the perimeter of the lawn, like big faux versions of the cattails over in the reeds, and which, in reverse, made even the cattails look fake.

But when the clouds closed over the low-ball sun brilliantly stalled behind the black trees, and the bugs rose up out of the earth like teeming, tiny messengers and rushing carriers of the gathering darkness, the torches were lit, and there was nothing unreal about the mad faces of flame breathing black fumes upward in their flickering ring around the people, and imparting fire's primal paint to the faces disappearing into the dim and the din. Lobsters, of course, for dinner, dished out on plastic plates, and corn on the cob, and as soon as they started serving, a civil, loose, long line formed, going straight back from the table and sagging with the slight slope of the lawn down toward the pond, where it still seemed a little lighter, over the water, and kids laughed in the open field beyond, boys chucked rocks up in the air to try and draw down the swooping, darty bats—or hit them—hunting bugs with their radar, show off to the girls. People at the end of the food line didn't move ahead right away, but stood where they were in clusters, and continued talking as the rest of the line inchwormed forward.

Timmy carried Bennie, zonked out on his hip in his little button-up wool sweater and matching hat with earflaps. Bennie looked like a little old man no matter how much they dressed him up like a baby, and he opened his eyes when people touched him, or spoke too loud, and after giving them a no-nonsense, grandfatherly gaze, plainly annoyed, his eyes rolled back and he fell asleep again.

North Island Wool, he repeated each time he was asked where they got Bennie's excellent outfit.

Oh, that place is great, more than one person said. And:

They do a really good business, mail order catalogue, biggest employer on the island—as if everyone here didn't already know all about it.

Most of the people here were summer people, of course, and of course it was islanders working the food table and bars and everything else. There were some islanders invited as guests, too—a few. Just as the church up on the hill in town where Timmy and Anna got married was for summer people in the summer, and the islanders used it the rest of the year, but moved to a shingle summer church in the middle of the island, out by the Grange, for the summer—the social life on the island was mostly divided along the same lines. While this party was going on at the Prices' place, like a resort with full open bar and lobsters free, the islanders were having their own party, a bunch of them, mostly men, out at Mullen's Head, out near Burnt Island, with a few barbecue fires going for burgers and hot dogs. Beer, mostly Bud, and plenty of it, and a pretty big fire on the beach. Mostly pickups were parked under the trees and out into the field that was enlarged by the storm last year.

Victor had some steaks and stuck some onions right into the fire, still in their skins, which he caught some shit for, but when they were done and the eating was great, poppin' those suckers out of their skins, he said,

Yah eat *that,* and got some laughs, like almost anything did, now that they were settled in, feeding and half gone, like the light, and the light from the fire took over, leaping and lighting up their baby faces, under caps and beards and those brown-tinted glasses glinting.

Both parties were in full swing and fire-flickered darkness after eating and drinking, talking and waving mosquitoes away, when the siren alarm in the middle of the island went off in its little gilled box with a horn on the roof of the firehouse, three long rising and falling whoops, like some prehistoric bird, but loud enough, easily, to loop over the ends of the island and everyone outdoors and in, TV going, a radio, conversation, or just the refrigerator's *hmm*. The islanders knew the alarm didn't go off if it wasn't really something, and not without jokes and pokes at each other wasted no time, though some of them were pretty goddam wasted! piling into their trucks and heading in a headlit armada line rumbling over the Mullen's Head road, raising a ton of dust like smoke. There was already a bunch of guys there standing around the new lemony lime fire truck outside its garage, idling with its headlights on, but not the spinning red light on top. Turned out there was a fire all right, and a real *doozah,* out right where they just come from, out past Mullen's Head, and they looked at each other, kidding, like don't look at me. But no one seemed to know where it was exactly, except: Mullen's Head, out past Mullen's Head. Right where they just came from. So they waited, smoking.

Meanwhile, at the other party, there was less worry that it was really a fire, except among the Martin men and their guys doing the food and bar tables, who took off right away without saying anything to anybody except each other. Fires were serious business on the island, *by Jesus.*

Meanwhile, the first men assembled at the four-garage-door firehouse, and when Eric came out and announced where the fire was, they piled onto the truck and into their own trucks, as the second alarm sounded, and headed back out to where they just came from, leading and following the fire truck in a long train, connected by headlights, that snaked swiftly over the island road. The red light was spinning on top, splashing emergency into the trees, but they didn't bother with the siren. When the road stopped, they stopped. A dirt road ran down to the left into the trees just in from the shore, and the fire truck, after sitting for a minute to think how to do this, tried to take the turn by backing up, then going forward, then back again. Maneuvering tight like this, it made the turn, crunching branches and sweeping and snapping off more, and burrowed into the darkness brightly tunneled by the bright halogen bloom of headlights fisting ahead up the stony dirt lane between near evergreen walls. Roots crisscrossed the twin dirt paths of the road and a grass strip ran down the middle like a long brush, and both and the bumps were eaten by the eyes and the bulky box of the truck as it ate its way in, just fitting. A fox or a cat scurried across the road ahead and into the woods. It didn't look like any fire was coming, while they were heading in there, nor when they got to the clearing. The headlights swiped across the Cottingham cottage, its red and roofed low shape, the white trim, hidden snugly back in the trees, and the headlights flashed back in some of the windows. The fire was supposedly over on Burnt Island, right across the water here—not fifty yards, mudflats at low tide, eternally good clamming. But there was no sign of any fire from here, and they wondered if it weren't a goddam prank call.

But Eric said the call came from the coast guard, and their call came from a yacht anchored for the night off Calderwood. Burnt Island almost touches North Haven. Double dotted lines on a topographical map indicate where a road used to run on a causeway over the rocks and mudflats fanning out into parabolic coves in opposing directions. Now there was no trace of the causeway, just hairy seaweed covering the barnacled ledge; but the straight stretch of the road built up level through the tall woods on Burnt Island was still there. In that picture in the downstairs bathroom in Manchester of Dad standing in that part of the woods with Simon with a crew cut on his shoulders, there, barely discernable, if you knew it was there was the old road hidden and blended in time under the needle blanket floor going off behind them.

There was some debate as to whether the fire could jump across to North Haven if, say, Burnt Island became a full blaze.

There was some debate as to whether that would happen. The older guys thought it could jump the water, and the younger guys, who hadn't seen really big fires, hadn't worked the dump fire in the seventies in the middle of the island, thought there was no way, they were just being old guys. Some beer made it from the trucks, and a couple of guys went over to Mullen's Head to get the rest and clean up there. Even if nothing happened, they'd have their end-of-summer party right here.

Down at The Islander the room was packed and the band was in full swing, with people standing along the walls and two and three thick at the bar, and on the dance floor, dancing, couples and girls with girls in a group. The singer and lead guitar was a short guy with long sideburns who kind of ran in place like Bob Marley and grinned a lot, looking over at his lanky bass player now and then like they had some delightful secret between the two of them surfacing in the music. His big grin seemed held in place between his bushy sideburns, like that's why they were there, his grin-straps. He was really into it, and the house loved these guys, and hooted it up after every song. The place was going nuts when the song "Coconut"*(Put the lime . . .)* ended, and, as if joining in, or like someone at the fuse box, the house lights blinked, the lights on the band and the bar and the fairy lights strung around both rooms just under the ceiling, strung for Timmy and Anna's dinner the night before they got married, two summers ago. The guys in the band looked at one another, smiling, and people milled and stood there and moved to their drinks to wet their whistles. The lights stopped flickering and came on full again, revived, then after a beat went brown, surging dimly, like the juice was leaking out, and then the lights went out altogether, and everybody cheered.

Fat little candles came out and the little angel flames floated around the room, and someone lit a joint, and someone loud went,

Oh, Jeez, Brewstah—now you done it! Which raised a little laughter.

Guys got up and came together by the candle cluster at the end of the bar by the door and, suddenly calm and plenty sober, conferred. Clayton behind the bar tried the firehouse, and Randy Hooper and Forest Hooper, and they were all busy.

Try my wife, said Bud Beverage, she's over at Hands', she'll know, they're right there, 'r can go right ovah.

I'll try your wife, someone behind him called out, but no one laughed.

They could smell the fire, and in a quick couple of hours could see the glow outlining the serrated treeline across the dark water. A few guys went and got in their boats to go check it out, and by radio the message came back that yes, by Jesus, North Haven was in danger, and they sure could use a fireboat, by God, which in fact was already on its way from Belfast. The glow grew orange and ominous, and they could see smoke hurling crazed forms up into the night over the nest of trees. They agreed to wait there and see, had to, and when it got closer, to hose down all the trees on this side, and that, hopefully, should do it.

Over on the water side a number of boats were sneaking back and forth, and some were sitting there floating, engines cut, in the middle of the Little Thorofare, watching the show, and it was spectacular. It had munched well into the island, and back toward the dock. More craft were arriving all the time. Randy Hooper patrolled back and forth in his lobster boat, *'Bout Time,* keeping people away, sounding all official with his baritone down east accent through his bullhorn, wherever he got that, and he shined his mounted spotlight in people's faces who came close in spite of his orders, and they brought their hands up to their eyes and moved away. The fire was fantastic, like some psychotic maniac leaping up from the underworld, totally out of control, beautiful, wild hell-hair flaring up, bright, awesome, crunching and crackling, its monster appetite devouring the island remarkably fast. It was savage entertainment, primally presented, hypnotic, cinematic, *live,* and so incredibly potent, it was chaos unleashed, but also really graceful, with this great slow preconscious grandeur. A small, familiar fire radically enlarged and reflected on the water, lighting the beach and the air around, so bright you could see all the boats and people and their white faces lit, looking, and the colors of their clothes, and when you looked away it was so pitch black, by sudden contrast. Even from far away you could feel the heat and hear clearly the prodigious heat, with crackles and crashes coming out of the furnace roar, like wind, and it was thrilling how high it went, twice as high as the trees, sometimes leaping three times as high, cowled by surges of smoke disappearing upward into the darkness, and when black columns toppled into the heart of the burning city, sending up with an excellent crash a skyward rash of sparks like birds and bright bees, onlookers cheered, boats gammed together on the molten glass, some floating apart; but mostly they stood silent, transfixed by this exquisite destruction, this fabulous ancient spell of god the fire, the first god, the first TV.

Some of the guys around the fire truck held the theory that wetting down the trees and shore would actually *feed* rather than hamper or dampen the fire, because it was so hot that as it got there it dried the zone in front of it, and the oxygen out of the H_2O was actually fuel for the fire, because that's what fire fed on, and would then just as soon suck up them two dried *H*s, too.

Jeez, Josh, I sure hope the ocean don't catch on fire, then, *pffft* of a beer opening. Then we're really screwed.

A light drizzle, more a mist, a gentle mizzle, came sprinkling down on them, sitting and lying in groups on the ground, around the time they could first hear the fire, faintly wheezing, then louder as it got later, crashing and popping through that steady griddle crackle gradually approaching. Some of the guys left to go sleep, ready to return whenever they got the call. As it got lighter it turned out to be a white, misty morning, faintly foggy—or was that only smoke?—and out of the shrouded woods on the Burnt Island side some deer came peeking out through the curtain, one after another, looking around with sharp head movements and lovely, large, terrified eyes. When there were six standing there, one, and then all of them, walked carefully in single file over the mudflats and sea-weedy rocks, heading right toward the North Haven guys crouched on their shore.

Go grab my gun.

Just what we need here, start killing each other.

'N' you know there's more to come.

Aint huntin' season, Ray.

I thought huntin' season was year round out here.

The beer was gone and it was morning and the fire wasn't there yet, and even if it came there wasn't much else they could do except madly start cuttin' all them trees down at the last minute, so half the guys still there went home, get some Zs 'n' come back later for the action. Norm Drigg was the one guy there who was truly worried the fire would leap to North Haven, and he wasn't about to leave the scene of the coming battle, and didn't want anyone to go, but wanted to get more guys there right away, not guys keep leaving, and everyone get their chain saws and get to it.

Where we gonna put all the trees, Norm?

They'd been giving him shit all night, but he was still serious, and later in island lore the fire's leap over to North Haven that never happened lived on as the Norman D. invasion. More deer did come, in groups and pairs—none solo—and the remaining guys watched them silently step out of the woods and pick their way across the mudflat, adding to the dot footprints. All told they counted thirteen deer, nimbly tiptoeing to safety, white tails then bouncing off into the North Haven woods.

Most of the boats were gone by daybreak, but a couple still floated there, still watching, one of which was Timmy, in shock, and some buddies with Steven in Steven's boat. They'd agreed to stick it out however long, and had a full bar below to support their resolve. But a couple of them were passed out, and they were almost out of butts, and the fire had moved to the far interior of the island, and the misty morning seemed as depleted, raw, and devastated as the charred, smoking corpse of this side of the island, floating in its own smoke before them, so they decided they'd go back after smoking one last bone, but still didn't budge when the roach burned the last fingertips and was tossed. When the white sleeves of approaching fog began to enfold them and the island, they were about to leave when they saw, above the fire in the far heart of the island, this incredible chimney effect, so they stayed for a while longer to check that out. The outrageous heat and upward thrust of the fire burned a huge hole in the fog, consuming it and sucking it in and upward, like this huge sort of air volcano doughnut, and through the fire and smoke going up you could just get glimpses of blue sky in there. They took out a chart to get some compass readings for the way back through the fog. William got up on the bow, holding the painter for drunken balance, to look out for rocks, and Timmy and Steven both piloted. As they edged past the last ledge by Burnt Island a group of cormorants stood on the rocks like burnt-out tenants, and seeing them standing there, forsaken, drenched, and skinny, completely black, Katherine, with her Bulls cap pulled down and her jean jacket collar up, said,

Looks like those guys got crispy-crittered.

Zwirner couldn't blame Simon this time because it was Red's fault, he learned when he got the story from Will Deery. So he played it cool—or tried to—and tried to act like it was no big deal and to make light of it, make a joke when they met in a side room before court.

Guess you guys had a little shopping spree, he tried to josh, though there was no lightness in his tone, just the spoiled tinge of sarcasm.

Red had seen the paper with room service breakfast in bed—she gobbled every last morsel—at the Ritz, but Simon hadn't seen it yet, because Dad got only the *Globe* delivered anymore. That he grabbed and looked at in the car, but didn't read really, because there was nothing about him and nothing very interesting, except that guy Cone got traded or signed somewhere new as a free agent. Baseball was starting up again already, down in Florida. On the news and in the paper there were pictures of players sitting on the grass trying to touch their toes, or with the bottoms of their feet together and their knees apart, working on their tans. Baseball is such a breeze of a sport—but that's what Michael Jordan thought, and look what happened with him when he tried to switch over.

The stickers on the Plexiglas partition showed it was the same car company out of Revere as Red's limo he took home alone the day before, but this time it was just a regular car, and this different driver didn't wear a suit and tie or cap. He wore sunglasses, and it was a navy blue Cutlass Supreme with no frills except tinted windows, if that was a frill.

Simon saw the driver checking him out in the rearview mirror. The bright day flashed by like cross-section samples of the whole mystic picture wrapped bright and full in that hopeful, depressing shift of spring in the air, soon to be released, but mostly it's still inner loveless March, frozen mud the main message on the surface, alternating, sometimes softening out, with the lift of thin light in the pale chill and glints of better weather, when windows and coats open and the breasts come out, bouncing under blouses and dresses showing knees, buds on the branches swell slightly red and stores open their doors to sales, paint their trim, while the band of green growth and balmy relief creeps, in fits and starts, up the country from the slower-mouth South, led back to life by the million birds swarming up their flyways, the buried noses of crocuses along walkways, followed soon by daffodils, wider spread, vivid yellow flags, along moist black driveways and in funereal fieldscatters, nodding, sleeping, still standing, through the fat last snows, or a frozen mizzling daylong silvering of all the trees and towns of southern New England, ending in squinty, slap-sharp sunshine, so everyone can see and appreciate the exquisite handiwork glitter, while across game board counties homecoming cars skid in slow motion and crash into one another and into trees with every single outstretched branch sexily encased, down to the last Q-Tip buddy twigs, their twinkling ice-earring drip-tips cinematically poised for the sudden crash of metal and shattering glass bashing through the engine-humming safety sound track of radio music and voices spewing ads between banter and bits of news like the report that night on TV with clips and figures of the numerous crashes, pile-ups, and rubber-necking delays due to the lovely ice-out—

And then that day, like spring herself, there was Katherine in the back of court. Like a flower popped up out of the darkness of the year. She was pale and pretty, wearing pants and a baggy coat she kept on inside. When Simon turned around during one of the delays it was to look right at her, and she was looking right at him. She looked kind of pissed, or like she just woke up, but Simon lifted his hand by his hip in a little like flipper wave, accompanied by one of his almost imperceptible little nods a notch up. Her eyes changed a little, but the rest of her expression stayed, as she opened her hand breast high in a brief signal hi back, which infused him with this sudden new high season of the self, it was like a bong hit, right when he needed it, and as he was sitting there, like transformed, he thought, That's God, not a god like everyone thinks, like behind the sky, watching, and ignoring us, but in people, like who do that to your life, or, like, something happens.

He couldn't go out to see her during the break, and after lunch she wasn't there, but there almost in her place, which was weird, but a couple of places back, in the back row, under the clock, was that guy Pete. Their eyes met, and without any movement of greeting, or the slightest hint, they acknowledged each other, and Simon felt like now, one two, things were working the other way, up, for him.

There were delays all during those transition days of moist early spring splattered in alternation with late winter malingering in the mushy gray palette of your mood. Jury selection began for real the day after Easter, which Simon definitely saw as a good sign. Easter was like a daffodil, coming like Katherine out of the muddy dead grass of thawed winter, and daffodils always made him think of Mum, and Mum's coffin, which was covered with them, though she wasn't even really in it—wasn't she cremated already?—though you could picture her lying in there, either way, totally mashed up beyond recognition—

A friend of Mum's from the area invited him over for Easter, with a message on the machine he took down from Dad and Ginny's room, or Mum and Dad's room, as he still thought of it, and he left it without a message, just a blank and then the beep if you called, on the tall stool on the way into the kitchen, hooked up to the wall phone and plugged in around the corner with a white extension cord plugged into a brown older one he got down in Dad's workshop. He took it from the low ceiling in the cellar infested with Dad's pretty dangerous, Dad, do-it-yourself wiring job.

On that Friday, Good Friday, there was a call he didn't feel like listening to till Saturday, just to stop it blinking every time he went by, and it was Mum's friend Mrs. Windsor, who gave her first name.

Hello Simon, if this is you there, this is Ceci Windsor calling, to see if you'd like to come to our house Easter Sunday,
early afternoon. Aaron and Rob and Alexia will be here, and
some cousins and friends. It'll be sort of an informal buffet outside on the terrace, if it's warm enough, with an egg hunt on
the lawn for the grandchildren, and I hope you can make it,
we'd love to see you. Around noon. Do come! *Eeeeeeep.*

Shyeah right, Simon thought, and called Timmy to tell him.
Bennie was wailing in the background, Timmy said wait a second, and Simon was so glad he didn't have other people's lives.

Are you going to go? Timmy asked.

No way.

You should. Timmy sounded upbeat, double-chinning the
receiver, his voice was throatily hearty in life. They're nice.

What does that girl Alex do? Simon asked. She's pretty.

I don't know . . . Timmy trailed off doing something else
with clanging kitchen sounds, but then he did know: graphic
artist, computer stuff, lives in Cambridge. She spent a lot of
time in and out of McLean's.

This made Simon like her more—McLean's was the preppie
nut house. He always had a crush on her, at least he did twenty
years ago, yikes, and he felt her name and her hiding place in
him light up when Mrs. Windsor said it. He saw her a few times
in her upper teens, she had a really good body and short hair. He
would've gone nuts, too, if he grew up in that family. They were
like a parody of stuck-up rich people. She was cool, though, like
a rebel from way early. Got stoned a lot, Simon knew, though
only once or twice with him, and whoever else, like at Singing
Beach some summer night, or like winter woods, where?

She's a really good skater, he told Timmy, though Timmy
had all the same childhood information as him. She used to go
in figure skating competitions, and she was really good at tennis, too. Simon remembered her playing pond hockey with the
boys, with her ponytail up pert in the back of her head, bob-

bing really like a pony when she'd stride, thrusting straight forward, sort of kick-skipping off the star tips of her blades, the way figure skaters do, bouncing a little, instead of pushing off each side like with hockey skates, or now Rollerblades, which Simon had done once, on Timmy's, in Brooklyn, in that Prospect Park, but he didn't have his own, couldn't afford them, he wasn't into fads, anyway. Though he was into skateboarding, actually, back then, but that was more like a whole lifestyle, and could do a handstand on one still, no problem. But so maybe he'd go Rollerblading with her sometime like in Cambridge, or some country road, find a smooth one, like if they went on a trip, like up to Vermont, or maybe Maine. She looked like a deer, a doe, with her long eyelashes and long neck.

Though the next message was from her, too, telling her number, Simon didn't call Mrs. Windsor back to say he would or he wouldn't come, but on Sunday, surprising himself, he called the car company and ordered a car to come pick him up at noon.

The sprouty message of spring. Dark branches, smoothly extended and intertwined overhead, their little buds swelled like nuts with minutely shingled shells, the great green money of summer stocked inside at the ends of all the niggardly, skeletal, little, like, pickpocket fingertips bobbing in the breeze. The ocean, gray today, came in and out of view along the curvy way, between big houses and long lawns. John Updike lived back in one of those. Mum always read his books. Simon remembered coming with Mum to the Windsors' house sometimes during the day, doing errands, and how he hated it there then, just waiting around, not unlike his life now, or ever since, actually, and now here he was going back there, why? If he was driving himself he would have kept going, past the brick wall and stone pillars of their driveway entrance, and gone on like to Nick's Roast Beef, or just drive, but since he would have had to say something to keep this girl going, they ended up turning in when he said, and went up the long tree-cave driveway like in a dream.

Their house was a brick mansion set back from the sea—Salem over on the right, the smokestacks bigger from here, and Misery Island from a different angle than he was used to, Bakers behind—surrounded by a lawn like a golf course, already getting green, with hedges hiding the beach, and at one end, going into the garden that had white statues standing around and a fountain in the center, he remembered now, with a circle pool, lily pads and orange goldfish in the brown water he tried to bomb once with golf balls, with What's-his-name, the son his age, Rob, who's probably like a lawyer or stockbroker now, like all those guys he grew up with, and like fat and married and rich, which he already was, two out of three, as a kid. He used to have a Band-Aid-colored patch over his eye, like under his glasses, for a while, like for years, to like strengthen the one, or like punish the other, for being dominant, or weaker. Normally he never would come here, but today, for some reason, like, namely, Alex, or more like, maybe these days he was open to things more, like whatever opened themselves to him—What he liked about the Eastern religions or mysticism or whatever, as he checked them out in his way, nibble by little bit, as the pieces came deeper, was not just the wisdom of it all, but the way they had their ancient sayings about how to live, and like maxims on enlightenment, and how to be, that were just like how he already was, so they were like corroboration and reinforcement of his wisdom and whole, like, inner detached way of being he already had.

Three of the five parked cars were dark Mercedes, and one a Lexus, goldy silver, and one a red, the rebel, Honda, the newer, rounder, style, like now all the cars were turning into the same car, and past them on the lawn were two boys, obviously brothers, in the same dress-up corduroy pants with cuffs, and collars sticking out over their sweaters, standing there looking at a new bright blue plastic soccer-sized ball, bought, you could tell, for them to play with, here, now, but now here they were and they didn't want to play, maybe because the lawn was wet and they had on dress-up shoes. The little one with a cowlick was squinting and talking away, his head tilted and moving a little with what he said, and the older brother listened doubtfully, with the same squint and a skeptical small mouth, arms crossed and his head tilted the other way. Beyond the brothers and the broad lawn the ocean was bluer now, tinily textured with a breeze over it, and the pillowy clouds were now opening up, big mappy patches of cold cobalt behind, between, coming through, on and off, with the wind, and patches of shadow, by the arriving acre, slid over earth and sea. You couldn't see it from there, except the beginning of the waves breaking, but Simon remembered, now, the beach down there that went out pretty far, veiny rivulets at low tide and shells embedded in the hard granular sand, slappy wet closer to the water. He felt like going down there, or just leaving, but just stood there looking, and the driver said out her window, still sitting at the wheel,

Will you be here for a while, or for how long? Simon looked at the driver with her dark sunglasses, oval like glasses were now. Because I'd like to go get some cigarettes if there's time, if you don't mind.

Yeah, okay. But come right back. I'm maybe not gonna stay here very long. He looked at the house. What the fuck was he doing here? She pulled forward, munching the gravel, and he raised a finger to stop her.

Go left at the end of the driveway and that takes you into the town. He felt like getting in and going with her, get out of there, go to Nick's Roast Beef, but just then the green front door opened and out came an old woman in a dress to her knobby knees. As the car curled around the circle and crunchily crept away, bye, she approached Simon with a manufactured smile like she smelled something bad and didn't want to show it. She came right at him over the wet grass in her teal shoes with a gold thing on them instead of out the flagstone walkway and then over.

Simon, hello. Welcome.

Once she spoke he recognized Mrs. Windsor, disguised in there, in this shrunken old lady. Wrinkles were written around her same, but sadder, sort of hollow eyes, and her mouth and even her neck, and she reminded him of the Cowardly Lion, except pruned and spotted with moles and tan-and-white splotches Mum used to call grave spots, look who's talking. Her voice was the same, though, like the same friendly soul, she was a nice lady, except croaky like she could cough, or like bark, and her eyes were the same Tootsie Pops licked down to the round brown core.

I'm glad you could make it, she took the hand he held out to hold her off and bonily gripped it like he was saving her, and then she came in for the kiss on his cheek in spite of him. She smelled strongly of her perfume and makeup powder, and he thought how he could like live on her ring, encrusted with rocks, ditto the earrings, and pearl necklace, for like ten years.

The house was a big house you could call a mansion, but it seemed to Simon small, actually, compared to his house in Manchester, or compared to what he remembered, like it was a semi-shrunken version of the original. Same with her, it was a little bit of a shock she was so old. Some people in their sixties were totally in their old age, but others were just, like, silvering, it depended on how you weathered and wore down, how much you worried and abused yourself and like built up bad karma.

Indoors a light party murmur came from down in the sunken living room off to the left. White lilies, their sticky pistils and stamens loaded with yellow pollen powder, were lined up along the wall in the front hall in flowerpots wrapped in colored florist's tinfoil. As they went in past two big mirrors with chunky old gold carved wood frames, she chatted chirpily, How are you, I'm so glad you came, how's your family, like he wasn't on trial for murdering his father, her friend, and her dead best friend's husband.

Everyone, she stepped down the two steps and Simon trailed behind like Bill Murray being a scruff in some movie. These people were wearing coats and ties and dresses. He didn't know any of them. Kids were off in the other half of the room by the shut French doors going out to the lawn. You remember Simon.

They all faced him and she said who they were, from left to right. Now he recognized the brothers, his age and just older, the childhood pecking order stays. The one guy Rob's glasses were just the same, the black frames, which was a clue, and was funny, but otherwise what a porker, he was right, and already that old and bald.

The father stepped over, still the same long-legged guy with butterscotch glasses, but now gray and creaky like a great blue heron. He said hello heartily, with direct eyes, and held the handshake long, for a meaningful second, and Simon liked the guy, like he used to, for being friendly, genuinely, instead of a typical oblivious rich adult, though he was so far from Simon's type, and his world. He was a big financial guy, his father used to be secretary of state around World War II. There was a question about him on the SATs Simon got sort of in trouble for because, after the first few questions, he made a fish pattern with darkened dots on the answer sheet, he saw it emerging, instead of reading and really answering the questions. Mum liked the guy, too, and Simon knew it was totally her, why they invited him, but so what, maybe that's why he came, too. The father asked how he was getting along, and said if there's anything I can do please don't hesitate to ask, and Simon thought nyeah, like how about some money, but he also felt a more appreciative maybe, thanks, you never know, and sort of filed that one away. He talked to that guy Rob, who, he was right, was an architect now, but was between firms right now, and was thinking of going out on his own, like if he could get a commission, which Simon knew what that meant, he was living off his trust fund. The cheese hors d'oeuvres, baked and puffed on crunchy beds of white bread toast, were pretty good, and he ate lots of them, and drank cider like he was trying to get drunk on it.

The wives of the brothers he didn't talk to, but he was surprised, they weren't totally preppie, but kind of cool, for there, and one of them looked maybe Mexican, pretty sexy, actually, with a slender neck and long fingers, and she kept looking at him with her white and dark eyes, not followed by a smile. Alex wasn't there, and he didn't ask about her, because who would he ask, and what would he say, and what if the news was bad? Anyway, she was in her own league to him, separate from them, he didn't like to think of her as one of them. He still wondered about her.

The kids by the French doors were putting together a kite on the floor. Simon went over to look at it and told them what they were doing wrong. It was a box kite, and they were trying to fit the diagonal support sticks inside before they squared all four sides, so it kept collapsing when they tried to do the next thing.

You have to do all the sides first, Simon said, standing over them with his cider. Then when you put in those inside ones it all like pops out tight.

The older girl in charge looked at him with a little frown, doubtful, or resentful that he was moving in on her territory, or both. The littler sister, same red shoes, a bird barrette, sitting on the floor with her little legs apart, knelt up right away and did just what he said, and it worked. They attached the string where Simon said, then took the kite outdoors, with the three other kids watching following, and no grown-ups, except Simon.

How come you didn't have to get dressed up? said the little one carrying the string, while her older sister carried the kite. The grass was a little drier already from the sun, but it was still soggy earth underneath.

Sylvia, the older sister shot her a mean look.

I did, said Simon. For me.

Noooo you didn't, the little one wrinkled her face.

Yes, and anyway, when you're grown up you can do whatever you want.

They tramped out to the middle of the lawn making a trail of darker green wetness.

I wanna be grown up, said Sylvia, talking to him, Simon could tell, only because her little sister was.

It's not so great. You can do whatever you want, but also you have to do everything yourself, Simon explained. And if you don't do them, then there are lots of things missing. And if you do do them, then you don't have time for anything else. They stopped and Simon had an audience. Being a kid's like a long paid vacation and you're totally free, so you better enjoy it.

'Cep for bedtime, she pointed out, and all the rules, and Simon nodded, yep's true.

And school, Sylvia added definitively.

The little one got the kite up by running where Simon said, with it raised on her arm, the way he showed her, and letting the string out as it rose. It stayed up like it's supposed to, shaking, and moved like uneasily in place, and when a gust came it shimmied up and up, the paper drumming loud, and tugged hard, alive, trying to fly away. The girl squealed, and the others laughed, except Sylvia, who marched, fisted, toward her and demanded,

Let me hold it.

Not yet, said the younger, and a shade of concerned expertise creased her face as she concentrated on the kite. It was like a fish, fighting hard to get away, tugging and swimming all over the place, resting for a minute, then, trying to trick you, it would jerk suddenly, and swoop off again, up or down, to either side, like it wildly wanted to get away. Twice it dive-bombed, like shimmying, almost to the ground, but swerved up again like it didn't want to die, but out of control. The third time up, pretty high now, because she was letting it out and letting it out like Simon said, it dive-bombed, faster and faster, quivering in a long arc to the sea side, and crashed into the lawn with a loud crack. But didn't break, the little crew discovered, amazed, when they got to it, running over, led by Sylvia, who slipped once, her arm shot out, but didn't fall, and kept going, full speed.

You need a tail, Simon said, and for a second the girl didn't get it, she thought he meant her, then she nodded.

What shoo-ey make it out of?

Well if you don't have a leopard handy to cut one off of, he said, deadpan, get an old sheet or a shirt and we'll rip it.

She went inside while the others trooped back with the kite, and came back out running with a pillowcase bannered behind in one hand and a pair of scissors in the other he could see her falling and falling on, if she slipped, but she didn't, because he thought of it first. Her cheeks were so rosy when she got back to him it was like fake, like makeup, and same with Sylvia, who was more of a tomboy, you could tell, even though they both had on the same dress and red shoes, thin white cotton socks folded over the same two inches, except Sylvia's were pushed down.

The pillowcase was perfectly good and Simon felt like keeping it, instead of cutting it, but he didn't have an apartment now—but he had a whole house to himself, actually, and a whole closet full of sheets and pillowcases and towels, like a lifetime supply. The pillowcase had initials embroidered on it, bumped out like a scar, and no hole or stain or anything wrong with it, except it was maybe a little frayed at the open end, but fine with him, he stabbed it with the scissors and tore and cut it into a good couple of long tail strips. Holding the scissors at the tip he flipped them firmly, like a knife thrower, deep into the lawn. The kids were impressed by that. He tied the strips together and made some more knots to give it some heft, and split one end to tie the two pieces together around a corner of the kite that had a little tuft of grass and wet dirt on it from the crash landing, then held the orange bikini building model aloft and tossed it up and stepped back a few steps as the sisters together cried,

Hey!

The box kite rose and tugged and spined up the invisible. The grown-ups stepped outside onto the flagstone puzzle pieces and watched. They held their drinks and wives by the elbow or the eye and watched Simon Curtis send up the kite. Whatever they said they said to themselves. Simon saw them, and sensed something, but ignored them. His shirt was the same one he wore in court and on the news on the steps on the way out on Friday, Good Friday. His pants had paint by the pockets and on the lap especially, on the left, from touching with his left forefinger or fingertips together, and wiping it off, and were punched out at the knees from not being washed for a while, which the seasonal cleansing sea breeze ballooned up, somehow, the ankles, he was a kite, which were bare with no socks, in his green sneakers with their curled Velcro flaps. The kite drew vibrating ovals of live orange up there against the cobalt spring opening its map of hope over everybody watching. A gull slid sideways out over the beach. The water was bluer by another royal degree now, with the inevitable dispersal of the breakaway cloud nations, and the fresh dominion emergence of the old king sun.

With their cousin followers clustered around them, the two

sisters stood by, first pleading in bleats, then trying to be good, and get it that way, but Simon kept flying the kite into smaller and further remoteness. He glanced over at them by the house like a jury of peers, not his peers. Mrs. wasn't out there, Mr., maybe, either. The kite climbed and like clawed and claimed its spot up there on high by the dot moon, the worn nub end of a bone, and Simon said,

Okay, what's your name?

Lizzie.

Okay, Lizzie, he handed her the roll of string, making sure she held on tight. Don't let go.

I won't. Her mouth was determined and she set her feet apart with her fawnlike little legs in an A.

And don't let it pull you away up into the sky, which scared her a little, but she tried not to show it, and he didn't tell her he was only kidding.

Yeah or you'll keep going into outer space, her sister teased.

If the gulls don't get you first up there, said Simon.

No-o-o-*hoo*, Lizzie crooned into a whine, part play, part plea for real.

Their beaks are sharp.

She stood rooted to the spot and held on tight. The kite also stayed right where it was, up there by the bone moon. It was a perfect day for flying a kite, but who were these kids, who were these people? It was fine, and fun, even, but the unself-conscious balance dissolved when the older brother of Rob came over, Aaron.

Good, Liddy, he sang as he approached with his drink in his hand almost gone. He seemed nicer now than the closed-off Groton snob he was before, but Simon still didn't like him, and felt like, what am I doing here with these people, though a moment ago the good enough answer was, flying a kite with these kids.

Lizzie had her own reaction to her father approaching, which was to back up and away, to clear her base position for flying command. She slipped and clicked her shoes together and fell back on her bottom. She let go of the string by mistake as she fell. The roll of string bounced away across the lawn and unraveled as it went. The knot of kids, after a hesitation, agape, went running after it, but couldn't catch it. Simon could have caught it, but just stood there and watched and felt like, there it goes. The kite shimmied up more as it pulled away, then wavered wildly, and then like slipped and went all over the place, under the dot moon, like it was frantically writing a Chinese character saying *Save me* or *Get out of there*. Then it went into a wiggly free fall, fading away, and the string took off faster across the lawn, way beyond the kids going after it.

The kite either came down on the beach, unseen except in patches past the hedge, or it went into the water, maybe, where the waves were breaking in. Lizzie still stood there with her mouth open, a little *o*. The brother father strode toward the break in the hedge where white railings led between naked rose hips to the stairs down to the beach, and the gaggle of kids swarmed over to join him and head, giggling, down to the beach.

Lizzie looked up at Simon and said in a troubled little voice, Sorry.

It's okay, it's your kite, was Simon's not exactly comforting solace. He knew that kids knew, and were more serious and clear-eyed about right and wrong, and the worried life in between, than adults, and so he didn't soften his dealings with them, which in a way was a kind of respect. Though he also was gentle with them and could enter into their tenderness and total, like, perception walled with pure emotion. Like the time on his hands and knees in Brooklyn with Bennie, both of them watching a tiny bug with six legs and antennas making his ordeal way patiently over the bumpy carpet planet surface. He remembered exactly what it was like to be a kid, because he had never lost it, and in a way was still very much there, whatever that charmed immediacy is, kind of naturally stoned, which was part of what he thought of as his kind of enlightened like existential grace and gift advantage and special mental-spiritual space, but was also, let's face it, his built-in disadvantage and like mental retardation.

Lizzie was looking right at him. He looked right back with his eyebrows lifting his shut-mouthed face, like, What?

Did you kill your father? she asked him matter-of-factly.

Their eyes remained locked without any confrontation or tension. She was the fist person to ask him this.

Nope, he answered calmly. She seemed satisfied with his answer and now was done with him for now, probably forever, and said,

Can I go and get the kite too?

Sure, Simon said. You can do whatever you want. You always can. You should remember that.

She took off with her fists pumping and her bare little legs going like fingers under her dress.

Back at the house the others drifted inside. Simon saw Mrs. in the window to one side, looking out like a portrait in her frame, looking trapped in her life. Right then Simon's car returned, took her long enough, and stopped where it stopped before in the turnaround. The girl driving had her sunglasses on and didn't move or get out. He headed over there, pausing to glance into the garden enclosed by hedgerows. It was like he remembered it, except smaller, with no flowers yet, the beds of dirt covered partly with straw, flattened and gray from the winter on it. A few robins ran up and down the strips of grass between the beds, pecking for worms. The statues were gone. The fountain, not going, was a swan with its neck extended, looking straight up. The pool had a black stone rim. It was dry, with spidery cracks in the concrete, matted with dead leaves over the drain. The new air and this particular sky, the sun not very high this time of year and racing island clouds, and this place here where he last was with Mum, were all right from his childhood, like everything these days, around here and in him. It was like his life was on trial, like open season on Simon, so the full file's open. But right now, this moment, especially, with a conspicuous presence of then, and just as much Mum, her obvious but kind of overwhelming absence—

Sticking to that side of the lawn, he went toward the house, but didn't cut over to it, and didn't look over as he revolved the bulk of the house past him and got into the Crown Victoria and said,

'Kay, let's go.

Simon said the same thing now he said at the beginning of the summer, when asked what his plans were for after the summer,

I don't know, I'll see, even though now it was already after Labor Day. If he didn't want to talk about it, fine, but it seemed like he did, in spite of himself, when he added, It depends.

On what?

On what happens, shrug.

What do you mean, what happens?

It was like an interrogation every time. He invited it.

How much money I have. The defensive, dismissive tone said leave me alone, but the lean of silence after, something brotherly, tacit, said more, please ask me, help me.

But don't you know how much money you have?

He shrugged, but nodded yeah, pretty much.

Or couldn't you make a list right now of the money you've got coming and add it up?

I *could* . . .

Well, what do you still have coming in that you don't have yet?

Well I have three sort of commissions, this lady who's a friend of Ginny's friend over in Rockport wants three of the Camden Hills, or like one or two of the Camden Hills and one of her view out to here—

And how much, like about four hundred for each one?

Yeah, up and down, but yeah, about . . .

Okay, then say you do them all, that's twelve hundred—

And two people haven't paid me yet for ones I did, and Steven wants another night one . . .

Okay, then you'll have two thousand dollars if you do them all.

Yeah, but I might not.

Why, you might not be able to finish them all?

Oh I could easily, but I just might not, like if it's a nice day I'll go out and do another new painting somewhere, maybe . . .

Well it's in your hands.

Yeah, not really.

What do you mean—if you want to do them, you can.

Yeah, but that's not how I do it, I go with the flow and see what happens.

Well if I were you I'd make sure I'd do them, so I could plan.

Well that's you.

The light and the wind direction had changed the way it always does right on schedule right after Labor Day, like somebody flipped the big switch and summer's over, and the windy morning ripping the wrong way up the Thorofare had that desolate emptiness, like something wrong was revealed in the different light and sharp shadows hiding nothing, and people were going or gone.

Well say you had two thousand dollars at the end of the month, where would you go?

I don't know but I've got a couple of people who haven't paid me yet, too, but Steven I still owe some to and it'll be more for September because I can stay there still.

Oh so you're not coming back here when Dad leaves?
He cracked a smile in his brown paper face and lied,
Nope.
Yeah right, but he stuck to his lie, his life. But so what are
the different possibilities you've been thinking about?
Southwest.
That's pretty vague. He shrugged slo-mo like so what, it's
pretty. Where do you think, like Arizona?
Yeah or New Mexico or Texas. He bristled uncomfortably in
his chair like the question like spiked his clothes, but he
answered readily enough, and could have left if he felt like it, or
just stopped talking, like he usually did most of his life. I like
like Texas, and I've never even seen the Rockies. Except, for
that I'd have to get a car.
That would take your two thousand right there.
Knocks not quite hammering were Dad out there, then it
stopped, but the presence persisted.
Or I could go to Boston, I was talking to Katherine.
Oh yeah? Do you have something going with her?
No way, he winced like his back hurt. Or I don't know,
maybe New Orleans . . .
I thought you hated it there and never wanted to go back.
I don't hate it there, one slow shoulder coming up to his
turned chin like inner flexing, or constricted stretching, like in
a yawn, there are some good things about it, too. I was just in
kind of a rut.
Could you get your old place back?
No, that's gone, but it's no problem getting a place there.
He pinched at the wax drips on the candle and the scab where it
pooled on the glass candleholder like a melt-rounded ice cube.
Rent's so cheap down there I can live on like three hundred dollars a month.
If you finished the paintings you said, and get paid, you
could live for six months.

And I can sell paintings down there, I have people.

Sounds like maybe you should do that, but Simon's face didn't rise to it. Finish those four paintings and get paid, take your money down there, and you're set for the winter—you won't have to get a job.

I never have to get a job, he said, offended at even the word trying to be associated with him in a sentence.

Okay, fine, but if you went anywhere else with just two thousand dollars, it seems like you'd have to work.

I get by.

Okay, fine—I'm just saying, it might make the most sense to take your two thousand dollars down to New Orleans and you'll be all set for the winter.

Simon didn't exactly do back flips over the plan.

Anywhere else you'll have this whole thing hanging over you of not knowing how you're going to make it through the winter.

I can sell paintings.

Yeah, maybe, but that's such a risk, and you're putting so much pressure on yourself, creating anxiety.

He sort of smiled blithely, but weird, like no pressure could ever touch him from this world, even though you could see it touching him heavily at that very moment, most moments.

Whereas if you go to New Orleans with that money you'll know you're set, and then if you sell paintings, good, that'll be gravy, and you can live like a human.

If I take that money down there I'll just gamble it away at the track, I know myself.

Well just *don't.* He was resigned before the fact, before the act, like a self-convicted felon knowing his fate way beyond the reach and like parental range of any court.

You could pay your rent like six months in advance, and then you'll have it taken care of.

I'd never do that, I need the money.

He poked at the sore under the corner of his lip, and grazed the bacon surface with loving little fingertip brush taps.

Besides, if I doubled it at the track then I'd have twice as much, just like that, in one bet.

The washing machine started, in its final spin cycle, to bang away like a marching band drum.

It's like you don't want to help yourself, Simon.

'Zackly, he smiled in his way like a strange, proud enigma, instead of being perplexed or worried or wanting to change.

Well it's hard to want to help you if you don't want to help yourself.

Fine, I didn't ask for any help.

Well you did, by bringing it up and talking about it, and anyway—

You're the one who asked all the questions.

Yeah but you invited them, Simon, you wanted to talk about it to help you figure out what to do.

I don't need any help from anyone, he said, getting up, leaving his plate with toast crumbs and a red jam smear on the table, went into the kitchen and the washing machine went off with a bang, so he went through into the laundry to take his things out of the washing machine and put them in the dryer. He stood in there, still, after the dryer began, with his fingers playing like on a keyboard, or like drawing a little on the front edge of the dryer, and stayed there, framed in the window, in the dimness under the shed slant roof, partly indoors, partly out—just standing there like that.

It rained during jury selection, days of the same. And the same girl, day after day, drove him into Boston. They talked a little, and Simon liked the foreign curl, a nice lilt in her voice, like French, or Caribbean, like both, but different. He asked her, and she said she was from Madagascar, and he loved that. They got to be kind of friends, not really talking, but she was his regular driver to the trial, which was taking its sweet time. Headline news, even when nothing happened. Finally the big show began.

The prosecution's case was predictable and strong. First, led gently by Sandra, came Gail, the traitor caretaker cleaning person, who told how she found Dad. Then Sandra trotted out the state's team of crime scene Keystone Kops, detectives, forensic and medical examiners. They took a week.

Then came Janice. Simon was surprised. He knew she was on the witness list, but no one had said anything since, especially her. She smiled at Simon as she sheepishly took the stand, almost tiptoeing, like apologizing for being there. Simon didn't smile back, but looked her right in the eye. He didn't have a good feeling about this, and the way her forced, half-hearted smile wilted on her face. After that she didn't look at him, but kept looking to Sandra Gorman to ground her and help her along. She told about being friends with Simon in New Orleans, how she always liked him, and still did, and how last summer he came to stay in her barn in Rockland.

Did he tell you why he needed a place to stay?

Yes he did. He said he'd had a fight with his father—

Objection.

I'll allow it.

Did he tell you about the fight with his father?

Yes he did.

What did he say?

That they'd had an argument about their island, which his dad had given away—

The same island that someone burned later in the summer?

Objection, Your Honor. There is no—

Sustained. The last question will be stricken from the record.

Okay, go on. You said they had an argument about the island . . .

Yes they did, and about a number of issues that had apparently been building up tensions between them for years. At least for Simon.

Such as?

Well, such as Simon's dad's alcoholism, and his remoteness as a father.

Go on.

And about the fact that Simon was staying at his father's house against his father's wishes when no one was there. This was why he came to stay with us.

There seems to be a pattern here—

Your Honor—

Continue with your questioning, Miss Gorman.

We'll get back to the island, and the alcoholism, and the fact that Simon stayed in the house against his father's wishes—but first, tell me, was there anything else they argued about?

Yes there was. They argued about Simon's mom's death. And money from a lawsuit connected to the accident.

Go on.

Well Simon apparently overheard his mom and dad having an argument before she died in the accident?—in which Simon heard his mom say to his dad that if he didn't quit drinking she'd kill herself. And then soon after that when she was killed in the accident with the train, Simon was sure she'd killed herself, that she'd driven into the path of the train on purpose . . .

She looked down and you could sense her concentrating on not looking at Simon; then she couldn't help it anymore and she glanced up at him. Her mouth moved in a weird way, her lower lip and chin like rippled and opened on one side, and there was a fleeting plea in her eyes. He looked back at her with a flat, not very friendly expression, and she looked away with a flustered little shake, then looked at Sandy Gorman, who got her back on track by nodding encouragingly, *Go on.*

So from that Simon felt that his dad was to blame for his mother's death.

Do you remember exactly how he expressed that he held his father responsible for his mother's death?

Yes. He said his dad killed his mom.

This is really sick.

I know, Timmy whined, I *agree*. Over the phone, like this, or in person, it didn't matter, it was the same. Anna seemed to blame him for the recent twisted turn. He heard the baby in the background and wanted her to get off and go get him. He was glad he wasn't there. The *Post* headline read,

THE WIFE DID IT!

The *Herald,* in Boston, ran,

CURTIS
SHOCKER
WIFE HIRED HIT

Both tabloids had pictures of Dad and Simon—the same two pictures—and of Red. The words were different in the two articles, but the story was the same. Inside sources say evidence points to Virginia Curtis, widow of murdered Richard Cary Curtis, conveniently off in California at the time of the crime . . .

As the single beneficiary of the deceased's hefty insurance policy and his will, the dishy socialite, savvy Democratic Party operative, former assistant to Lieutenant Governor Tommy O'Neil, and special assistant to Governor Michael Dukakis during his run for the presidency, Ginny Curtis had everything to gain by her husband's death.

Freedom, among other things, from his alcoholic tyranny.

Sources say there is evidence that she hired someone, through contacts, to commit the murder. Questions remain as to whether she intended to have the murder committed in such a way as to frame Simon Curtis, who was staying at the house in secret after she left, or whether his presence there was unknown, and a coincidence.

Simon rolled into the kitchen around eleven and let out a loud *Ha!* when Timmy showed him this. Timmy slept till ten for the first time in ages up in Phoebe's canopy bed, and was now on his third cup of coffee and third English muffin. He felt like Simon. There were no eggs.

You think it's funny?

Tchyeah. Simon glugged o.j. from the carton.

Well I think it's sick.

Simon did his smooth slow shrug.

Maybe that's the way it happened, he said, staring, still asleep, into the refrigerator zone of being. You don't know.

Simon, you're lucky I'm even here! Timmy shook.

Touch-*ee*. Yeah really lucky. Thanks a lot.

Simon, what do you— Timmy stood up. How can I—

You can't, so just forget it.

Do you want me to just leave?

I don't care, do whatever you want.

In the stung silence zinging between the old yellow walls of their original kitchen, where it all began, shrunken now by their hulking adult ghosts, something softened, or Simon relented, enough, at least, for Timmy to say,

Simon, so many times I look at your life and it breaks my heart—I think of how Mum would feel if she saw how you live, I think how there's no one else in the world I grew up with but you, we played all the time and fought and totally formed our personalities around each other, and even if you don't care about me anymore, I'm not like you, all hardened and weird, I think of your life sometimes and I feel like, *What happened to you?* and I feel so sorry for you—

Timmy was tearing up, his voice going that way, too, and Simon said,

Don't, not meaning don't cry, though that, too, because look when he said it, but meaning, don't feel sorry for me. I choose to live this way, he added, gently sort of grabbing Timmy's hands clenched in front of him as he said, *I'm okay.*

This killed Timmy, and he cried worse, shaking his head with his face contorted. He talked through it:

And even though you act like you don't like me, I cherish our childhood and I love you and wish we could get along, out of all the people in the world, you're the one I grew up with, I have you in me, and—

Simon was welling on the bursting edge of crying himself, now, but busted out of it by saying,

Don't feel sorry for me.

But I *do*! Timmy's voice was straight, but his face was crying freely. How can I not? Look at the situation you're in!

No cat came by, no Mum came home in her car right then. This was the only blue world left.

I love you more than anyone—even though you're so hard to get along with.

Well I don't love you more than anyone, I love everyone the same, and I love everything the same.

You love everyone the same?

Yup. And I love a tree the same as I love you.

Well I love you more than a tree.

Look I'm glad you're here, okay? This he offered like an apology, or like a conciliatory way out, as he noticed from the almost empty pack, folded in half, how many English muffins Timmy ate.

Well you don't act like it.

Timmy was relieved and grateful, but too upset, still, to just let him off like that. He felt like pushing it a little more.

Why do you want me here?

You're my brother, okay.

There was no bite or edge or defensive resentment in his voice, nothing sarcastic, just a flat direct acquiescence that was almost a plea. Timmy read this right, and after a pause, breathe, gave him back,

Okay, and gulped the rest of his coffee down, and rose to refill it from the automatic drip by the sink. The custom blend beans were ground and frozen, from Ginny, in a gold foil unlabeled bag, it was really good. Really good.

The *Globe* had a normal article about the trial getting under way. Since the opening statements concluded so succinctly the day before, they had the day off today, Friday, and then the weekend.

Wanna go to Crane's Beach? Simon asked, while working his way, standing, through his series of English muffins, the last ones Timmy left. He put sliced roast beef from Henry's in a packet on the last two, call 'em lunch, with mustard and a leaf of almost white lettuce on the last.

Are you allowed to go there?

Timmy didn't want to go to Crane's Beach with Simon. He wanted to just take it easy here, make the best of it, since he'd agreed with the lawyers and Red to stay with Simon for right now—Simon didn't know this. But he also just wanted to leave, but not go right back to Brooklyn yet. He thought of Katherine in Jamaica Plain.

They don't care where I go.

Simon.

'S true.

Simon, it's your condition of bail.

They just said all that in court for court. But they don't really care.

He didn't say he'd seen the cops and they'd seen him in town and at the beach the other day, and that they didn't say or do anything, but that's what he was thinking. And the way it took them so long to get the electronic surveillance set up, the monitors and the bracelet. He showed it to Timmy.

Actually it was an anklet, not a bracelet, and more like a plastic hospital one than the metal clamp he pictured when they first said. A wire band went around inside the middle of the sort of turquoise bluish plastic, doubled over for about two inches where your name would go. They put it on him down at the police station with this clamper thing the FBI used, when it finally got there, that melted the plastic together when it made the clamp. He didn't know if there was an extra little thing inside there, besides just the wire band, like a trip wire or something, or a chip. If there was, it was tiny, or really thin, maybe to try and trick you, like if you tried to cut it or take it apart. They made him take off his shoe and pretty raunchy sock to put it on, and told him go ahead and do anything you ordinarily would, like take a shower or a bath, and don't worry about breaking it, but whatever you do, don't cut it, or it'll set off the alarm, and you'll go straight back to jail.

The alarm was in the police station, the same one fancy security systems in expensive houses in the town were hooked up to. Dad and Ginny never got one, like a lot of people in the eighties did, like the Hunters next door, they figured why bother, the house was too huge, you'd have to put those little things on all the windows and doors, tap in on the keypad every time you came home, fast, before it went off, and besides, they never got robbed all those years, except a few times by Simon, like the silver that got reported to the police by the antique dealer in Essex because one of the things had Dad's name engraved on it, his and Mum's wedding date, and ushers' signatures. And then, well, this last time.

Also down at the police station, in the same room, on its

own metal table on locked wheels, was a black box monitor, more like a video game than a computer, with four white dot blurs apart in a trapezoid constellation on the blue lit screen, and one other finer dot between them, which was Simon, sitting at home watching TV, or moving around, wherever he went. He had to go like five hundred yards for it to move like an inch. No one ever actually told him he had to stay inside the dots, or exactly what the rules were, except go home and stay there was the idea, obviously—at least he was like officially welcome there now, Dad. And though they argued in court a little about the phrase "home vicinity," and the parameters, after it was supposedly settled and they let him out, no one said anything else—except like Zwirner, who he didn't listen to— even when they were hooking him up to this whole monitor system. The four dots were what the techno guys setting it up called *the fence,* though they didn't really make a fence, except like by dot-to-dot on the screen, which were the borders, though nothing happened if you passed through it, like an alarm or like an electric zap on your ankle, except you saw the dot Simon cross if you were watching. The only way the alarm went off was if the wire in the bracelet, as they kept calling it, even though it was on his ankle, was cut. But what if it was cut out of range of the home monitor, like outside the fence, Simon wondered, there's no way it would ever know, except what, like by satellite? And so it really was only a monitor, he felt like, not an alarm/alert like electronic jail you wear, or a fence to really keep him at home, and it was only a monitor if you looked at the screen, which hardly anybody ever did there, he bet—

The four blurred dots came from four beetles, they called them, mounted around the property, all actually on town-owned land, technically, right along the road surrounding their property as best they could from the road, which was why it was that fallen trapezoid shape. One was on a telephone pole

down by Smelly Beach on the track side, right where Boardman
Ave begins and the white sign with black lettering saying,

PRIVATE WAY

RESIDENTS ONLY

hangs from the granite sort of entrance block. Simon went
right down there the first day they hooked it all up to check it
out, they didn't say not to, and he found it like a kid playing
army, climbing up those rusty sort of wickets sticking out of
the pole like bones out of Frankenstein's neck, up to near where
the wires were, and there the little sucker was, no bigger than a
flashlight-sized battery, except squared off like those old radio
ones with the weird little tongue-touch male and female nipple
top. It was attached to the telephone pole by two bands of wire
like an inch apart that were screwed tight with a couple of those
screw thingies with notches on the wire band to tighten it with,
they look almost like movie film, but made out of metal, going
through a reel. How the thing sent out signals or received anything was a mystery, because it wasn't like a little dish receiver
like you might picture, it was just this little like pud.

The other ones were by the bottom of the driveway on the
post they stuck in near the hydrant with one of those orange
square metal signs raised from it for the plow. That one they
half hid in the rhododendron down there gone wild over the
years like Tahiti or something. The third was on the telephone
pole past the other driveway below the valley of the Hunters.
That one he spotted like bird-watching, there it is. He couldn't
figure out how they got it up there, the pole didn't have those
ladder handles. Just go up like a coconut climber? They must
have used a ladder, one of those cherry pickers from a truck.
The last one was down by the railroad tracks, right near Mum's
crossing, almost like they did it on purpose, or if not them,

then whatever it is out there that's the pattern maker of life, with all its mysterious little connections, which who can say what it is, exactly, God, but it's definitely there. If those were the kinds of signs and like ontic alphabet he could read, or at least try to, maybe, like a dog with an inkling giving a sheet of math on the sidewalk the sniff test to verify it, then no wonder he wasn't worried about what was happening around him, and sort of to him, they wished, these days, or ever, because it was all like water in the river flux, or ashes in the blown veil of maya, himself included, like in that pretty new Bob Dylan song, "Man in the Long Dark Coat"—*people don't live or die, people just float.* Except all people did, really, was worry and rush around, with worry and rush their fuel and fate.

They were sitting in the kitchen, not deciding, when a car pulled up and slowed to a tentative stop in the middle of the driveway. It was a blue Nova, classic sunken uncertain like bachelor worker's car of America with Mass. plates. The window went down halfway but the face stayed undeveloped inside. Simon watched from the very side of the kitchen door over the porch and rhododendrons with their fat arrowhead buds just starting to get sticky and swell. The dog was at Gail's now, Ginny's orders, so no semi-watchdog service out there wagging and not barking.

Timmy looked up from the paper at Simon peeking out, almost hiding, and was struck more by this sneaky performance in his own sort of home than by the other little mystery of who it was out there, arrived in the blue nerve of the morning rolling brightly over already into another afternoon—

Who is it? Timmy asked and Simon, without looking back, answered with his hand pumping down slow for Timmy to stay put, compadre.

It's not a delivery cuz those guys get right out. His breath whitely, barely evanesced on the glass by his lips like Dad's, and Dad's father's, plumpish cherubic and sort of senatorial-voluptuous. And the paper's already here, both of them.

The engine stayed on and it was like that Massachusetts movie the other night he kind of liked a lot, *The Friends of Eddie Coyle*. The car was lurking, kind of like a shark, and looked unemployed and definitely not from friendly waters. Simon was wearing red weird jeans and a red T-shirt like a person from that cult in Oregon, which wasn't so far from him, actually, except it was being with people. Timmy looked at him and wondered why his brother was so weird. Simon's mouth was hinged a little open, oddly askew, his eyes were cupped back in bone sockets, his arms hung oddly like a Neanderthal.

Guy's just sitting there, Simon said and opened the door and went out.

Timmy didn't continue to read the paper, nor did he get up to look out the window and watch. Simon was out there for a while. When he came back inside, Timmy, just heading out of the kitchen, acted like he could care less who it was or what they talked about. Simon waited for him to ask, but he didn't, so he said,

Yeah, so that guy was kind of weird.

Who was he? Simon followed Timmy through the coat corridor into the front hall, where Timmy, like Dad used to, looked through the mail on the brown thing, heaped there where the blue bowl used to be, his brow-heavy image in the mirror perfectly copying his movements and every little move.

I don't know, some guy.

What was his name?

I don't know, something.

The name went in one ear and out the other, or was like stuck somewhere in between. Rick, he thought, or Rink, which he knew wasn't right, so he didn't say. Timmy kept his reflection's ghost-guy counsel. He looked at his hands holding the mail—Dad's—bills and who knew what, not his business really, except if he didn't deal with it, who would? Simon?

Simon, you talked to him all that time and you don't even know who he is?

So.

Are you really that stupid?

Simon made a fleeting stupid face at him with a jelly jaw and *uhhh* mouth and annoying eyes.

He was probably a reporter.

Simon froze for a second then convinced himself on the spot that he thought of that before and decided, that guy, no way.

That guy wasn't a reporter.

How do you know?

Did you see him?

No.

Well if you did, you'd know, too.

Simon picked at a little something between the side of his chin and his lower lip, making it worse.

Witness, in his permanent permanent press tuxedo and stoned state, blinked awake from a quick sideways nap into a languorous yoga stretch and then poured himself nimbly off the couch. Like a couple after a little spat, the brothers both stayed there and felt a little better.

So you wanna go to Crane's Beach? Simon floated.

He kind of did want to go.

Well I have to call Ann, see when I should get back. I should probably get back pretty soon.

I thought you were going back tomorrow.

He pushed the problem he was working on out with his tongue and tried to crush it that way, between thumb and forefinger. He winced.

Yeah, well, I have to call Ann and see . . .

Like the cat, but upright, large, and less languid, Timmy retreated into the shadowy cool of the TV room.

I know what we should do, Simon said when he emerged from taking a pee, standing there in the bathroom for a while with it hanging out, looking at the different pictures from different times in their lives. Like Dad's father's team picture, the jerseys spelling the mantra of this whole tired legacy that made them and kept them in its numbing continuity:

ANDOVERANDOVERANDOVER . . .

We should go to the Red Sox game. They're playing Toronto. They've already lost like six straight, and that was after losing the first four, but Clemens is pitching and he's still good, though he's getting old. Y'know, he squeezes rice to strengthen his grip. You squeeze really hard and they crunch together a little bit.

Timmy looked at Simon Rajneesh in red lounging on the brown couch like a human cat in psychoanalysis, Timmy the reluctant shrink/brother, unwilling and unqualified . . .

Are you allowed to—

Don't worry about me. I go to Boston every day for court, don't I? It's the same parameters.

Simon was picking up the legalistic lingo with a curious adhesion. His phrasing and sentences also took on at times an awkward aping of technical legal expression, like cops or ordinary Joes on TV, or on the stand, anywhere self-conscious, trying to sound really professional and intelligent and by the book, which always came across as stupid and wooden or, like, trying to sound smart and official. Add that to Simon's already odd articulations, and you get his own curious brand and blend of legal and Simonized language. Like when Timmy said what about tickets, and Simon answered,

Don't worry, I'll take care of the tickets, Mr. I'll-Handle-It, suddenly. I'll make a call and then we just pick them up prior to the game.

Prior to was one of his new phrases he stuck in there whenever he could, like he was more on top of everything and the way the world works than before, when he just said *before*. Another one was *at this time*. He knew from ads on TV during the games how to order tickets. Call 1-800-SOX-TKTS.

How'll you pay for them?

I said I'll take care of it. Simon shut his eyes.

Simon had Red's Visa number, expiration date, she wouldn't mind. She wouldn't notice.

And we should ask Katherine if she wants to go.

Timmy didn't say no; he actually liked the idea. But he didn't want to call her because Anna would be pissed if she knew he called her to ask her to go to a Red Sox game, especially after they sat in court together the other day—the papers called her an unidentified woman friend. He knew she'd be pissed even if they went to a Sox game with her—she with them—but he was willing, in fact eager, to do it, and argue and suffer the consequences later, if it came to that, a guy has to live, please—so long as he could say he didn't invite her, Simon did.

So Mr. I'll-Handle-It-Prior-to-the-Game took care of the tickets, and then got her number from Timmy and called Katherine. She said sure, great. They'd pick her up in Jamaica Plain before the game. Timmy was quietly amazed. Simon never took initiative like that. Except like getting pot. And especially with a woman. He'd never had a real girlfriend before. Maybe he'd learned something, sitting around the last couple of months ordering food over the phone from Cooper's and Henry's, and calling the car service when he needed it. Reserving the tickets was incredible enough. But to say he was going to call Katherine, and then to go right ahead and do it, was astounding. Timmy wouldn't've been surprised if this was the first time ever Simon called up a girl, or a woman, just like that, in his life.

When Mr. Take-Charge/Charge-It called the car service for a ride to the game, Timmy stopped him in the middle of it, saying:

Simon, we don't need a car—I have a car. I'll drive.

Simon considered a second, then pushed down the button on the phone, hanging up without saying anything else to the person on the other end at the car service.

Then, on second thought, Timmy decided to leave his car here and drive Dad's instead, why not, why rack up more miles on his when he didn't have to, especially when the Escort wasn't working so well, these mysterious knocks when you slowed down, like someone trying to get out— So they took Dad's car.

Smoked a bone.

You didn't get directions?

Timmy drove and Simon sat there being driven beside him, his arms crossed with his thumbs in either armpit like a swimmer cold after swimming. Timmy wondered if he was cold, or if he was just holding himself like that, sort of slumped-stoned there, strapped into himself like a cocoon. When they left, Timmy suggested he wear a coat or something, since it still got cold these nights, but of course Simon said, I'm fine, Timmy, and stuck to his defiantly scant Rajneesh outfit.

It was getting lighter out later these days, and it was a nice, like, glowing dusk, the trees blushed by light green or a buddy rose haze in there, and commuters heading, thicker, half with lights on, the other way, as these two characters headed into Boston on the deeply ingrained, for both of them, mental track of 128. Timmy asked Simon the directions, to decide which way to go.

I have the ad*dress.*

But you don't have directions?

When they sailed past the Route 1 exit—Timmy decided to go the 93 way—Simon said,

Why're you going this way.

I think it'll be faster . . . But I don't know how you expect us to find Katherine's without directions.

Just go to Jamaica Plain.

The radio was on WBCN. BCN was good again, playing kind of alternative stuff, like they used to, after over a decade of being too commercial and pop. Most of the bands and songs that came on Simon didn't know but he didn't feel like ungluing his stasis and reaching over to look for other ones. Timmy knew a lot of them.

Somewhere along 93, the gravestone cluster of Boston buildings sticking up, still small, behind the faint greening fake fur distance of trees, Timmy realized that the last time he came this way was on the way to Dad's burial. He felt like time stopped then, though the world kept going, mercilessly, and here he was, still, in both, stuck in between. Everything meant motion except him. And Simon sitting there not saying anything.

Neither of them really knew how to get to Jamaica Plain.

Just go to Brookline, it's near there, Simon said, when they had to choose, in the sudden stoned convergence of lanes and the tricky turn, above the Boston Garden, for Storrow Drive. Timmy didn't really know how to get to Brookline, either, exactly, so he took the turn and went the way they went to the cemetery. It was too bad they weren't just going right to Fenway Park, because they were heading right now for the big CITGO sign outside the outfield.

At a minimart gas station in Back Bay, or maybe Brookline, Timmy got directions to Katherine's street. It wasn't far, though the directions were a little confusing.

Y'know Mum used to live in Jamaica Plain, as they crept along looking for the light after some Irish bar to turn at.

Yeah I know, Simon, she was my mother too.

Once on their way back from Christmas, or maybe Thanksgiving, in Brookline at the ponderous old place where Dad grew up, they stopped by the side of the road to look at the house Mum grew up in. It was sort of Tudor, not very big, with rough-cast cement painted off-white, and brown beams showing in structural triangles. It had no connection at all to Mum, no matter how much you tried, it was as impossible to think of her living there as it was to imagine her as a child.

A car in front of them, pronounced *kah,* had three caps lined up in the rear window like a storefront fan display: the Red Sox B, CELTICS rounded over a little green Irish guy wearing a derby spinning a basketball on his finger, and New England PATRIOTS. No Bruins, Simon thought, but Boston was like that, you were either basketball or hockey.

Katherine's street was basic working-class houses, just the same, lined up not quite touching, but very close, with gaps in between some for a driveway or a dog patch or little carpet strip of lawn surrounded by cyclone fence, and hers was one of them, painted mustard bad sienna with brown trim, like some of them were, like the Bruins.

The numbers on the doors were hard to see in the gloom and murky palette of the houses and the lives they housed.

Both brothers got out to go in, and Katherine came out before they got to the door—probably, Timmy thought, because her boyfriend was inside. A motorcycle rested aslant next to the stairs up to the porch. She wore braids and looked really pretty, and also pretty happy, which was nice for both of them. A dog chained to the neighbor's house barked loud in hoarse, harsh salvos of four, and she called out some like Spanish name for it to shut up, but it didn't. She wore cutoffs folded up to the knees and Teva sandals, like it was already summer. Simon looked at her legs and her, like, nice shape.

You should bring a sweater or something, he said. It was chilly out.

Oh, like you?

Simon had his arms crossed, clenching/hugging himself.

I should of. Simon's self-hug went into a shrug and a cute smile. Learn from my mistake.

She was convinced, and stopped on her way back inside, silhouetted and framed, to admiring eyes, in the light in the doorway:

Do you want something, too?

'Kay, if you have something.

Timmy in his gray Patagonia fleece, like he was on a climb, inspected the mica chips glinting in the black rock ledge they cut into a wall for the sidewalk and built the little lawn on top of. Water trickled down in a darker stain getting wider lower down. Maybe the whole hill was made of this rock and this was just an outcrop. He felt like Dad thinking that. Simon checked out the bike.

Katherine came back out after a pretty long time—boyfriend again, Timmy was sure—with a zip-up hooded sweatshirt and another top, and told Simon to choose one, holding them out, one in each hand, by the scruff of the necks, scarecrows with the life gone. Simon chose the more female of the two, even though the zip-up hooded sweatshirt was like it was already his, except without his holes or paint on it or just like dirty around the marsupial pockets. The one he took was sort of a Tyrolean pullover he put right on. It was tight on him but fit fine. He looked to Timmy like a fag street hooker who instead of a blow job would like roll you, like he said he used to do in the bad days in New Orleans. Katherine said no, it's all right, when Timmy said for her to sit in front, but then did when he insisted.

Now she was wearing blue jeans with a red patch under one buttock.

Y'know my mother used to live in Jamaica Plain, Simon, leaning up from the backseat, told Katherine.

Our mother, Timmy said.

They drove and got lost and got near. There was tons of pregame traffic and no parking places.

Let's just park like at a bus stop, or like that hydrant right there, Simon said. So what if we get a ticket. Meaning, it's Dad's car, so what can they do?

Timmy let that one pass. It was easier with Katherine there. He wanted to park in a lot, which meant they'd have to walk a ways. And pay. Katherine ended the quibble when a car behind them honked to go already by pulling out a ten-dollar bill and floating it like a leaf onto Timmy's lap.

I'll pay the parking.

From the street, as they walked toward Fenway Park with the streams of others coming together, the light glowed like there was extraterrestrial life behind the high walls. They couldn't find where to pick up the tickets, so Katherine asked a cop, and they walked halfway around the stadium to Reserved Tickets.

Coming out the alley to the seats and the field below, aglow, so green and bright, the clean cinnamon dirt and crisp white lines, was like a childhood revelation. It was incredible how hard and how far in a straight line the players could throw the ball while they were warming up. Their uniforms were beautifully chaste white, with the red lettering, and they all had fat thighs and pretty impressive arms, this close. The seats were on the first base side, behind the Sox dugout, about ten rows back. Great seats. Life was suddenly not so bad at all.

How much do I owe you? Katherine asked when Simon handed her her ticket, as the geezer in his conductor's hat and red coat showed them to their seats.

Nothing, it's on me, said Mr. Moneybags.

Timmy didn't say anything, but wondered how much the tickets were, looked at the price, and thought, Jesus, Simon, but was glad, too, they were good seats. Simon went off to get some hot dogs, instead of waiting for the guy to come around. Timmy wondered where Mr. Moneybags got the cash, and checked his wallet, not sure how much he had before, but he thought he had at least forty more. He and Katherine both got a beer with a cellophane lid held on to the sweating plastic cup with a rubber band. Someone had to put all of them on. And then when they swept up the stadium after the game, all the rubber bands.

Simon returned with three hot dogs, a big Coke, and a pack of peanuts stuffed into his pocket, and a big stoned grin at this bounty. He was chewing, just finishing his first hot dog.

Ont one? he offered them both, hoping they'd both say no or at least just share one of them. All three dogs had onions and pickles and mustard on them. Timmy took one and wolfed it down as fast as Simon devoured his second one.

You guys are going to die of a heart attack.

Not me, said Simon, though he didn't expand on why or how not.

Katherine asked a lot of questions, and commented on the colors and the light and how supernaturally vibrant and charged it was. She called the players studs.

Really you've never been to a game before?

Well, the Portland Sea Dogs.

Tseh.

Tseh nothin'. They're good.

They're minor league, like the way farm team for these guys. None of them'll ever make it here. Maybe one.

By the third inning the Sox were down three-zip on a single and a passed ball and a sacrifice fly, and then a two-run homer where no one in the stadium said a word, it was this really nice, sort of eerie, silence, with that sinking feeling of: Not another year like this again. It wasn't the Blue Jays like Simon said, but the Seattle Mariners. And it wasn't Clemens pitching but some Puerto Rican who looked like he knew he was going to lose, or like his back hurt him, he had this sort of mince in his walk, and this little wince on his face, the wispy little mustache custom made for the wince. When he got in trouble almost every

inning till they took him out in the sixth, he'd take off his cap
and wipe his brow with his biceps sleeve, then put it on again
and puff out his cheeks as he peered into the intensified zone of
the moment to the catcher squatting there flashing no-escape
finger signals against his crotch.

Simon told Katherine rules and little details, and Timmy, on
the other side of her, talked with her about her life, her wait-
ressing job, her art, her boyfriend. They were driving up to
Maine tonight, after the game, on his motorcycle.

Tonight? After the game?

Well, we were going to go tonight, like right now, but then
I wanted to come here with you guys. So we'll go after, no
biggie. He's taking a nap now, after work, so he'll be fresh.
We're both night owls, and the highway will be empty, smooth
sailing . . .

Did Jeremy get mad you wanted to do this?

Yeah, no. He gets mad at anything I do, she laughed, so I
just do what I want. Relationships are so fucked. She tugged on
her cigarette and spoke through it in a way that made smoking
look really good. But he's great.

Timmy didn't say a word about Anna the whole time, and
neither did Katherine or Simon, until after the seventh inning
stretch, when Katherine said how she and Jeremy were going
on vacation to Texas later in the summer, and Simon said,

Chyeah Timmy's on vacation from his wife, can't hack having a family.

Timmy looked at him appalled and incredibly pissed, and
wondered where that came from. Simon realized it was kind of
a nasty thing to say, and tried to like ride over it with,

So really you're going up to Maine tonight? You going to
North Haven?

Well, we're going to Portland, and I'm driving from there
tomorrow morning to Rockland to get the ferry.

It was seven to one in the eighth inning when they left, like half the other people there crowding out to beat the crowd. They heard the last inning on the radio. The Sox in their last wraps rallied for three runs with only one out, then it ended on a double play from a line drive caught on a reflex lucky leap, then fired to first before the runner even stopped to try and get back.

Rumor *hezzit* that kinda crazy Curtis, the painter, done it, was some *pissed off* about them givin' th' island away.

Dad came padding into the kitchen from outside. He looked left to Timmy with a nod of greeting, then looked right and saw Simon and turned away, and was about to walk away but stopped, and with head bowed made himself turn back to him again. Simon in the window stood facing the booming dryer not hiding but not looking at Dad either. Dad stepped toward him and opened the paned door to the laundry, letting out the booming twice as loud, as if the drumbeat of their tension doubled.

Do you know where the Whaler is?

He must have seen Simon take it, because he didn't ask Timmy first, nor did he assume Timmy had taken it over like he said he would.

Yeah, I took it over to Brown's. Simon turned his head only.

Oh—okay then, Dad replied. Brown's was the closest dock to Steven's apartment, above the Gal Gallery, where Simon was staying, and he obviously planned to keep the boat for his own use.

Dad looked trapped to Timmy, taking in the scene from the next room, as he pivoted partway to leave, his face a big brown frown, looking down, then turned back and spoke further to Simon over the slow, two-beat booming of the dryer, sneakers in there, a zipper clanking around.

What are your plans? Dad managed, if you don't mind my asking.

I'm going to Portland, Maine, Simon came up with, for a few days . . . and then I'm going to Boston, and maybe New York, and then I'll see . . .

Where are you going to live?

I don't know yet, Simon said quickly, and took this opening to ask, Can I stay here Columbus Day weekend? Which to Simon's presumed entitlement, Timmy knew, was already decided, no matter what Dad said, and not just Columbus weekend, but also the time until then, and no doubt after . . .

Elaine will be coming then, too, so yes, you may. Dad's bunched brow didn't soften.

How about next June, Simon tossed out while he was at it, can I stay here then? which he also knew he was going to anyway.

June, no, Dad managed to utter, and finding it not so hard, after all, to say, backed it up with a less authoritative mumble. And, folding and molding his hands like dough, his mouth set, he left.

During their encounter the rain began, and now was beating in light thrumming gallops, diagonal dashes and dots appeared on the windows, the fusillade of soft bullets pelted the house, and the thousand needles pinpricked the water with little coin prints everywhere, and when Dad left it came down harder, really coming down now, lifting a light whiteness over the surface of the water. Simon came out of the laundry place and got some potato chips up on their corner shelf and came in to Timmy, who didn't want to get into Simon's plans, or the boat, or anything Simon, so he didn't say anything. Simon, standing there, crunched his potato chips one after another, then opened his mouth wide for a bunch of them, broken pieces, and said, his mouth full and crunching, and wiping his hands on his pants,

So you're leaving tomorrow?

Yup.

That was all, and Simon withdrew, going through the living room, and as Timmy brought his bowl to the sink to rinse, saw him out in the rain-dark corridor down by the door jauntily throw back the curtain of the closet, a big purple Merrimeko flower pattern, totally Mum, like a cocky conquistador with his cape, and pull on the light within and stand there with his legs apart looking in at the stuff in there. Timmy shut off the gushing faucet, which sprayed him again because it was either on, gushing out too hard, or off, no gentle middle, and right then heard Simon say softly, but out loud,

No raincoats.

Timmy left the morning after they went to the Sox game, Saturday, midmorning, before Simon got up. He said good-bye when he went to bed, in case, and he also left a note.

Simon—
See ya.
Good luck this week.
Call me.
Love, Timmy

How come people said love in a note when they'd never say it like face-to-face, real life, out loud?

Love. It wasn't like he suddenly thought Katherine was perfect or anything, not at all, that's part of what made it so cool, it was just there, now, above everything else, for the first time he admitted it to himself, or let it come through all the way, and he couldn't help the new feeling, no matter what he thought or tried to think about her. It was like she was him, now, too, magically, with him, in him. When they dropped her off last night she kissed Timmy on the side of his mouth/his cheek, then leaned over into the backseat and kissed Simon smack on the mouth. And it's like, that's all it took. Then when she got out of the car, he got out, too, to get in the front seat, and give her the sweater thing back, and as they parted she squeezed his hand, their eyebeams locked for a split second in the animal dark and the instant highest dimension. And starting from then, though it had been starting all that night, and all those years kind of below the taut surface . . .

He couldn't help it, and he didn't want to. He felt like a new person, and also like himself the continuum, same person and floating force as when he was a child and ever since, and now it was like water came into water warmth, just right, and deep as the wait. Maybe it was extreme, but so what, love was extreme. He felt like everything was different now, like a blessing reward for his patience and the long, like, pause his life was up till now. A lot was changing these days, and now here was this, too, like he always knew. You couldn't just sit there, suddenly he was like everyone else, he had to act.

But so what was he supposed to do? He knew her, at least, which was a real advantage from other times, like when he didn't even know the girl. Which also made it realer, maybe— definitely. Often what usually happened with him was he'd see some girl he liked, like working at the artist supply store, or behind the cash register at some store in New Orleans he'd start going to a lot, or just walking in the street, like along St. Charles or Carondolet, he wandered around a lot, or like in Audubon Park, he'd have to go up to her cold and just say something, which was really hard, for him, especially, especially with a woman he liked, but he'd do it once in a while at least after years of not being able to. If he was painting at the moment at the site, it was easier, he could say like, This is my painting I'm a painter I'd like to paint you, and maybe they'd like his painting and be impressed and flattered or think he was interesting and say okay, like happened once with this

Guatemalan girl, she was really skinny, possibly very young, like possibly fifteen? though it seemed like, from what she said, she had a baby— But anyway, she said okay, and she came over and sat on his balcony, and he painted her profile, sitting there, and the leaves and branches and curlicue wrought iron railing, and shadows of them on the side of the house. She was barefoot and tiny, really beautiful, but you could tell that she'd lived a lot, with her quiet hardness, like she was made of stone, sitting there, but soft inside, like pudding, and no surprise in her eyes, she was like him, she was so little he could twirl her around on his finger, or like on his—

But with Katherine he didn't have to break the ice or like get to know her. It was already all in place, almost like by itself. No way would he tell Timmy a thing, he'd be totally jealous, and however he'd wreck it, he'd wreck it.

He could call her tonight, late, but what would he say, and where, actually, she wouldn't be there yet, anyway, and if someone else answered he'd hang up and then not call again, because they'd know it was him before. Witness kept following him around, so okay, Wit, c'mere, you wanna do something, let's go, and they went down to the cellar with this idea he half had, half-baked, before, but now here it was whole loaf, and got to work with Witness his willing accomplice. The power tools and a lot of the good things were gone, but there were hand tools on their nails on the wall above the workbench, and odds and ends in jars and coffee cans, and in a cigar box full of bits and things, he found a razor blade rusted on one side but sharp still, it was fine for what he needed it for. He got some pliers, too, and some wire snips, and some wire, and black plastic electrical tape, and a hammer and a little nail, and took them up to the TV room, with Wit following, fully aware she had a big role in this scene.

He sat in Dad's place on the couch, and with the TV on CNN, negotiations in Bosnia breaking down, he pulled his

ankle up on the other knee, and in the light he put the corner of
a paperback book tight in the gap between his actual ankle and
the anklet, and, trusting that it would work and not set off the
alarm down at the police station, since he wasn't breaking the
circuit, he hammered a nail, in one hit, through the metal
band, and the plastic coating, into the book maybe twenty
pages, perfect, as far as most people read, then he punched
another above it, same way, and then, half an inch away, two
more, just the same, so the four made a square. Then he used
the razor blade, with a little help from the snips, to cut away
the bracelet plastic between the holes he punched, so the wire
was showing. It should work right, if that show was right,
which why wouldn't it be, about these guys, or one guy, who
they never caught, who derailed an Amtrak train in like Arizona. The track is wired so if any of the ties come apart, so do
the wires, and an alarm goes off. Simon knew about train track
alarms not working. But so for this guy the solution, which
worked, was simple: you connect another, bigger, like loop,
piece of wire in two places to the wire you're going to cut, and
then you cut the wire between those two connections, so the
circuit is kept alive on the main wire, and so nobody knows it
was cut. They did that, then pried the rails apart, so when the
train got there, that was it. The news guy called the connector
wire a leader wire, and if it worked there, it'd work here for
Simon, especially with the train connection, and so that's what
he did now. He made a couple of like three-inch leader wires,
then attached them, twisting wire to wire. Why do they show
things like that on the news, so some other person, some psycho, can see how to do it, and go do a copycat disaster, caused
by the media, who covers that one, too, talk about making
news.

Then, like bracing himself, he snipped the wire in the home
detention device, as they called the bracelet. He knew it
wouldn't do it, but imagined the alarm going off in clanging

whoops, right this second, in the room down at the police station, and he half expected, but not really, to hear sirens in a
minute, and for a cruiser or two to show up, fast, with a skid-
stop out on the driveway, and out they'd hop, with their hol-
sters unsnapped for the first time ever, that rookie kid again.
But after about ten minutes, when nothing happened, he knew
what he already knew, that nothing would, now or ever, in this
whole thing. He waited for about half an hour and then taped
up the connections. Again after five or ten minutes of Bosnia
when nothing happened, he knew it was okay, it worked, like
he knew, he took the thing off his ankle and crowned Wit,
curled beside him like a pillow, and when she tipped her head
to paw it off, he pulled it down over her ears, pressing them,
collapsed, down, then popping up, one then the other, and
then he overlapped the taped part and taped it like that, tight
fit, just right, lovely necklace, Wit, now you're me.

This woman came on CNN, reporting from Sarajevo, she
was cute, kind of intense. When she was done she said her
name, and CNN, and she had an English accent, but her first
name was French, and her last name like Pakistani or Arabic,
and here she was on CNN, American, in Bosnia, reporting to
the world—

They took Dad's car last night and nothing happened,
except of course everything happened, too, in this awesome private universal expansive way, and so without deciding exactly
what he was doing, he got into the car, after taking care of the
cat, feeding him and then putting him out for his own adventure, and thought the car to town and through, right past the
police station, like a test, like so catch me, which he passed no
sweat, like he was invisible, like invincible, and went on where
the road went to Essex, past the boats in their marsh marina
across from Woodman's Eat-in-the-Rough clam and lobster
place, not open yet, and the antique stores with their stopped
time like their broken old clocks, and then past Ipswich, still

like the fifties, or Maine, on the Main Street, it was like you were closer to New Hampshire and north now, getting away from Boston and home and everything happening back there. Kids from school used to come all the way from here on the Newburyport bus, every day, and then all the way back to the massive white pines and firs up here, open arms out, each one like an explosion radiating from the human trunk and frozen in all their magnificent branch gestures along the roads and the highway lined up like psychic guardians, many deep and strong, welcome, safe, to New England the more Northern, where it hasn't changed and the workers' cars are rusted and the accents have no *r*s. Welcome to New Hampshire, and he knew he was a felon, now, after the blue sign marking the state line, but the friendly woman at the Exeter tollbooth sure wasn't on the lookout for him, and actually you weren't a felon if they didn't catch you, were you, and they never would, why would they, it wasn't like he was going to go rob a liquor store, or go on some rampage ending in a chase scene with gunshots. He wasn't even speeding, the other cars were rushing past him, actually, like bats out of hell, like on a mission from the devil, south, like go find God, north, or in flight just from life back there, or maybe some catastrophe, it seemed like, like Boston was burning, good, let it burn, maybe it was gone. Over the river and into Maine it was like another degree freer, and the smaller green sign, more modest, less state, more statement, said *Welcome to,* small, then in bolder white letters, the presence and place and, for Simon, supreme state of mind,

MAINE.

BCN faded, and the other Boston stations, before the main Maine one, WBLM, came in with its staples, still, of seventies rock, which for them wasn't like a seventies revival, like everywhere else, with them it never went away. Led Zep they still played, all the time, and Aerosmith, and like the Cars or Jethro Tull. It was a nice day, late morning, midspring, crowded over earlier with darkening, lowering clouds that would rain soon, and later on, but the light right now was nice, like sourceless ambient, with a glow that came and went and made the white lines on the gray highway highlighted bright, and the Stones came on, the drum stumbling in, one of their best songs,

I'll never be . . .

At the Burger King that used to be the HoJo's, on both sides of the highway at Kennebunk, he inhaled two Whoppers with bacon and cheese and a large fries and a strawberry shake, and then got another large fries for the road, with a handful of ketchups. He didn't know why he was so hungry, but sometimes you just were, and he didn't know where he was going exactly, except that he was definitely heading, like, north, like obeying another, huger hunger. Maybe he'd go out to North Haven on the last boat, he knew Katherine was there, to him she was everywhere, it was like her face was printed on the sky, and wherever he looked, her face, like that glow out there, he knew it in her eyes, and the way she paid attention to what he said, and little things, that she had him in her, too, same as him, and it made him feel like more like himself than ever before. Now he really believed in reincarnation, or like *be*-incarnation, because this wasn't just him and her, this was their souls together, you could tell, it was incredible.

The trees up there were behind by like two weeks, with more buds than leaves, just buds on some, and the grass along the highway had green coming up through the winterslept dead grass. The marshes now and then you passed, between the main population of trees, weren't green, they weren't ever green, they were the same old marsh grass light wheat color, windswept in one direction, bending or like matted down. Portland he never really liked, he blew right by it and then got off on the coastal route, Route 1, and after Brunswick like along that river, and over the bigger one in Bath, and beyond, it was like another, deeper degree of home nature arrival, and he felt that liberating feeling he always got when he got up here, like relief, like love in the air, a different kind than the highest one he had now, too. He got gas, almost didn't notice he was on empty, in Wiscasset, before the turn into town, the downward slope to the bridge winging across the river, the schooner of the bet Mum won.

Rockland had limp flags for some sad hopeful tourist scheme along Maine Street. Two pickups and two cars for the ferry, and a tarry green dump truck with a black tarp over the sand, that was maybe in line, maybe wasn't. He cut the engine in one corner of the lot and sat with the radio off, kind of vibrating, or feeling the stop, after driving so much, and he thought about the next move here. The next ferry, the last one of the day, was at four-twenty, and now it was around two. It still hadn't rained, and the clouds had moved up to a smooth marble ceiling. Maybe one of those cars was Katherine's. Maybe she was already out on the island. Simon always wanted to get married, don't laugh, but it was always not yet, no way, but now he could see it, totally, with her, they'd go to North Haven in the summers and both paint, live around Boston the rest of the time or more like Costa Rica, or maybe Portland, even, with her it wouldn't be so bad. Their kids would definitely have red hair, between the two of them, and would wear bare feet a lot, and be kind of little hippies, and maybe when they got older be musicians, or maybe like physicists or like doctors, the rebellion went like that sometimes, backward from laid-back liberal parents into real conservatism, so maybe they'd be like these little Republicans wearing bow ties and make some money, good, someone had to. He knew he'd be a good father because he knew still, totally, what it was like to be a kid, and how to be playful with them, but also be the boss and pay attention to the little things that matter to them so much. Also he knew, like firsthand, how kids tried to get away with things, so he wouldn't let them. Kids were like dogs, they were much smarter and knew much more than people realized, and they just wanted to be told what to do and to play.

He saw a guy he knew, whatever his name was, Ray, who worked for the plumber, walking in his beat Timberland boots and skinny blue jean long legs down the hill of the lot toward the ticket hut. He went in. He was skinny and pretty scrawny as a kid, blond like parted bangs, and an overbite, slight, but handsome, sort of, like a blond Kennedy, or one of the Bee Gees, but now, after like twenty years of lifting propane tanks and carrying them over his shoulder to the truck and doing whatever else for work, his arms were pretty big, and his chest, and he was still blond, but less and sort of boyish looking, still. He knew Katherine, they all knew each other, but she wasn't one of them, only she came from them, but she was different, like in a pearl category all her own.

Two hours till the ferry, forget it, plus what if she wasn't out there, or what if she was there, what, would he just walk up to her house, her parents', he didn't even know which one, it was one of them clustered up that road on the way to the golf course, and what would he say, and where would he spend the night, it would be too cold at home, and not fixed up, no food, he knew, he ate it all in the fall, except like some macaroni and cake mix, and no more gas, hey Ray, and the water wouldn't be on— Forget it. He kept going. Love could wait if it was love, and it was.

He went to McDonald's again, full order, drive-thru, to be safe. He was like a bottomless pit lately, it was weird, in the same way that life had endless possibility opening now, he had to like fuel it. He was gaining a little weight. Two pairs of his pants, he had only four, didn't fit anymore around the waist, not even close, in fact, suddenly he was getting kind of chunky, in fact he was getting kind of fat, though he kind of ignored it, but he had a bigger gut, he was thicker in the middle and thighs and arms and neck than he'd ever been, and he could feel it in his face, his cheeks, and like this gross chin-strap like bib layer, double chin, like Timmy and Dad, he hated it, and his hands, licking and looking at them now, greasy on the wheel and his lap, were thicker, and his fingers were sausagey, like Dad. His arms like this looked stronger, bigger biceps in a T-shirt, or crossing his arms, massive, and his neck was a little thicker, too, like a football player, or a bouncer, or some enforcer type. On TV he looked strange, which was just TV, he thought at first, which it was but also no way around it, he had his input, he was definitely fatter. Just from those few months at home, that's all it took, free food all the time, all you can eat, and he ate it all, boy, all day.

He kept driving, rural roads, woods, towns once in a while with a neon beer sign in the minimart window. Canada before he knew it. Jackman, the border, hardly even a question. Then Quebec like a whole new world, so close. He and Katherine could live here, have kids. Some hayloft life. Paint, eh? Farms, silos, really organized countryside. St. Everything everywhere. Gaz . . .

Simon didn't decide what he was doing until he had to, and in a way it was decided for him, which was often how it was with him, which actually was fine with him. It was getting cold up there, especially nights and rainy days, which was most of them, lately, and about a week after Columbus weekend they came and turned off the water and drained the pipes, so he really had to go. Columbus weekend Elaine came up with her boyfriend and this weird guy who didn't say anything or even look up, but just read the whole time, like he was under a serious deadline. Her boyfriend was this middle-aged guy with shaggy eyebrows and intense eyes who was this real estate wheeler-dealer and also definitely a drunk, but the kind who includes everyone in his expansive good party feeling. He had some buildings in Boston, and though Elaine's eyes were maybe trying to tell him at dinner to stop, he offered Simon the possible deal of an apartment in one of them, in Central Square, in exchange for painting it, and, month to month, painting the others, too, an apartment per month, for rent. Simon said,

Yeah, maybe, but wasn't that thrilled with the idea of Boston, though Katherine was there, at least, and said it was pretty cool, and some guys from Middlesex he hadn't seen for years, and actually didn't even really want to, who like never left. One of them used to be a national champion skateboarder, and was also really into Frisbee, and showed tricks to Simon, who was a real natural, too, after getting stoned together all the time, and now he was a painter, too, with a gallery in Boston and his own gallery that he ran on Martha's Vineyard. Simon kind of hated Boston, but he definitely didn't want to go back to New Orleans, which was like the city of his streetwalking depression, stoned the whole time, alone, like a hungry cat. Actually he had a cat there, who got shot. One day the little guy dragged his body home, walking just with his front legs, like pulling the rest of his blood-drenched body along, and then looked at Simon half like, *sorry,* half like, *help me.* He left there so glad to get out of there this last time, like a real low, it would be such a drag to go back there again, like with his tail between his legs . . . He didn't really have enough money to go out west to the Southwest because he had to have a car for that, at least when he got out there. Maybe he'd get some money in Boston and then head out there for winter. This deal with Owen was good because it was just month to month and he could take off whenever he felt like it, if Boston was really bad, or maybe he'd sell some paintings and go to like Hawaii, or Central America.

So when they turned off the water Simon called Elaine and got her machine, and so he hung up. But then he thought about calling her later, and her maybe not wanting Owen to give him the place, and just having to talk to her on the phone, and so then he called back right then and said to the machine in his slurry monotone,

This's Simon, I was wondering about Owen's apartment in his building, and hung up.

Owen called back that evening saying,

I know I know I know, like over his shoulder to Elaine as Simon picked up, and they talked about it, and Owen said it was still there and the offer still stood, if he wanted it, and he should come to Boston to make it definite. So Simon left that day on the late boat, sort of putting off packing all day, waiting till the last hour to start sorting through his clothes and paints and trying to figure out what to take, and when it was getting close he just stuffed a bunch of things, like a random selection, into a duffel bag, from Mum's closet, whose zipper didn't work, and some of his paints and brushes and things into brown paper bags, and then those into a garbage bag doubled up, so he was like a Santa Claus garbage man with a big black sack, getting onto the ferry at the last minute, giving the guy to tear the North Haven–to–Rockland half of a crumpled ticket he still had.

It was sunny and cold but nice out, and the island and the little islands in the Thorofare drew past like they were lying low, and by the Sugarloaves these near little cotton clouds, like shreds of fog, pulled past and partly over the sun, it went in and out and like pulsed. The White Islands were hunched down, like ready for winter, like hunkered down, and the Camden Hills, gray as the off-season bay, and blue, were half rubbed out like sleep. When the ferry pulled in, the bus was waiting at the top of the hill. Simon went right to it, without rushing, and the driver, who he'd had before, told him to go get a ticket down in the ferry ticket hut, so, still without rushing, because the guy was the one making him do it, he went down and got one, and some munchies from the machine, and went back to the bus.

The apartment building was five stories, brick, with stores

on the street level whose Arab like fish-people inside the like aquarium window waved to Owen as they went past the windows. The stairwell had a banister coming loose from the wall because they tried to just screw the supports right into plaster. The muffled *thmp-thmp* of rock bass came through the first door they passed, mouse-sized TV talk show clapping came through the next, something really sad tried to make these the sounds of his new neighbors he knew he'd never talk to, he knew he'd never really live in this place. Owen tried different keys on his over-full key chain, fiddled with the lock, then got it and pushed the door open. The apartment smelled like the ghost of old food trapped in there to die, but it wasn't a bad place, after the first sinking glimpse of any empty place. The kitchen had a window looking over a corrugated sort of shed stuck on the roof of the building next door with tar painted over the seams and slapped around, and rust bleeding down from the bolts. Over that was like a bank building, farther away, with the little blue symbol of sailboat sails and digital time, *11:11,* facing itself in white like palindromic lightbulb dots on a black rectangle sign, and, over that, plenty of open sky, cold cobalt today, but city, but still, so morning clear and hard it could crack. The other room had a window facing the same way, some bookshelves built in, and that's all, and it opened in a sort of double-sized doorway without doors into another room that would be the bedroom with no window, but one wall brick, exposed. It was pretty small, but it was okay, and to paint it would be like one day. A room to sleep in and have a TV, and a room to paint in, and a kitchen was all he needed. The light wasn't great, with only the one window in the studio room, but it would be okay, for now, it would have to be.

So could I move in now?

They agreed to do it month to month, with a month's notice. He could move in at the first of the month. He'd start by painting one of the rooms now. He would paint an apartment each month for rent, whether it was one of the one-bedrooms or the two-bedrooms, whatever order it worked out in, depending on the tenants letting him in. The two-bedrooms would count for one and a half months' rent. Already he was thinking okay, I'll do a couple of those right away, and that's four months free rent right off the bat, including this first one. Owen took Simon to the hardware store, where he had a charge account, and introduced him to the guy and said he could sign for paint and whatever supplies. Simon would come by later and pick up some gallons of that beige, rollers, pans, drop cloths, etc. They drove in the Audi back to get Simon's sack of stuff. Simon asked Owen if he had an extra TV or radio. . . .

The next day he walked around the streets and down to the Charles River, where two dogs looking for trouble hooked up with him. They were mutty city dogs, like with Irish Boston accents, but good dogs, probably hungry and dishonest, and he felt like taking them back with him. They didn't have any tags or names, maybe, either, anymore, if ever, and they followed him, even when he told them not to, but he decided not to take them back, too bad, doggies, sorry, get out of here, stop following me, but they followed him anyway, still, till traffic cut them off, honking, and someone yelled out their window at Simon and gave him the finger, whipping by, but he ignored him, but what an asshole, what a world, he hated the city, though there were vicious people everywhere.

He picked up the paint and a roller and pan and drop cloth and brush, and a scraper, one of those five-in-one things, and taking it all, in a box and bags, across the street, he felt like he was getting a new start on life, even though it felt like it wasn't very exciting, that it wasn't really his life, and wasn't really a new start. He spread out the drop cloth and got it right up against the wall, got the paint can open with the knife and fork Owen gave him, bending the tip, and poured the paint, sweetly smooth, into the pan, like melted coffee ice cream, pure and like purely factory manufactured. Rolling was fast, nothing like getting right to it. He got up on a chair. He tried to get the edges up at the ceiling with the roller, and almost could, but got some marks on the ceiling, which was white and didn't need to be painted. He tried to rub them off with his hand, and then his hooded sweatshirt sleeve, and tried with spit, it was latex, but the marks were up there, kind of a mess the more he tried to fix it, but not that bad, from far away. So after the first room he left the edges to do with a brush, after, and same with the corners. This would definitely take more than a day to do the whole apartment, but still he had a few days, or two.

Now he needed to figure out where he was going to go, and be, for the couple of weeks till he could move in here upstairs. Maybe he'd go out to Martha's Vineyard, or like Vermont, or down to New York, but all of those would take up money, and half of it he didn't even have yet. He should call those people who owed him or at least tell the post office in North Haven where he was, so if a check got sent to him they'd forward it. Probably he could sell some more paintings to the mothers, Mum's friends, out on the North Shore, so maybe he should do a trip out there, but it was a drag setting that up, calling them, and having one of them pick him up at the train, and then like having to see them. Like last time, they gathered at Mrs. Kendrick's for like a tea party with Simon, with him eating barbecued potato chips from the bag, and he showed them photos he had of paintings, and some of them bought some, and though they were rich, and Mum was dead, they were all real cheapskates, when it came down to paying, like they'd try and sweet-talk him down.

The phone was still on, good, from the person before, so he tried Red and her machine wasn't even there, and then tried Timmy. Anna answered. She tried to be nice, but he felt like she was fake, or too tight, or something about her really bugged him, as usual, and he gave her just one word answers.

So how are you?

Fine.

Where are you?

Boston.

She handed Timmy over, just getting out of the shower, and he asked the same things, and he gave the same terse answers, but when Timmy asked where he was staying, he explained further,

I'm at an apartment of Owen's I'm painting for rent.

Who's Owen?

Elaine's boyfriend, his tone like, *It's your own family and you don't even know.*

Oh him, oh yeah, Timmy had met him once, two summers ago, one weekend up in Maine.

There was nothing else to say, so Simon tried out one of his possibilities,

So I was thinking of coming down to New York for a while—but that didn't exactly get a standing ovation, so he tried the next—or maybe go out to Manchester, sell some paintings.

Dad's gone now, I think, for a week out to California, Timmy said and immediately regretted it, and then later *really* regretted it. He then overplayed a pause where he had to listen to Anna, to show her she was interrupting him, like she always did when he was on the phone, as if he had two ears, which, with his new haircut, he especially did, like sticking out like little elfin fins.

Oh, no—Dad is there, Ann says, just Ginny's gone for like two weeks to visit her mother, who's sick.

Well I wouldn't stay out there anyway, just go out for a day, Simon said, but after they hung up, he thought that maybe, actually, he would stay out there. Maybe Dad really was gone and Timmy changed it, because Anna like shook her head no, and like hissed, Don't tell him, and that's what they talked about in the pause.

The truth was he only had like five hundred bucks, actually, on him, minus the trip down, so he better be careful, but he'd figure it out, he always did, or if he didn't, which was a lot, or, in fact, most of the time, still it figured itself out, somehow, something would happen. Like, look, after all the times in his life he had situations or like problems way worse—here he still was. The next day he called Manchester to check if Dad was there, and he was surprised when he was,

Hello? and even more surprised when he spoke to him, instead of just hanging up, like he told himself he would if he answered.

Hi, Dad, this is Simon.

Simon, Dad said, and swallowed it. Hello.

Hello, Simon said back, with a hard edge in it. Dad waited a moment, because the pause was Simon's, it seemed, then said,

What's up?

Not much, I'm in Boston.

Boston.

Yeah I've got this apartment in Cambridge.

Cambridge, Dad echoed. Splendid.

Yeah, Central Square.

Splendid. Simon could picture him on the phone on the way into the kitchen, standing there in front of the bulletin board, maybe a cat lingering by his feet wanting to be fed.

Yeah, but the thing is, I can't move into it till November first, so I was wondering if I could stay out there in my room until then.

Simon, Dad hesitated, wondering what to say, and how to say it. You don't seem to understand you have to take responsibility for yourself. You're a grown man. Purportedly.

I take responsibility for myself fine, Dad, that's what I'm doing, just I need a place to stay, for like ten days, till my apartment opens up, and I thought, y'know, maybe I could go, y'know, *home?*

I'm sorry, but the answer is no, absolutely not, and stop asking. The *no* came rounding out, baritone, like pompous, and something about it drove right into Simon's sore spot against Dad, and he answered with an evenness in his voice that hid the real rage under its surface, except it quavered out a little at the edges.

You're just sitting out there in this big huge empty house by yourself, and your son wants to come home for a little while, because he needs a place to stay, and you say no— Well thanks a lot, and he hung up.

He rolled a joint and toked away the bad Dad vibe. Then he rolled the remaining walls and went and got a cheese steak sub, with onions and green peppers, for lunch. The cheese stuck to the tinfoil when he unwrapped it. He felt like he could live here, for a while, at least, and the sub was really good, though the limp green peppers, in with the onions, looked really like worms. The cutting in with the brush took forever into the night, but he had to get it over with, so he kept going. Really the ceiling should have been painted white again, to cover over those holidays, but it didn't have to be perfect, it was just some cheapo rental apartment.

He called Timmy again, which was more in a row than he usually did, but for some reason he wanted to tell him he talked to Dad.

Yeah, so? Timmy sounded asleep, or drunk, and not very interested.

So I asked him if I could stay out there, cuz I need a place till the beginning of the month when my new place opens up.

What did he say?

No.

What do you expect?

Nothing, but y'know what? he decided on the spot.

No, what, Simon? as if he could give a shit.

Fuck him, Simon said, I'm going anyway.

And so Simon took the train out to Manchester from North

Station, the beat-up bottom drawer of the rusty old Boston Garden, where the Bruins played and he went to games as a kid, with the big four-sided scoreboard hanging from the ceiling and championship flags from old Celtics and Bruins hanging from the rafters. At a Clash concert in there once he saw a guy fall from the balcony. His girlfriend was screaming at everyone to help, you *motherfuckers*! Finally they came and took him away, like dragged him, maybe dead, in a blanket.

It was after the commuters coming in, and he got there just in time for a train, which he took as a sign that this was meant to be, and he was doing what he should, which he already knew, anyway. The miles going out of Boston were such a mess, it was like the Industrial Revolution wrecked by the Civil War, all these burnt-out factory buildings and this wastescape of rusty heaps and glittering broken glass and rubble lots and abandoned buildings no one wanted to clean up because now we were busy getting on with the computer age, hurry up, and just don't look at the mess they made up till now, it's their mess, not ours—as the one love one world spins off in desperate runaway—

Going over the Salem Bridge into Beverly the sun was really bright out on the water, not glittering with separate sparkles of sun-shot, like the broken glass, but glaring, like with this one wide-angle sheet of glare. It was windy, so maybe that was why, and with the sun lower in October, with the creeping long light and short, helpless days. The wind made a molten texture, and whitecaps on the outer blue, so blue from the cloudless sky. Shadows were black, beginning this time of year, but the land still had its colors, but faded, and fading, merging darker. The buildings in Beverly seemed so puny, this was like the closest little city when he was a kid, when he'd come with Mum to get new shoes, or skates, or go to the doctor's appointment at the hospital where he was born up in one of those windows.

Familiarity deepened into the prickly unconscious on this last home stretch, and he got off at Beverly Farms, though Manchester was the next stop, because this was actually closer to home than Manchester, and this is where they always got off. He had clothes at home, unless Dad threw them away, so, carrying nothing, he headed up the tracks, walking with his sneakers sort of flexibly feeling the chunky gravel between the two directions, and balancing for as far as he could, pretty far, a bunch of times on the polished blade surface of the rail, smooth as a cheek, touching it, cold, and silver from use, while the rest was rust. Those spikes like big nails, if you chucked them end over end, went *thoom* into the water like torpedoes, age ten, around then, when he was like Huck Finn. Which he still was, true to himself, except now it was held against you.

Next morning, it seemed like two seconds after he crashed asleep, when it was getting light out, Simon was awakened early by the phone, which was lucky, because he could've easily slept through it, he was amazed he didn't, and slept who knows how long, and he had to be in court at nine. He didn't answer it, or even get out of bed. Usually these days he woke up at the right time from his internal clock just knowing, which almost always worked, which was good, because he didn't have an alarm clock, never did except his radio one as a kid, listened to music late into night. He went totally groggy zombie naked with a boner sort of bouncing into the kitchen passage and played back the message on the stool. It was Red and she said,

Hi, Si? Are you there? Please pick up if you are. Or okay, if you get this soon, it's seven-thirty Monday morning, call me at the Ritz, and he looked at the number written on the bulletin board at the same time she said it. He didn't know she was here. He didn't call her back, but the phone rang again while he was standing there, and again he let the machine get it. It was

Red again, and instead of listening to her again, he like made bold and picked up.

Si, you're there.

Yeah where else would I be, he croaked.

You're in a little trouble, sonny boy.

Tsyeah I know, he almost laughed this early, but she didn't with him, so—

Are the police there?

What do you mean, why would they be?

Well if they show up, don't say anything, and don't be a wiseass. She was like all business, but not unkind or bossy, just like direct and assertive. Where were you, Simon?

When?

Yesterday, last night.

I was around, why?

She sighed. Have you seen the papers today?

Why, what?

You violated bail when you went to the Red Sox game, Simon.

How'd you know about that? *Timmy?*

Simon, it's headline news. His hard-on was gone and now he really had to pee, bad. He was marching in place, slo-mo agony, like Bob Marley.

Really?

She waited for him to say more and he did.

They can't prove anything, and bes—

There's a picture.

He laughed a little nervous relief.

'S not funny, Si.

No I know I—

And what was that little stunt with the cat?

You know about that too, wow.

Zwirner's really pissed at you, Simon.

I don't care.

Well, you should care.

Why, he's a jerk.

Your life's in his hands, that's why.

My life's not in anyone's hands, he said to himself, and kept to himself. He was definitely awake now, like tiger avid, like the world was one way and he was another, it was back to that whole thing again.

Look, Simon, her voice softer, sweeter, her again, the side he liked that liked him. I didn't call to rag on you. I called because I'm concerned about you, I love you, and I want you to know I'm with you. Okay?

Barely audible, 'Kay.

It's just that sometimes you make it really hard, you know?

He really didn't know, but he played along contrite quiescent,

Nyeah, even softer, like a bleat below language.

Red sighed. Lifted them both out of the inquisition but into the place it came from, the worried world. So I'll see you soon, Si.

Cape.

I mean, technically speaking, we never worked out specific parameters of the home detention, except to agree on the use of the electronic device and the phrase *home vicinity*, Zwirner spoke with his mouth full.

Fenway Park is the home vicinity of the Red Sox, Jack, not of your client, Sandra quipped, also chewing with her mouth open, knees apart like the men leaning toward the table, in the judge's chambers, with the old yellowed map of Cape Cod under the glass under the pizza cartons.

He stretched the same lame but possibly valid excuse for the cat shenanigans with the electronic bracelet—that they hadn't defined, specifically, the parameters of the home vicinity—and perhaps they hadn't adequately spelled out the rules and bounds of the home detention monitor system.

He took the thing off and put it on the cat, for chrissakes. He's flagrantly flaunting his disrespect for the court.

Look, I don't claim that my client's a model citizen, and frankly, I don't claim that I can control him. But if he gets sent back to jail, it will send an unequivocal message that he belongs there, and I'd be forced to argue for a mistrial—which I don't want any more than either of you. This seemed to resonate with the pizza eaters. I mean, come on—do we really want to start this whole thing over again from scratch?

It was obvious the judge had already made up his mind what to do before they sat down to lunch, purportedly to discuss the matter. He'd hardly finished chewing when he pronounced,

Okay, here's what we'll do. The defendant will remain under house arrest, but from now on it will be a supervised house arrest. The court will appoint a guardian to insure and monitor his stay there—to make sure that he stays. This afternoon we will recess early, at three o'clock, and at four-thirty we will meet here in my chambers. At that time you two will have agreed upon a qualified individual who will perform the service of court-appointed guardian. This service will be rendered at the defendant's expense. I want someone to live there at the house with him until the conclusion of the trial. Understood?

Will Deery told Simon, sitting in the barred room eating Chips Ahoy, what the judge had decided, and Simon immediately responded,

I know who to get.

Who?

That guy Pete the detective from Maine they got to get stuff on me up there. He usually works for defense lawyers but this time he was with the prosecution.

Good idea, Zwirner said almost without hesitation when

Will Deery told him Simon's suggestion. If the state used him to gather background, they can't object to him. Get him.

Simon was glad about this. He'd been meaning, sort of, to call Pete, and maybe get him to dig up some stuff, so good, now he'd have him right there, like his own live-in, one-man like undercover staff. To the news organizations in the coming weeks, Pete was Simon's bodyguard, though the court papers quietly released, amid others apposite, after the weekend, revealed in craftily concise, inchoate, arcane lexicon, the precise terms of his position. The *Globe* picked up on this, and ran a wrap-up piece that described Pete as the court-appointed monitor of Simon's home detention. The *Herald* went with another picture from Fenway Park, Simon chomping on a hot dog, cheeks bulged, explaining that Pete was Simon's bodyguard, appointed by the court to keep him from going to any more Red Sox games.

This guy Pete, it turned out, in a curious twist, used to be a prison guard up in Maine, at the Thomaston Prison, of all places, that Simon passed all his life, passed just the other day, and always looked at and wondered about, and so when he thought of prison, like the word *prison,* or just the abstraction prison, it was there that he pictured, and now here he was not in prison, but at home, instead, Dad dead, with a guard from Thomaston Prison of all places, it was weird, watching TV and eating tons together.

Simon was really relieved they didn't know he went to Canada. That could have been pretty bad. He almost felt like he didn't really go, it was more like a private dream excursion, so it wouldn't be fair if he got nailed and like sent back to jail for that, for what?

This guy Pete actually was a really good guy, and it was like he was just waiting up there on the edge of events, where Simon passed right by him on his little northern junket, like to go get him, like tag him on the map, and now here he was, two hundred miles south, two hundred bucks a day, he got for twenty-four hours a day, some of the days which he spent in court, others just hanging out with Simon watching TV.

In court Pete sat in the front row with Red or Timmy, or whoever that day, or sometimes back one row, or sometimes way in the back, and then he'd leave, next thing you'd know he was gone. He looked tougher than if you knew him, he was actually really nice, but he also actually really was tough, too. He told Simon over the weeks all kinds of stories about growing up in East Boston, and then the marines, where he was the second youngest drill sergeant ever, at eighteen, then Vietnam, on the roof of the embassy, guarding it when they evacuated Saigon in helicopters, like in that movie, he said it was exactly like that, when it started getting hairy they brought in him and his guys, this elite guard unit—

Simon wouldn't listen to Zwirner, forget it, as we know, or to Timmy, or even Red, really, he never listened to anyone, starting at the top, which was Dad, which was the bottom, which was the whole problem, but he listened to Pete, lo and behold, right from the start, like from the moment in the urinal he knew, and they became like this buddy team people all saw coming and going, Mutt and Jeff go to court.

The zip of the opening days of the trial, all the big excitement and heightened expectancy, was soon replaced by a pervasive boredom, affecting everyone, from the spectators and press to the jury and the tired old judge and even the lawyers—and especially Simon. He couldn't believe this was what a trial was like, it was so slow, so many delays and recesses and little decisions and stupid little sidebar arguments and mini rulings, why didn't they just get to the point, he would if he were them, he'd be a good lawyer, either side, either getting out of it or nailing the person. If this was how it was, and this was how they were going to convict him, he felt like it was no sweat, there was no way. It was like everybody agreed there was really no definite proof, except the flashlight, and even that wasn't proof, but so like they agreed to go on and on with all this other stuff anyway, just to make the trial a trial, and not just a trial but like this big show trial. More than anything else this whole thing, like most of life, was just a lot of waiting around.

Zwirner still left the courtroom with Simon, for show, but left him with Will Deery, and now Pete, too, as soon as they got past the phalanx and the gawkers out on the steps. And now that Pete was there, Will felt absolved of his baby-sitting responsibilities, today, at least, and as if he were in a rush to be somewhere else—another career-making trial?—he hurried off without so much as a glance or a wave good-bye.

Where's he off in such a rush to? Simon asked Pete, not really expecting an answer.

A woman, Pete answered, the man with the answers.

Half the reporters, after the initial crunch, went running after Red. The others trailed Simon and looped around in front of him, running, to cut him off.

Halfway down the stairs Simon stopped and Pete put his hands up in front of him. Questions flew.

Why'd you do it?

What do you think your chances are of getting off?

Did you do it?

Will you take the stand?

Did you do it for the money?

The money's mine, Simon said, loud enough for them to hear, and the shock that he spoke shut them up. He sounded pissed off because he was. Not because they assumed he did it, which they did, you could totally tell, or because they were asking him questions instead of leaving him alone, but because the mention of the money pissed him off, because he'd recently learned from Pete that there wasn't any money anymore, like he thought, it almost all got eaten up by inheritance taxes, because Dad did his will wrong, instead of like giving them ten percent every year with nothing taxed, like he could have over the last however many years, and what little was left would go to the lawyers, or actually to Red, to pay her back for paying them, though maybe she wouldn't make him pay her back, maybe she could just like write it off, she wouldn't know the difference, so maybe at least he'd get some little bit, a lot to him. But so it wasn't that they were asking him about it that pissed him off, it was the money, it was gone, it was Dad again, typical.

Pete woke Simon the next day, dropping the paper open on his chest. Now that Pete was there, Simon wasn't sleeping in Dad's bed anymore, but down in his own room again. Pete slept in Dad's bed, the only one big enough, and he slept at a diagonal. Pete was six-five and over two-fifty. Coffee was his main fuel, besides tons of food, especially like now, like Simon, when it was free and unlimited. He drank a pot of coffee to himself first thing like someone else would have a mug. The first breakfast/brunch they had together on Sunday, Pete ate his own whole pack of bacon by himself, most of the pieces slimy, almost uncooked, the way he made and liked them, which was why Simon didn't have any, he made his own, crispy, and he thought he had an appetite.

The black block tabloid blared:

SIMON SAYS
THE MONEY'S
MINE!

It wasn't like Pete was mad, he was just showing him. Like check this out, or here we are today, hombre.

Simon on the phone went on with Katherine about how they didn't have anything on him, it was totally circumstantial, if anything it was more like he was the one who had stuff on them. But when she asked him what he was talking about, he went mysteriously blank, like sorry, top secret, even to you. He asked her if she was going to come to court, or maybe they could go for a meal or something, or like a movie.

I'm in Maine, Simon, I can't, she said, and hope weirdly illumined his like groping, strangulated thing of trying to talk even though it was the opposite of yes, you.

Well when you get back, he said, and the illumination, instead of the opposite, intensified when she said,

I don't know if I'm coming back, or when.

What about What's-his-name?

I don't know—I don't know right now.

She didn't tell Simon how he had been part of their arguments, and how she stuck by him.

'Kay, well I don't have any big rush, Simon said pretty tartly, and abruptly hung right up. That he was hurt more than rude, she had plenty of time to think about, alone in her room painting, days in the downstairs floor of her gallery building like a box of peace in the middle of the fog-wrapped bay, where she could paint her inner whiles and stop for a cigarette, the radio on community radio all day, cassettes scattered on the table.

A beautiful summer night after rain. The anger had been unleashed and now it was washed out and calm after the rocking thunder and rain and blue cracks of lightning in which the house felt like a big ark fort up there on the hill, like ready to float them out into the ocean when the waters rose, and now the ocean dripped in the trees, little smacks onto the wet driveway, you could smell it intensely atomized into the air like out of one of those plant sprayers that sprays mist, or one of those perfume things Mum used to have, you squeeze the bulb. She would sit in her slip at her three-mirror dressing table getting dressed to go out, and she'd spritz a little under either armpit, then she'd touch some quickly between her breasts and dab either side of the neck like under the jawbone, raising her chin just so, and then she'd squeeze a last cloud in front of her and, eyes shut gently downward like an angel, walk into it.

Pete and Simon were going for a walk around the block, as Simon called it, which Pete thought was funny, because it meant down one driveway, along the road by the ocean, and up the other driveway—there was no block. Mum and Dad used to walk around the block after dinner like this—and they called it walking around the block—Simon told him,

Like the only thing they ever did together.

Except raise a family.

Yeah, well.

It's hard to raise a family.

Pete had a son, five, and a baby girl, up in Maine, whom he almost never talked about, but almost never stopped thinking about. His wife grew up in a trailer in Maine, and she lived up there now, in a trailer he paid for, back near her parents. They weren't divorced, but they weren't together. She gained like sixty pounds after they got married and had the first kid, and with the second kid put on some more, and she was never going to lose it. She looked like the baby, they were his little porkers and he loved them. He missed them. But Boston was growing back on him, this glimpse of the big time, and maybe they'd never get back together and work it out. He didn't know if he wanted to.

Pete had hundreds he told Simon all the time, but Simon had never told him a single real horror story of growing up, and he concluded that whatever happened to derail Simon's life wasn't caused by terrible treatment, but by his own twisting within that maybe did, maybe didn't, have legitimate grounds in parentage and the way he was raised. Sure there was some benign neglect. But this guy didn't realize how privileged he was. In spite of his constant critiques of his background, the sick poverty of the rich, his favorite theme. Of which Simon was a living casualty. To walk every night after dinner around a dripping paradise beside the ocean like this and call it a block was most people's dream. Now here Simon was moaning about it, Pete and he walking around the same block, like the parents, except smoking a joint and pacing the vanishment like soldiers revisiting a battlefield, except all that Simon did here, as far as Pete could tell, was play war, or play whatever, and feel lost and alone.

Simon had wanted to play catch or Frisbee out on the lawn this summer a bunch of times, and a few times they had, but Pete got all sweaty pretty fast, and said my back, and went and sat down on the terrace and read the paper, just like Dad not wanting to play catch, or not for long enough, and Pete smoking now was like Dad with the orange dot glowing every hit, he'd move it around like writing in the air, when he was putting them to bed, and he'd do the big wheel with the orange glow making a circle the radius of his arm, getting smaller and smaller, and getting faster as it got smaller, till it was this hyper little scribble. *Good night, now, boys.*

Pete got his pot from Laugh. It was strong. First hit or two and you were in Asia on paranoid patrol alert, and Simon wanted to hear about Vietnam, but Pete hardly ever said anything about it, especially now when Simon didn't ask. Pete looked weird when you got stoned, like Frankenstein in a shaved bear's body with clothes. His head was a massive skull, and when they got back inside it was like illuminated. They ate another meal.

Simon admired Pete but also thought he was too passive. Pete wasn't a bad cook, yes he was, but the few things he cooked were all right. He and Simon were pretty much on the same level there. They ate a lot, in front of the tube.

Simon wasn't painting anymore during this period, life was taking over the dimension.

Pete, like Dad, wouldn't come in all the way to wake Simon, he'd just appear in the doorway, filling it, and his looming would wake you, maybe, then he'd say what time it was. This morning, though, was different, he came in and stood like inside Simon's radius, disturbing the meshing, but offering a peace offering compensation of another joint, since they were both still a little burnt out from last night. It was raining out again, or still, whatever, the light applause.

Big day, big guy.

Pete lit up a fat one and grinned. He was already in his suit and tie, his hair combed wet.

Simon sat up all crusty and took the joint when Pete handed it to him. The cat came in, too, for the action, like hey, you guys, what's going on in here?

Got to start off de mornin' on de right side of jah bed, Simon croaked in a rasta voice, which he could do pretty well, you know mon.

They both grinned. He held the hit in.

On the way in to Boston they smoked another bone with Laugh, who had one ready behind her ear, the ends squared off, like the perfect driver. They had to get some hash browns and Eggamuffas, they kept calling them, ordering into the speaker and laughing, except for Laugh, and lots of ketchup and a strawberry thick shake, each, for the balanced breakfast for your balanced day.

There were more of the mobile unit vans than usual parked out in front of the courthouse, with the big like ray guns on their roofs, the wire snaking around the pole, or satellite dishes like ceramic flowers with a metal stamen in the middle pointing to outer space, to beam you out and back into millions of homes and pixilated minds.

Zwirner started off slow. His usual courtroom aggressiveness was artfully held in check, and what came across was a well-tailored, double-breasted self-assurance. His arrogance was belted and tucked in—noticeable, but, like the handkerchief in his breast pocket, nicely folded and smoothed back with the sartorial suaveness of his new blow-dried haircut. Red had a haircut, too, and so did Sandy Gorman. It was like Haircut Day at the trial. Or like a movie, with the stylists grooming the principals a few degrees beyond ordinary preened humans. So that in contrast, Simon's slept-on fuzz ball, like more dandelion than dandy, looked like, who let him in here? Well-fed of late, as we know, Simon was getting round, fast, and today, really baked, he looked like Mr. Gonzo Sleepyhead dressed up to pass for formal normal.

Though he looked buggy alert and alive as can be with coffee and ambition, Zwirner's voice was still coated with the woolly batting of sleep, and was as low and tenebrious as Henry Kissinger's. Alcoholic, was Simon's verdict again.

The first defense witness was a forensic pathologist, an old guy with a shiny head and bristly white hair on the sides where he still had some. He wore a bow tie, and seemed totally sure of himself, calm. His responses were slow and deliberate and more lawyerly than the lawyer's questions. For this reason it was hard to pay attention to what he was saying.

The experts came up with varying interpretations of the evidence. One held that, okay, Simon hit him, but that's all. Dad didn't die from the blow to the head, but from a heart attack. And even if the heart attack happened out of fear at the attack—can you convict someone of scaring someone else to death?

Or another version claimed Dad wasn't even hit on the head by Simon, or by anyone else. He wasn't even close to murdered. He just died of a heart attack, period. The bump on his head came from falling down the stairs. He fell down the stairs because he was drunk, and had a heart attack at the bottom of the stairs, induced by the shock of the fall. Or he fell down the stairs because he had a heart attack. Stabbed and electrically jolted by the first pressure and groping spasms in his left side, in his whole body, he tried to get up as if to get away, and collapsed onto the boat frame on the floor a few feet away, where he was then throttled by further, deeper, final convulsions, and, half in, half out of the boat, as if to be borne away, kicking against the last dull cannon shots, he choked from lack of oxygen, and died.

Pieces of evidence were like scattered words, Dr. Kramer explained.

Kramer's interpretation of the crime scene and what happened there, based on the physical evidence and its disposition, was simple: Dad came down the stairs, encountered someone there in the basement, and was hit on the head by that person, causing him to fall, unconscious, into the partially built rowboat on the floor. Kramer spent the rest of his testimony on the flashlight.

When Simon was showered with the usual daily battery of questions out on the courtroom steps that afternoon, he handled the daily ritual with the ease of an actor, with a calmness too blithe to be real, with Pete standing right behind him in his dark beer glasses like a communist president and Secret Service guy combined, hands clasped military guard style over his belt buckle, feet planted regulation shoulder width apart. Simon squinted and saw little midges milling in the air over their heads like another swarm of reporters, alive for only a day, this was their big moment, the minute fluffiness of each lively bug-soul catching the late light and sort of glowing. All the questions were versions and repetitions and spin-offs of the same thing, so when he heard this one voice in the frenetic mix, whomsoever's it was, blunt, like sort of bleat out again,

What's Zwirner up to?

he made a mouth and sort of shrugged,

Beats me.

According to Dick Kramer, the fingerprints on the flashlight, along with all the other physical evidence and its disposition at the crime scene, pointed to one possibility. Someone else came into the house, which was not locked, encountered and hit Richard Curtis on the head with the flashlight, and left. Simon had nothing to do with it. His fingerprints on the shaft of the flashlight could have been put there any time—weeks, months, even years before that night.

Timmy was staying out at Manchester for the night. Things had changed since he was there a month ago. The dog was back. The lawn was mowed. The refrigerator was full of weird Simon things, like Dad would have, too, plus Pete stuff, like big soda bottles, a salami log with the white circles of fat.

A card table was set up with a chair in the living room where the Christmas tree used to go. This was Pete's office, nice ocean view. Timmy assumed Pete was responsible for all the order that had amazingly swept through the house like an antistorm. The sofa pillows were puffed and the windows were squeaky clean. But after being there for a while he realized it was Laugh—what was her real name, anyway?—who was behind it all. She was like Simon and Pete's den mother. Or like Mum. She made the house shipshape, made them get a cleaning lady, who cleaned up everywhere, it was great, plus changing the bedsheets and doing the laundry and putting the boys' clothes away.

The boys watched TV together with dinner heaped on plates on their laps.

Laugh didn't live there, but she stayed there sometimes, and sometimes brought her daughter Gloria and her daughter's cousin, or at least that's what they called him, a skinny little white guy named Mike. The room Timmy usually stayed in was changed around into a room for the kids. There was a poster of a scowling Arnold with a big machine gun and a belt of bullets bandoliered across his bulging chest, a maelstrom of fire exploding behind him. Also a bright green and black dart-board with Velcro dart balls stuck to it, and a little Nintendo game on the bureau. On the closet door mirror where Timmy used to do his Partridge Family rock 'n' roll routines, pointing the hairbrush microphone at himself at eye level as he swiveled his hips, were some sort of mutant superhero stickers, mixed in with a few YEAH and SIMON SAYS. Timmy lay down on his old bed with his shoes on, and when he closed his eyes felt the bed tipping back, fairly steeply, like a sailboat, it felt like he might slide off headfirst, like a sea burial, like Mum, *The Mutiny on the "Bounty."* And in the tilt back was a pleasant slight spinning sensation, like he could feel the centrifugal pull of the earth and all its events.

When he woke up, Simon was standing in the doorway looking at him. This used to be their room. It wasn't dark yet, but dusk, and the sourceless light sort of suspended there in time, eased and half erased them in the dim, so the presence and pressure between them was less, and the room was their old room. Think how many years here, all the times they talked. What did they talk about? Going to sleep at night, explaining the world, making it up, starting in again in the morning, after breathing together all night, every night, lying in the two beds, the window like a huge gridded painting between them of the day or the night or the klepto violet hours between the trees out there, the same old red and white striped curtains. One waking and stumbling in pajamas with a little boy boner to the crack of light of the bathroom door, the light always on in there, to pee and see yourself, your mussed and puffy head, scrunched face, in the bottom of the mirror over the sink, the toothbrushes in their slots and the Crest Simon squeezed out from right near the nozzle and never put the cap back on.

When you die you can come back if you think it while you're dying.

No way.

Yes.

You don't know.

You don't know.

Yes, if you do it right they can't stop you, or sometimes anyone can go like for a visit.

No way.

Yes way.

How?

It's easy. When you're ready you just go when nobody's looking, and it's easy because you don't have a body anymore.

Breathing through his nose, little Timmy con*thid*ered this.
In the darkness, just voices, the occasional rustle, they were like
the bodiless souls in heaven they were talking about: it was not
hard to imagine.

Well—but then—how do you get back down?

That's the part you have to know. 'Cause they can see down
here from up there, that's all they do. But to get down you have
to go into a bird.

Really?

Yuh. Or sometimes the rain, and when you get down in little pieces of drops you get back together in a puddle!

Really?

Yeh, that's what puddles are . . . That's why they have puddles.

Even when he didn't speak, you could hear Timmy's lisp, the
way he breathed.

Then what is it if it's a really big puddle?

Then it's like two people down together.

Like *thex*?

Kind of.

Wool what if it's like a whole pond?

Then it's like a whole bunch of people like who all get killed
together like in the war. Like Germans.

Or what if it's a whole like lake or the ocean (th' *o-thin*)?

Same thing, but like the whole war, instead of just a village,
or like other histories nobody even knows, but they're there.
All the way back to dinosaurs.

Do cavemen count?

Yup.

Animals?

Nope.

Yeth, dogs.

Nope. Just dolphins.

Little Timmy con*thid*ered the brutal injustice of this. Simon gave him a break:

Dogs are snow.

Simon could have been Dad in the doorway, with his hip leaning out, ankles and arms crossed, like parked there, kind of caryatid of the house, he'd circle his cigarette in the dark, but what Timmy thought of was Mum, before Simon said anything, coming in to kiss them good night, and this one time he hadn't thought of since, till now, when she came in almost fairy dancing in the grainy getting-dark with her hair brushed out, like all frizzed and puffed out and floating up with electricity, like a ghost, and she was that way, too, all airy in her seethrough nightgown, dancing around, her face straight, arms out like fluid underwater, and the gauzy flower of the nightgown out in this like vision visitation. He was so without her Timmy forgot how she used to play around like that, like tickle-attacking him like she did, all in a good mood, on the couch in the TV room the night before she died. The last time he saw her.

Sorry, Simon said, you can't stay here. It's not your room anymore. He was joking. But Timmy didn't think it was funny.

I'm just kidding. Simon made a long face like Timmy's. When a sibling acts like the other one to the other one, there's an implicit, uniquely sibling critique and presentation: this is what you're like and you know it, so if you don't like it, good.

Timmy said nothing. Simon didn't exactly soften, but said,

You should come down for supper. We've got some of those good little barbecue chickens from Henry's. Everybody gets their own.

He smiled a big-eyed stoned grin, and Timmy realized how baked he was.

Pete still had on a tie, loose, suit coat elsewhere. He addressed Timmy in a very soft voice, like an assassin holding it in, but really about to blow your head off, Timmy felt like. But that feeling went away during the dinner, and over the weekend Timmy learned that Pete was just like this big soft bear you could practically hug. They hadn't really talked before. But now Pete asked Timmy how Bennie was, and told him he had a son that age, too. They whipped out their wallets and exchanged pictures of the little guys. Both—amazingly, Timmy thought, especially since Bennie lived in Brooklyn—wore little Red Sox caps, shading their squinty little flesh-ball faces. They talked about the greatest feeling ever of the little guy laughing with you and you're the father. Lying in bed or on the floor and he stands on your stomach balancing and losing balance, and laughing, both of you, as he grips your two forefingers for balance, claws at your face. And in the eternal nature of fatherhood, there they both were, away, with the son in mind, while the wives, at that very moment, were washing and putting the babies down to bed.

They blew a bone and drank Beck's out on the terrace till the bugs got too bad, and then when there was nothing good on cable, the three of them went down to the video store.

Not Chuckles, Reese's Cups. We've got tons of Snickers at home, and ice cream, but . . .

Timmy in his newfound and induced looseness like drifted away. Pete had a bemused smile when he was stoned that stayed on his face like his bellwether buzzed expression, his eyebrows stayed up like he was tasting a fine wine in the air, and life was not so bad at all up at that particular altitude.

Timmy had parked not in an actual parking place between painted lines, but stopped right in front of the lit entrance to the video minimart, and of course two seconds after they disappeared inside, a cop car pulled up behind and loomed near, its high beams flooding into Simon. He could tell without looking it was a cop car.

Just go around, Simon said out loud.

As if in response, after a moment's pause, the driver's door of the cop car opened and shut. The knock on the window was a loud double tap, hard enough to break the glass, it seemed like, made with the butt of the black metal flashlight, the kind we know all about, which he flipped around and shined into the car, taking in the two beers on the front seat like they were driver and passenger, then shined in Simon's face in the back. Simon put up his hand.

Open the window, the cop said, louder than he had to.

Get the flashlight out of my face, Simon said, too soft.

The cop kept the light shining in Simon's face long enough that it didn't seem like he was giving in or being told what to do, then lowered it and boinged the beam all over the place looking around inside the car.

Open the window, the cop said again. Simon rolled it down halfway.

That's a twenty-inch Mag-Lite made in Ontario, California, Simon said. The cop was a kid. Simon and his pushover rookies.

Where's the operator of this vehicle?

Where do you think?

The kid looked back at the cruiser to get his partner's eye, but only got the double headlight glare.

Get out of the vehicle, please.

What for, I didn't do anything.

Now the partner was there, older than Simon, a big man in the wider sense of the word—big gut. The two cops conferred for a second. Inside the fluorescent store, Timmy passed the door, then Pete, carrying like Doritos, like five bags of them, but neither looked over. The head of the older cop was backlit as he leaned down to the window and looked like a roast beef, but with a mouth moving to eat itself.

Smells like a brewery in here.

He was trying the direct but friendly familiar tack, and though Simon saw the little act, he sort of went along with it.

I know, he said. 'S not my problem.

Now Pete was there, mysteriously, without having come out the doors. He was way bigger than both the cops, and ten times as tough, but came on soft and respectful.

Hey guys, Simon half heard him saying, I'm the one you want to talk to.

They turned to Pete, and now Simon couldn't hear what they were saying, just Pete's purr. Pete took out his wallet and license and kept talking. He leaned in the window and muttered,

Suburban Boy Scouts, and told Simon to grab the registration, and to get out of the car if he motioned for him to.

The car was still registered to Dad and so wasn't strictly legal. Who knows what Pete was saying, but he chattered on and even got a laugh out of the boys in blue. Timmy came out downloaded with a twelve-pack of Buds and a grocery bag overstuffed with the puff bags of chips. He stopped, startled, right outside the doors. Some other people were coming in from their properly parked car and ordinary evening, and had to say *Excuse me* to get him out of the way. Pete gestured, ushered him forward into the scrum. Simon in the backseat *tsk*ed at Timmy's blanched like *Tim*id expression.

Pete introduced Timmy to the cops like it was an ordinary social setting, and Timmy chin-nodded greetings and tried to play along. Then Pete gestured with his left hand flippering, slo-mo, for Mr. Snicker ensconced in there to come on out of his capsule and meet the men and the moment.

This is Simon, Pete said. Simon, Officers Roake and O'Neill.

The two nodded to Simon's slightest, and the rookie, his

green apple face polished with excitement in the presence, shot out his fresh bread hand to shake, which Simon dispelled with a lifted finger of limited greeting that looked as much like a warning. Officer Roake looked more like a regular person than a cop. Like a coach or just some townie father, which he was. He wasn't charmed or impressed by meeting Simon face-to-face, but still he did have that enhanced expression, whatever it was, like he felt the lift, and liked being part of the bigger picture/ other echelon, even if only for this intersection second. It was irresistible to everyone, including the judge and the prosecutors and everyone involved, or not, on down. Everyone, it seemed, except Laugh, though probably her, too, she just knew how to not show it. Or maybe with her it was the disdain built in, though she didn't show that, either, to Simon, at least at him, but at anyone rich and white, which Simon totally agreed with, for having the world on a platter, while most of the rest of the world was still in different degrees of slavery and misery under them.

Pete did the talking in cop talk, assuming the right tones and insider assumptions. Timmy and Simon stood half aside in identical stances—one leg straight, hip jutting, the other leg a little bent at the knee—like they'd practiced and perfected this growing up. A fat couple with flattened, upturned piggy noses, both of them—brother and sister, or they found their true mate—passed by and stuck their piggy noses inquisitively into the gathering, and instantly recognized Simon. They looked at each other like puppets, gasped, and since there was no crowd to hide in, sidled on inside, reluctantly, when Officer Roake looked at them. Pete made the guys laugh one more time, then,

So I guess you guys have to write me up—

Yeah, nah—

But whatever it has to be, if you can keep these clowns out of the press on this—like they were big city cops in a movie, hip to the press—then I'll be able to keep my job. Know what I'm saying?

Yeah, we'll let this go, no problem. You guys go home and eat your chips.

Pete nodded Simon and Timmy to the car.

Thanks, Timmy said faintly, and Simon frowned at him and made a disgusted mouth like, You jerk.

Pete muttered a few more buddy remarks, and to the last, as the three parted, all grins, Roake said,

Yeah, Sox are already down three zip.

The boys stopped off at West Beach on the way home to smoke a joint, parked in the empty parking lot, looking over the low-tide expanse of sand and the water dribbling in like dark, watered-down syrup, smeared out to the islands and the counter's-edge horizon, barely discernible, the pepper-grinder lighthouse briefly becoming itself each minute or however long it took the beacon to go around and blink past them in its long circumferent sweep. And of course who pulls into the parking lot a few minutes later but the other boys in their toy cruiser. They pulled up right beside Dad's station wagon. Pete's head had like floated to the top of the open driver's window. He greeted his friends with a big stoned Frankenstein grin he didn't try to suppress to more ordinary proportions.

The rookie was driving and Roake was right there, face-to-face with Pete.

Sox are down six-zip now, not smiling but not unfriendly either. I think they need you guys back home pulling for 'em.

The sweet concert smell of pot came cooking illicitly out. Pete knew to not even try and hide it.

Roger, was all he said, collecting himself a little, at least in the face, and started up the engine, which, Dad's car, even though it'd just been running, Dad, coughed a couple of times, like Dad, before it started. Then, catching Simon's dead eye as he looked back to reverse, Pete made and had to make out loud the Roger cross-reference. He leaned back to Roake,

It's not Roger on the mound, is it?

He's getting shelled, Roake nodded them home.

Just as they were crunching out of the half gravel parking lot, "American Pie" came on the radio, and each of them loved it—

Three men I

—and the calm stasis that encircled them and extended like great wings of night and safe camaraderie—

I can't remember

—when Pete cut the engine, at home, and they sat there in the driveway to hear out the rest of the song, each in his own perfect, reminiscent way.

The Sargent portrait of his great-grandmother in the governor's office seemed to have changed. Now she wasn't just there in the painting, framed in her time for him to gaze into, now she was there in the room with him, another consciousness—and a stern, imposing, moral consciousness. The change was remarkable. The turquoise pendant on her chest now appeared more green, and seemed to stand out not merely from her pale proud cushion chest, but to have subtly popped out one more dimension, out of the plane of the picture and into the world, just inside the real rim of the room, and her eyes did the same thing, even more subtly, but with a pellucid, paranormal insistence. He had met her eyes thousands of times before; but now new double dots of watery white glisten had appeared in them. Now there was someone there. And her lustrous, silvery silk dress now seemed, disconcertingly, to be falling off her shoulders and chest, as if her breasts, like a single matronly bolster, had deflated a little, she had become disrupted and *déshabillée* in the stepping-forth transformation, this strange emergence from the brown murky background and heritage. Indeed, she had become positively *louche*. Like the picture's frame, gilded with floral, carved curls that smattered also across her dress in spectral imprints, the empty carved chair beside her to which she eternally gestured—welcoming, showing him the way, offering him the throne, or righteous rest—now seemed prohibited by her pose, reaching protectively over its arm to the back, and the imprecation in her newly direct and present gaze suggested, with atavistic disappointment hardening her berry-full Cary mouth, that she was now guarding the throne, her domain, not so much presenting it to him, perhaps, as now—was she?—barring the way. He read the brass plate screwed into the ornate frame. It seemed to be a glaring headline. Usually he overlooked the actual title—it was invisible to him—and, like someone looking only at himself in a group photograph, looked always to the last line.

John Singer Sargent
American, 1856–1925
PORTRAIT OF MRS. CHARLES PELHAM CURTIS
née Ellen Sears Amory Weld

Simon sipped a joint and Timmy tipped his beer back, and the unseen evening steeped up from the purple sea. Side by side, like animals everywhere, the brothers breathed their transience.

After inhaling his other appetizer, ice cream soda, Simon heaved a sort of *here goes* sigh, with a little grin and accomplice eyes, and Timmy appreciated that he was acknowledging his fear, and was trying to step through it here, bolstered by *a, b* and *c,* b here being brother; and to Timmy, believe it or not: *not.* This softening amounted to friendliness. What was happening?

Katherine? Hi this is Simon. He sounded normal for him.
He nodded at the lengthy reply and let the information pulse
punily in.

Okay, well could you tell her to call me?

He hung up like he always did, without saying good-bye.
Timmy didn't say anything.

Pete appeared large in the screen door top half and said
behind them,

You boys behaving? like Dad. Except Dad never would've
checked on them. Simon slurped the rest of his appetizer. The
phone rang and Simon and Timmy exchanged a pot-paranoid
look of *I'm-not-gonna-pick-it-up,* and both laughed, or smiled at
least, and neither picked it up. It rang there between them a
few times, nearer to Simon, and stopped ringing sooner than it
should have, and now their look was, Good, there, that's gone.
Then Pete appeared in the door again, like a butler, and said,
stentorian, the voice of the unavoidable,

Simon, it's for you.

Brows popped up wow on both brothers. Simon picked it up
after enough time for Pete to get back to the phone in the
kitchen.

I've got it, Pete, is how he greeted whoever it was.

Oh hi Katherine, he looked at Timmy, then gazed off, kind
of glazed, into his closed bet for happiness. He smiled and
didn't and smiled and didn't, like he and his mouth couldn't
agree on a reaction as he listened.

I thought you weren't there.

I just got back.

Sure, he thought. Though she was breathing hard—but why
would she be breathing hard just because she just got back? She
didn't jog, he didn't think. It was her little act probably. But
she called, anyway. Still, he felt like hanging up. She sounded
flat.

So how are you?

He hated when girls tried to be all cheery. It made him act the opposite.

I'm okay.

This wasn't the first time Timmy was sitting on Simon's silent side of a phone call, but here he was. But now, instead of just being annoyed, he was sympathetic, and he said, joking, but also meaning it,

Simon, you should say something.

But he didn't speak, and Timmy knew Katherine was waiting.

You're the one who called her.

No she called me.

What? said Katherine.

No, I'm talking to Timmy. Timmy be quiet I'm talking to Katherine.

She called you back.

Simon glared at him, like exaggerated, exasperated, and Timmy got up and walked over to the garden like Dad, smoking a new cigarette, the renewed vantage point and fresh safe start they give you, every time, centering him enough, here on the old home hill. The garden was overgrown, though some of the perennials were there, but past their prime and gone a little wild from neglect, like they had turned to weeds under the bad influence, gone to seed like the whole house, beneath Laugh's surface order—like Timmy, too, under Simon? Though the lawn was mowed and the house was clean, the soul of the home was already gone. It was just a sort of real estate purgatory—of realty and reality: Timmy as a kid, seeing signs, read one as the other. But soon the trial would be over and the real reality would take over again. Maybe then he'd feel back on track. And stronger than ever, and his marriage and everything would be better, art would rise out of the nowhere he was breathing now, like this was one of those mythic ordeals you had to go through, the rich fallow phase of trial and tribulation.

After the first nervousness Simon felt fine talking to Katherine. Simon had never been in love with a woman who was in love with him at the same time, and he had never made love like that, in love, so in fact he had never made love. He had this big grin now, like a grimace he didn't even notice.

Until she said, So I guess you heard your lawyer called me.

What? No. Why—what'd he say?

Timmy's cigarette glowed like a firefly over by the garden, he was like a statue, or a ghost of Dad, just standing there in the going indigo, with his junior dad belly a little bit out, and the ocean was a ghost, too, world-weighted, pulling at the whole downward-slipping, darkening sky.

I don't know, it was weird. He didn't say much.

What did he say? Simon's tone was outright nasty.

Jesus, Simon, she could bite right back. Don't get pissy at me, it's not my fault.

Okay, *Katherine,* the testiness still there. Just tell me what he said.

I told you—not much. She paused and he heard something knock in her room, or like, she dropped the phone. Maybe she was lighting a cigarette. She and Timmy took drags off each other's cigarettes, like they were a couple, and maybe they were—they were, he knew it—definitely.

Are you still there? after the exhale. She definitely was smoking.

Yup. I mean Jesus Christ, Simon. I don't hear from you for all this time, and then I get a call from your lawyer, who like grills me, and then the next day you call and get pissy. Thanks a bunch.

Wool what'd he say? He grilled you.

Yeah, I mean, he was trying to be all friendly about it, but when I got off the phone it was like, What the fuck was that?

Was it Zwirner?

I don't know. Your *lawyer.*

Yeah, he's such an asshole.

William someone—

Will Deery?

Now Simon really felt conspired against. Will Deery. And that exact moment he noticed Pete looming there in the screen door, unmoving, massive portrait listening, for how long? At least he wasn't listening on the other phone. Simon busted up any anti-Pete thoughts and blurted to him as a full insider ally, *Ptseh.* Will Deery called Katherine and was like grilling her.

Pete didn't move, except his eyebrows up a little, almost unseen in the almost dark.

Katherine, let me call you back, Simon said, and hung up without listening to her reply.

What's Will Deery's number?

It's on the list, Pete shrugged.

Simon, suddenly Mr. Action, called Will Deery at his home number, and after three electronic chirps he picked up.

Hello? he said softly, like he was taking a nap, or lived alone—both were true. It was a Sunday. The week was about to turn again on its late Sunday heavy hinge into another week.

This is Simon, no hello like no good-bye, the other end of the same thing.

Si-*mone,* how goes it? His breezy chumminess seemed to Simon like such an act now, especially when, to Simon's bull-breathing silence, he added, What's up?

Why'd you call Katherine?

Why did I call. Katherine. He repeated slowly. I give up. What are you talking about? Who's Katherine?

Don't give me that. She said you like totally grilled her.

I talked to her whatever, maybe six months ago. You mean your friend Katherine from Maine.

It went back and forth like this till Simon mostly believed him that it wasn't him, and then Will Deery was asking the questions and Simon was answering them.

Well then somebody questioned her, posing as me. Who? Why?

Simon talked to Katherine again that night, and then three more times in the next two days, talking all the time, of course, about this, as the pretext, and then whatever else. And then when the article came out in the *Herald* about her and Simon— it was that guy, again, from the porch—they talked a bunch more times, Simon going on and on about how they could sue the *Herald* and win, like, millions of dollars.

A museum curator took the stand, an expert on Chinese porcelain, identified and appraised the "Curtis collection," as she called it, and ventured that a complete set would certainly include the bowl in question, whose value she put at around ten thousand dollars. She estimated the worth of the whole set to be maybe ten times that. Simon's and Timmy's eyes widened. An insurance appraiser followed and seconded her estimate.

And then, what everybody had been waiting for, but had stopped believing would happen—Red took the stand. She hadn't been in the courtroom that morning or the past few weeks, so everyone watching, including Simon and Timmy, was surprised when she came clopping up the center aisle when her name was called, next witness, after the lunch break. She wore chunky-heeled shoes that were almost sandals and a loose pants outfit with a sleeveless semi-see-through shirt that made Sandy Gorman's Filene's Basement lady lawyer pantsuit look like Kmart.

She crossed her legs and spoke softly in her lowest voice into the microphone. Everyone leaned forward to hear as if they were all on a boat, and the boat were listing: listening. To an opening series of easy yes-no questions she answered, *Definitely,* five times in a row, followed by an even firmer *Absolutely.* She looked wan, her voice weakened or softened by distress. An act? People said she didn't look good. They liked saying that, feeling privy and concerned. Zwirner asked her nothing about Simon or Dad. Only a few questions about the blue bowl, and about the lack of security in the house.

Sandra Gorman, firmly friendly, lost ground by sheer character comparison every second she questioned Red in cross. She seemed to sense this, and after quickly circling a few times around the blue bowl, briefly, ritually, as if unsure of herself, she confined her questions, to questionable effect, to establishing the theme of the necessary distance Red must have from her family. Red didn't resist, but didn't agree with what Sandy was getting at; then Red contradicted her directly.

Actually I am quite close to my family precisely because I have to keep a distance from the general public. I lead a very private life, and my friends and family are at the heart of that—like anyone else.

Okay. How would you describe Simon's relationship with your father?

Oh please, she coughed into her hand, the other cupping the mike. Sorry, she added, and answered: It was always hard for both of them. They loved each other, but just didn't see eye to eye. It actually wasn't a very contentious relationship, though. Dad and Simon are very alike—both keep things in. I think Simon's resentments—which are his business, not mine, not yours, not anyone else's—were legitimate. Dad was not a very present, hands-on father. But whatever the troubles between them, their relationship was mostly a nonrelationship—they kept their distance from each other.

Before anyone knew it, the big excitement was over, not so exciting after all.

Timmy was next.

Why didn't you tell me? he whispered curtly to Pete after Zwirner said,

The defense calls Timothy Curtis.

They did tell you, last week, Pete tipped his head to Timmy.

Yeah, but I mean *now,* today. Christ.

Pete shrugged with a good-natured *Sorry, buddy* smile, subdued, and Simon turned around and grinned at him. Timmy didn't have a tie on today, just his normal clothes. When he got up to the stand and looked out at everyone looking at him, he saw that Red was gone, and felt kind of abandoned. He didn't even know she was coming, and now, like that, she was gone again. Reporters and gawkers swarmed after her as she swept out of the courtroom and into the elevator held there for her by one of the court guards. No one else was allowed in, and when the elevator doors parted downstairs, a swarm was there, but she wasn't.

This was the day Simon spoke on the steps for about fifteen minutes, instead of his usual little Simon Says quip. Among other things, he talked about Katherine, and said yeah, he loved her, what's it to you? And he talked about the blue bowl. He spoke enigmatically, and repeated what he said before, that the blue bowl's the key to this whole thing.

The next day the big Simon Says story came out, and the day after that Katherine was there. She didn't even say she was coming. It was great she was there. After court Simon said why don't you come out to Manchester with us for dinner, you can stay the night, we have tons of beds. She glanced at Timmy, who didn't meet her eyes, as the elevator door opened and they had to scramble past the hustling scrimmage of reporters, cameras, gawkers.

Well I could, I guess, Katherine said as they hustled down the steps, Pete leading the way to the waiting car, Laugh at the wheel in her shades, looking straight ahead, her expression too-cool-for-school. Pete held the rear door open for them and they piled in, then he got in the front with Laugh. They had hardly pulled away from the crowd and the location vans when Laugh, watching the dishes and antennas on their roofs shrink to toys in the rearview mirror, took a fat joint from behind her ear and

lit it with a single, long, seed-popping suck. Pete took a monster poke, held it in with a cough that tried to escape out his
nose but didn't quite, and passed the joint into the backseat.
Simon took it first, then Katherine, shrugging, took a sippy little toke, followed, without exhaling, by another just like it, and
when she handed it to Timmy he shrugged and figured whatever, might as well.

They got roast beef sandwiches—*twelve* of them—and tons
of fries at Nick's, and had the first course, first round, in the car,
then, stopping for ice cream and beer and cigs at the Store24 in
Beverly Farms, had a second meal, same as the first, in front of
the TV at home. They watched themselves on the news—lots
of laughs—and then watched a stupid cop movie on HBO, one
long car chase, it was pretty good, actually. Pete sat in Mum's
place, log legs extended, and Laugh lay curled on the couch
with her head on his lap, zonked out, her mouth open like a
dead fish. Every once in a while she snored, and Pete would
hold her nose, or tickle the tip till she snorted, wiping away the
phantom fly, getting some laughs from the other three slouched
on Dad's couch, Simon in Dad's place, Katherine comfy in the
middle between the two brothers. Laugh woke all the way and
punched Pete on the chest. They went up to bed. He carried her
over his shoulder like a caveman carrying his zonked little cave-
woman.

Even though he was sweetly stoned like everyone else, still
Timmy couldn't relax all the way with Katherine right here
beside him, her leg touching his, but leaning toward Simon.
When the maze of his mixed thoughts and feelings gave him an
opening he finally got up.

I'm going to bed.

Yeah, you should, Simon said, meaning it as a joke, but also
meaning it. He smiled a loopy grin. Timmy didn't smile back.
As he headed up the stairs out in the hall, Katherine folded her
feet under her where he'd been sitting and laid her head on

Simon's lap. As she wriggled to get comfortable he got an instant hard-on going against her temple and her ear. Simon loved it with her head there and all her hair, but to be like polite he tried to sort of adjust it out of the way with one hand in his other pocket. She reached her hand and touched his hand through the pants, and then touched his cock with a friendly little stroke, meaning it's okay, leave it there.

Summer was on its last lap! Office buildings were filled with tans standing out nicely against crisp white collars and sleeves, heads fresh full of outdoor colors, ocean waves, and corn on the cob eaten outdoors, kids playing on the lawn. Planes trailed banners and left white words expanding on the blue-skinned sky over weekend beaches and over Fenway Park. The Sox were going down fast. Simon, some felt, was, too. Others thought he'd definitely get off. He had the expensive, expansive lawyers—that was all it took.

I'll tell you exactly what happened, Simon said.

You should tell the court. Katherine stroked the nice boyish curve where his butt met his lower back. She believed him.

Okay, I will, Simon said.

I'll tell you exactly what happened, Simon said to the court.

This abrupt turn of events made everyone nuts with excitement. Simon stood up and said he'd like to speak. Zwirner shut him up and approached the bench, gritting his teeth. Clearly he could not believe this was happening. He was a control freak, especially in court—and especially in the execution of his defense. He had virtually finished his potent, polished summation, and was about to rest his case, when Simon just—*stood up.* They broke for half an hour. Zwirner swore at Simon in a vicious stream—heatedly refused to condone this move, as the *New Yorker*'s behind-the-scenes account put it. Simon just sat there, waiting for him to shut up. His almost impassive expression and patient, leonine bearing showed how thoroughly sick of this guy he was, and how with his resolve he had risen above him and his stupid face like a catcher's mitt.

I want to testify, Simon said.

Absolutely no fucking way are you going to ruin my whole goddam—

I'm going to testify, Simon said calmly.

You still don't get it, do you, you pathetic, stupid little motherfucker—

You're fired, Simon said.

Oh—I get it! Now you're going to—

You can stay with me if you want, Simon said over Zwirner's rant to Will Deery. Will Deery laughed and raised his hands, like he was caught.

I can't, he mouthed softly, as Zwirner continued spewing his piggy punk rock jeremiad.

Simon shrugged.

Don't do this, Will Deery said without much conviction, though his face, his friendly—was it collusive?—expression, said the opposite. To Simon his eyes said, *Do it.*

Simon got up and walked out of the room. He told the bailiff trying to listen at the door to tell the judge they were ready to resume the proceedings. That was his phrase:

You can tell the judge we're ready to resume the proceedings.

Though there wasn't any *we* anymore. It was just Simon.

I woke up in the middle of the night hearing something. I sat up in bed and listened and heard something again in the room right below me.

Simon sat up in bed now as he had then. They were like cats, lying there together, him suddenly pert and alert, eager to tell his story, Katherine beside him stretched long and languorous, looking at the play of candlelight on the ceiling over Mum , and Dad's bed, listening. The room was getting lighter, dawn already.

All right, so I went to sleep late after watching TV in bed, right? And woke up when I heard something. It was like a knock, or someone knocking around down in the playroom—Dad's workshop—right below me. I got up and went to go see what it was.

The courtroom was tipped forward, all ears. Simon didn't speak into the mike, but it picked up his voice, and if people had to strain to make out every word, it wasn't because his voice wasn't loud enough, it was because he spoke fast, in spurts, in his run-on way of speaking, and blurred and blended words into one another.

At first, when I was still in my dream, it was a soldier like on patrol with one of those bayonets on his gun. Then when I was more awake I thought, Oh, it's just a raccoon, because they get into the garbage down there all the time. Except wait a minute, this was definitely inside. Was it a raccoon inside? Then I woke up more and it seemed too heavy, the couple of footsteps, like a bang, and then dragging, and when I listened from the top of the stairs it stopped for a little while, like it knew I was there. I knew it was a person.

Simon spoke loud, and Katherine didn't try to tone him down. But she felt like someone else in the house, Pete or Timmy, could wake and hear him. She thought of Timmy asleep in another room.

I thought it was Dad, really drunk. Down there probably to down some more whiskey. He kept a bottle, a big half gallon jug, down there like hidden with the paint cans and turpentine, as if anybody was watching. The lights were out and it was dark. There was moonlight coming in the windows. I could sort of see enough to go down the stairs. If Dad wasn't so drunk the lights would've been on, so he must've been really wasted.

Simon cleared a thingie from his throat and took a drink of

water from the glass they had there for him. Right then Zwirner came in through the doors in the back of the court-room with that priest guy Father Ryan. It was totally packed in there, but people saw who it was and made room in the back row. Will Deery came in a second later and stood beside them against the back wall like an usher with his hands clasped at his waist. People turned and murmured at their arrival. Simon thought of saying something, but didn't. Instead he said noth-ing. For like thirty seconds he just sat there staring at them. People started to murmur again and the judge said,

Would you like to resume, Mr. Curtis?

Mr. Curtis? Simon said. I'm not Mr. Curtis—Dad's Mr. Curtis.

Laughter charged and won the room.

As you wish, the judge replied, unruffled, sounding like Dad. Please continue.

Okay, so I went down the stairs in the dark while they were making noise, then there was no more movement down there, like they knew I was coming, and like froze. And so at the bot-tom of the stairs I froze too.

Katherine reached for the pack by the bedside where maybe Dad used to keep them, before he quit, if Mum let him smoke in bed—no way; but she did, he did—and lit a cigarette. She was really sexy, rolling over and reaching like that, and Simon, sitting there on Mum's side, kind of squat like a gargoyle, liked how he could see her pussy, from behind, like a little nub bud, nestled up in her excellent buttocks, but he felt like she wasn't paying attention, so he paused and kind of coughed, to make that point. She lifted her chin and exhaled toward the screen window above the head of the bed.

Go on, she smiled.

My pubic hair's redder than yours, Simon said.

How about that? She extended her arm like a queen and, without looking, flicked the ash behind her head into the win-dowsill well.

But your hair on your head's redder than mine.

Yeah, wow.

Mine's bushier than yours, too.

Harassment, Your Honor.

She tickle-nudged him with her foot and he grabbed it. They both smiled. He stayed sitting up.

So anyway, at the bottom of the stairs I could see pretty well, with the moonlight coming in the window, and like onto the floor. There was someone in the middle of the room with a flashlight. I couldn't tell who it was, but the breathing sounded like Dad, maybe, through his nose with his mouth closed—but why would Dad have a flashlight, and not just turn the light on? I just stood there, and so did the other guy, shining the flashlight around. I slipped back to hide when it came to me, but it caught my head and saw me, so I stepped out and went toward the guy, as he came toward me, shining the light right in my eyes so I couldn't see anything.

Simon saw Zwirner whisper something to the priest and smile. Simon glanced at Timmy and Red and Pete, then looked at the jurors because they were the ones he was telling this to. They looked like they were watching a movie. The guy who looked like James Taylor, with his long arms and legs crossed, had a really serious expression.

When he got close, like in a split second, he lifted the flash-light and tried to hit me on the head with it. I saw it coming and moved my head and hit his like forearm, but it got me, like right on the cheekbone, near my eye. I sort of stepped to the side from the blow, but then, like in that split second before he could hit me again, I came around with a big roundhouse and hit him really hard on the side of the head. I got his ear so it must've hurt. It hurt my hand.

Simon was up on his knees, acting out what he described to Katherine. The room was even lighter now, the gray sky out the windows pulling pink. To show hitting the guy on the head, he did first the swing, in slow motion, and then, again in slow motion, the swing into his own head, hitting his own ear. He opened his mouth in a well-acted grimace of pain.

The guy dropped the flashlight and left. He turned around and went right for the door and was gone. He didn't run, but he went fast, like direct, and didn't bump into anything on his way out. He went out the door and was gone. I could see the movement more than, like, the man. But it definitely wasn't Dad.

Simon took another sip of water. This time his throat wasn't dry. The room was like high-altitude mountain stillness. He stopped because he thought he was done. Then he realized there was a little more to tell, and so he told it. This made for a nice dramatic pause. Runs in the family, someone said later. He waved Katherine's smoke away from his face.

The flashlight was still on and I picked it up. I felt the side of my face to see if it was bleeding, and it wasn't, but it felt like it was. I went after the guy, out the door. I couldn't see him with the flashlight, and listened and couldn't hear him, and then I could. Footsteps over to the left in the parking area of the driveway. There are bushes in the way, so I couldn't see him, but then I heard a car door open and close, and went out to see. But by the time I got to the driveway the engine came on and the guy was driving away. I couldn't see what kind of car it was, though I could see it moving away. I think it was like a sedan. The flashlight beam was strong inside, like indoors, or even like against the house, but shined like into the night to see the car it didn't do any good, it was too far away. When it turned to go down the hill, the car turned its lights on, and I watched it go down the hill, then chucked the flashlight into the woods and went back inside. I went up the stairs to the porch and into the kitchen and drank some orange juice, then went back to bed.

But first I went to the bathroom and looked at the bump on my face. It didn't look as bad as it felt.

Why did you throw the flashlight into the woods? Katherine asked, her face studious, the sheet pulled up to her chin. This was also the first question Sandra Gorman asked when she got up to have her go at Simon in cross-examination.

I don't know, he shrugged, cuz the guy was gone and I had the flashlight, so good riddance, and he made a heave-ho throwing motion.

Simulating the throw he made a mouth that made Timmy smile at the familiarity and shake his head: it was like you do when you want to look like someone with no teeth, pull your lips back in between your teeth so they disappear and look like gums. Simon did this when he was concentrating on a pitch or a Frisbee throw or some tricky maneuver, like spinning a pillow on his finger.

Why did you walk toward the intruder—

I don't know, I just did.

And why did you go after him?

Same thing—I don't know. It's just what I did.

Weren't you scared?

Kind of, but it's like, fight or flee, a moment like that, and so I guess I fought.

Didn't you throw the flashlight away because you had just killed your father and now you wanted to get rid of the evidence?

Sandra Gorman made a frustrated, like desperado, jab for the heart. Simon sort of smiled.

That's a leading question, but I'll answer it anyway. No. It happened just like I said. You can ask me a million questions, but it won't change the truth of what I just told.

Why didn't this come out during the presentation of your defense?

'Cause my lawyer didn't know what really happened, because he never asked me what happened. Even when I tried to tell him, he didn't care and didn't want to hear it.

Is that why you fired him?

Yeah—no—well, kinda. I fired him because he wouldn't let me tell the truth of what happened.

And in the presentation of your defense—

Listen. It wasn't my defense, okay, it was his defense. I had nothing to do with it.

Okay, then—

That's why I fired him.

Got it.

Katherine moved close and tried to snuggle and caress him, calm him and comfort him, but Simon didn't exactly reel her in. So she curled around him, just touching, and stroked his calf repeatedly, softly running her thumb along the meaty side of his shinbone. His leg hairs smoothed down under her hand and then popped up, all curly again, when it passed. His hand rested on her head, then softened and went exploring into her hair, the soft surprise of it, so thick and so light, and pretty tangled, especially the back, where there was this serious like nest from fucking. The room was rose-tinted now.

Your hair's totally tangled back here, y'know.

Yeah, thanks to you, mister.

He felt weird for a second, like she was Red saying that. And a bunch of times already, over the night, he had the feeling, like he did often anyway, that she was sort of Mum. Though it always went away again, like almost right away.

Why did you go and stay at home without your father knowing it, if you knew he didn't want you to be there?

Because I knew he didn't want me to be there.

This got a few laughs and maybe emboldened Simon's wiseass side.

So you just went anyway.

Yep.

Why?

Because I *needed—a—place—to—stay.* Simon said it slowly as if he were repeating something for the tenth time to a child with attention deficit disorder.

So you did it in defiance of him.

That's right.

He said this as one like liquid word, in a dismissive, superior way he often did that drove Timmy mad, leaving out and like slurring over the *ts: Thahszrigh(t).*

And you stayed there in the house for all those days and nights without his knowing it, hiding and sneaking around—

Yeah but I didn't kill him.

This comment stopped Sandra Gorman in her tracks.

You expect us to believe you did everything leading up to the murder, but didn't—

Look, I didn't do anything leading up to any murder. I was just there sleeping.

She shook her head in disbelief.

You expect us to believe—

I don't care what you believe. I care what they believe—he nodded to the jury—and I know they believe me. Because it's the truth and they know the truth when they hear it.

Sandra seemed to consider whether she was losing ground here. And Simon felt like he was gaining, so he added,

Especially compared to everything else they've had to listen to this whole time.

You seem mighty sure of yourself, Simon Curtis.

That thing was happening again. Thoughts were weird things, if you thought about it. They just came flying in out of nowhere.

Yeah, well, I am. Because I have the truth on my side.

If you are Mum, hi Mum, I know you're always there . . .

And the judge was just like Dad, while we're at it, sitting up there at the head of the table not saying anything, thinking he's in control, but while everybody else does the talking.

Simon, I'm afraid you've left one essential thing out of your story.

This wasn't a question; she was baiting him—and it worked.

Oh yeah? What's that?

Your father.

This time he didn't say anything. His face said something more agreeable than adversarial. He sure didn't look like he felt cornered or worried. Or even concerned. Sandra Gorman threw her hands up.

How do you account for your father?

I don't, Simon shrugged—and added, Who does?

A little laughter prods a small smile. Katherine shifted and now stroked his thigh. She grazed the ol' sleeping soldier, and it didn't take much for it to awaken and start to nod up to attention.

So why do you think your father wasn't there?

I know, it's the weirdest thing.

He lay back and his cock flopped, three-quarters hard, over to one side. He closed his eyes and explained,

I think he was right there. I just didn't see him.

But you said it was light, there was moonlight.

I know, but I just didn't notice him, I guess. I was watching the guy with the flashlight, and then the light was in my face. Then the guy left, and then I left. Dad must've been right there on the floor the whole time, like lying there in a heap right beside me. I could've tripped over him.

So he was already dead when you got down there?

I dunno. Probably.

She tongued the pink helmet, red around the rim, then like melt-attacked her head down over the whole thing. It was like a snake when they eat a whole little animal, whole. The first few times going down she took him in really far without gagging. He felt like pushing her even farther, and like really fucking her head, like really hard. But wow, she beat him to it, like reading his cock's mind, and began a pretty aggressive bob up and down, exactly how fast he wanted, though not quite hard enough, and not really far enough, but still, it was great, sure beat beating off! He did little thrusts a little deeper, holding her head over the ears when she was farthest down, even though he was afraid he was hurting her, and she responded not by gagging or pulling back, but by going that little bit deeper each time, with violent little gag-jabs, like plugging herself. She was on her knees, leaning over his legs, sticking her ass up like a cat crouched, like stretching, so he lifted his foot against her pussy, so the top part fit right in, like stop-action kicking a soccer ball, and she was really wet, and started like grinding on him, like sliding a little bit back and forth, lubed, like fucking his foot, it was great, while she kept on sucking him. It was perfect like that, and even though he'd already come like a bunch of times in the last couple of days and nights, he was going to again, and he was just getting to that last like plateau of effort and opiate letting go into the like rising tickle-stream before you come, when she stopped and looked up at him, with her head and hair all wild. She was like this really beautiful new kind of animal-angel, off in her own passion-dimension, and her face rose up toward his, like enlarging with her eyes, kind of serious, but watery and faraway, and even though she was so like right there, and her mouth, already wet and like rubbed out, like rubbery and ready from the blow job, latched onto his mouth like an alien and sucked and like ate him alive, and he met every move of her mouth with his own like chewing lips and wrestling tongue. Then in sort of a surprise, but not really, she was over his cock for a quick but patient positioning feel, line it up, and then she almost like threw herself down on him, pretty hard, like a professional wrestler body slam, and in that one excellent move he was all the way deep in her, she was really like lubed and writhing around. In only about five bounces up and down, with her breasts bouncing the opposite way, she started to moan like she never did the other times, low, like in pain, or like she was possessed by some man-beast, and that made him almost come again, and again she like paused and shifted what she was doing this time to switch from a like kneeling position on top of him to a squat upright right over his hips with her feet on either side almost like she was taking a shit except she was in ecstasy bouncing up and down with her head tilted back a bit and her eyes softly closed and he came before she did and she kept going even though he held on to her hips to try and like stop her. She came too right after like with that moan again going deep and gravelly, possessed, into her throat and like larynx opened up from before kind of brutally.

Never allowed in the room again, Mum never left. In the house in his head in court in her bed in this inquiry intimacy inhabiting Sandy Gorman? in a way in the world and like Katherine in the heart in the body. Simon remembered this one time Mum asked him to sweep off the porch. He must have been somewhere between like twelve and fifteen, when she died. It was summer at the end of the day. He started sweeping, starting over by the kitchen door and the doghouse. She was on the porch, too, watering the hanging fuchsias and geraniums and like picking off deadheads and tossing them over the railing into the rhododendrons. After a minute she goes like,

That's not how you sweep, give me that, and she grabbed the broom and started sweeping really fast with like Mum anger. She missed a couple of places and when she gave him the broom back he went back and got them without looking up at her and continued to sweep his same way as before though not as slow maybe but still really mellow and extra deliberate compared to her all like frenetic. She could be like that sometimes, like really impatient, which of course made him be the opposite, like slo-mo mellow man for the rest of his life, but also she could be the warmest person in the world even when you didn't want her like cuddling and tickling you. When she died it was like the sun went behind a cloud and he didn't realize it stayed that way and never came out again until now when it did like with Katherine and also in a weird way with all the attention and like his star rising lately, even though it might have seemed like the opposite.

Katherine smoked again kind of out the window where sunrise put color in everything and lifted the tops of trees past the lawn in a crown glow like of hope surrounding the house. Like you are sometimes, Simon was settled and alive in the moment at the center of his life, and everything felt righter than right. He even felt like God was part of it, like crouched right there, couched with him, in him, and in all this, instead of that private high thing he could secretly get to while everyone else wasn't even close.

I had this dream I was in the middle of this like party of animals where everyone was themselves but they also looked like the kind of animal they looked like. These little girls with zebra aprons and little bras on were the parking attendants pointing where to park in this big garden and then inside they were the waitresses getting drinks for everyone and serving food. It was at Sky Farm in North Haven overlooking this incredible sunset with great big gray clouds piled up and the sun getting under them all orange spilling across the whole sky and staying like that with shifts and shafts and deepening variations after the sun slipped behind the blue woman of the Camden Hills lying there on her side like in bed with the sheets the bay all ruffled and dark with wind and cold night, almost like winter approaching across it, coming fast with the wind right at you.

What is the general feeling in this dream? Describe the emotional climate.

Sandra Gorman was not a therapist, but Simon would never go to therapy. Katherine was not a dream!

I don't know, Simon reflexively resisted with his habitual skill and ease at avoidance. But it changed into this like chase scene where they were after me for murder.

They were after you for murder?

Yeah but it was just a dream.

Who did you murder?

In the dream.

Yes, who did you murder in the dream?

I don't know. Maybe no one.

If you did murder someone, who would you say it was?

I don't know but you'll probably say some part of myself.

Did you murder your father?

What, you think you're tricky?

Sandra Gorman was Mum and Mum already knew.

You think I'm going to like oops, *duh,* just like admit it suddenly?

Who was after you in the dream?

I don't know probably you.

I'm not trying to catch you. I love you.

Love was not something Simon had ever discussed with someone he maybe loved and who possibly loved him and he wasn't about to do it now except by saying,

Yeah but you're after me you're trying to catch me in that way.

I don't know, Simon, I think you're the one who's been after me, trying to catch me.

Yeah well I did.

And I'm glad.

The jury deliberated for two days, a Thursday and a Friday, and it was expected—from the usual signs that it's going to take a while, such as requests to review significant chunks of testimony—that they'd take up some or most of the next week, at least, to come to a unanimous verdict. So it came as a surprise when, on Friday afternoon around four o'clock, the jury's foreman, the guy who looked like James Taylor, accompanied by the bailiff, after knocking and receiving a croak in response, entered the judge's chamber, where the judge was snoozing unabashedly, sockless, on his couch, and announced they had arrived at their verdict. And it came as a real shock, even though lots of people were expecting it, or at least hoping for it, when they found Simon guilty of second degree murder.

The James Taylor guy read the verdict slowly, clearly, without looking up, until he was done, and sat down. A bolt of mental lightning ricocheted around the room, lifting a rumbling thunder of reaction, and struck Simon on the back of the head, sending a jolt of mortal recognition down his spine and up again where, like one of those test-your-strength things at a carnival you hit with a sledgehammer, it rang the bell of his skull and sent shivers over his scalp and his skin to the tips of his fingers and the air-licked rims of his lips like an incredible awful orgasm. And like a dazed boxer when he hears the bell he stood up without thinking and with his mouth hanging open stunned turned to face the roomful of people. Judge Word smacked his gavel to shut everybody up and told Simon to sit back down. The room got quiet but Simon seemed not to hear the judge. Instead of sitting down he stood there and raised his arms and held them outstretched like Jesus with the palms upward in a gesture open to multiple interpretations.

Everyone there had their opinion about what it meant, just as they all had their opinions about his guilt. And soon everyone else had their opinions about the gesture—as well as about the verdict, and subsequent rulings (sentencing, appeal)— because its image appeared on front pages everywhere the next day. Someone snuck a camera into the courtroom and got a shot of him. The image in the papers—and of course on the news and in magazines and on the Internet—looked more like a shrug than it did to those who witnessed it. His eyes, in the famous picture, were almost shut, lidded like an angel, only the underside whites showing, just a slit, so it looked like, eyes rolled back in his head, he was drunk, in a trance, or like in some third-eye state of meditative grace.

To those present, it seemed like a gesture of supplication or sacrifice: *You got me. Now are you happy?* His face was stricken, sad, calm, almost stripped of affect, as if blanched by shock. When he first turned he kind of winced, then his face knotted, clenching neck tendons pulled taut. As he let go it looked like he was starting to smile on one side of his mouth, but it went another way, and his face relaxed with the emotional strain or strangeness melted into and out of it as he raised his arms, and he stood there like that for a while, pilloried, enigmatic as ever, for all to see and ever wonder about.

Katherine was there in the front row between Timmy and Red and her presence there meant everything to him and nothing. The jury just found him guilty.

Zwirner got up from his place in the back row and left the courtroom. Will Deery stayed sitting there with that guy Father Ryan, who looked at his hands folded on his lap.

It was as if all the blood and life were suddenly drained out of everything. A few deadly days later Judge Word sentenced Simon to ten to fifteen years in prison, but allowed him to stay in Manchester, still guarded by Pete, pending the appeal. The media went insane, everybody everywhere was talking about it. Zwirner was back, confident as ever. Father Ryan went for a walk with Greg Gregory along the Charles between Harvard and MIT. The sky was like a video screen with Dad's face on it looking preoccupied, bemused, saintly. Where was Mum? She was in the river, she was in the ocean, she was the rain. She was not Katherine. Simon cried a lot but not in front of anyone. To other people he acted like everything was fine, he could handle it no prob, which was true, he felt like, but when he was alone he got fucking petrified and couldn't sleep and couldn't see hope or the mystic anywhere except like the inverse, the black core of his wicked distress closing in. Timmy went back to Brooklyn, hobbled, lost, and Red left again. When Simon asked Katherine to come on out to Manchester again, she said she couldn't, her boyfriend was back in town.

I thought you were with me, Simon said.

Well I was, Simon. But I still have a boyfriend. We're going to try to work things out.

You're stupid, he said flatly. I'm going to get off on appeal.

I hope you do, Simon. Her voice was tiny and hurt. I have to go now, she peeped, and hung up on him the way he always did her.

Zwirner acted like the guilty sentence was all Simon's fault and none of his own. He still didn't explain what his strategy was going to be for the appeal, and why he was so sure he was going to flip the conviction. He had lunch with the governor's brother. The panel of three appeals judges was chosen with the same mysterious alacrity that had sped the trial along from the start. A date was set for October 21—Mum and Dad's anniversary. And also, that guy from the *Globe* detected, the same day, a year ago, that Simon went home to stay in Manchester without Dad's knowing it. Makes you wonder.

Zwirner smiled, in fact could hardly suppress his seemingly inappropriate glee, as he began to present his case to the appeals judges. It took less than three hours. The conviction should be overturned, he argued persuasively, because the only object of evidence tying Simon to the crime—the flashlight—was obtained in an illegal manner. The state trooper, who learned of the flashlight's existence from Simon soon after Simon was arrested, and thereafter initiated a search for the crucial piece of evidence in the woods surrounding the house, learned of its existence in a wholly illegal manner, through harassing and aggressively attacking the defendant, which was witnessed and described in unequivocal detail to the Court of Appeals by an officer from the Manchester Police Department, who was standing right there, *trying to stop the fight,* as he put it in his own words, *before it got out of hand.* Officer Murphy's testimony clearly indicated that state trooper William "Biff" Toomey inappropriately provoked, taunted, and threatened the witness. Thus the single piece of key evidence was illegally obtained. And therefore the conviction of the defendant, Simon Cary Curtis, of murder in the second degree, must be overturned, and he must be set free.

The Court of Appeals agreed, and Simon was, indeed, set free.

Simon now knows.

Before I pull another disappearing act, I might as well tell you what happened.

I was at the house. I went there, pretty drunk, on the last shuttle from New York to Boston, rented a car at Logan Airport, and drove (wove) out to Manchester.

The house was dark. I didn't know what I was going to do I just knew that somehow I'd wake up Dad and get him to discover that Simon was in the house. That was my muddled mission. It really bothered me that Simon was staying there, and I went there to put an end to it. The jig was up.

I went kind of noisily in the front door and caught myself in the mirror above the Brown Thing. I emptied the mail and money from the bowl there and took it outside and put it on the passenger seat of my rental. This wasn't planned, it was spontaneous, like everything that night: I always liked that bowl, and I wanted it, so I took it. I went back inside, again letting the door clatter shut. This time Dad was awake, he heard me, I heard his door open upstairs, and he called out coarsely,

Who's there?

I didn't answer him, but walked audibly through the front hall and down the coat corridor toward the kitchen and Simon's room. It was dark, but blue with moonlight, so you could see, I know the place by heart. The kitchen didn't seem to make sense, so I went down the stairs to the basement. I flipped on the light down there and saw Dad's whole boatbuilding operation, the boat—skeleton drawing on the floor in Magic Marker, the tools on the workbench, and the bent struts all over the place. I was pretty drunk, and for the sound and fury of it, kicked a cardboard box out of the way. It had Dad stuff in it that spilled out, extension cords and whatever else, and, one by one, I kicked that stuff out of the way, too. Then I think I grabbed a piece of wood and knocked on the ceiling to wake Simon. I wasn't sure he was up there, but I knew. I heard someone coming. I grabbed the flashlight in its wall clip next to a mini fire extinguisher. I shut off the light and waited, like a spider in his corner.

I expected Simon, but Dad came down the stairs first, like a ball coming down its chute. As soon as he got to the bottom of the stairs I shined the flashlight in his face. He had his glasses on and a towel around his waist.

Who's there, dammit? he growled.

He looked befuddled, scared, drunker than me. I didn't have a plan; but what came to me right then was to get out of there, get Dad to find Simon somehow, and get out of there. I had to flush Simon out.

Dad came at me, I couldn't believe it, he was a bull.

It's Simon, I said, trying to sound like Simon.

God*dam* you, he said, stepping into me now, but I stepped aside like a bullfighter. He smelled sour, like his father when

I'd go over to his bed in the summer as a boy, and, in his pajamas and bathrobe, belted, he'd tell me stories about the green monkey.

Give me that, he said, as if to a recalcitrant child, grabbing the flashlight. I jerked it away and his hand caught my wrist and gripped, pretty hard. One or two of his fingers caught in my wristwatch as I pulled my arm away. He didn't let up, he jostled further, wrestling, like he was trying to tackle me. I couldn't believe it, he was fighting me! I wriggled free and pushed him away, but he held on to my shoulder, staggering. He hit me with a roundhouse on the side of the head, hard, catching my ear and my jaw. There was a burst of brightness with the shock of the blow, and my head was ringing. It was like he hit the fight switch in my head: I swung back, and hit him on the side of his head. I shined the light in his face, and he looked scared, lost, wincing, and came at me again, his mouth agape like he was toothless. I hit him again, hard, get him off me, and really connected, with the flashlight, with the side of his head.

He went limp, like he was kidding, and fell on the floor. His eyes were open and his mouth was open. The towel had come off, and he looked like a big round baby, his belly, his butt, lying there half curled. One arm was bent the wrong way. His glasses were still on. I couldn't believe he attacked me.

Now came Simon, he must have heard. I just wanted to get out of there, and turned and went, but stumbled over the box and the junk I'd kicked out of it. I turned and shined the light in Simon's face at the bottom of the stairs, just like Dad. I stepped past Dad and kept the light in Simon's face. He came right at me, and this time I didn't wait, I swung at his head with the flashlight, but he blocked it, partly, with his arm, and grabbed onto the flashlight. He wouldn't let go. So I pushed him and let go of the flashlight and got out of there.

One more thing. This whole blue bowl thing. I've talked to Simon about it. About how he said it's the key to the whole thing. There's the actual blue bowl. As evidence, whatever. Okay. Then there's what it represents to Simon. It's like the sky. The blue bowl the day. The blue bowl the bay. The natural world and his rightful place in it. In his family. In this life. What everybody wants. And everybody deserves.

Acknowledgments

Gratitude to Melanie Jackson and Victoria Wilson, for being great, for hanging in there with me forever. And love/thanks to Kristin, Paul, Joe, Mike, Eddie, Willem, Liza, Woog, Amy, Scott, Martha, Giulia, Giada, Maddalena, Angy, Peter J., Boohoo, Steve, Marie, Ira, Alec, Yaddo, Jiva, Lisa, Spo, Kath, Can, JCS, HRC, Whitey, Sri, Lola, JSK.

A Note on the Type

The text of this book was set in Garamond No. 3. It is not a
true copy of any of the designs of Claude Garamond (ca. 1480–
1561), but an adaptation of his types, which set the European
standard for two centuries. It probably owes as much to the
designs of Jean Jannon, a Protestant printer working in Sedan
in the early seventeenth century, who had worked with Garamond's romans earlier, in Paris, but who was denied their use
because of Catholic censorship. Jannon's matrices came into the
possession of the Imprimerie Nationale, where they were thought
to be by Garamond himself, and were so described when the
Imprimerie revived the type in 1900. This particular version is
based on an adaptation by Morris Fuller Benton.

Composed by NK Graphics, Keene, New Hampshire
Printed and bound by R. R. Donnelley & Sons,
Harrisonburg, Virginia
Designed by Iris Weinstein